BORN PARIAH

The ship was old. Even at its best faster-than-light speed, the trip through space seemed endless. Before Anthony Saunder's eyes, the star fields showing on the monitors dimmed and brightened. The effect was lulling.

Anthony stared in boredom as the ship spanned the light-years, letting his thoughts drift, thinking vaguely of Procyon Four, his home world, and the sight of shallow waves from his main room window, then of another beach back on Earth at Saunderhome.

Saunderhome, when he was five years old and secretly listening to servants.

"Clones. Right out of test tubes, they tell me. Hatched 'em from surrogate mamas, but they ain't *real* kids."

They'd been speaking of *him*! Anthony the illegal clone, not a real human being—not even now, after all these years!

By Juanita Coulson
Published by Ballantine Books:

Children of the Stars:
    Book One: TOMORROW'S HERITAGE
    Book Two: OUTWARD BOUND
    Book Three: LEGACY OF EARTH
    Book Four: THE PAST OF FOREVER*

THE DEATH GOD'S CITADEL

THE WEB OF WIZARDRY

*Forthcoming

LEGACY OF EARTH

BOOK THREE OF THE SERIES

CHILDREN OF THE STARS

JUANITA COULSON

A Del Rey Book

BALLANTINE BOOKS • **NEW YORK**

Library of Congress Catalog Card Number: 88-92172

ISBN 0-345-28180-2

Manufactured in the United States of America

First Edition: April 1989

Cover Art by David Schleinkofer

In memory of Judy-Lynn del Rey, whose idea it was, and who insisted that CHILDREN OF THE STARS be done, and done right.

When the barriers are broken,
And the last taboo is done;
When the final NO is spoken,
And the hurdles all are run;
Then shall Adam's children muster,
Free of kings and priests and guns,
Where a thousand races cluster
Round a multitude of suns.

—*Apodosis*, Canto XII
Anonymous

Table of Contents

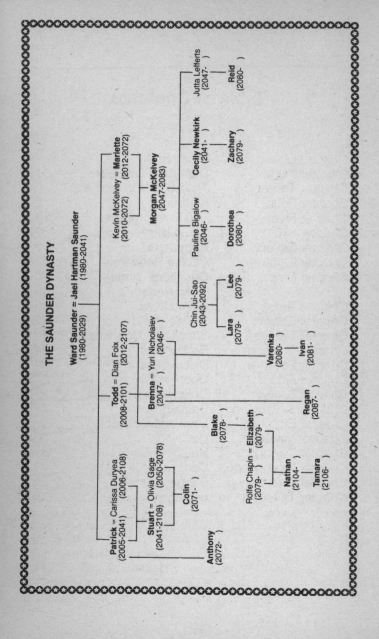

THE SAUNDER DYNASTY

Ward Saunder = Jael Hartman Saunder
(1980-2029)   (1980-2041)

Patrick = Carissa Duryea
(2005-2041) (2006-2108)

Stuart = Olivia Gage
(2041-2108) (2050-2078)

Colin
(2071-)

Anthony
(2072-)

Todd = Dian Foix
(2008-2101) (2012-2107)

Brenna = Yuri Nicholaiev
(2047-) (2046-)

Blake
(2078-)

Regan
(2087-)

Varenka
(2080-)

Ivan
(2081-)

Rolfe Chapin = Elizabeth
(2079-) (2079-)

Nathan
(2104-)

Tamara
(2106-)

Kevin McKelvey = Mariette
(2010-2072) (2012-2072)

Morgan McKelvey
(2047-2083)

Chin Jui-Sao
(2043-2092)

Lara
(2079-)

Lee
(2079-)

Pauline Bigalow
(2046-)

Dorothea
(2080-)

Cecily Newkirk
(2041-)

Zachary
(2079-)

Jutta Lefferts
(2047-)

Reid
(2080-)

CHAPTER ONE

✕✕✕✕✕✕✕✕

Tour's End

Anthony Saunder glanced at the figure lurking in the darkened wings. Lighting effects from the stage beyond revealed the hidden watcher's openmouthed wonder; the local merchant was mesmerized by the drama—and by the emota-sensors the actors wore. Jesse Eben, too, had noticed the play's impact on the uninvited guest. He leaned toward his friend and whispered, "Tell me, kid: Is that the same mold-brain who refused to order our new releases?"

The younger man nodded sourly. "Because, he said, our sensors wouldn't add anything to an ed or entertainment package. He *also* said the only reason he wormed his way in here for React Theater's final performance was to be polite."

"Uh-huh." Jesse snickered, sharing Anthony's contempt.

Since they'd landed on Settlement Clay over a week ago, they'd been wining and dining that vid distributor, pressing the flesh and pushing Saunder Studio's products hard. The merchant had countered with a litany of doom and gloom. Business had been terrible lately. And Anthony's vids cost too much; sure, they were good, but not that much better than the competitors'. Besides, the distributor wasn't confident the settlers would want to

1

buy these new emota-enhanced chips. Maybe next year, if sales improved, he'd think about increasing his order.

The old song and dance. It had gone on for centuries between Terran suppliers and their retailers. The difference nowadays was that a company boss and his colleague had to travel a hell of a lot farther to touch bases with their markets. Light-years farther, in fact. Expenses had steepened proportionately, as well, in the interim. Painfully conscious of that last, Anthony and Jesse had economized to the bone on this survey tour. For months they'd shared transport and accommodations with the React Theater troupe. Their itineraries were the same. Most of the performers had worked for the Studio in the past and hoped to again in the future. They wanted to stay on Anthony's good side, and added several of Saunder Studio's best-selling dramas to their repertoire as free advertising for him. In return, he and Jesse had assisted with backstage operations at every stopover.

And at that moment their expertise was needed. Anthony heard an anomaly in the sensors' carrier waves. Potential disaster! With Jesse at his heels, he made his way through a clutter of boxes and luggage. The crew member tending the emota-apparatus looked up gratefully at his approach and stammered, "I . . . I'm sorry. It got away from me."

The tall, dark-haired man with the unusual pale-blue eyes smiled reassuringly and forbore to comment that it frequently did get away from the stagehands. Hassan, React Theater's actor-manager, was too cheap to hire qualified personnel and over-worked his employees, with predictable results. "Let us handle it," Anthony said. He took over the boards, deftly tightening circuit feeds and smoothing out glitches. Meanwhile, Jesse fine-tuned the monitor link. Then the three of them peered anxiously at the view screens showing the audience out front—nothing but rapt expressions there. The spectators hadn't detected the momentary bobble in the signal, thanks to the emota-sensors' effect.

Emota technology was a recent one, dating from a scant seven years ago, at the turn of the Twenty-second Century. Its original purpose had been medical, helping doctors treat the severely injured and mentally ill. Anthony had been among the first to realize the bio-boosters had other applications. Modified, the sensors greatly enhanced an actor's or instructor's words and gestures. Taking a gamble, Anthony had installed the gear on all his Studio's production lines. Eventually that might prove him farsighted, not foolhardy. So far, balance sheets weren't encouraging, and this market tour had meant still more red ink on the ledgers. But he and Jesse had no choice; they'd had to make the trip to keep sales healthy.

The stagehand sighed in relief. "Glad you're here to take care of this stuff." She waved at the delicate sensor control boards. "They throw me every damned time. Nice having someone with your know-how to make sure the troupe wraps on a high note."

They'd do precisely that. Sophisticated tiny emota-sensor relays were attached to each of the actors' costumes, gathering brain waves, pulse and breathing rates, and temperatures. The performers' feigned responses to the drama translated into emanations of joy, fear, anguish, and rage. Combined and concentrated, the signals were broadcast to the audience, seizing it by its emotional throat.

React Theater had chosen a guaranteed crowd pleaser for their big finish. *Vaughn's Challenge* was Ian Dempsey's most popular melodrama. Critics on Earth had flayed it, of course. But here on the frontier, it pushed all the right buttons: carving out a Settlement on a hostile planet; brave pioneers resisting pressure from unfeeling, callous Charter sponsors, who lived safe and secure back on Earth; natural catastrophes; star-crossed lovers; violent death; remorse; and, of course, victory!

Veda Ingersoll, the troupe's long-in-the-tooth leading lady, delivered a lengthy, tear-jerking passage. Greedy for the spotlight, her co-star Hassan almost walked on her lines in his haste to get to his own character's passionate declaration.

"Milking it outrageously," Anthony noted, wincing.

"Nah! Not milk," Jesse said. "They're churning out something my ancestors couldn't have touched. Not kosher. Too much ham."

Anthony chuckled, but kept his attention on the readouts. Whatever he thought of the play, he had to hold the controls at peak efficiency. The more skillfully he did that, the greater the emota-sensors' impact on the audience—each member of which was a probable local customer for Saunder Studio's vids.

The drama ended in triumph. History tapes gave a grimmer account of these events and what had followed. For the characters acting out their story amid solid-looking holo-mode scenery, time was frozen at 2083. Mankind was on a threshold, just beginning to reach out from the Solar System. The Saunder-McKelvey star-

3

drive, invented by two of Anthony's relatives, was available, but still a risky means of travel. Yet Captain Vaughn and his settlers had accepted that risk and numerous others. They'd conquered Wolf 359 Three, a world since renamed in Vaughn's honor. And those settlers were still burdened with debts owed their sponsors. So were thousands of other immigrants, including the citizens of Anthony's planet, Procyon Five. That was why the crowd loved the play; they identified with its theme and the characters' struggles and hopes.

Vaughn's Challenge rolled on. For Anthony, though, truth intruded on illusion.

2083. What had he been doing then, while Vaughn was taming a world?

In 2083, I was eleven, trapped on Earth, dreaming of escape to the stars. I made it, but I'm still trapped, in a way, running as fast as I can to avoid failure. At least it's a trap of my own making.

Kilometers away, a heavy-hauler shuttle launched. The muffled roar could be heard even through the hall's thick log walls. No one seemed to hear that reminder of the here and now. As the rocket's sound faded, Hassan, Veda, and their supporting cast spoke the play's final lines. The last poignant emota-sensor signals were beamed to the spectators. Actors posed in a defiant, heroic tableau. The crowd was breathless, not wanting to break the magical moment.

Gingerly the backstage crew brought up the lights and erased the scenery projections. The actors were left standing on a bare, makeshift stage. Only *then* did the audience erupt in whoops and cheers.

The performers basked in waves of adulation. The rest of their team, however, was busy tearing down and packing. The company had an outbound flight to catch. As the actors stepped into the wings between curtain calls, the wardrobe master detached the emota-sensor devices and brought them to Anthony. The costly little gadgets were locked and sealed in the case, readied for transport. Equipment and baggage accumulated by the hall's rear door. Gradually the area was being stripped. Nothing but the rented monitors would remain when the crew was done.

The spectacle out front amused Anthony. Hassan and Veda were third-raters, their cast a bunch of has-beens and never-will-bes. On Earth or the Colonies, they would have drawn sneers,

4

not this kind of adoration. Charter Settlement Planets' audiences weren't fussy. These locals didn't know—or care—that what they'd seen was a badly acted chestnut. They were thrilled and grateful. Emota-sensors had supercharged their enjoyment. React Theater was an exciting change from much-used vids and, most important, it was right here on Settlement Clay. Touring acting companies this far out in the Terran sector's boondocks were exceedingly rare.

Little wonder the crowd was eating up the show. Those faces on the monitor told the tale. These people were pioneers, uncouth, uncultured, and tough; weaklings didn't emigrate to the stars; they weren't willing to deal with the frontier's dangers and isolation. The hall was jammed with agri and forestry workers, teamsters, road builders, carpenters, medical personnel, shuttle pilots, cooks, butchers, merchants, and local government employees. There were a handful of Space Fleet troopers on furlough and some independent planet scouts, looking as rakish as old-fashioned pirates.

Not a jaded critic from Earth among them!

Nonhumans also had attended the drama. Five Vahnajes clustered on the far right side of the cavernous room. The tall, gray-skinned lutrinoids were the guests of a Clay politico. He was explaining the play's fine points to them. The Vahnajes responded with pointy-toothed smiles, their heads wobbling atop their snaky necks. On the opposite side of the hall, as far from the Vahnajes as they could get, were four Whimeds. The felinoids' crests and bright clothes made them stand out vividly among the humans.

Now and then the Vahnajes scowled at the Whimeds, and the Whimeds returned the favor. That was a common situation. The Vahnaj Alliance once had owned an exclusive trade deal with Terra. Then the lutrinoids were the only e.t.s. mankind knew. But today, in 2108, *Homo sapiens* was out on the starlanes and learning that other races were interested in interspecies commerce, too: Lannons, Rigotians, Ulisorians, and especially the Whimed Federation. The Whimeds were real go-getters, moving boldly into markets the Vahnajes used to have all to themselves. Whenever the two races came into contact, they tended to bristle at one another. Fortunately, from what Anthony had seen, things never got any hotter than that. He supposed the aliens had watched the play—despite the chance of bumping into their rivals—for the

5

same reason he and Jesse had played the PR game with that vid distributor.

The e.t.s. were a magnet for the eye, but no concern of Saunder Studio. Anthony had produced some language packages and docu-vids about relations between the stellar civilizations, but they weren't major items, and profits were minimal. He had no plans to expand the lines or push into non-Terran markets. Charter Settlement Planets Council strongly supported what it called "cross-species cooperation." Anthony, however, had decided they could get that from businesses able to bear the cost of such do-gooder enterprises. *His* wasn't.

The applause seemed to go on forever, but finally the crowd was sated. The actors rushed backstage into their portable dressing rooms. Those cubicles would be the last paraphernalia loaded, once they'd been telescoped down into their traveling boxes. People bustled about, bumping elbows, cursing, trying to do everything simultaneously, rushing to complete preparations. They worked amid floating crop residue, the leavings of beasts of burden, and the pungent odor of disinfectant. The backstage area was actually a hastily converted loading dock. Most of the time this place was used to store harvested *purgatio*, Clay Settlement's "green gold" export.

The vid distributor bumbled his way through the confusion. "Saunder! Eben! About that order I gave you. I want to add five gross. Can you supply that much?"

Anthony raised an eyebrow and said sarcastically, "We'll try." Jesse managed a pained smile and made an entry on his mini-ledger.

"Great show!" The merchant pumped Anthony's hand, behaving as if he were facing the man responsible for React Theater's success. "You definitely got something going in that emota-sensor rig. Knew it all along. Sure grateful to be in on the ground floor. Hey! Veda! Hassan!" He galloped off to fawn on the troupe's stars.

The men from Saunder Studio swapped tired glances. "I hope our accounting department doesn't panic," Anthony muttered. "We could be buried in profits from such a windfall."

Jesse scratched his little salt-and-pepper beard. "Oh, he was really impressed with our stuff, all right. A couple more customers like him and we'll go broke. Come on. Let's get out of here."

6

As the company poured from the building, they were forced to slow to a crawl. React Theater's stay here had been an SRO smash. Locals who couldn't get seats in the hall had paid to watch the final show—and feel the emota-sensors' effect—via meters-high view screens ringing the plaza. Now they clamored to see the actors in the flesh. Town militia held back the mob with difficulty. All of the performers reveled in the admiration, but Veda Ingersoll hogged the attention shamelessly; she flounced and tossed her blue-dyed mane like a starlet half her age, earning glares from her co-star and cast.

Anthony snorted scornfully and edged past the bottleneck. He himself was vid-star handsome, and his face and name were well known throughout the sector. There had been a time when he could have stolen these hams' thunder without trying. But that period of his life was over. He was a businessman now. His job lay behind the lenses. Hassan and Veda could wallow in their fans' embrace, for all he cared.

Someone grabbed his arm and wouldn't let go.

"Saunder! Anthony Saunder!" Heads turned, and recognition bloomed. People nudged one another as the grabby stranger blurted, "I can't believe it. Come all the way out to this back-world hunk of rock and meet *two* Saunders in one day!"

Grimacing, Anthony braced himself for a familiar ordeal—the name-dropper. The Saunders and McKelveys were Terra's most famous family. They touched the lives of billions. Some citizens were leeches, sucking up to and latching on to any member of the clan unlucky enough to meet such parasites. Actual ranking within the Saunder-McKelveys didn't matter. Kinship alone was a touchstone of sorts. Anthony wondered idly which other Saunder this loudmouth would claim to have met.

The man was certainly no local. His broad accent, fancy lace shirt, and exaggerated pantaloons were dead giveaways; he was another slumming tourist from Earth. Pioneers tolerated his sort for the credits they injected into the Settlements' economies.

"What a coincidence! They booked your cousin Colin into that grungy hostel where *I* stayed. What a nerve, but he never objected. You colonists are full of surprises."

Onlookers stirred, growling. "Colonists" was a term reserved for inhabitants of Mars and Earth's other neighbor planets. Beyond the light-year boundary, Terrans were "settlers," and proud of it. To them, "colonists" was a mild insult.

7

Anthony mulled something else the tourist had said. Colin? On Settlement Clay? That was a surprise, an unwelcome one.

"Guess I should expect you people to do crazy things," the boor went on, "considering the way you have to live. Grubbing in the dirt alongside these stupid yokels. Tell me, Saunder: Doesn't that make you feel like an animal?"

Anthony wrenched free of the buffoon, but couldn't get away. The mob hemmed everyone in too tightly. Pointedly snubbing the Earthman, Anthony stared over the tourist's head—and locked gazes with a Whimed. Felinoids' pupils had an umbralaca shape, not slitted like a cat's but resembling miniature stars opening in large irises. The e.t.s.' scrutiny could be unnerving. As if mutely apologizing, the alien blinked, then turned and vanished into the congested plaza. Anthony felt oddly annoyed by the brief encounter, and unsure why.

Meanwhile, the Earthman was spewing calculated insults and a steady stream of false buddy-buddy chatter about the Saunders and McKelveys. Abandoning any pretense at subtlety, Anthony snapped, "Colin isn't my cousin." It was not true, technically, but maybe it would shut this clown up. He should have known better.

"So okay. He's the bastard. You're the clone. Not much to choose. Must be why the pair of you came out here with all these cretins, eh? With *your* family connections, you wouldn't be stuck in these Settlement stinkholes otherwise . . . Hey! Quit shoving!"

Shoving wasn't all the crowd was doing. Pawing and buffeting, they knocked off the tourist's cap and stomped it in the dust, snarling that they intended to do the same to the cap's owner. His veneer of smug bravado peeled away, and he bawled for help. But his guide had mysteriously made himself scarce. Disgruntled militiamen had to rescue the offworlder from his own folly, hustling him none too gently through the mob and out of the plaza.

Anthony and Jesse had grabbed their chance, making good their own getaway and scrambling aboard a waiting bus. The React Theater's crew was already settling in there, yawning and fidgeting. They weren't going anywhere yet; the troupe's actors were still sharing a love feast with their fans. Jesse keyed his mini-ledger and began updating his records. Anthony leaned back in the carriage's grass-stuffed seat, applying biofeedback to his fury, trying to calm himself.

The tourist had called him a clone. Few people did that to Anthony's face, though he knew there was plenty of gossip. "The

8

high and mighty Saunders. Uncrowned royalty, the newscasters say. Hah! That family's got plenty of skeletons in its closets."

Anthony was one of those skeletons.

His reflection shimmered in the bus's window. A dead man's face peered back at him—Patrick Saunder, martyred hero of the Crisis of 2041, savior of humanity who nobly gave his life for mankind's future.

He was dead, yet he lived on—or his genetic copy did.

Cloning human beings was illegal today as it had been back in the Twenty-first Century. Nevertheless, Patrick's widow Carissa had purchased five replicas of her slain husband. The boys were pawns an in intrafamilial struggle and, when that conflict was over, they were excess baggage. Anthony was the only one of the five to survive to adulthood, the only one to emigrate from Earth. He couldn't escape his past, though. Being a clone was a lifetime sentence. The tourist had merely pointed out what everyone knew—that Anthony Saunder wasn't a *real* man, just an artificial product of secret labs and Patrick Saunder's DNA.

"Relax," Jesse said softly.

He'd seen the younger man's clenched fists and whitening knuckles. Biofeedback techniques weren't working. The rage was still boiling. "I wanted to kill him," Anthony said incredulously.

Jesse pretended to read his ledger a moment longer before he replied, "Anyone would have."

"Anyone *human*." The response to that was a disapproving frown, and Anthony dropped the topic. "I—I suppose I'm tired. How long has it been, anyway?"

The non sequitur didn't bother Jesse. "Six months and five days, kid. Quite a tour we've had ourselves."

"I'd forgotten what an ordeal this was. Haven't undertaken anything similar since—"

"Since we were with Li Lao Chang's company," Jesse finished. He smiled, reminiscing. "God, but you were green when Li first told me to show you the ropes. Green, but damned good. You could have acted rings around—"

"Don't."

"Those porn shows and shoot-'em-ups you did for Li were just stepping-stones," Jesse persisted. "If you'd stuck with it, you'd be the sector's top actor by now."

"Don't," Anthony repeated, more firmly. Why did they keep

9

rehashing this pointless argument? Around and around and around, going nowhere. Jesse was so sharp about other things. Surely he must see that the youthful acting career he treasured in his memory had for Anthony been solely a means to an end. That stint with Li's troupe had taught the young migrant from Earth all the tricks of the trade he'd needed to develop into a master *behind* the vid lenses, not in *front* of them. And that was where he intended to stay—as boss of Saunder Studio, acknowledged expert in handling emota-sensor equipment and directing. *Not* as an emulator of vain, shallow, posturing puppets like Veda and Hassan.

He *had* taken something useful from acting—biofeedback techniques and knowledge of how to fake emotions. With time, the processes had been so polished they'd become almost second nature to him. But they could never be first nature for a *clone*.

The only exception to his established façade was his friendship with Jesse. That was genuine, the only relationship he could trust, the only one worth the effort. The rest of Anthony Saunder's life was a magnificent performance, carefully staged in order to survive in a universe filled with normal human beings.

"Well, finally!" Jesse said. Veda, Hassan, and the supporting players were climbing into the carriage, finding their places amid luggage, backstage crew people, and their traveling companions from Saunder Studio. Grumbling with impatience, the driver slammed the door and clucked to his team. Swaying, the vehicle jounced across the cobblestoned plaza and out onto Clay Settlement's main street. Some of React Theater's staunchest fans loped alongside the bus for a couple of hundred meters or so, waving their farewells. Veda blew them kisses.

The carriage rocked over uneven pavement and into potholes. The scene on every side was typical of a recently tamed frontier world's capital: wooden houses; tents; squatters living beneath the elevated boardwalks; kitchen middens; smoke and stench from open fires; and humans, Vahnajes, Whimeds, and several large, furry Lannons.

The shuttleport area was equally chaotic. Horse-drawn vehicles of all kinds jockeyed for the best place in the lines to the cargo and passenger terminals; farmers stood beside the road selling food and drink to passing drivers and riders; and competing merchants haggled over their outgoing shipments of processed *purgatio*, trying to wrangle the best prices from the trip jobbers.

By the time Anthony's caravan reached the main gates, the group was sweaty and irritable. They hauled their own bags and theatrical gear inside and fought through a tangle of other arriving and departing travelers. The terminal, like most of Settlement Clay's public facilities, was built of logs and smelled of mold and wet conifers. The interior atmosphere did nothing to ease Anthony's temper.

The sight of their assigned staffer from the Visitors' Bureau did, however. She waved to catch their attention, drawing them out of the noisy, seething crowd. The combined tour's tickets were in her hand, and she knew exactly where the group needed to be. In seconds, they'd left the cacophony of the main concourse behind and were walking down a quiet, cool hallway.

Anthony resumed an interrupted conversation with the woman, bantering slyly. She laughed and nodded, savoring, as he was, the memory of a dalliance they'd shared this past week. It was standard form for Anthony, on a journey or on his base planet. Affairs had always been easy, with rules spelled out in advance. Nothing weighty, nothing permanent—just fun. The staffer had been a charming diversion, as he'd tried to be for her.

Now he was doing his best to leave her with the feeling that she was glad she'd met him. The staffer seemed to be playing the same friendly game: "So long. And look me up again, if you ever head back this way."

Neither of them was paying much attention to where they were putting their feet. They had almost reached the departures lounge when they hit a wall.

CHAPTER TWO

⊙⊙⊙⊙⊙⊙⊙⊙

Departure Delayed

No, the wall had hit *them*. It had been a wall of local troopers, boomtown brawlers wearing uniforms.

Anthony helped the Visitors' Bureau staffer to her feet while he eyed the goons warily. The man giving orders to the roughnecks wore the same Bureau badge as the woman assisting Anthony's tour group. The two confronted each other.

"Stand aside! My party has a clear pass!"

"So does mine! Full clearance from Ops!"

Anthony considered putting in his credit's worth. If they didn't straighten out this snarl fast, the troupe—including him and Jesse—would miss their flight.

Their escort shouted, "I've got reconfirmed reservations for the React Theater company and Anthony Saunder and—"

"So have . . . *Anthony* Saunder?" The staffer's counterpart did a comical double take.

At that instant, a blond man emerged from the nearby lounge. His elaborate feathered headdress shook in the breeze of his hurried pace as he demanded, "What's the problem here?"

Jesse spotted the distinctive hat and groaned, "Damn. Colin! Our own personal bad penny. It *would* have to be him."

Colin Saunder's liaison tripped over his tongue trying to smooth over the mix-up. When he mentioned Anthony's name, the blond stiffened, but quickly recovered his aplomb. His brown eyes searched the crowded corridor until he spotted his kinsman. "Anthony!" he cried in sham delight. "I didn't know you were here!"

"Really?" Anthony took a proffered hand. "I've been expecting to see you ever since I spoke to a lovely man who kept quarters at the same hostel you did."

The shorter man's square, boyish features twisted with distaste. "That non-contrib chud. What an obnoxious mess." An uninformed observer would have thought the pair were amiable conspirators, trading a joke, as the kinsmen donned their best manners, concealing years of animosity. Colin nodded to the React Theater bunch. "I heard your shows were terrific. I intended to catch a performance, but just couldn't find the time."

"We'll sell you a vid," Jesse volunteered. "That is, if you'll ease up on those trade restrictions that limit our Studio's sales on Procyon Four. Never saw so much red tape as your Settlement's people crank out."

Colin seemed amused. "I'll see what I can do. And how are you, Jesse?"

The question was a formality. Jesse, though, took it as a wedge. "Better than Anthony and our liaison lady, after your goons mauled them."

The rising young merchant prince from Settlement Procyon Four had to respond to the challenge. He spun on his heel, making the feathered headdress billow colorfully. "Nesbitt? What about that? Did your men use force?"

"We—we were only protecting your privacy."

"I said nothing about brutalizing anyone. Be assured I will report this to my friends on the Council. It doesn't reflect well on Clay's officialdom. Not well at all." The chastened staffer blubbered abjectly. Colin was widely acknowledged as the kingmaker of the Charter Settlement Planets Council. His candidate, Myron Simpkins, was supposed to be a sure bet for the Presidency. Colin could indeed do this erring bureaucrat considerable damage, perhaps ruin his career. Nesbitt bustled about efficiently, getting rid of the troopers and soothing ruffled egos and feelings. His mood mellowing, Colin bowed to the React Theater's liaison. "I do hope those brutes didn't injure you, my dear."

"Uh, no. But . . . but what are we going to do about these duplicate reservations?"

The merchant's smile would have melted a glacier. "I'm certain it's merely a programming error," Colin said. "Easy to see how someone made the mistake." He shifted his focus to Anthony.

Saunder Studio's head adopted his kinsman's urbane tone. "So it would seem. But then we've been getting in each other's way for years, haven't we?"

Colin's mask slid off for a second. He corrected the lapse at once, saying lightly, "Oh, I wouldn't call it *that*. We'll clear up this misunderstanding in no time." It was obviously a meaningless dance of words.

Anthony already had assessed the beings crammed into the departure lounge. Vahnajes and Terrans, well-dressed V.I.P.s with luggage IDs that indicated they were advance teams for the upcoming Interspecies Trade Conference. This Solar Year, for the first time, the meeting would take place in the Terran sector. *Homo sapiens* was coming of age among the star-roving civilizations. The e.t.s had admitted that by giving the hosting job to Colin, a human. He'd spent heavily and politicked ruthlessly to achieve that coup, and nothing was going to interfere with his plans now. Come hell, high water, or nova, he'd be shepherding that roomful of V.I.P.s to his base planet, Procyon Four—the site of the Conference. He certainly wasn't going to yield his reservations to a relative he detested.

But for the time being, the show had to go on. Colin snapped his fingers imperiously and commanded the Visitors' Bureau employees to check log-in times on the two sets of tickets.

"Someone's going to get bumped," Jesse said. "I think it's us. I count twenty-nine in that ready room—"

"And Colin makes thirty," Anthony finished, nodding.

Hassan was complaining loudly, hoping against hope—in vain. Anthony read the Visitors' Bureau liaisons' faces and knew before they announced it that Colin's reservations had been filed first. The blond spread his hands in a gesture of gracious regret. "Well, there it is. Sorry. Perhaps we can work out a compromise."

"Sure," Jesse said. "We'll draw straws to see who sits on whose lap."

Colin bared his teeth in a strained grin. "Very funny."

"You have the fait accompli, correct?" Anthony said. He shrugged elegantly, taking a casual, unconcerned stance. Colin's aides and the React Theater were visibly impressed, and again Colin's mask slipped a trifle. He shot Anthony a glare brimming with hatred.

"This is . . . embarrassing. I hadn't planned this . . ."

Anthony waved aside the stumbling apology, deliberately adding to his kinsman's irritation. That looked like the only satisfaction he was likely to get out of this sorry situation. Fait accompli, indeed! All the one-upmanship in suave manners in the universe wouldn't cancel out the fact that Colin was going to take that shuttle—and Anthony and Jesse weren't.

Veda Ingersoll had been dithering, more and more agitated by the moment. Now she trotted toward Colin and began simpering shamelessly. "Oh, Mr. Saunder! Don't you have at least two extra seats to spare? I'd be ever so grateful. A terribly important series contract hinges on my getting to Loezzi Settlement to meet my agent by a specific date. My hairdresser and I *must* make those connections."

Jesse winked at the prima donna's disgruntled fellow players. "The rest of you peasants can sprout wings to make *your* outbound flights," he teased.

Stung, Veda retorted, "*I* am a star. Can I help it if my public demands my presence?"

Colin was trying to cope with this unanticipated development and turn it to his advantage. "Uh . . . Veda Ingersoll? How wonderful! I'm a big fan of yours."

"Has been since he was a baby," Jesse put in, "and since Veda was way too old to play the ingenue."

She ignored the crack. Without a hint of embarrassment, the actress turned to Anthony and asked sweetly, "You don't mind if I ride on ahead with your kinsman, do you, darling?" Under other circumstances, he would have guffawed derisively. That ham! Her blue hair was artfully disarranged, her pout exquisite—if she'd been twenty years younger.

Veda gushed, swamping Colin in coy compliments, extracted from the hundreds of rôles Veda had played in her career. The merchant prince looked slightly glazed. He managed to shut off the twittering verbal flow by ordering Nesbitt to add Veda and her dye specialist to the passenger roster. The actress shifted her effusive expressions of gratitude to the rattled Visitors' Bureau staffer.

A paging bell sounded. A recorded voice announced that those in the V.I.P. lounge should prepare for boarding. Aides scampered about gathering luggage and herding Colin's guests toward the debark tunnel. Veda and her hanger-on didn't need to be prompted twice. The room emptied rapidly.

Procyon Four's merchant prince lingered, staring at his cousin. Slowly, with apparent reluctance, Colin began to retreat. "I'm sorry things worked out this way, Anthony. I hope we'll meet again soon, under happier conditions."

"I'm sure we *will* meet again. We can't avoid it, can we? Have a safe trip."

The blond's face was a map of resentment and malicious triumph. The second reaction won out as he turned away, hurrying into the corridor at the far side of the lounge. Colin paused and threw a gloating parting glance over his shoulder; then the door shut him off from those left behind. There was a shift of air pressure as gates opened and closed in the shuttle gantry's elevator access. A few minutes later, Anthony heard the rumble of machinery shifting the gantry away and clearing the shuttle for launch—the shuttle Anthony and Jesse had planned to ride.

The stranded travelers moved into the now-vacant V.I.P. room, for all the good that would do them. They were well aware they were likely to be stuck here for some time. Passenger service on boomtown worlds was irregular, at best; cargoes got preference.

React Theater's remaining star performer railed dramatically against the fates and anyone Hassan could find to blame. "Dammit, Anthony, why didn't you use some Saunder-McKelvey muscle on him? How could you let him steal our tickets that way?"

"Colin's a Saunder, too," Anthony said tiredly. "Remember? And his reservations numbers *were* lower than ours. Maybe you should have tried Veda's stunt. *She* got on board."

Getting no satisfaction there, Hassan struck out in alternate directions. His troupe had learned how to dodge his tantrums, but the Visitors' Bureau staffer hadn't. This wasn't the first time Anthony had witnessed the actor's bullying, and he was in no mood to put up with it now. Locking horns was no solution, however.

Gradually, talking all around the knot that was rubbing Hassan

16

raw, Anthony shunted the man's anger and mollified the shaken liaison worker. Soon Hassan was exchanging commiserations with his people, channeling his energy into imaginative ill wishes aimed at Colin Saunder. The woman from the Visitors' Bureau, inspired by fresh enthusiasm at being off the hook, charged out to light a fire under the terminal's reservations division. "I'll get you replacement tickets!" she promised. "Right away!"

Anthony doubted it, but he continued smiling until she was out of sight before he let his dejection show. Heaving a sigh, he flopped down onto a bench beside Jesse and settled in for a long wait.

Well, at least things are quieter in here now. Hassan is behaving himself, thanks to me. I jerked his strings pretty neatly, if I do say so myself.

He was good at manipulation, at playing survival games. When he was very young, living on Earth, Anthony had used that game to placate the adults who controlled his life. He suspected he'd inherited the gift through Patrick Saunder's DNA, along with the long-dead politician's golden voice, handsome features, and hynoptic pale-blue eyes—none of Patrick Saunder's wealth and clout, though. The clone had gone out into the universe with good looks, dazzling manipulative skills, and damned little else. It was ironic that Patrick's natural grandson, Colin, had followed the same route. He and Anthony were *both* skeletons in the family closet.

"The bastard did it again."

Anthony craned his neck, peering at Jesse. He didn't need to ask what his friend was talking about. "Low blow. Colin's not responsible for his being illegitimate."

"Hell, that's not what I meant," Jesse said. "Sure, his mama was dumb for not pinning Stuart down with a marriage certificate before they went romping. But that didn't make her a criminal. It's Colin's fancy airs and actions that make him a bastard. Merchant prince! Kingmaker! That bunch of feathers! I'll bet you credits to seaweed he rigged things so we'd be stuck here."

"You're diving for clams without a helmet."

"Am I? Did you see that look he gave us when he was walking out? I'm going to check those reservations records." Jesse jumped to his feet.

Anthony trailed him to the door, arguing, "Even if you're right, what good will it do to find out?"

"It'll help me keep score. Sooner or later we'll square things and pay him off, kid, one for one." The associate producer shrugged off the younger man's hand and stormed down the corridor.

Fighting a headache, Anthony massaged his temples. Words rang in his thoughts:

The bastard versus the clone! Fate had put them on a collision course from their births and made them pawns on the chessboard at Saunderhome, the family's legendary Caribbean island complex.

Patrick's widow Carissa ruled the complex and her husband's vast fortune from there with pale, steely hands. But she couldn't always rule her son Stuart, that rakehell, degenerate spendthrift. Colin was the love child of Stuart and his mistress Olivia Gage. For a while it had looked as if Stuart might cut the apron strings and start his own dynasty. Carissa stopped that cold by buying the clones, which threatened Stuart's inheritance. Then she'd bribed the courts to "lose" Olivia Gage's proofs of Colin's paternity. Stuart's little rebellion was finished. Checkmate and game.

From that point on, Colin had no legal right on Earth to call himself a Saunder. Until he'd emigrated to the Charter Settlement Planets, he'd been known as Colin Gage. Out here, names and paternity were a lot less important. And Carissa didn't care what name he went by—out here—as long as he *stayed* on the frontier.

Anthony was the other surviving pawn left over from that cruel game. He'd been a tool. And when a tool lost its usefulness, Carissa Duryea Saunder discarded it. Or ignored it when it ran away to the C.S.P.

The Terran sector was light-years wide, wide enough for the clone and the bastard to go their separate ways. And yet they met with surprising frequency. It was as if they were being pushed together by forces beyond their control and were still pawns, not of outsiders, this time, but of their own pasts.

Colin, the bastard, the exile. Never legally acknowledged by his father, he was cheated out of his inheritance by his grandmother. His mother was a suicide, his only other relative a drunken ne'er-do-well of an uncle. When that man died, Colin had shipped out to the stars. He'd climbed steadily ever since, a true by-his-bootstraps overachiever.

Anthony, the clone, the exile. A trump to top Stuart's claims as Patrick Saunder's heir, he was another of Carissa's rejects. He, too, had worked his way up from nothing out here in the Settlements. In his early years of freedom, Anthony had earned his bread as a brawn laborer, as so many other young emigrants had. Then he'd stumbled into Li Lao Chang's acting company—and had met Jesse. That had initiated a big change for the better. His career in action vids and erotic dream dramas had been short, by Anthony's own choice. But that stint with Li had given him the training to graduate into operating his own vid studio. It had taken years to accumulate sufficient funds to set up his business, though he had eventually made it. The clone hadn't climbed as far as the bastard yet, because Anthony had gotten a later start. Now if he could only hang on financially a while longer, he'd be over the top, matching his kinsman's success—or near enough to satisfy Anthony's hopes.

"I was right." Jesse had returned from his errand. He ran a hand through his grizzled mane and repeated, "I was right."

"Colin bribed the reservations programmers?"

"Nah! Nothing so petty. He just pulled a few strings," Jesse explained. "These Clay settlers know which side of their Charter Contract the credit flow is buttered on. They owe Procyon Four's export pipeline plenty. That means Colin's outfit—"

"He damned well *is* petty," Anthony interrupted, "when it's my head he's holding under the water!" Hassan's group stared wonderingly at their fellow passengers. Anthony forced himself to speak more calmly as he went on, "Colin's so convinced we're fighting him that he feels he has to drown us."

"Why?" Jesse demanded. "Come on, kid. Not *that* again. It won't dry. Colin's playing dirty simply because he's a rotten bastard. Why should it make any difference to him that our Studio's located on Procyon Five?"

"Because we're right next door to *his* HQ on Procyon Four," Anthony said with icy logic. "Swiping our reservations is his way of paying us back for swimming into his territory."

This debate wasn't as familiar as the one concerning Anthony's getting out of the acting profession—but it was equally heated between the two men.

Jesse's scorn was withering. "Are you through? We've been over this a hundred times. How the hell are we crowding Colin? Procyon Four or Five, so what? His product lines are precious metals and exotic pharmaceuticals. Nobody on Procyon Five is in competition with him—especially not *us*. Most of our companies

19

deal in undersea manufactures. And he doesn't have any investments in—"

"I still think he feels pressured," Anthony said. "I told you we should have found another site for the Studio."

His friend threw up his hands in exasperation. "Will you listen to yourself? Be sensible, kid. The reason we picked Procyon Five was that we didn't have a lot of options. It wasn't because we were trying to stick a sand burr in Colin's ass. Settlements weren't exactly begging us to sign leases with them, you know. Five just needed our taxes more than most."

Anthony hardly heard him. "It wasn't so bad until we built the Studio. Before then, there was some nastiness whenever I ran into Colin, but nothing ugly. We'd paste on our silly grins and one-up each other playing Mister Smooth. Now he's getting mean. I can't help thinking he's reacting to being pushed too hard."

"That's *his* problem, if true," Jessie retorted. "It's time he grew up and quit acting as if he's the only guy on the block. He doesn't operate his business empire that way."

"He's not *related* to his customers," Anthony muttered.

"I repeat, that's *his* problem." A grin split Jesse's homely face. "And I also repeat that I'm keeping score. Don't worry about it. Someday when he least expects it, I'll pay him back with interest."

"When we can *afford* to pay him back. Did you find out how much this delay is going to cost us?"

Jesse winced. "Don't ask. We'll have to sell a few more gross emota-sensor packages, kid."

His friend's offhanded optimism made Anthony chuckle sourly. A few more gross! Sure they could! Nothing to it.

Well, what was done was done. They were stuck here. And whichever outbound flight they managed to link up with, they'd have to pay the fare—and the extra expense of rearranging connections further along their star route. They might as well make the best of the situation and sit down to a long haul of waiting.

In fact the wait wasn't nearly as long as Anthony had feared. Their ally with the Visitors' Bureau performed small miracles. After only five hours, she wangled them a replacement passage. Anthony pulled out all the stops, projecting warm sincerity, thanking her profusely.

When he got a look at the transport his group would be riding, though, he wasn't so sure the woman had done them a favor. The craft was an ill-equipped rust bucket. But lift-off was nominal, in the spacers' slang. Anthony hated the leaden sensations and vibration of a launch from a planetary gravity well, so he psyched himself through that leg of the trip, imagining he was a pilot, not concerned about all that clanking and thumping surrounding the passenger cabin. His scenario actually wasn't too farfetched. There *were* accomplished space aces on the Saunder-McKelvey family tree—his kinswoman Brenna, for one. She was the test pilot who'd broken the light-speed barrier, giving the stars to Terra. No doubt she'd feel right at home here.

Settlement Clay's oxygen-rich sky darkened as the ship spiraled upward, reaching toward escape velocity. Passengers rubbed their med patches, compensating for the stress. It was still a rough ride, getting up to the forest world's artificial satellite.

Docking was a tooth-jarring jolt. The crew was used to handling cargo, not people. Anthony clung to his safety straps while the linkup was completed. After another tiresome wait, the passengers were permitted to take the tube "up" to the spaceport's lobby. Even with compensation meds, the transfer to a rotating torus affected the travelers severely. Looking as frazzled as they felt, they commandeered chairs in an empty alcove and sat down to wait—again.

Jesse checked the Port's reservations counter and reported back. "That starhopper we were going to take is long gone, naturally."

"Naturally," Anthony said, not bothering to hide his disgust. Long gone, with Colin aboard. That still rankled.

"But we got lucky," Jesse continued. Hassan's troupe perked up, interested. "There's a ship here in the station finishing repairs. They lost their scheduled payload because of the layover for that. Now they're happy to take us and some other passengers on instead of a *purgatio* shipment. Anything. Just so they can head on out and pick up a consignment at their next port of call."

"Which is?" Hassan demanded.

"Polk Station. We can make connections there for Loezzi, then to Beno—where *you* guys can hop for your home base and Anthony and I can grab a straight shot to the Procyon system."

"That's awfully roundabout," the actor whined.

"It's the best you're going to do," Jesse said. "If you don't believe me, try to do better." The grumbling subsided. Over the past months the troupe had come to trust the associate producer's abilities in these matters, as Anthony had done years earlier.

There was another wait, of course, while arrangements were finalized and the cargo hauler readied for launch. The travelers sprawled in the alcove. Some dozed. Others tended to small chores with their luggage or bought snacks or gossiped. Anthony and Jesse collected relayed messages from the Port's com office and started going through a somewhat dated backlog from Saunder Studio. Nothing called for instant, expensive replies. All the same, this remote version of contact with their co-workers holding down the home fort was very welcome.

Home—not too much longer, with luck, and they'd be there. Star roaming was new and exciting to tourists from Earth. But many of those who actually lived in the Settlements often found themselves drawn to a single world, a base planet where they could stay put and call that their own.

A high-pitched raspy voice cut into the men's conversation. "Thor-i-sad? You Saun-der kin-dred? Urr! An-thony Saun-der!"

CHAPTER THREE

○○○○○○○○

The Long Way Home

With effort, Anthony mastered his surprise and got to his feet. He faced a quintet of Vahnajes. None wore a translation device, so he spoke at a very slow, measured pace. *"Mejuo*, yes. I am Anthony Saunder. I give you hello."

As they bowed and bobbed, he studied them curiously. There was little sexual dimorphism among lutrinoids; the only way to distinguish the quintet's two males from the females was by the males' erectile sideburns. All five were tall, thin, and wore the flowing robes favored by high-ranking Vahnajes. Unlike others of their species Anthony had been acquainted with, these painted their gray skins a stark white with thick layers of ugly cosmetics. He supposed that was a fashion peculiar to their particular ethnic group within the Vahnaj culture. The five also were exuding a musky odor, which betrayed how new they were to the Terran sector; generally, lutrinoids who dealt with humans were polite enough to neutralize their exhalations and sweat. These e.t.s apparently were ignorant of that protocol.

The group's leader sidled closer to Anthony, assaulting the Terran's nostrils. "I Fal-Am," he said. "Us . . . urr . . . del-e-gate. Urr . . . in-ter-shpecies . . . urr . . . Con-fer-enta. Yes?"

23

Anthony overcame an urge to shove the Vahnaj downwind and said in a rigidly correct tone, "I am honored to meet you, esteemed delegates."

"Us . . . urr . . . do not . . . urr . . . wissh dis-turb . . ."

"You do not disturb me, *Mejuo*," Anthony lied. The Vahnajes bowed and bobbed and grinned inanely, forcing him to respond in kind. He knew that whatever they wanted wouldn't be arrived at quickly. Face paint and stink aside, this fivesome seemed as methodical as all their race were.

Anthony couldn't recall a time when he hadn't known a Vahnaj. Ambassador Quol-Bez, the Alliance's first representative to Earth, had been a frequent guest at Saunderhome. As interspecies contacts enlarged, other lutrinoids had visited the humans' sector and the Caribbean island. Vahnajes—all e.t. civilizations, in fact —regarded Saunderhome as a shrine and the Saunder-McKelveys as the premier Terrans. That attitude dated from the mid-Twenty-first Century, when Todd Saunder's code-breaking attempts had established mankind's initial communication with beings from other solar systems. The breakthrough had put the Saunder-McKelveys solidly in the forefront of human affairs, a position they'd never relinquished. Since those early days, others had challenged their preeminence, but none had surpassed them, in or out of the Terran sphere of influence.

Fal-Am patted his three-fingered hands together. "You . . . urr . . . traaa-vel . . . urr . . . Con-fer-enta. Yes?"

"No, *Mejuo*. I travel to Procyon Five."

"Oh! Wissh . . . urr . . . safe journey." The last word came out as "churneeee." Typical Vahnaj pronunciation of the—to them —difficult human tongue, Terran English.

C.S.P.'s Linguistics Division employed full-time staffers to translate supposedly already translated Vahnaj dispatches. To a degree, that wasn't the lutrinoids' fault; their vocal apparatus simply wasn't designed to handle alien words. But it could be done. Ambassador Quol-Bez, exceptional in that area as in many others, had overcome the handicap. The majority of his fellow Vahnajes, as often as not, still mangled even the names of their interstellar neighbors. They rendered "Ulisor" as "Yulshor" and "Whimed" as "Feemaid." Anthony had it on good authority that a very prominent Vahnaj diplomat consistently addressed his human counterparts as "Trerrians." Even Ambassador Quol-Bez had difficulty with certain sounds. It had been a long time after his assignment to Earth before Terrans learned that one race of e.t.s was named the Lannon, not the Trannon. To this day, the Vahnajes' elder statesman was unable to make that shift.

Bows and grins followed, with bursts of flowery titles and compliments.

Anthony followed suit, knowing the drill. Despite the elaborate courtesies, he remained wary. Experience had taught humans that not every lutrinoid was as trustworthy and admirable as Ambassador Quol-Bez. He was his species' best. And as was true with humans, aliens came in all varieties—superb, terrible, and indifferent. Anthony had no way of guessing which these five were. An intelligent Terran remained on guard around the grayfaces—or whitefaces, in this case—until he'd thoroughly sounded out the Vahnajes in question.

If any alien needed a trans device, it was Fal-Am. "Us . . . urr . . . stay Porta. Urr . . . temp-o-rare. To traa-vel Col-in Saun-der. Our ssship . . . urr . . . broke. Ar-rife . . . urr . . . not time enough. Wait 'struct-shuns . . . urr . . . gov-ment . . ."

"I understand, *Mejuo*. Most unfortunate. I trust you will find alternate transportation soon."

Suddenly the quintet began chittering furiously. The males' sideburns flattened, a sign of extreme tension. The Vahnajes peered intently across the torus's corridor at a Whimed who was pretending to read a monitor. Sensing their scrutiny, he turned, glowering. It wasn't the same felinoid Anthony had seen on Clay, but this one's starburst stare was just as riveting. In lockstep, the Vahnaj males approached him. The Whimed backpedaled, yelling an obvious warning. They didn't heed it or stop. He ran.

Anthony watched this performance in astonishment. He was awed by the Whimed's coordination. Running in a space station wasn't an easy trick for *any* humanoid.

And the Vahnajes were enraged! He'd never imagined their race being capable of such fury.

The Whimed vanished around a bend in the torus. The Vahnajes halted, swiveled, and came straight back to the place where they had been standing. Fal-Am smirked and resumed his conversation as if nothing had happened. "You . . . pleash . . . An-thony . . . will . . . urr . . . be of Pro-cyon Five del-e-ga-tion to Con-ferenta?"

Still rattled by the strange encounter he'd witnessed, Anthony said, "Uh . . . no, I will not attend."

That triggered a loud round of babbling apologies. Taken aback, Anthony assured the Vahnajes they had nothing to apologize for. "There is no offense, *Mejuo*. Honorable Fal-Am, no offense."

Unconvinced, the e.t.s continued to retreat, bowing and bobbing and chirring abjectly. After one final mumbling grovel, they fled, their robes flapping comically.

Jesse frowned and asked, "What the hell was that all about?"

"Damned if I know. For a moment I thought we were going to see a slice of interstellar cold war right here. Did you notice that hot pursuit earlier? I guess what set off this last session of apologies was my telling them I wasn't attending Colin's Trade Conference."

"Wish you could," Jesse said. "It would be great PR for the Studio."

"Forget it. We haven't been invited."

"Shoulda been," the older man insisted. "It's a business conference, right? And the Studio's a business."

"A very small one, compared to the big guns that will be hopping over to Procyon Four in a month." Anthony went on, "Anyway, Colin isn't likely to ask me to join the crowd. He's been cocking his feathered hat to host this brawl for years. And spent who knows how many thousands of credits to swing it. Nothing's going to throw a cloud over his moment of glory. My presence there would definitely be a cloud for him."

"It's not his decision to make." Jesse sighed, looking glum. "But you're right. We're out, though we shouldn't be. Five's guilds and trade associations have been cordial to us. Didn't invite us into last season's Planetary Industrial Exposition, though, until you threw 'em a whale of a sales pitch. Snobs! We belong up there with those big guys."

Anthony said slyly, "If you're in a hurry to join them, we could cut corners—go the Tracy Rutledge route."

The suggestion, even in jest, made Jesse shudder. He shared Anthony's opinion of that notorious case. Rutledge had been Settlement Alpha Cee's top trader of rare botanicals, alien gems, and esoteric sporting events. He was going places at top speed. Then he'd become entangled in a messy bribery scandal involving a Charter Corporation development project. A lot of risk takers had indulged in similar shady deals, throughout the history of Terrans in space. The practice was winked at if no one got caught.

Rutledge had been. His fall was spectacular, his mercantile empire collapsing almost overnight. That example had served as a warning flag to Anthony even before he'd set up Saunder Studio. He had resolved to keep *his* business dealings strictly clean, with no whisper of anything illegal. And Jesse agreed completely. They'd let fools play those stupid games—and pay the consequences.

Suddenly they had no more leisure to contemplate the Rutledge tragedy. Port control announced that the travelers could now board their starhopper. Quickly—before anything *else* might delay them—the group gathered their gear and hurried to the departures gate.

Halfway there, they passed Fal-Am's quintet. The Vahnajes were whispering to one another and watching two Whimeds from a safe distance. This time, however, there was no attempt to get any closer to their opponents.

Anthony glanced thoughtfully at the Whimeds. Unlike Vahnajes, felinoids exhibited plenty of sexual dimorphism. This pair was definitely male and female, the male taller and heavier, the female hippier, though bustless, as were all nonlactating Whimed women. The cat folks' facial features were identical, underlining their kinship. Twin births were the norm for their species, according to those "meet your alien" edu-vids Anthony had produced for C.S.P. Council.

Vahnajes and Whimeds glared daggers at each other. The effect was that of two sets of espionage agents, each casing the enemy. These humanoid aliens were in a heated mercantile rivalry, struggling for dominance in the Terran sector. Anthony hoped their conflict would remain at its present stage and out of the political arena. *That* might threaten instability, and instability was bad for business.

Then he was entering the descent tube and had to put the e.t.s.' quarrels out of his mind. As he moved away from the outer wheel, gravity diminished. That was the only clue that he was heading "down." The tunnel's interior was a bright, circular passageway, distorting perspective. Anthony clung to guide rails, following signal arrows through a series of pressure locks until he reached the starhopper. He, Jesse, the React Theater company, and an assortment of other people settled themselves into couches and secured their safety straps.

Anthony was glad to see that the ship was owned by Saunder-McKelvey Enterprises Interstellar. When he'd first left Earth, nearly every FTL vehicle in the Charter Settlement Planets had been registered to SMEI. His kindred's patents on the stardrive had given them a big head start in the transport field. Nowadays they were being crowded, though all the other companies also had to use SMEI's designs; those were the only ones available, or ever likely to be. Profit still poured into the well-lined pockets of Anthony's relatives.

Like a good many starcraft, this one had been constructed to carry cargo. For this jump, one of its holds was converted for passenger use. In an emergency, the compartment could be sealed and jettisoned as a lifeboat. That was the plan, at any rate. Everyone knew that if a spaceship ran into serious trouble, there was rarely time to jettison *anything*. Settlers tended to be fatalistic on that score. There was not much need for worry, however, on this ride. SMEI starhoppers had a fine safety record.

Air locks cycled, whining and thumping. Tethers and boarding tunnels disconnected as the craft buttoned herself up tightly. Tugs shifted her out of her berth, pushing her antisunward from Clay's space port. Despite the heavy multiple hulls, the travelers felt the casting-off procedures. It took a lot of power to overcome a starhopper's inertia. She had real-space propulsion units, of course, but it was cheaper to tow her out to her FTL takeoff point. During these stages, a few blasé passengers actually slept, floating in their couches, restrained only by safety lines.

It took nearly a solar hour to reach launch mark zero. On the cabin view screens, Anthony saw fading blips crawling out of the frame—tugs, getting clear before the big ship's graviton spin resonance engines switched on.

The screen blurred, and a tightness gripped Anthony's skull.

They were underway.

He'd always had to endure that painless pressure when a starhopper began to break the light-speed barrier. Once he adjusted to the effect, the sensation eased.

There was no feeling of acceleration. Popular science vids—many of them produced by Saunder Studio—explained that when an FTL ship engaged her main drive, the vessel didn't travel any faster. Instead, she slipped in and out of "real" space and time, shrinking the universe.

For hours Anthony napped, catching up on much-needed sleep, reenergizing tired muscles and frayed nerves. During the following wakeful period, he and Jesse resumed their work with accumulated com messages and their business correspondence backlog.

Many hours in the ensuing days of ship's travel could be filled sleeping and eating. More work was followed by vid production shoptalk with the React Theater troupe. And of course there were workouts in the ship's exercise cubicles, counteracting the long stretch of weightlessness.

After all that, there was boredom.

As travel time dragged on, Anthony thought increasingly of home. And he thought increasingly of Colin and of how the merchant prince had gloated when he'd stranded the men from Saunder Studio.

The FTL drive dimmed and brightened the star field showing on the monitors. Its effect was lulling. Anthony stared as the ship spanned light-years, his thoughts drifting, blurring . . .

Anthony seemed to be sitting in his house, watching waves lap at the main room's window wall, waves of a shallow inland ocean, younger and less salty than the sea girdling Saunderhome . . .

Saunderhome—on Earth.

He was five years old, listening to servants.

"Clones. Right out of a test tube, they told me. Hatched 'em from surrogate mamas, but they ain't *real* kids."

"Don't let the boss lady hear you talkin'. It's supposed to be a secret. She don't want nobody to know they're clones, even if everybody *does* know."

". . . say she paid plenty for 'em, so's she could keep sonny boy in line. Serves Stuart right for getting mixed up with that Gage woman. *She* had her nerve, that whore, claimin' her bastard was the boss lady's grandson."

"Doctors say he is. Blood tests and all."

"Stuart never signed no papers. It ain't his, legal. He may be a mean son of a bitch, but he's no dummy. Miz C. sure stomped him and that whore good, hee-hee! Yep! Just flattened 'em with her bought-and-paid-for judge. Got Stuart's money locked up tight. He has to run to mama for every penny now . . ."

"Hush! There's one o' them clone babies. What you doin' here, honey? Where's your brothers! Lord! I hope them two littlest ones didn't wander off again. They're so pitiful stupid they'll drown if it rains. We better find 'em."

"Dunno why Miz C. wants the poor li'l things. She don't need 'em any more, now that sonny boy's behavin' hisself."

"Can't put the babies back in the test tubes, you fool. She's keepin' 'em as insurance, in case Stuart gets hincty again. C'mon. Let's round 'em up, like we do Miz C.'s lap dogs . . ."

The gossip session ended abruptly in Anthony's mind, because five-year-old Anthony had refused to listen any longer.

Miz C.—Carissa Duryea Saunder, Empress of Saunderhome.

Sonny boy, that degenerate brute—Stuart, her son.

At the time of that overheard conversation, Stuart Saunder was merely going through the motions of rebellion. There'd been little fight left in him by then. He was beaten; but, like a beached water breather, he kept thrashing spasmodically—and futilely. His ill-fated dalliance with Olivia Gage and Colin's birth had been Stuart's last hope of breaking free from Carissa. She'd ended those dreams before they'd really begun. Later, Carissa had arranged what she deemed a more suitable match for her son with one of Earth's wealthiest heiresses, Felicity Emigh.

Felicity, another of Carissa's pawns, had died recently after decades of a loveless match, and Carissa's scheming had come to nothing; there'd been no issue, no legitimate grandson to take Colin's place. With Felicity dead now, Carissa and Stuart lived alone in their castle by the sea—seething in their mutual hatred.

It had been years before Anthony fully comprehended his rôle in their private war. Understanding started when he was a toddler. He'd met Olivia Gage briefly. She had sweet-talked her way around the Saunderhome guards in a desperate attempt to get to Stuart and convince him to defy his mother. Olivia had brought four-year-old Colin with her. On the grassy terrace fronting that Caribbean palace, Anthony and Colin first came face-to-face. They had stared at each other with the unblinking intensity of very small children. Anthony remembered that Colin's big brown eyes shone with fear, and that Colin's hair looked silver-gold in the tropic sunlight. As Colin sucked his thumb, the dark-haired, pale-eyed clones goggled at him. Anthony could smell flowers, feel the Caribbean breeze . . . and hear nasty little dogs yapping in the distance. The Empress of Saunderhome, accompanied by her bodyguards, was coming to evict Olivia and her young son from the island.

That was the last time Anthony had seen Colin until over a decade later, after they'd both emigrated to the C.S.P.

At least Olivia Gage hadn't had to suffer that long, as Stuart's wife had. Olivia died by her own hand when Colin was seven. Her brother had anticipated living in the lap of luxury because of his sister's liaison. Instead, the embittered man was left with the custody of a bastard kid and no money. Rumors were that he took out his frustration on his nephew in blows, kicks, and vicious emotional abuse. Perhaps that was why Colin had grown up to be such a smiler to one's face and an expert backstabber.

Carissa's agents hounded Olivia to death. And they drove Olivia's son and her brother far from Saunderhome. The fugitives found a haven, if it could be called that, in the Brazilian mining camps. While Colin's uncle slowly drowned himself in liquor and drugs, the boy had acquired a trade. When the Charter Settlement Planets came looking for recruits, he had a miner's regs and a skill to sell. Colin had shipped out and never turned back.

Anthony, a year younger than his kinsman, had to wait months before he got the same opportunity. He'd spent a childhood in hell, a hell disguised as a tropical Eden. No servant dared befriend him or his siblings. The clones had no money, no freedom to move, and were under constant surveillance. Five little clones and how they grew!

Carissa needed only one viable genetic copy of her husband to thwart Stuart's plans. But she'd paid for extras, just to be sure. Her scientists were happy to experiment at her expense. They had cold-bloodedly allowed five fetuses to develop to term, even though prenatal monitoring revealed that three babies were defective, physically and mentally retarded.

After several years the retardates began to disappear, one at a time. They had always been sickly, needing frequent medical treatment and around-the-clock supervision. Sometimes they had fallen critically ill and had been rushed to Saunderhome's private hospital for emergency care. Repeated crises weakened already fragile minds and crippled bodies. Anthony had known at a very early age that his brothers needed protection and he'd tried to shield them. In the end he failed, or felt he had, because they were taken away; he and his one normal brother never saw them again.

Throughout his life he had been troubled by recurring nightmares of shadowy figures entering the closet-sized room at Saunderhome where the little clones slept. The shadow shapes would pick up one of the sickly retardates and vanish into the night. In the morning the others would waken and wonder fearfully where the missing one had gone.

And sometimes, in his dreams, the shadow shapes turned toward Anthony. He dreaded those moments, certain that this time they had come for him. *He* would disappear, as his brothers had. He'd go into limbo. Carissa's employees would erase him, and he would never have existed. No loss—after all, he wasn't a real person. He was just a clone, expendable.

Colin, clutching his mother's hand and gazing at Saunderhome, must have imagined what glorious fun it would be to live in such a paradise. He saw Anthony and his brothers as rich kids, his lucky rivals who'd stolen his birthright. He envied them, not knowing how deprived and miserable they actually were. Colin, resenting his bastardy, blaming Carissa and the clones for his exile.

There were worse things than illegitimacy. Out here in the Settlements, many people shared Colin's uncertain paternity. And no one gave a faint damn about such matters.

Being a clone, though, was a permanent stigma that followed Anthony from Earth to the stars. He was forever set apart from all legitimate and "natural" children such as Colin. He and his brothers had been different from the start—not quite human.

Once there were five. Then Drake disappeared. Then the shadow figures took Bart, then Eddie. For a long time, it was just Carl and me, because our genes hadn't been damaged during the cloning and gestation processes. Carissa used us. So did Stuart, in a way. So did everyone else at Saunderhome. We were pets, and not treated as well as Carissa' dogs! And one day when we were fifteen, Carl couldn't take it any more. He walked into the surf and let the current grab him. I remember how much I envied him. That was when I knew I had to get away from Earth before I was destroyed, too.

I made it. I escaped.

So did Colin. He left earlier and he isn't a clone, so he's climbed higher than I have. Hotshot! The bastard proving himself. He's way ahead of me . . .

But I'll get there. I have to. It just takes time—time, and a hell of a lot of luck. I have to keep swimming. The surf pulled Carl down and killed him. But not me! I'll beat it. Swim against the tide of public opinion and debt.

Someday . . . someday . . . I'll stand on the shore. Free! No more shadow figures. They won't get me. Never!

Colin and me. On the lawn at Saunderhome. Looking at each other. Envying. Wanting to be the other guy. Imagining that the other guy's better off. That hasn't changed. Colin still wants to prove he's better than I am and get even with me for his losing his inheritance. And I still think he was the one who had it easy, being free of Carissa and Saunderhome, free to go somewhere else . . . anywhere else . . .

"Anthony?" The voice was a gentle intrusion at the edges of his consciousness. He rose out of his memories, coming to the surface, orienting himself. He was on a starhopper, floating against his safety straps, and staring unseeingly at a view screen full of distorted stars. Jesse was on the adjacent couch, watching him with concern.

"I'm all right," Anthony said, his words strained.

"Sure?"

A smile tugged at the younger man's mouth. "Sure."

"Want to talk?" Jesse invited.

They wound their way carefully through verbal mines, back to nondangerous subjects. No mention was made of Anthony's yesterdays or of their present financial worries. They discussed plans for the Studio, of seeing co-workers again, and calculated their remaining time till the upcoming ETA.

Warning alarms shrilled. The sound froze the soul.

The ship was in her "wink" phase—momentarily out of FTL mode. Sudden unscheduled deceleration made some passengers black out. Anthony fought a wave of nausea as the starhopper yawed sickeningly.

"Jesse! You okay?"

"Right here, kid! It's . . . it'll be okay. They'll get on top of it, any second now."

Pep talk for both their sakes.

Gradually that gut-wrenching motion abated. The big vessel steadied. Travelers groaned, daring to breathe once more. The sirens shut up. Silence was as stunning as the previous clangor had been.

Crewmen swam into the compartment from the control area, towing emergency gear and checking for injuries as they went. Anthony, Jesse, and the acting troupe had come through the up-

33

heaval with little more than bruises and upset stomachs. Some of their fellow passengers weren't as fortunate. Cleanup was still underway when Hassan gawked at the view screen and pointed. A spot of light that had been a mere pinpoint an instant before now was expanding, half filling the frame. "What . . . what's that?" the actor squeaked. "Is it a nova?"

"Never mind what it is," a crewman said tersely. "Let's get these patients secured."

The ship's pilot was a bit more talkative. "We're heading into Polk Station as soon as we complete a hull-integrity check. Everybody's going to be fine. Just follow the rules, settlers."

They did. But they didn't stop speculating. By the time the spacecraft had reached the Port's zero launch mark and met her tugs, a variety of theories were being tossed around. Despite the crew's denials, most of the riders were sure that the light *was* a nova. Anthony thought otherwise. He'd overheard the mutterings of another passenger, a retired pilot: "Seen that before. Some poor bastard blew up out there. Drive and all gone." That made sense. Too damned much sense. It explained, too, the shock wave that had hit the ship and why the crew had clammed up; it would be sticky business to tell a cabin full of frightened people that another ship had exploded close by.

A med boat came alongside and off-loaded the injured. They'd be rushed ahead to the Station for treatment. Tugs towed the starhopper herself in at an unhurried rate. When she docked, her crew was escorted away for debriefing by several Space Fleet officers posted to the satellite. Civilians, though, were left utterly in the dark, still knowing nothing for sure.

The mysterious light had been seen on the Station's monitors, too. Its lounges and corridors were abuzz with gossip. Irked by the lack of any solid news, Anthony went to a checkpoint to get some answers. He broached his questions to the staffer on duty at a bad time; she was already rocky from coping with other travelers' queries and rounded on Anthony with a waspish "No! I don't know what happened! If they tell me, I'll pass it on to . . ."

She broke off, paling, seeming to see Anthony—and identify him—for the first time. "Oh! I . . . I'm sorry. You . . . you're . . . Anthony Saunder, the . . ." Another pause. The staffer gulped, regaining her composure. "How . . . Is there anything else I can do for you, sir?"

Anthony's viscera were in a turmoil, and not solely due to the emergency on the starhopper. What had the woman been about to blurt? "Anthony Saunder, the clone?" Her expression, now, was brimming with eagerness to please. No trace of animosity or revulsion showed at confronting a fake human. Anthony said tonelessly, "Thank you. I believe you've told me what I wanted to know."

"Oh, sir, I really would like to fill you in, if I had any details at all. I *do* have an update on the condition of the injured passengers. They're out of danger," she said, beaming like a child hoping for approval.

He muttered an incoherent acknowledgment and walked away. It was several seconds before he realized that Jesse was tagging after him. The associate producer had overheard the exchange and was whispering, "Hey, kid, she didn't mean it like you think."

"No?"

"Nothing to do with your being a clone." Jesse went on in the same *sotto voce* style, "She just reacted when she spotted you as a Saunder-McKelvey. Hell, your picture's been in thousands of family PR items over the years. How could she *not* recognize you? Head of Saunder Studio, and so on. The lady figured she might lose her job for yelling at one of the high and mighty. That's all. It wasn't—"

"Drop it," Anthony growled. "Just drop it."

Jesse grimaced, but he didn't press. He knew better. In the older man's view, Anthony was paranoid about his origins, seeing insults where none existed. Anthony disagreed, certain *his* interpretations of words and body language gave the true version of how others felt toward him. Arguing, though, simply opened old wounds. He preferred to bury the subject as fast as possible whenever anything like this occurred.

A few hours later, while Anthony and Jesse were cooling their heels in the Port's canteen, a trickle of information finally began to leak out of Space Fleet's Station HQ—not heartening news for travelers. A temporary blockade of Polk System's starlanes was imposed, with no particulars offered. No further questions would be answered. Civilians must stay put and do as they were told. They'd be notified when it was safe for them to continue to their destinations.

The Port wasn't equipped to handle the lengthy layovers of so many transients. Aliens complained to their various on-station reps. Terrans bitched uselessly to *their* reps and to each other. People slept in the lounges, lined up for turns at the sonic sanitary facilities, and seriously depleted the satellite's food and entertainment stores.

When an all clear came at last—after more than two local days—Anthony and Jesse had missed yet another connecting starhop and had to reschedule again. They and the React Theater company finally departed on an independent ship of dubious ancestry. The vehicle's iffy reliability, the accumulated delays, and the building tension ate at everyone. A few travelers behaved like raw greenies, fresh from Earth; they jumped at the slightest noise and became testy over trifles. Spouses, old buddies, and longtime co-workers were at each other's throats. Their sole escape from friction was brooding silence. Anthony resorted to that often, lest he snarl at Jesse and say things he'd later regret.

Dammit, wasn't this trip ever going to be over?

As they neared Loezzi Port, things changed for the better. The formerly surly crew started catering to its passengers, especially to Anthony. View-screen readouts showed that the ship was being reclassified as priority traffic. They'd bypass the usual line and zip on through to Docking. Jesse, half in jest, said, "Did you put them up to this, kid? We can't pay for such preferential treatment—"

"Pull the plug on that," Anthony pleaded. "I'm floating without a tether, same as you."

Now it was first class, all the way. The React Theater troupe was torn between delight and resentment. They enjoyed the pampering, but assumed that Anthony could have twisted arms to obtain the cushy treatment on the earlier legs of the trip, if he'd wanted to. He didn't disabuse them of their illusions. He was having enough trouble making sense out of the situation himself. The crew responded to all his inquiries with shrugs. They didn't know. They obeyed the Port authorities. It wasn't their job to ask why.

When the passengers emerged from the ascent tube of the Port, smiling staffers awaited them. The puzzled show business people were shown into a refreshment-stocked top-grade lounge. Jesse's teasing went into hyperdrive. Anthony *must* have paid off someone! Aggrieved, he denied the charge, running out of witty comebacks and increasingly uneasy. *Was* he going to have to pay for all of this stuff and the posh service?

A uniformed SMEI security guard came to the door of the lounge and beckoned unobtrusively to Anthony and Jesse. They detached themselves from the ongoing feast. The guard touched his cap respectfully. "Good day. Captain Saunder requests that you join her and her party."

CHAPTER FOUR

❖❖❖❖❖❖❖❖

Kindred

The mystery was solved. *Captain* Saunder meant Brenna. The title wasn't honorary, either; she kept her pilot's regs up to full status. "Of course," Anthony said. "I assume she's responsible for the special treatment we've been enjoying, as well?"

Nodding, the guard gestured toward the corridor. They followed him through a series of interconnecting halls and rooms, heading into a restricted section swarming with uniformed and civilian SMEI personnel. Brenna Saunder never traveled alone. It took a large support staff to handle her far-flung business interests and protect her family from favor seekers or less friendly types. A luxury suite lay at the core of the miniature defense system. Two women, a man, and a Vahnaj male were in residence. "About time!" the older woman greeted the new arrivals. She jerked a thumb at Anthony and asked, "He been behaving himself?"

Jesse played along. "Sure has, Cap'n. I keep him in line."

"Good man! Can't let these kids fly too high or they'll singe their wings!"

"Mother! Give them a chance to sit down and catch their breath," the younger woman begged. She and her half brother

38

commiserated with Anthony, chagrined by their elders' corny jokes.

He went through the social forms. "Happy to see you again . . . Brenna . . . Regan . . . Ivan . . . *Mejuo* Ambassador."

Quol-Bez's bald head bobbed in reply. "I give you hello. This encounter is pleasant but . . . urr . . . unanticipated?"

"Lucky accident," Regan explained. "We hadn't planned to stop at Loezzi Port at all."

Ivan picked up the story. "But that shoot-out and Fleet blockade at Polk System threw us off vector. We diverted here to regroup."

Anthony and Jesse swapped startled looks. Shoot-out? So *that* was it! Maybe now they'd get details. Brenna had a direct pipeline to Space Fleet. If any civilian knew what was what, she did.

Captain Saunder noticed their reactions. "Didn't they tell you? Fleet nailed the smugglers who've been running illegal alien drugs down to Polk Settlement. That's *one* bunch of chuds we won't worry about again." Anthony remembered that veteran spacer's comment and felt cold. *"Some poor bastard blew up out there."* Shifting suddenly from her bloodthirsty comments, Brenna bent over a monitor terminal and complained, "Where's that caffa and food I ordered? What am I paying you people for?"

"Jump when I say starhop" was captain's style. Carissa Saunder shammed helplessness in a little-girl voice, never lifting a finger if she could avoid it. Brenna was loud and straightforward. She worked hard and expected the same from her employees.

When an aide delivered refreshments, Regan played hostess. Anthony relished this chance to unwind. He made idle chitchat, snacked, and updated his impressions of the suite's occupants.

Brenna was sixty, but looked twenty years younger. Her figure was as straight and slim as her statuesque daughter's. The only gray in Captain Saunder's hair was two attractive white streaks.

Her children were chips off the same adamantine block. Ivan, Brenna's son by Yuri Nicholaiev, her former copilot, had his father's open, Slavic face. But there was plenty of steel behind the young man's easygoing façade; Ivan's terraforming company was in the upper ranks of humanity's industrial giants, though he hadn't yet turned thirty. By all accounts, his sister, Varenka, who managed SMEI's Earth-based divisions, was just as much of a go-getter. Regan was Brenna's daughter by a man Captain Saunder refused to identify, a secret she had kept for two decades now. The affair and its result—Regan—were acts of defiance. Brenna had gone against prevailing Saunder-McKelvey custom and scorned to hire a surrogate mother to carry her younger daughter to term; Captain Saunder had performed that old-fashioned chore herself, as if to prove she could do that as well as conquer the light-speed barrier.

Ambassador Quol-Bez looked very much the same as when Anthony had last seen the alien. The Vahnaj diplomat was a little balder, these days, his neck a bit more wobbly, and his pointy teeth blunted. Retired after a long career, he was completely at home in Terran society. Unlike most lutrinoids, he had no musky body odor, spoke good if not perfect Basic English, and wasn't bothered by the usual Vahnaj cultural idiosyncrasies—such as their horror of being seen while they were eating.

Brenna broke into the idle chitchat, rounding on Anthony. "Why didn't you call me—collect!—when you ran into flight schedule problems? If one of my techs hadn't spotted your names on a passenger manifesto . . . I can't believe you rode that stinking scow!"

"Maybe we ought to drop a memo about it to Griffith's inspectors," Regan said. "They should clamp down on those fly-by-nights."

Ivan chuckled. "The media would love that, little sister. Us? Leaning on a C.S.P. Department? Telling their enforcers to stomp one of SMEI's scrimp-poor competitors? Terrific PR!"

"You know I didn't mean it that way," Regan said, blushing.

"I know what you meant," her half brother teased. "Shame on you! Pretending to be so interested in Malcolm Griffith's election campaign, when it's really his curly-headed son you're angling for."

"I *am* interested in Griffith's program," Regan argued hotly. "The issues are vital to—"

"That's enough!" Brenna stabbed a finger at Anthony. "As I said, *next* time you're stuck, give me a call. Hell, if I can't help out a kinsman in a crisis, what good's my money? I'm taking care of those travel snags right now."

"It wasn't a crisis," he began.

Captain Saunder was a juggernaut, flattening his objections. "It's all set up. One of my ships will take you boys directly on to the Procyon System. Oh, and I've arranged for separate passage for those theater people you've been splitting the ride with. Done! I won't take 'no' for an answer."

There was an awkward silence. Short of staging a scene, Anthony couldn't reject Brenna's gift.

Ambassador Quol-Bez said, "This is . . . a correct gift from one Saunder kin to another?"

"Damned right!" Case closed, as far as Brenna was concerned.

Anthony resigned himself to being the recipient of her largesse —again. He'd started owing her when he was a teenager; she'd paid for his passage off Earth. Earlier, she'd been equally generous to Colin, sending him and his uncle money to tide them over and to pay the youth's passage to the C.S.P. During that period, Captain Saunder was far from rolling in wealth herself. SMEI was still a struggling new company then. Yet Brenna had insisted on aiding kin who were even further down the financial ladder than she was. Anthony had appreciated her magnanimity—and hated it. He'd slaved to repay that first loan, but knew better than to try that in this instance. By now Brenna had become a billionaire several times over. Any attempt to return her gifts nowadays brought stern lectures on comparative wealth and how she could easily bear such expenses and he couldn't, all painfully true.

Ambassador Quol-Bez gently reproved his patron. "Friend Brenna, perhaps this is . . . urr . . . demeaning to Anthony?" His accent was heavy, but quite understandable.

Brenna was startled. "Well, yes, I guess things could be interpreted that way. Didn't mean to step on your toes, Anthony. You have your own business and resources, sure. But hell, let's face it—you didn't settle out here with a fortune backing you. No fault of yours. I'm just trying to make up for the rotten deal Carissa handed you. You're entitled to perks. You're a *Saunder*."

He swallowed a laugh. Lack of prejudice was one of the captain's most admirable traits. Some of his kindred held a very different point of view. Carissa had told him—often—that a mere clone wasn't entitled to anything. "I feel guilty taking up your time and money," Anthony said, softening his obvious resistance to Brenna's gift. "You already carry so many responsibilities. Your family. Morgan's . . ."

Captain Saunder was a superb caretaker. Her cousin Morgan McKelvey, her partner in the FTL project, had been horribly maimed in a failed spacecraft test. A few years later, after his death, Brenna made certain that his posthumous heirs grew up well cared for and rich. By now her kids and Morgan's were all adults, fledglings who'd left the nest and were firmly established, dominating every field of endeavor throughout the Terran sector. But Brenna still kept a maternal eye on them and on less closely connected relatives like Anthony, too.

"Nonsense! Those aren't responsibilities," she exclaimed. "I *like* giving my own a helping hand. Jesse, you make sure he uses that ticket." He grinned and threw her a mock salute.

Satisfied, the Captain steered talk onto other matters—the upcoming C.S.P. elections, business, the military's crackdown on smuggling, and power wheeling and dealing. Most of the conversation was an exercise in the abstract to Anthony and Jesse. Even if they were optimistic about Saunder Studio's future, it would be years before they were in the same league with Brenna. If worse came to worst, Anthony mused grimly, they wouldn't be in business at all.

"I wish you carried full credentials to the ITC," Brenna was lamenting, nodding at Quol-Bez. "You should really be leading those Vahnaj delegates."

ITC, the Interspecies Trade Conference, Colin's big event. The thing haunted Anthony, slapping him in the face everywhere he turned.

"It would not be . . . urr . . . suitable, friend Brenna. It is sufficient my Alliance honors me. How is it termed in your language? Emeritus? I rather like this designation."

"You deserve to head up the whole lutrinoid herd," Brenna grumbled, but didn't pursue that particular topic. Humans were very aware of the Ambassador's ambiguous situation. Before he'd undertaken his mission to Earth, his government had performed secret "excisions" upon him to ensure Quol-Bez would not reveal, even under torture, any of his species' weak points. Quol-Bez had willingly accepted the sacrifice for his people's sake. The "excisions," however, meant he was forever set apart from his own race. The Vahnaj Alliance revered him and had granted him a handsome pension. But he rarely made the return trip home, now that he was retired. Apparently such visits were too painful. Instead, he had become a semipermanent member of the Saunder entourage.

"At least you're going to be there in an advisory capacity,"

Brenna said. "I need *one* reliable voting member among the Vah-najes. It's going to be tough enough to pilot my reps, without opposition elsewhere. Hope to hell the conference doesn't fall apart before we get things straightened out, or we'll run into worse messes than that shoot-out near Polk. The next time, inno-cent bystanders like Anthony and Jesse might not be so lucky. They could get splattered like the smugglers."

Regan's face was ashy. "Oh, it wasn't *that* close, Mother."

"Don't fool yourself, girl. It damned well was close. You saw the C.O.'s report. I don't want anything like that happening again. We Saunder-McKelveys aren't immortal."

No, they weren't, Anthony acknowledged silently. Morgan died as an aftermath of the stardrive experiments. Mariette and Kevin McKelvey, his parents, were killed instantly in an earlier FTL test. In the Crisis of 2041, both Jael Saunder and her son Patrick had died in a fiery explosion which leveled the original Saunderhome.

"This latest incident worked out okay," Regan said, trying to put a cheerful view on things.

"Might not have," Brenna snapped. "The really ugly part of the operation is that the smugglers tricked some Lannon traders into being their patsies on the contraband deal."

Ivan shook his head. "Damn them. The Lannon Financial Treaties League is complex and unpredictable, anyway. Pro-cyonids don't define commerce or law quite the way we do. And some of their rulers are having bad reactions to this affair."

"Such an intriguing species!" Regan murmured. Anthony had seen her glowing expression before—in vid documentaries of planet scouts or scientists announcing their latest discoveries.

"Your 'intriguing' Lannon could turn this into a sloppy inter-stellar boilover," Brenna commented acidly.

"Griffith's cooperating with the Fleet, and they got the Lannon to safety before—"

"Grow up, girl. You're no novice or greenie. You've got a couple of years of working with your own division of SMEI under your belt by now. You know what's involved. Or are you too wrapped up in your romance with Griffith's son to see the obvious?"

Regan was offended. "I'm conscious of the larger picture."

"I hope so! An important section of the Lannon worlds are really insulted by this incident. They've lodged a protest with the

C.S.P. Council, and some procyonids are threatening to pull out of the Interspecies Trade Conference altogether. Out of *all* future treaties and negotiations. That could have damned serious repercussions, if we don't stop it, fast."

Anthony inhaled sharply, appalled. The six stellar civilizations had signed mutual peace pacts. If any race abrogated the conventions . . .

There had been no war in the Terran sector since the abortive Earth-Goddard-Luna civil conflict of 2041. However, history vids showed what even such a limited clash meant. The alien races, too, had gone through internal baptisms of fire, teetering on the brink of self-annihilation. Supposedly they had risen above that to be star rovers, highly developed and peaceful.

But the Lannons' warlike era was only recently behind them. If this shoot-out with Terran smugglers somehow dragged them into a major blowup and dissolution of the treaties . . .

Brenna read Anthony's horror. "Uh-huh. That's why we're here. Ivan has to head on to Settlement Noviy; there's a terraforming crisis there, and he's needed. The rest of us, though, are going to an extraordinary session of C.S.P. Council. Trying to hold the line, keep the Interspecies Trade Conference on vector. The C.O. on that smuggler smash said the Whimeds' Outer Satellite Faction was sniffing around the edge of that dirty deal, so we want to bring the felinoids as well as Quol-Bez's people in on the parley. You can bet, if the Outer Satellite bunch was there, Fal-Am's spoilers were, too."

"Fal-Am?" Anthony blurted in surprise. "We met him at Clay Port. He and his party didn't look like smugglers."

His kinswoman pounced. "Why were they on Clay?"

"Uh . . . Fal-Am said they planned to rendezvous there with Colin and accompany him on to Procyon Four. But the Vahnajes' ship had malfunctioned, and they were awaiting new instructions from their government—"

"No. Is not." Ambassador Quol-Bez's high-pitch denial slashed across Anthony's words. The lutrinoid's sideburns were flattened, stiff streaks along his gray jaw. "Fal-Am told you untruth, friend Anthony. He is chief of . . . urr . . . power-ful delegation to Con-fer-ence. He instructs others. He does not ac-cept instruction. He is . . . Biyelin Vahnaj." The Ambassador spoke that last with disgust. Anthony had never seen the aged e.t. so upset. "Biyelins . . . urr . . . are . . ."

44

"Troublemakers," Regan finished for him.

"Just so. Also trouble-makers are Whimed Outer Sat-ellite Faction. These elements . . . urr . . . bell-i-cose? Is that term? They disregard treaty honored by their peoples."

Anthony realized he and Jesse were being let in on some very hush-hush info. Brenna turned to them. "Did you see any Whimeds while you were at Clay Port?"

"Yeah, we did." Jesse described the puzzling scene they had witnessed.

Brenna grunted unhappily. "Espionage agents! Spying on each other. You warned me about this, Quol-Bez. These damned troublemakers are becoming active in the Terran sector now, even heading up delegations at the ITC. The main-branch Vahnajes and Whimeds have got to put lids on their die-hard reactionaries."

The Ambassador resembled a figure from an ancient tragedy —the sage, foreseeing disaster and helpless to prevent it. "Biye-lin are most . . . urr . . . violent. As are Whimed counter-parts. It has not been possible for my Al-liance to . . . urr . . . discipline Biyelins. In past, they . . . urr . . . confined their op-erations against Whimed Outer Satellite Faction to stellar re-gions where . . . urr . . . their terri-tori-al claims overlap. It ap-pears they ex-pand their . . . urr . . . aggressiveness." His frequent stammers and pauses revealed how concerned Quol-Bez was.

"Somebody better give 'em the word," Brenna said, scowling. "They won't be allowed to play their cold war games in *this* stellar region. And we damned well won't let them wreck the ITC!"

Whimed belligerent factions bumping heads with trouble-maker Vahnajes! The main lines of their species were already in heated mercantile competition on the starlanes. So far they'd played by civilized rules. But what if not *all* felinoids and lutrinoids did so?

Again, Brenna read Anthony's mind. "Tough to take, isn't it? We thought we had our neighbors figured out. And here they were giving us a tidied-up picture of what they're really like."

Anthony smiled at the irony in that. "Fair enough. We hide *our* warts and blemishes as well. My Studio produces propaganda vids for C.S.P. The glories of Terra. No mention of Earth's brushfire wars. None of smuggling, the growing tax rebellion in the Settlements, the political cutthroating, and the no-holds-

45

barred business practices—no mention at all of less-than-perfect human behavior."

"Because we're hiding such details, we're still woefully ignorant of each other," Brenna said.

"Communications," Regan said suddenly. "Free exchange of data. That would help." She sought support from Anthony and Jesse. "Your Studio should produce vids that tell the *whole* story, and we should insist the alien civilizations put their cards on the table, too."

"Good luck, girl," her mother said. "But it's a hell of a job. Differences in opinions, biology, languages, religions, social customs, and attitudes . . . xenophobia. Mankind is still leery of the people from over the next ridge or on the next planet. Why should we be experts at coping with the warty secrets of our alien neighbors—or they with ours—when we can't deal with differences within our own species?" She poured herself some fresh caffa and went on, "You know, I used to dream that some day Terra would arrive at a golden age. Be really worthy to stand up alongside the mature stellar races. The ITC was supposed to be humanity's rite of passage: Now we're full-fledged partners, recognized as such by the merchants and politicians of the e.t. worlds. But I'm learning there *is* no golden age—for us or them. They've just had more experience at covering up their festering sores than we have."

Gradually the conversation shifted to Terran politics. The ITC would provide a forum for preelection vote seeking and speeches. Colin, using the clout of a Conference host, would be playing kingmaker for his candidate, Myron Simpkins. Brenna's branch of the family, Regan in particular, were backing Simpkins' opponent, Ames Griffith, for the Charter Settlement Planets' Presidency.

The results might be interesting to watch, but Anthony's contact with the ITC would be limited by a seconds-long signal lag between two neighboring planets. Nevertheless, the decisions made at the Conference would affect his future, and that of every Terran in the sector. He envisioned a meteorite plunging into an ocean, sending shock waves thousands of kilometers, touching people and habitats far from the impact point.

Brenna was telling Quol-Bez, "I'll help you keep those Biyelin Vahnajes in line, and I suppose I'll assist the Whimeds' top cats in squashing *their* troublemakers. But I'd be happier working with the felinoids if they weren't giving a boost to my chief business competitor." Ivan and Regan attempted to interrupt, dismayed. ˌTheir mother plowed on, heedless. "Serge Bolotin's a money-grubbing sneak! His father never would have broken Hiber-Ship's accords, the way Serge is doing."

Gently Regan said, "It's not Hiber-Ship Corporation anymore."

"Well, Bolotin Charter Settlement Corporation, then. It *used* to be Hiber-Ship Corporation. I remember the day Yan formed the company. Good man. Tough rival, but honest. He's hardly cold in his grave, and his son's hiring Whimeds to annul everything Yan lived for. Disgraceful!"

Brenna made a disparaging noise. "I admit I'd probably do the same if I were in Serge's boots. That snail-whale of a ship he inherited is costing him a fortune while she waddles out to the Kruger 60 System. If the Whimeds can soup up her antique engines and make planetfall twenty years ahead of schedule, Serge will be able to recoup. He always *was* greedier and more practical than Yan."

New Earth Seeker, filled with volunteers in frozen stasis, had launched from Jovian orbit scant months before Brenna had made her FTL breakthrough. Her success had rendered the hibernation ship obsolete, but by then the asteroid-sized craft was on her way. And her passengers had signed a contract forbidding their awakening before they arrived at their destination—even if FTL was developed while they were en route. Yan Bolotin had honored that pact, despite the grievous expenses it entailed. When he'd died, though, his son found a way out of the dilemma. The Whimed Federation had a lot of experience in altering old-fashioned photon ramjets. They were accelerating the sleep ship, cutting her ETA drastically. From Serge's point of view, he wasn't breaking the original deal; the volunteers remained in stasis. However, they'd awaken and establish their Settlement much sooner than planned—and Serge would begin reaping profits much sooner.

Brenna's involvement was very personal. Before she had married Yuri Nicholaiev, there had been another man in her life, Captain Derek Whitcomb, now in stasis aboard Hiber-Ship. He was Kruger Settlement's leader, handsome, blond, and thirty years old. He'd still be thirty years old at planetfall, twenty years hence.

Ivan and Regan worked hard to shunt their mother off her sour-reminiscence track. "Okay, okay," she said grumpily. "But one more credit's worth. I *do* approve of one thing about Serge —he's a progressive. You won't catch *him* voting for Simpkins and those status quo Mother Worlders at ITC." She pointed challengingly at Anthony and his friend. "Speaking of that, are you delegates?"

Jesse peered at the ceiling, whistling softly, handing the thorny question to Anthony, who said flatly, "No."

"Why not?"

Mildly annoyed, he retorted, "Because my Studio's small-time, from the point of view of Procyon Five's major industries —and they are the ones selecting delegates. Besides, Jesse and I have been on a market tour for months; we're out of touch."

"Don't give me that false modesty garbage!"

"I'm not being modest. I'm a contributor. I pull my own weight for my Settlement. Saunder Studio turns out solid, basic products—how-to and entertainment vids that the majority of ordinary settlers need and want. But I'm *still* too small-time to be a likely nominee as an ITC delegate."

"I've seen your vids," Brenna said, nodding. "You're right. They are solid. Nothing flashy, but the stuff the pioneers have to have if they're going to domesticate their planets and not go nuts from boredom while doing it. I could use someone like you at the ITC sessions."

"To provide on-site propaganda for Ames Griffith's campaign?"

Brenna shrugged, acknowledging the suggestion. "That and much more. Assembling the straight story on the Charter contracts fracas, for one thing. All these Settlements trying to kick loose from their agreements, disavow their debts to their sponsors, and go independent. If they do—"

"We'll have more Ardens," Anthony said.

"Arden was a fluke," Ivan insisted. "Those immigrants were back-to-nature fanatics before they ever left Earth. Nakamura should have known that batch would go native and head for the tall trees—literally! He had to write off his entire investment and abandon the world to the Ardenites. Things are different, elsewhere in the sector."

"Not *that* much different," Regan countered. "Eventually most of the other Settlements will try to split away from their

Earth-based spnsors, too. Except for a few really established worlds, like Colin's Procyon Four, most of the frontier planets believe that Earth is never going to understand their problems or give them a millimeter of development space."

Anthony eyed his young kinswoman with respect. "Correct. We're not indentured servants any longer. The system has grown too broad for that, with more and more self-generating economies, looking outward for markets beyond the Terran sector. Meanwhile, the Charter Companies turn deaf ears to our pleas for an adjustment in those financially crippling contract terms we're carrying."

"That's too one-sided," Brenna protested. "You younger settlers have no sense of history. Dammit, those Charter sponsors made it possible for the Settlements to get started in the first place. Without their seed money, we'd be stuck back in the Solar System. The pioneers want to cut the economic lifeline and leave Earth drained—"

"As she's draining us," Anthony said sternly. "For example, my Studio pays backbreaking taxes, taxes no businessman on Earth would tolerate for a week. But I have to help feed Procyon Five's treasury so she can try to reduce her debt to the Charter sponsors. It doesn't matter whether we signed a contract with them or not. *I* didn't, as you know; I worked my way here, with the help of the outbound ticket you gave me. The sponsors don't care who pays, or that the Settlements are being forced to impoverish themselves in too many cases. The fat cats stay snug and safe on Earth and bleed the Settlements dry, then act astonished when the frontier planets rebel."

He'd spoken with more heat than he'd intended, possibly because one of the most notorious fat-cat Charter Company investors was Carissa Saunder. She alone owned enough stock in the C.S.P. worlds to cost the Settlements millions of credits annually.

Brenna nodded reluctantly. "Legitimate gripes on both sides. I guess that's always been true, down through the generations. But couldn't we, for once, learn how to compromise before so damned many people get hurt? And that's what's going to happen if the Settlements try to cut the ties and go independent."

"We can try to compromise," Anthony said, "but the process is already underway in a hundred subtle areas. Jesse and I see it taking place in our particular field. We have to re-record our standard fiction and nonfiction vid issues regularly, adjusting for the drift in dialects and local customs among our customers in the Charter Settlement Planets. We have to issue fourteen major versions, one for each established Settlement, altering references for local flora and fauna and terrain, local heroes, local history, and slang. Frankly, sometimes I think our vids, subspace news network broadcasts, and FTL transportation are the only thing keeping the frontier from separating into dozens of isolated outposts. And if *that* happens, a lot of them will die. We're too weak to stand alone yet."

"How true!" Regan cried. "What a shame you're not delegates!"

"Indeed," her mother said. "They're sharper than 90 percent of those chuds who *will* be attending the ITC."

Anthony gritted his teeth. Why did she keep harping on that subject? "I doubt if we'd be much use there. We steer clear of politics."

"I'm not asking you to run for office," Brenna said waspishly. "You think. You express intelligent opinions. You *have* intelligent opinions. Those are rare items, sad to say. Are you for Griffith's monetary reform package? Good! I wish Colin was. But he's too wrapped up in his import-export quotas and his commercial ties with Simpkins's standpatters and Procyon Four's Vahnaj trading partners."

Regan said, "When we get our voting blocs aligned, we'll make dents in Simpkins' support."

"I hope so. His policies would be a disaster. Anthony put his finger on it: We've all got to give some and pull together. With Colin's party calling the shots, only the thoroughly established Settlements will benefit. They won't see that the entire C.S.P. association is disintegrating until it's too late." Captain Saunder sighed despairingly. "If only you two were delegates. I'll bet you support all of Ames Griffith's legislative proposals . . . Enough heavy talk. Hey, we aren't doing justice to this food!"

The remainder of the time Anthony and Jesse spent in the suite was relaxed and pleasant. They were genuinely sorry when an SMEI staffer came to announce that their assigned ship was ready for boarding. Anthony and his friend thanked Captain Saunder at length for her generosity, and there were promises all around that they'd meet again soon. That was iffy, in view of Brenna's peripatetic life-style. She and her children saw the men from Saunder Studio off with warm good wishes.

There was another, lengthier leave-taking from the React Theater troupe. The actors and stagehands were ecstatic at the unexpected upgrading of their travel plans. Captain Saunder wasn't there to accept their thanks, so they gave them to Anthony.

Hassan made parting easy. He hammed up his farewells, playing to an audience of curious onlookers in the Station's nearby corridor. "Don't forget us. We'll always be available for any of your productions."

"I'll remember," Anthony said, waving to the others, and he and Jesse escaped into the descent tube.

The ship Brenna had reserved for their journey was a further extension of the luxuries in her suite, a late-model craft with posh appointments and attentive crew. The other passengers were SMEI execs. It was one of those uncommon situations when Anthony got a heady taste of what it would be like to be an upper-echelon Saunder-McKelvey. He had no illusions. The execs didn't see him as Brenna's equal. But Anthony *was* her kinsman, and because of that, he rated preferential treatment on this ride.

The big vessel eased away from Loezzi Port. Specially hired tugs guided the craft toward her FTL launch point. Often, the sole indication of movement was a shifting scene on the cabin's monitors. Attendants swam through the compartment pampering the travelers as the ship progressed toward her starhop zero mark.

The tugs retreated, and a thrum of power built deep inside the SMEI spacecraft. Then Anthony felt that familiar painless pressure nudging his skull and knew they were heading home.

CHAPTER FIVE

✿✿✿✿✿✿✿✿

The Entrepreneur

Even a top-of-the-line SMEI starhopper took several days to make the jump from Loezzi to the Procyon System. Ample time for the passengers to become acquainted, log sleep sessions, and work out in the ship's exercise chambers.

A star voyage contained far too many hours of leisure in which to brood on potential financial disaster. Anthony tried to push away those gloomy thoughts, seeking diversion. He turned to the individual miniscreen near his couch. The crew was piping in commercial channels for the passengers' convenience—a luxury not available on the cheaper transports Anthony and Jesse had ridden on earlier legs of their tour. Selecting a newscast, Anthony floated against his safety straps and watched the recorded update.

A volcano erupted on Settlement 61 Cygni. Appalling footage showed great loss of life and an entire year's production of precious metals destroyed.

C.S.P. Council hearings on a bill to beef up Space Fleet were proceeding with minimal delay. Recent publicity about the smuggler smash probably helped the legislative process along.

Census findings showed half a billion humans in the fourteen major Settlements, eight minor outposts, and space stations.

Five recently scouted planets were being offered for development. Anthony wondered cynically if the Charter Companies would get many takers on those. With the growing number of rebellions against Earth-based sponsors, a lot of would-be emigrants were having second thoughts about indenturing themselves as earlier pioneers had done.

Medical news told of advances in *purgatio*-derived gravity and atmosphere compensation drugs, improvements in post-trauma grafts and implants, and miracle discoveries in prenatal gene manipulation to eliminate inherited flaws. But no progress was reported on beating the VN/HS-3 virus. That bug was a unique and very nasty one, capable of crossing interspecies bio-barriers. For Vahnajes, it was a venereal nuisance. Transmitted to *Homo sapiens*, by humans dabbling in exotic interracial sex, the disease was rapidly and agonizingly fatal. Quarantines had limited its spread in the Terran sector, but there was still no cure for its unfortunate victims.

Another, more upbeat story on the interspecies front came from the ITC. "Distinguished delegates from . . . prominent Terran and alien tradespeople . . . figures from political spheres . . . meeting to solve mutual problems in commerce . . . hosted by the celebrated merchant prince of Settlement Procyon Four, Colin Saunder."

Anthony muted the sound, telling himself he did so because the commentator's Terre Neuve accent annoyed him. The woman continued to mouth descriptions. The screen split to show a sprawling complex where the Conference would be held and portraits of Colin, presidential candidates Simpkins and Griffith, Brenna, and Ambassador Quol-Bez. Then came portraits of e.t. attendees, including a glimpse of Fal-Am.

Wanting to catch more background on the Vahnaj troublemaker, Anthony moved to freeze the news flow.

By the time he'd touched the controls, another image had replaced Fal-Am's. The picture was that of a hauntingly beautiful Whimed woman. A printout translation identified the alien as Yrae Usin Hilandro. He'd encountered that name in theatrical industry journals. Supposedly Yrae Usin Hilandro was *the* artist of the Whimed Federation, their "cultural treasure." Signing her to perform at the Interspecies Trade Conference ought to weld together the disparate felinoid groups in joint admiration of such a gem.

It would also be another feather in Colin's hat, since he was the Conference host.

Yrae Usin Hilandro's face was heart-shaped, framed by a fluffy cloud of red-gold hair. Her body was slim and androgynous. Her eyes seemed to reach out of the portrait and grab the viewer. Was that intense, hypnotic gaze part of her "incomparable artistry" touted in the accompanying printout? The stare was a potent tool for any actor, human or alien. Anthony was tempted to magnify the image more and discover what color those starburst irises were. Then he canceled the impulse. What difference did it make? He wasn't an ITC delegate; he'd never meet this fey creature in the flesh.

Irritably he wiped away the inset and allowed the broadcast to flow on, now showing Saunders and McKelveys in one capsule promo after another. The family had been a force in Terran history for nearly a century now. From the 2020s through the 2060s, mankind had been dominated by Ward Saunder, the inventive genius, his brilliant, ruthless wife, Jael, and their kids, Patrick, Mariette, and Todd. In the 2070s, Brenna and her cousin Morgan had paved the way to the stars via FTL. Now the current crop of Saunder-McKelvey princes and princesses were taking up the reins. The Saunders seemed capable of anything—including bending law and custom and getting away with it.

The Settlements generally disapproved of surrogate motherhood and other medical "trickery" applied to human reproduction. For the settlers, those methods were right only in agriculture. But they forgot that bias when it came to the top-ranking Saunders and McKelveys. Brenna, her siblings, two of her children, and her grandchildren had all been artificially conceived and carried to term by surrogates. That hadn't diminished their status a bit.

Right and wrong, it seemed, were subjective. On Earth, Colin Saunder was illegitimate, cut off from his inheritance, though he was the product of old-fashioned natural sex and birth. Out on the frontier, he had become a merchant prince. The settlers didn't give a damn how he'd come into being.

Would they ever feel the same way about a clone? If Saunder Studio finally achieved economic success, would Anthony Saunder be accepted as Colin's peer? Not likely. The pioneers regarded cloning as a *human* reproductive technique with even more loathing than they did surrogate parenthood.

54

Data on the monitors shifted. ETA was drawing nearer. On the nav grids, the Procyon System grew from a yellowish smear to a pair of stars. Gas giants orbiting the suns became visible as small spheres, though the terrene planets were still too faint to detect with the naked eye.

Hours later, the ship dropped out of FTL phase and entered real time and space. Tugs awaited her. Slowly they towed her toward the Port. The satellite loomed ahead, a twinkling metallic island in a black sea.

Ship's computers sharpened details. Procyon Four and Five began to be defined as worlds. Anthony glared at the image of his kinsman's planet. Colin had been at home for days while Anthony had been forced to take the long road back to *his* Settlement.

The feeling that he was being picked on increased when they debarked at the Port. The pampering ended here. There was a striking contrast in the Station staffers' attitude toward traffic headed for the system's two inhabited worlds. Ironically, Anthony's name cut far less ice here, in his home territory, than it had in space, traveling under the umbrella provided by Brenna's tickets. Here, businessmen and immigrants bound for Procyon Four got preferential treatment. Colin's exports alone brought enormous duty fees into the Port's coffer, and they were anxious to please. Procyon Five's trade, however, was second-class in the Station staffers' eyes. Their cut on Five's commerce was paltry. The intraorbital shuttles serving the two planets also reflected their difference in standing. Four's craft were spiffy and new. Five's were shabby refits. Before Anthony and Jesse boarded their downbound flight, they were in a rotten temper, smarting with resentment at the snobbery they had encountered in Port.

That bad taste lingered for hours until their shuttle was crossing the orbits of Procyon Five's moons and starting her entry spiral. Crew members gave the immigrant passengers a pep talk on their new Settlement, pointing out landscape features as those became ever more distinct.

Anthony watched the scene below with a proprietary air. He noted a glacier outbreak in the south polar region. That was not good; his stock in seabed exploitation ventures near there would slip if the ice thickened too much. At least the zoom lenses didn't show any signs of tsunamis or ocean floor volcanic activity this season. The shadowy outlines of undersea factories and pelagriculture depots looked undisturbed. On the few landmasses, terra-forming domes were pumping busily. Conditions on the surface weren't yet optimal for *Homo sapiens*, and wouldn't be for a century or more, when the terraforming stations had finished their work.

Monitor grids locked on to Equitoria, the Settlement's capital. The shuttle lined up, aiming for the peninsula lapped by epicontinental seas. There was nothing to see above ground, of course, except a kilometers-long landing strip.

Passengers secured their safety straps and boosted their med doses, countering the stress of reentering planetary gravity. Anthony was thoroughly sick of these routines Jesse and he had gone through so many times these past months.

Horizons were shrinking fast. Retros fired, and the ship's speed decreased noticeably. Her nose lifted and her tail settled. A bump and a surge of reverse thrust ended in a long, long roll to the end of the strip.

Heavy and planetbound, the shuttle lumbered off on her taxi lane. A maw opened in the black cliffs ahead, and she coasted down inside. Sunlight vanished, replaced by interior illumination. The travelers saw on the monitors that they were moving down a huge ramp blasted from the living rock. The vehicle finally stopped at the terminal gates. Tie-down noises rang through the cabin, wheels locked, circuits switched, and debark tubes connected to the hull.

A few overeager passengers undid their safety webs, lurched to their feet, and immediately sat down again. No drug permitted a star traveler to readjust to gravity *that* quickly.

Anthony and Jesse had no intention of looking like greenies. They paced themselves sensibly, taking their time collecting their luggage and descending the tunnel leading to the concourse.

Equitoria's Terminal, like the rest of the city, had a raw, unfinished appearance. Every frontier world had its distinctive traits, and Procyon Five's were water and subsurface living. Other settlers referred to the local inhabitants as troglodytes, a title they wore with perverse pride. Long-term residents took for granted the puddles dotting the concourse floor. Sea-wall seepage was a norm here. So were roped-off rockfall rubble heaps scattered throughout the big cave. To compensate for those eyesores, the Terminal builders had installed a spectacular window wall near the main entrance from the debark tunnels. Tempered plasticene set in Silurian stone offered a ten-meter-wide undersea-scape. Arriving immigrants stumbled to a halt, gawking. Their assigned guides assured them the window was unbreakable. Just the same, the new trogs recoiled when animals resembling giant octopi and crustaceans brushed against the far side of the transparency.

Dodging the sightseers, Anthony and Jesse entered chaos. The Terminal was an around-the-clock forum and junction for the natives and visitors, with people hurrying to and from their jobs. Human and alien merchants were arriving, departing, and conducting business. Boat taxi drivers advertised their fares, and vendors hawked their goods from colorful portable booths. Food aromas drifted from communal dining areas, mingling with the less pleasant odors of seepage and too many bodies. Amid the bustle and din, a number of trogs called "Welcome home!" to Anthony. Gratified, he returned the greetings. Media coverage of the Saunder-McKelveys had made even a minor clan member's face well known. But beyond that, the trogs saw him as a valued home world boy; Saunder Studio brought in badly needed credits to Five, plus the occasional thrill of a visiting vid star, here to act in a Studio production.

Suddenly a reception committee swarmed around the two travelers. Studio department heads and longtime employees slapped them on the back. "Who's minding the store?" Anthony joked.

"Aw, forget that for now!"

"Sure! We're just churning out reissues, anyway, until you loafers got back here and put us to work on something new."

Margaret Orr, Anthony's wardrobe mistress, hefted a basket and said, "We brought you a picnic. Sit down and eat! Get your planet legs before you try to ride the canals."

The men were happy to take the suggestion. They allowed their Studio family to steer them into the public dining room. As Anthony might have expected, Margaret had provided a little feast, well seasoned with cheery chitchat. During the market tour, Anthony and Jesse had maintained regular contact with the home team by com, so there wasn't a lot of business news for them to catch up on, but plenty of family gossip about births, marriages, romantic liaisons and quarrels, and amusing squabbles among Studio personnel. The only gloomy gus in the party was Chet Deverill, the company's accountant. He held his tongue as long as he could, then said, "Sure was a mixed bag of sales figures you shipped back to us. Real good on Vaughn, Hung Jui, and Noviy, but Morgan and Clay?"

"Lord God, Chet," Jesse begged, "wait till tomorrow to nag."

"Yeah, leave 'em be!"

"Take a recess!"

The exchange washed over Anthony. He was watching an odd assortment of onlookers nearby—some local uniformed officials and several others in mufti. They were blatantly eavesdropping on the picnic. A disturbing thought struck him. Were these snoops from the Charter Reps Division? Had these hangers-on overheard Chet's comments? That could mean a stiffer tax assessment for the Studio. Just what they needed!

Humans weren't the only snoopers hanging around. A Vahnaj and a couple of Whimeds were also keeping wary eyes on the picnickers. Anthony's experience on Clay Port made him uneasy about being under the e.t.s' scrutiny. He returned their none-too-subtle stares challengingly. That seemed to prod both them and the human snoops. The eavesdroppers made themselves scarce.

"I knew you boys would be tired," Margaret said finally. "Now you can go home. We'll hold the fort at the Studio a few more days. Take as long as you want before you try to get back in the harness. Go on! Shoo! Margie knows best!"

"You always did, love." Anthony planted a juicy kiss on her brow. His employees escorted him and Jesse to the taxi piers. They toted the returnees' luggage, haggled with the drivers to find the best fare, and saw their boss and his associate producer safely aboard the selected small craft. The taxi sidled out into the canal, rounded a bend, and the Terminal piers were out of sight.

Equitoria was bound together by an elaborate subsurface canal network. It linked the governmental core, commercial centers, and outlying residential areas. Taxis, buses, and private vessels plied the buoy-marked arteries. Genetically engineered native sea creatures provided an underwater glow of bioluminescence, giving the primary and secondary lanes an eerie, moonlit appearance. At every intersection, sanitary workers monitored other specially bred tiny animals—the "scrubbers", who disposed of litter and waste that had escaped the city's mechanical filters. Above the canal line, campfires shone from squatters' holes. Those damp, unhealthy caves had been occupied by the poorest trogs ever since Procyon Five's first days as a Settlement. The authorities looked the other way, knowing that the squatters had nowhere else to live. That was an all-too-typical situation on frontier worlds. Many immigrants spent all their funds on passage and arrived in the C.S.P. destitute. The less prosperous Settlements had limited housing available, so the bottom level of their citizenry had to make do with what they could find.

For more than a quarter of a local hour, the taxi chugged along watery corridors. Finally the driver throttled back, slipping into a dead-end lane. She cut the motor to idle, stopping by a stone pier. "Watch your step," she warned. "That seepage makes these old docks slippery." It wasn't surprising that she worried about taking chances; her scars and twisted legs showed that she, like many, was a former seabed miner who'd been crippled in an accident. Anthony flirted harmlessly with her, a game that pleased the middle-aged woman far more than the tip chit Jesse gave her. She was grinning when she revved her boat and backed from the channel.

Anthony activated the door lock with his palm print, and he and Jesse began hauling their luggage up the interior stairs. All residences on Equitoria were built well above the canal line as a precaution against tidal surges and sea-wall collapse. That made for a tiring climb after a long journey. The men halted in the foyer and prodded their med patches, boosting their energy with a shot of compensation drugs. Then Jesse carried the bags to the sleeping alcoves while Anthony busied himself at the house's servo readouts.

Everything was in order. The seaside dwelling looked much as it had when Anthony had left months ago, but it smelled musty. He tapped into the citywide aeration ducts to freshen things.

On Earth, this residence would have ranked as small and very modest. On Procyon Five, it was a mansion. Anthony thought of the squatters in their dripping caves and felt lucky. He never could have purchased this house at its original price. But the former owner, a pelagic industries magnate, had made the fatal mistake of arguing with a cephalopod. Other potential bidders at the death-taxes auction were superstitious, fearing the magnate's ill fortune would accompany his property. Anthony had no such doubts, and he'd snapped up a bargain. The place came with some nice little bonuses: carpeting and a refreshment island in the main room; moldproof paint there and in the two tiny adjacent sleeping alcoves; and a miniature version of the Terminal's window wall. The floor-to-ceiling transparency, flanked on one side

59

by a stair leading down to the house's sea-gate terrace, sat opposite the residence's canalside door. At present, the tide was low, and a too-bright sky dominated the upper portion of the window frame. Anthony shifted his gaze to the bottom section, where green water lapped at the plastic. The effect was very soothing.

With half an ear he heard Jesse in the foyer, checking the message recorder. Not likely that there was much on that. Without taking his eyes from the window, Anthony asked absently, "Anything?"

"The usual. Mm. Here's a note. Li Lao Chang's sixtieth anniversary is coming up late this year."

"The old porn monger will outlive us all," Anthony chuckled, remembering. It was true he'd formed his negative opinions of actors and acting while he was working in Li's erotic dream dramas. But he felt no animosity toward the show business veteran. Li was simply giving the customers what they wanted. And he'd taken a grass-green kid fresh from Earth into his company, giving him a break. He owed the old man a lot. "We'll have to find Li a nice gift."

A murky shape crawled across the black sand at the base of the window wall. Tentacles probed for edibles. Trogs called this species an octopus though it bore only a superficial resemblance to Earth's cephalopods. Procyon Five's variety had twenty arms, was garishly colored, and was covered with grotesque lumps. This particular specimen wore no ID tag. Obviously the medium-size male was wild, not one of the seabed installations' specially bred servants. With sinuous grace, the predator undulated, searching among the pebbles for goodies.

Belatedly Anthony realized Jesse was talking to someone—had been, in fact, for several minutes. "Oh? Right. If Zach McKelvey's in on it, the deal must be pretty firm . . . What? Well, actually, no. We just got here."

"Who is it?" Engrossed in his conversation, Jesse didn't hear the question. Curiosity prodded Anthony. The angle was wrong for him to see the tiny screen, and the voice at the other end of the line was indistinct, unintelligible. He didn't want to intrude on a personal call, but . . .

Jesse laughed and said, "Sorry you had to wait. Sure! Why don't you boat over? We'll get acquainted. Great! See you soon!"

As Anthony started toward him, Jesse broke the connection

and stood lost in thought a moment. Then he glanced up. "How you doin', kid? Meds working okay? No queasies?"

"You know they never bother me."

"So you won't mind a quick brushup and a change." Jesse led the way into the sleeping alcoves and yanked clothes off storage hooks. "Don't just stand there. Hit the soni-scrub."

"Why?"

"A visitor's coming." The older man hid his nervousness behind a brusque manner.

"Anybody I know? Anybody *you* know?"

Jesse smiled sheepishly. "Not yet."

"Oh-ho! And you'd like to." Anthony smirked and leaned against the doorjamb. "All the way home, you yammered that we wouldn't do anything for days after we got here. Now this. I assume the visitor is female. She's obviously rattled your hormones. But why do *I* have to dress up for her?"

"Quit playing detective!" Jesse slammed a wad of clothes into his friend's belly. "Get moving. This is business."

"Really?" Anthony feigned a yawn, draping the clothes over his arm. He made no move toward the cleanup cubicle.

"Okay! She's an entrepreneur," Jesse said, his homely mug twisted with exasperation. "Entertainment investments and projects. A bunch of Whimeds hired her as their Terran consultant. They want the Studio to produce a dramatic presentation they're staging at the ITC. There! Now you know as much as I do."

Anthony frowned, suspicious. "A legitimate offer?"

"Sure sounds like it. Governor Yamashita vouched for the lady."

"Yamashita. That figures." Anthony snorted derisively. "Our fearless leader has been drooling for a trade swap with the cat folks ever since they toured trogland last year."

"Can you blame him? Procyon Five needs alien markets. But Yamashita's no fool. I'm sure his staff checked our visitor out." Jesse cracked his knuckles, looking more and more fascinated by the prospect of meeting the mystery woman. Plainly she'd made an enormous impression on him during their brief conversation. And by all indications, she'd located the Governor's soft spot, too.

"It's scant weeks till the Interspecies Trade Conference,"

Anthony said. "The Whimeds and this entrepreneur can't hope to put together anything worthwhile in that short a time."

"We can at least discuss it, huh? Hell, we're not paying. They are."

"It's ridiculous—"

"Will you just get dressed?" Jesse pleaded.

Sighing, Anthony headed into the scrubber. He raised his voice to be heard above the whine of the apparatus. "Does this visitor have a name?"

"Pilar Gutierrez," his friend shouted. The scrubber on Jesse's side of the alcove started, drowning out whatever else he might have said.

Anthony refused to rush. He made a leisurely process of removing travel grime and getting dressed. But he was ready and waiting in the main room before Jesse emerged.

"I still don't see what this will accomplish," Anthony grumbled. "We've got too much to do to waste time on pointless discussions. Besides, interspecies material isn't our territory. The only stuff we've handled in that line were those meet-your-alien language translation vids for C.S.P. We ought to stick to our tried-and-true standards—quickie edu-chips and fiction for settlers and their kids."

"We're overdue for a breakout," Jesse said irritably. He fussed with the collar of his tunic. When the paging terminal rang, he lunged for it. "Hello!" Abashed, he cleared his throat and went on in a more normal tone. "Uh . . . come on up. Door's open."

Pilar Gutierrez breezed in. She and Jesse stepped all over one another's words in their haste. Backing off, they grinned and started fresh, introducing themselves. Then the entrepreneur turned to Anthony. "I already know you. No formalities necessary. God! You look even better than you did in those dream dramas from the Li Company. And those were made—what?— fifteen years ago? I own all of 'em," she finished with a charming smirk.

"Not exactly deathless literature," he said dryly.

"Who cares? They were terrific satisfiers, to use the pop slang of my girlhood. Thousands of females are *still* using them as springboards for their sexual fantasies, and don't let anyone tell you different. Meanwhile, the deathless prose holo-modes from the same period are languishing in institutional libraries. Your erotic vids were the best of their kind ever made. Haven't been matched since."

"Anybody got the equipment to move all this fertilizer?" Jesse teased.

Pilar's grin widened. "I'll bet *you* know fertilizer from the ground up, Eben."

They were off and running. The verbal joust went into full swing as Anthony led the way to the refreshment island. He handed around mugs of caffa and settled into a chair while Jesse and the woman bantered. Anthony stayed out of it, using the opportunity to study Gutierrez. She was a definite change from other entrepreneurs he'd met. For one thing, she was obviously a recent arrival from Earth; a distinctive lilt in her speech underlined that fact. However, unlike that boorish tourist on Clay, Gutierrez was doing her best to blend into the Settlement mainstream. She looked to be in her middle fifties, which made her Jesse's contemporary. And she scorned cosmetic surgery, relying instead on makeup and an attractive hairdo to counteract her too-square jaw and ordinary features.

When there was a break in her sparring with Jesse, Pilar peered curiously around the room. "I've read about this house and its past owner's melodramatic demise. Nice place." If she thought the residence spartan, compared to a company president's home on Earth, she didn't say so.

"You *read* about it?" Jesse demanded.

Pilar's dark eyes sparkled. "Sure. Read. You know. Little squiggles on the vid screen or paper. Or are you one of those people who never learned how?"

"Oh, I read just fine. Scripts. Contracts. Credentials."

The woman met Jesse's stare levelly. "Good! Then you won't have any trouble with these." She pulled a pack from her pocket and dropped the chips into the island's playback unit. As the men scanned the file, Pilar took a sip of caffa and leaned back wearily. "Damned glad to be here, fellows. I developed calluses on my rump, sitting at that Terminal hostel."

"Why didn't you send us a message while we were en route?" Jesse asked. "Would have cleared away the preliminaries."

"Too impersonal. My clients insist on direct contact. So we do it their way."

"*Maybe* we do it their way," Anthony corrected, and the entrepreneur bit her lip.

Jesse glowered at him. "Tell us about the deal, Pilar. We haven't seen any advance releases on it."

"That's because there haven't been any," she said. "The Whimed Committee is keeping a tight lid on it. No leaks until everything's set. They plan to stage a one-act live drama at the opening ceremonies of the Interspecies Trade Conference. Two performers. A felinoid woman and a Terran man—"

"Terran?" Anthony cut in, startled. "Who?"

"David Lavrik. He got rave reviews for a couple of low-budget vids last year."

"Never heard of him," Anthony said. Jesse glowered again, annoyed by his friend's rude manner. Inwardly Anthony admitted that he probably *had* heard of the actor Pilar had mentioned. So what? He heard of thousands of actors and read hundreds of reviews of two-credit vids turned out by little-known production outfits. Why should he pretend enthusiasm at a reference to one more such performer, merely to be polite?

The entrepreneur took a deep breath. "Lavrik grew up on the sector border, on a Whimed Protectorate planet. His parents are in trade, and he helped out with their import company when he was a boy. Speaks fluent Whimed, of course. Trained at a local arts school and later won a scholarship to Alpha Cee's Kinetic Academy. You *have* heard of that, I trust?" Pilar said, daring Anthony to deny it. The institution she named was the most prestigious in its field, barring its counterparts on Earth. "He starred with the Academy's touring company for several years, specializing in dance and ballet, but switched to dramatics for more scope. And he kept his ties with his acquaintances in the Whimed Protectorate all along, so they immediately thought of him when they were planning this project. The Committee can fill you in on additional details. Lavrik's really their discovery, handpicked for this role. They're particularly eager to costar a Terran in their play to compliment *Homo sapiens*, since the ITC is being held in our sector this session. They've also commissioned a Terran to adapt their drama, a Whimed classic. Ian Dempsey did a superb rendition—"

"Dempsey?" Jesse interrupted. "But he's retired. Lord! He must be over ninety."

"He's still got the touch. You'll agree, when you read his script."

Anthony ignored that puffery and gestured to the ident

64

vouchers. "According to those, Zach McKelvey is your principal Terran investor. How did he get involved?"

"As Dempsey's angel," Pilar explained. "He's the old boy's biggest fan. In fact, Zach's building a museum to house the playwright's show biz memorabilia. When the Whimeds approached Dempsey with their idea, he dragged in his buddy Zach. I've worked with McKelvey's firm before, so he gave me a crack at handling this deal. He wants to expand his interests outside the Solar System—and so do I. Ian insisted that you were the only possible choice to direct and produce this play. He loves what you did with his pop favorites like *Vaughn's Challenge*. Suits Zach fine, too. Your kinsman wants to keep the honors—and the money—in the family. You are the sole Saunder-McKelvey actively working in the entertainment industry. And your location is perfect for the Whimed Committee's purposes. Perfect match!"

Anthony had met Zach—the richest of Morgan McKelvey's posthumous heirs—only a few times. But this was the sort of venture the eccentric playboy doted on. Zach was a gambler. He could afford to be. Anthony couldn't. "Someone hasn't thought this thing out too clearly," he said. "We produce vids, not live dramas, and we don't do artsy stuff at all."

"Artsy?" Jesse said, snickering. "Ian Dempsey? Come on! He never touched a script that wasn't a tried-and-true crowd pleaser."

"This one certainly is," Pilar chimed in. "The presentation will be live, yes. But that's just the ground floor. Saunder Studio will record the play, with full emota-sensor enhancement. When ITC concludes, you'll have a license to market the package. Terran and Whimed versions. Plus a trade exchange consideration fee."

"With you, Zach, and the felinoids taking cuts off the top," Anthony muttered.

Pilar said, "There's plenty for everyone."

He shook his head. "It's a major diplomatic as well as mercantile project. Not the Studio's style. Over our heads."

"Oh, don't pull that," the entrepreneur chided. "You're good and you know it. When Dempsey showed the Whimed Committee your previous productions, they were sold right down the line. Forget artsy. They want a wowser. Artsy theatrical groups and recording companies don't know how to turn out a crowd pleaser in a hurry. You do. And nobody has your touch on the emota-sensors. Those are your special babies. We need you, your expertise, your high tech equipment, and your Studio. What could be plainer?"

Anthony raised an eyebrow. "Truth be told, that last reason is the main one, isn't it? Perhaps the sole one. Location. The Studio is the closest facility to the ITC site."

"That's important, yes," Pilar conceded. "Time is of the essence. But the other reasons are crucial, too."

"There's no way to meet the felinoids' deadline."

"It can be done, with you at the helm." Pilar leaned forward, talking earnestly. "It's a real plum. The spin-off potential for your company alone is huge. And the Whimeds are offering a fat nonreturnable retainer to sweeten the pot, right off the mark."

"Yeah?" Jesse brightened, abandoning any trace of a tough negotiator's stance.

"Slow down," Anthony said, irked. "We don't dive until we check the water depth. For all we know, Dempsey's put together a go-nowhere piece of junk. And the Whimeds aren't being terribly sharp, either. Asking *me* to direct and produce their big deal. Well, I suppose they don't know where the Terran bodies and scandals are buried."

Pilar was smarter than he realized and way ahead of him. "They know you're a clone, if that's what's bothering you. It's not a well-kept secret. Nor is the fact that you're sensitive on the topic." Anthony was chagrined. Was his touchiness on the issue such open knowledge, even on Earth? That was where Pilar must have picked up her info.

The entrepreneur softened her earlier remarks, saying, "You must have collided with some real cretins, if you think your origins would make an iota of difference in this matter. Not to my Terran backers *or* the Whimeds. You're blowing the problem out of proportion."

"Am I?" Anthony avoided her probing gaze, feeling awkward and increasingly cornered. "Even granting that, the project can't work. Too little time. Do you know how long it takes to mount the sort of production the Committee is proposing?"

"Hey, we've been in other mad rushes and made it in under the wire," Jesse said, exuding optimism. Anthony grimaced. Had the older man's common sense been washed overboard by a hormonal tsunami?

"Ian sent everything you'll need." Pilar replaced the wafers

66

with Dempsey's script, scrolling through it, pointing out key passages. "See? All the cues and playwright's notes are here. He says for you to follow the same method you did directing and producing his previous works. Shouldn't be any trouble. We know how fast you were able to turn those out. We checked." The woman's smile would have melted Procyon Five's ice caps. Jesse responded, solidly on her wavelength.

Anthony's expression was stony. He mulled the implications in Pilar's words. They had checked him out, a check probably not limited merely to his directing and producing. Gutierrez and her backers must know that Saunder Studio was teetering on the razor edge between success and financial disaster. They were using that, dangling a juicy carrot. Jesse, prodded by blossoming sexual interest in their visitor, had already taken the bait.

The project *did* offer tremendous promise—and tremendous risk. Dempsey's script *did* look like a wowser, in the right hands. But generous retainers and licensing rights weren't worth a damn if the play flopped. And there was a strong possibility it would. Bispecies dramas had been tried before, to very mixed audience reaction. Some of the adverse feedback might have been triggered by confusion concerning disparate art forms, cultures, and translations. Some might have been xenophobia. Whatever the cause, viewers had turned thumbs down more often than they'd applauded. And a director-producer bore the lion's share of the blame in those cases.

The deal offered prestige for Saunder Studio, big profits, and entrée into new outlets and markets, alien as well as Terran. No doubt Procyon Five's government would be grateful, and they might back up that gratitude with tax breaks.

Weighed against that were impossible time pressures, operating outside his and Jesse's normal working patterns, the complexities of a dual-species project, and the chances that the I'TC delegates would loathe the play, that the promised general vid release contract would die aborning, and that Anthony and Saunder Studio would end up in a deeper hole than they were in right now.

"Another five percentage points here," Jesse was arguing, pointing to a rough draft contract he and Pilar were mapping out on the monitor. Anthony stared at his friend in dismay. He wasn't sure he wanted to commit himself, even tentatively. Not sure at all.

From where he sat, Anthony could watch both the screen and the window wall. The contract being sketched was a bonanza in the works for Saunder Studio—or a potential catastrophe. Beyond the window, the cephalopod tried to rake prey into its maw—as Anthony and Jesse were being raked in by Pilar's lures. Could he elude capture? *Should* he? There was another side to the situation—what if he turned down the project and the Whimed Committee located a younger, hungrier producer and director who managed to pull off this deal successfully? That thought stung Anthony's pride. What if the result was a smash? He'd never stop kicking himself for being too hesitant.

Damn! What was he going to do?

Pilar gasped in mock outrage. "What more do you want, Eben? I've gone as far as I can. If six gross Terran-Whimed exchange units isn't enough for the retainer—"

The men spoke in unison: *"Six?"*

Butter wouldn't have melted in the entrepreneur's mouth. "Oh, didn't I specify the amount of the up-front fee?" She tapped the figure concealed in the fine print.

Not just dangling the bait. Setting the hook.

Six units would put Saunder Studio in the black for nearly a year. It would give Anthony breathing space while he built a firm base of general orders. But was this project's profit margin sufficient to tide him over *past* a year, if the deal turned out to be a terrible mistake?

He wished he could read the future as easily as he could read those numbers on the monitor.

"You'll be a *much* better creative representative for Terra than that Veda Ingersoll will," the entrepreneur began.

Both men stiffened. "Veda?" Anthony asked coldly.

Pilar consulted her reference packet. "Mmhm. Former C.S.P. President Pacholski will deliver the opening address of the Conference. And Conference host Colin Saunder has selected Miss Veda Ingersoll to assist the elderly gentleman by contributing interpretive readings illustrating key points in his speech."

"Interpretive, hell!" Jesse snarled. "The sweet ingenue bit, blue curls and all!"

"Didn't you just complete a market tour with Ingersoll's React Theater troupe?" Pillar said.

Anthony grunted. "We did. That's why we know what Veda's likely to do onstage. She was certainly busy on that shuttle ride with Colin, wasn't she?" he said to Jesse. The associate producer made no bones about his disgust. They blamed Colin for this more than they did the ham actor. Veda was Veda. She wouldn't have been able to resist the opportunity. Colin, though, was in a position of power. He could have chosen any top performer in the sector. But he hadn't. Colin hadn't missed his cousin's animosity toward Veda, during that brief encounter in Clay's shuttleport. This seemed like another deliberate slap in the face.

"Well, now we know," Jesse said. "It could have been worse."

Anthony's look made his friend and the entrepreneur recoil slightly. "Yes. It *could* have been Ali Hassan."

There was an awkward moment, then Jesse wrenched the discussion back to contract details. "This . . . uh . . . this matter of working with felinoids . . ."

"You've done that before," Pilar said sweetly, "making those Saunder Studio meet-your-alien vids. I understand you both learned to speak Whimed Basic as a result."

"We were dealing with two, count them, two felinoid diplomats," Anthony retorted. "With C.S.P. Terran interpreters on hand every minute. Hardly adequate preparations for weeks' worth of collaboration with a Whimed artistic group under a heavy deadline."

"Yeah, and what about their accommodations?" Jesse put in. "What about food and—"

Pilar laughed. "Quit fussing! They've brought their own supplies and polished their Terran English to perfection. No problems. They're willing to bend over backwards to cooperate with you. Really! Here, let me acquaint you with the top Committee members." She inserted another chip in the player. Tiny holomodes formed on the tabletop. Pilar pointed to each in turn. "Taisso, the star's manager and acting coach. Majlur, their chief of protocol. Kyinell, the star's dresser. And this is—"

"Yrae Usin Hilandro, cultural treasure of the Whimed Federation," Anthony quoted.

Pilar scented blood. "Would you like to meet her? She and her associates are waiting below, at your dock."

For an instant, neither man could speak. Then Anthony blurted, *"Here?"*

"Ready and eager to go," the entrepreneur confirmed.

Jesse looked heavenward. "Why the hell are they sitting down there in the damp?"

"Custom. Protocol. They insisted on riding along when I arranged this appointment and waiting outside, hoping I could lay the proper groundwork. Did I?" Pilar tightened her net, putting her hosts on the defensive. "*Are* you interested?"

Anthony took a deep breath. He felt as if he were about to leap off a continental shelf into deep water. "Ask them up," he said curtly. "We should at least be hospitable. After all, they've come a long way."

Pilar already had her wrist-pager to her lips, relaying his invitation, though in more courteous terms. As she finished, she told the men, "Governor Yamashita and his aide are with them. They trust you don't mind their tagging along?"

"Oh, let's have the whole Planetary Council in," Anthony said with broad sarcasm.

The Governor led the way up the outer stairs and immediately launched into flowery introductions, interspersed with phony apologies for intruding on what was essentially a private business meeting. Anthony was tempted to tell the little politician to scram, but didn't dare. Yamashita could be an ally in cutting red tape, if not on this project, on future Studio productions.

Opening conversation was careful, two species testing the waters. Anthony was fascinated by the variations the Whimed foursome offered on the felinoid somatotype of an hourglass-shaped torso, prominent elbows, and a large, crested head. Taisso was a talkative, chubby dark-skinned male. Majlur, a pasty-faced plug-ugly, resembled a sun-starved boxer. Kyinell was a tall, muscular older woman who tended to Yrae Usin Hilandro's wrap and fussed with the star's hair. *That* luminary was more petite and much more fascinating than her tri-di replicas suggested. Neither of the females was lactating and, typically for their species, exhibited little mammary development as a result; formfitting jumpsuits revealed the outlines of several sets of nipples high on their chests, but nothing more obvious.

Taisso chattered. Majlur, Kyinell, and the Governor's aide—taking notes—hovered on the sidelines, contributing a few monosyllables to the conversation, when they said anything at all. Suddenly Yrae Usin Hilandro stepped directly to Anthony. He moved a pace aside from the others as the Whimed actress peered up at him with childlike frankness. A surge of protectiveness struck him as he took her tiny, long-fingered hand, possibly because the alien woman appeared fragile. It was an illusion; Whimeds were a great deal stronger than *Homo sapiens*. "I have looked forward to this encounter," she said.

"And I have wanted to see you," Anthony replied, startled to find that he meant it.

CHAPTER SIX

✪✪✪✪✪✪✪✪

Yrae Usin Hilandro

The Whimed Federation's cultural treasure had kilotons of so-called stage presence. That contrasted oddly with her innocent manner. "I have reviewed your productions. You are a proficient operator of emota-sensor devices. Also a skilled director of dramatic materials. You are well suited to enhance Janyavee's immortal composition."

Had Pilar promised the Whimeds were fluent in Terran English? Yrae definitely was. Anthony would have to stay on his toes. He bowed in acknowledgment of her compliments—and distanced himself mentally, analyzing her. He began with the voice, picking it apart: peculiar, spellbinding qualities; sexy alto; good projection; and an exotic accent, but less distortive than Ambassador Quol-Bez's pronunciation. It was an ideal voice, all in all, for vids or live performances. "Thank you, *Irasten*. I am gratified to learn that the emota-sensor affects nonhumans as well as humans."

"Your control of these devices will be most useful at our presentation at the Interspecies Trade Conference."

She was wasting no time, and sounding cocksure that Pilar Gutierrez had already signed, sealed, and delivered.

72

"My participation in this project is not yet decided," Anthony warned.

Yrae's starry eyes widened. "You are not agreed? I do not understand. You dislike Janyavee's work which your Ian Dempsey has adapted?" Her stare was accusatory, rattling him.

"That is not an obstacle, *Irasten*." He didn't mention that over the years he'd directed and produced some incredibly puerile material for Saunder Studio's release—material that sold better in the Settlements than much more sophisticated fiction. "What I have read of the script is quite satisfactory. However, my associate and I have so far discussed preliminaries. Nothing is concluded."

The alien woman blinked, releasing him from that hypnotic gaze. Her sharp little chin dug into the hollow of her throat—an exaggerated head motion Anthony had learned was what Whimeds used for a nod. "*Aaa!* I comprehend now. Discuss. You are in accord with script. Matters of payment must be agreed next. Correct? And you approve my fellow actor?"

He struggled to keep up with her sudden shifts. "Your co-star? David Lavrik, Pilar said. I'm not acquainted with—"

"I will show you. Where is viewer machine?"

Anthony's earlier uneasiness was fading, replaced by amusement. Yrae Usin Hilandro was an enchanting blend of prima donna and gamin. He rather liked the combination and he definitely wasn't bored.

Jesse was doing his best to keep the others entertained properly. They played along with such vocal thumb-twiddling while the Whimed Federation's superstar and the boss of Saunder Studio held a tête-à-tête nearby. Jesse glanced questioningly at his friend, and Anthony shrugged. Misgivings or not, he knew they were sliding down the launch ramp headlong into this project. Well, the Whimeds were reputed to be fast workers. This proposal bore the rumors out. He gestured to the refreshment island. "A viewer is there, *Irasten*."

She didn't wait for him to escort her. Anthony hung back a pace, appraising her through a Terran audience's eyes. She had trim little buttocks, a narrow waist, very shapely legs, and a dancer's poised stride. Her felinoid characteristics didn't detract; they seemed more like elaborate theatrical makeup. In the spacers' slang, she was attractive riding material; the pilots also bragged that Whimed females were fully sexually compatible with Terran males. A few men Anthony knew claimed to have tried that experiment, though he hadn't.

As she reached the table, Yrae Usin Hilandro moved around to its far side, opposite him, and Anthony added expressive, piquant facial features to the scorecard he was compiling. She removed the script and contract wafers and took another from a bejeweled purse she was carrying. The actress inserted the chip —of Terran manufacture, he noticed—and motioned for him to stand beside her. Her imperious attitude suited her high rank and alleged talents.

He suppressed a chuckle and obeyed, taking a position close —but not too close—to the alien woman, and added another item to his actress-potential catalog—she was very short. Costuming would likely have to supply thick-soled footwear for her, or any clinches and two-shots she shared with David Lavrik would be comedy. Anthony doubted that was what Ian Dempsey and the Whimeds' classic playwright had in mind.

Images flowed across the screen. "This is not well arranged," Yrae complained. "Much was excised in the interest of brevity."

"Most career and background résumés are," Anthony said drily.

What he saw was impressive, nevertheless. A data crawl at the bottom of the frame filled in Lavrik's stats. Demonstration clips of the man's professional work occupied the rest of the screen. He wasn't particularly tall, so contrasting heights between him and Yrae wouldn't be a problem. The actor was handsome and, like Yrae, he moved with a trained dancer's lithe assurance. That was to be expected, considering his education at the Kinetic Arts Institute and a small but well-regarded prep school in the Whimed Protectorate region. The young man was no slouch at drama, either. Those low-budget vids Pilar had mentioned made Anthony wince, but because of the sloppy production values, not because of Lavrik's performance—*he'd* been superb. No wonder he'd garnered raves, examples of which accompanied the on-screen excerpts.

"I see why you picked him," Anthony admitted. "He's excellent. With the right packaging—"

"He is my choice," Yrae announced proudly. She nodded as Lavrik executed the demanding final sequence from the heart-wrenching popular musical play *The Stars of Home*. His résumé concluded with still more entertainment industry reviews and plaudits. Yrae reclaimed the wafer and put it back in her costly purse. "David is familiar with our culture, art, and language . . ."

"Not surprising," Anthony said, "given his upbringing on one of your worlds and his parents' involvement in Terran-Whimed trade. All that plus a KAI scholarship. He obviously knows his craft."

"You approve?" Plainly it was very important to Yrae that he second her choice of a co-star. She awaited his reply breathlessly.

For a heartbeat he was hypnotized by her nearness. Yrae's coloring wasn't remotely human; "pearlescent" was the word that sprang to his mind. Red-gold hair and a darker auburn crest framed those striking features. Winglike brows, extending to her temples, created a feral effect. And those eyes were hazel, with greenish flecks at the edges of eerie star-shaped pupils.

She was a saleable package, probably saleable enough to cancel out most interspecies prejudice—except for the Vahnajes'. Small loss, that. The Whimed Committee wouldn't expect miracles, just a solid success with the Terran ITC delegates. If they made points with some of the other e.t.s. there—though not the Vahnajes—that was an extra. They just might pull it off, Anthony conceded, thanks to their cultural treasure and a bright, up-and-coming human actor of David Lavrik's caliber. For the first time he began to wonder if the project might actually work.

Maybe.

A decent director could make all the difference—that and an expert touch on the emota-sensors to grab the audience . . .

"You approve?" Yrae repeated, frowning impatiently.

"Of Lavrik? Yes. He looks like just what you need. When can he start work?"

Yrae smiled. The impact was stunning. Stage presence to burn! "It was hoped David would accompany us to this meeting. However, his ship was delayed. He arrives on your world in five local hours."

"I sympathize. I know what it's like to have one's travel plans disrupted."

"It is of no matter," Yrae said, sighing prettily. "He is prepared. When do we begin?"

"In a day or two, perhaps. It will take me time to prepare, as director," Anthony explained. "Many things must be done before actual rehearsals can start."

Jesse had gradually steered the rest of the group toward the refreshment island. "How are we doin'?" he asked, having gauged the answer in advance from Anthony's expression and body language.

Anthony nodded slightly, giving his friend the go-ahead sign, then immediately had second thoughts, a stabbing pang of doubt. What in the universe was he letting himself in for? He must be crazy! But Jesse was already putting the wheels in motion. Pilar, the Governor, his aide, and the Whimed Committee were seating themselves. Kyinell dug into her purse—a plainer one than Yrae's—and passed pre-packaged food and drink to her fellow lutrinoids while Jesse served caffa to the Terrans. He took a chair and began, "We have a few details to thrash out. This clause, for instance."

Taisso squinted at the screen, reading the indicated item. "You wish not payment, please?" His accent was thicker than Yrae's. His syntax was garbled. But he was easily understood, just the same, unlike most Vahnajes Anthony and Jesse had met.

"Sure!" the associate producer said. "We just want to specify C.S.P. exchange credits, not Earth funds. We're a long way out from Sol. It takes forever and a day to convert their currency to anything useful out here. We prefer our own monetary system—Settlement units. Right, Governor?"

Yamashita beamed at this evidence of Saunder Studio's loyalty. Now if he'd reciprocate by offering them a tax break during the next business quarter . . .

"This be amended," Taisso promised. "Is fairness. Ethical." Majlur and Kyinell added fervent seconds, as if the chubby Committeeman had stated a religious truth. In a way he had, according to the meet-your-alien vids. Anthony had heard plenty about the Whimeds' obsession with their standards of ethics while he was producing those packages. For the felinoids, ethics weren't abstracts, and Taisso obviously lived by those principles. "Is reason for Interspecies Trade Conference. Yes? To define correct such misunderstandings." Anthony eyed the fat little e.t. with growing admiration.

"Sugarcoated reeducation, huh?" Jesse said. The phrase puzzled the Whimeds, so he explained its idiomatic roots. They grinned and nodded and he touched the screen once more. "We'll want Anthony's regular Studio crew on the roster. I assume you'll want the same for your people . . . er . . . your Whimeds."

"*People* is okay word," Taisso assured the humans. His smile widened. Anthony noted that the Committeeman had broad, yellowish incisors. Yrae Usin Hilandro's teeth were white and very even. Creative dentistry? He didn't know. And there was so much he *wanted* to know. There was a natural tendency for people of all races to fall back on stereotypes. It was silly for Terrans to expect Whimeds to exhibit catlike fangs, any more than *Homo sapiens* had the fierce canine teeth possessed by some of their anthropoid relatives. Plenty of other stereotypes needed puncturing as well. As Taisso had said, ideally the Interspecies Trade Conference would clear up a few of those misconceptions. That was one of the main purposes behind the Whimed Committee's dramatic project—to familiarize their stellar neighbors with what felinoids and their art forms were like.

". . . and the payee should read 'Saunder Studio, Inc.',," Jesse was saying. "We're a legal entity, registered with Procyon Five's Commerce Division."

"A most valuable member of our business community, too," Governor Yamashita added. Anthony and Jesse exchanged knowing, cynical looks.

"Another matter," Taisso said. He jerked a thumb at Majlur, and the protocol chief rummaged in a bulky case, extracting a shimmering assortment of echinoderm skins. They were local pelts, by-products of undersea food processing. Technically the creatures weren't echinoderms, but the trogs tended to call them that. And this particular variety was known as a silky, exemplified by these incredible hides. Anthony had never seen such large, intact, perfect silky pelts. Taisso glanced hopefully at Anthony. "We buy this here. Wish to make it . . . mm . . . cloak. Costume for David Lavrik in play. Can be done?"

Anthony goggled, silently making an educated guess as to the cost of such pelts and imagining their effect on an offworld audience. "Margaret Orr, our Studio's wardrobe mistress, is a superb craftswoman. I believe you will be more than content with her work." He touched the almost priceless skins gingerly, appreciating the symmetry of the faceted scales. This was the cream of Procyon Five's just beginning exotic exports industry—and the Whimeds were offering to include an exhibit of those products in their opening presentation.

Taisso nodded, then continued wrangling with Jesse and Pilar over arrangements and clauses: transportation for all necessary personnel to Colin's planet; specs on who would have responsi-

77

bility for what during the rehearsals and actual performance; rental fees on Studio equipment; and precise credit divisions on the vids that would be issued, after the ceremonies.

Anthony heard Yrae sigh wearily. He leaned toward her and asked, "Are you bored, *Irasten*?"

A smile tugged at her full lips. "Yes. I wish to see your residence. Our colleagues do not require our attendance."

"No, I don't suppose they do," he admitted in the same muted tone, as he offered Yrae his arm. She considered that, apparently searching her memory for a file on Terran social customs.

Childlike excitement lit up her alien eyes. "*Aaa!* Pleasure." Then she blushed a shocking pink. "Y-yes. I wish to have you . . . escort." Almost shyly she slipped her arm through his, allowing him to lead her away from the refreshment island.

"*Pleasure* is a perfectly good Terran English word to use in this circumstance," Anthony said. He meant to ease her embarrassment at a linguistic lapse. Her reaction, however, was surprising.

Yrae halted. Her crest became a thorny crown. Vahnaj males' sideburns were erectile mood barometers; among Whimeds, both males and females possessed erectile crests that functioned in the same way. Yrae said angrily, "You are amused by my clumsy employment of your tongue."

Whoa! It seemed it was okay for Taisso to correct Jesse on the use of *people* and for Jesse to spell out human slang phrases for their guests. It was *not* okay for Anthony to imply—even unintentionally—that Yrae Usin Hilandro's command of Terran English was less than phenomenal.

"No. I was not amused, *Irasten*," he said hastily. Then he was annoyed with himself. Why was he placating her? Pilar said the Whimeds were the ones who'd adapt in this partnership.

Yrae's starry eyes and stiffened crest were transmitters, beaming her anger at him. The C.S.P. edu-vids had hinted that felinoids were very low-level espers, under certain conditions. The effect shouldn't have been apparent across the species barriers, but it was. Yrae was a living emota-sensor broadcaster, and her emanations made Anthony shiver.

He tried to read that pale face. It wasn't easy. Her expression reflected little of the turmoil betrayed by her voice and crest. He put himself in her boots, empathizing. Yrae's profession demanded she manipulate an audience. At the moment Anthony,

78

her director and producer-to-be, was her audience. And she was afraid she'd goofed, spoiled his opinion of her, right out of the launch tubes.

Because of a minuscule slip of the tongue in a language foreign to her! This lady was a demon perfectionist!

"I wasn't laughing at you," Anthony said earnestly. "Your knowledge of English is excellent. I'll make a mess of Whimed when I attempt to speak *your* language. I hope you'll be patient when that happens."

Yrae blinked. Her crest softened. Her smile was a supernova.

Anthony had dealt with mercurial human actors, but this alien woman's mood changes made the most unstable Terran appear placid. "I will not laugh at you," she said.

He eyed her crest warily, seeing it as an emotional barometer. Now all he had to do was learn how to read the thing—while directing her and Lavrik, a man he'd never met.

Yrae cocked her head, studying him. "You plan to speak Whimed? This is not necessary. Translation devices will be provided at the Conference for those passages in the drama where David and I must utter accurately other species' languages."

Momentarily nonplussed, Anthony said, "I—I wasn't thinking solely of the final performance. From my experience, rehearsal requires a lot of verbal exchange. It's helpful if I'm able to direct with phrases familiar to the actors."

"Not necessary," Yrae repeated. "The official language of the Conference is English. I have mastered this."

"Of course. Mastered, indeed."

She took the compliment as her due. Yrae peered down, scuffing her boot across the pseudo-black-sand carpeting. Her behavior reminded Anthony of a child's, probing even unimportant items in a new environment. He pointed at the *real* black sand beyond the window wall, and Yrae walked closer to the transparency. An echinoderm—too small yet to be in danger of losing its hide, as the former owners of those pelts had—crept along the window's base. "I believe you name this animal a spike arm?"

"Yes. It's a remote relative of the silkies—the creatures who will provide Lavrik's cloak in your play."

"Always water," the woman said. Her non sequitur took Anthony aback. "The view port at the Governor's quarters also showed us your ocean. Do not mistake me. We are grateful for

79

the Governor's attentiveness; he showed us much courtesy, escorted us . . . on your canals."

"There's nothing much to see on this planet's surface," Anthony explained. He didn't describe Procyon Five's terraforming efforts. The Whimed Federation was familiar with that science. A star-roving humanoid civilization *had* to be. He didn't want to come across to his visitor as foolishly boastful, talking about his race's technological achievements when those achievements were nothing extra.

"The oceans of my birthplace world are very different from this one," Yrae said.

"I understand. I, too, was born near another sort of sea, saltier and richer in animal life. Procyon Five has no mammals or true fishes. Cephalopods are our most advanced native species. Yet despite this planet's strangeness, it is home to Jesse and me."

"The host of the Interspecies Trade Conference is your kinsman," Yrae cut in. "Is he also native to your world?"

Anthony's gut tightened. What was she up to? Yrae had proved she was well briefed. Surely she knew the answer to her question. "Colin Saunder and I were both born on Earth," he said coldly. "But we didn't live in the same region. He was raised in a jungle area. I spent my childhood at Saunderhome. You've heard of that?" he finished challengingly.

Yrae looked wary. Smoothly she shifted back to the previous topic. "I must become accustomed to many environments if my Federation is to enlarge its trade. Your world will be my residence while we rehearse."

Now that she'd quit digging about Colin, Anthony was much more at ease. "Would you like to observe our sea creatures at close range?" he offered. "We can stand on the bottom without getting wet." A Whimed's eyebrows and lashes grew together at the temples, and those furry points in Yrae's face turned downward into a suspicious frown. Anthony smiled and said, "It's quite safe."

She nodded assent, her small hands moving up and down in rhythm with her head. He knew that was felinoid body language with some Whimed cultural groups, an emphasis of her agreement.

They descended the steps to the terrace dome outside the house. A cramped pressure lock connected to the underwater bubble. When they walked onto the black sand beyond, Yrae sucked in her breath and gazed up wonderingly at the elongated miniature dome. Most offworld visitors had that reaction when they realized that they were standing beneath kilotons of water.

An invisible roof held the sea at bay, the water magically suspended. Anthony and Yrae Usin Hilandro were warm and dry inside a green capsule. Three meters above them, sunlight sparkled on an inland sea. Anthony showed her the shadings between the bright upper waters and the darker lower levels nearer the window wall.

"The tide's rising," he said after checking the dome's monitors. "It'll reach the top of the window, at its height. At low tide, there's a lot of sky showing. I rather like that. It varies the scenery. Naturally we *do* lack a few things, like a starfield or darkness at night . . ."

"Because of your star's companion sun," Yrae said absently. Once more she'd reminded him that the Whimeds were veterans on the stellar frontiers. They were very familiar with binary systems. He'd been about to tell her something she already knew.

Yrae explored the dome, examining everything, picking up a handful of black sand and letting it trickle through her fingers. Nothing was too insignificant to draw her attention. Anthony chatted idly. "It's nothing spectacular, but Jesse and I enjoy the view. I hope to buy a minisub someday, and perhaps a couple of specially bred riding octopi for seabed excursions. They're expensive, though. Out of my reach for the time being."

At that moment a wild cephalopod emerged from the seaweed forest beyond the dome. A smaller native species that the settlers called a bobber was swimming into the octopoid's visual range. The globular, jellylike bobber was unaware of its danger. Tentacles lashed out, grasping at the prospective meal. The contest was even. Bobbers had nasty stingers, and they'd fight if they must. How much bobber venom could the octopoid tolerate? Waters churned, plants swaying, black sand motes dancing. The octopoid anchored itself on seaweed with its free arms and tightened its hold on the bobber. As the smaller creature resisted, the octopoid flinched. Blue stains muddied the green water, proof the bobber's stings were inflicting damage.

Anthony had begun to think humans and felinoids were actually very much alike. That attitude was swept away.

Yrae froze—not in the motionless stance of a Terran mime, nor in that of a human religious mystic, but different. There'd

81

been no mention of such a Whimed tendency on those tapes Anthony had made for C.S.P.

The alien woman didn't seem to breathe. She didn't blink. The texture of her skin changed from living flesh to marble. Alarmed, he took a step toward her, then paused. Yrae said nothing, but he knew as clearly as if she'd screamed at him that he must not touch her. Her expression was utterly blank. Yet she projected savage defiance—as the bobber beyond the dome was doing. The beautiful Whimed female and the bulbous aquatic native of Procyon Five were sending a warning: *Approach me at your peril.*

Slowly, keeping his distance, Anthony circled Yrae. Her pupils were enormous black stars. The green flecks in the irises glinted ominously. Was this a trance? It *looked* like a trance to a Terran. To Whimeds, it might be a completely natural state.

Hair prickled on Anthony's nape. He had a bad case of the jitters. What should he do? On impulse, he interposed himself between Yrae and the battling sea creatures, blocking her line of sight.

Despite the fact that she could no longer see that death struggle, she remained locked in her living-statue pose. Anthony was afraid to attempt any further intrusion on her peculiar condition, not wanting to precipitate a crisis.

"Stransir fo cheleet, Usin Hilandro . . ."

It was a male voice, alien, harsh, and shocking in its suddenness. Anthony swiveled, staring toward the pressure gate. Majlur, the Whimeds' protocol expert, stood just inside the dome. Anthony hadn't heard the man enter.

The tactic of getting between Yrae and the fighting water creatures had no effect. But Majlur's words did. Yrae flushed, losing her awful pallor. She whirled, pinning Majlur with a furious stare. Her crest was fully erect. The man took an involuntary step backward. So did Anthony, even though Yrae's rage wasn't directed at him.

This was no low-level esper ability. Whatever the talent was, Yrae possessed a lot of it. Her anger was tangible. In a split second she'd gone from trance to wide-awake wrath. She shouted in Whimed, not a shriek but an alto roar. Anthony couldn't translate, but he could make a shrewd guess. Except for the language, Yrae might have been any hot-tempered Terran actress, ripping up an oafish subordinate who'd spoiled her concentration.

82

Was that what it had been? Intense concentration?

"Briala thur. Ji! Ji! Nulow dush!"

If she'd been shrill, the explosion wouldn't have been so unnerving. Her low-pitched roar created instinctive fear. Anthony sidled away from the woman, trying not to attract her notice. Majlur cringed, bending over, spreading his fingers and extending his arms at waist level, groveling while still on his feet. He spoke in Terran, "I not mean disturb."

Anthony felt sorry for the alien. He'd beg forgiveness, too, in Majlur's place.

Yrae also shifted to Terran, saying less loudly than before, "You did disturb. I am not please. Pleas*ed*!" she corrected herself, stamping her foot. "I am Hilandro. You may not do this."

Majlur's pasty skin reddened. He stretched his arms out as far as he could without toppling onto his nose. "You—you requested attend. Taisso requests this." Anthony raised an eyebrow. That, at least, was a tactic that didn't differ from one species to another—when in trouble, blame someone else.

"Taisso!" Yrae exclaimed scornfully. "He does not command me. You will remind him I am not a servant." She inhaled deeply and went on, "You will tell him I will attend when I choose. He is not to request this again." Majlur nodded and retreated hastily through the pressure lock. Gradually Yrae's breathing slowed. Anthony suspected she was using a form of biofeedback, the same sort of self-calming techniques he'd learned years ago, during his short stint as an actor.

She smiled, calculated, brilliant, patently false—but very beautiful. "They wish me to return. We have much to accomplish before rehearsals," she said sweetly. Her crest was soft once more. She behaved as if the trance and her outburst against Majlur had never happened. Anthony didn't ask what all that had been about; he wasn't certain he was ready for an answer.

Physical attractiveness and her esoteric charm had made him forget for a time that Yrae Usin Hilandro's species had evolved on a planet light-years from Earth. She wasn't merely a Terran actress wearing extreme makeup. The starburst pupils, her strange hair, and her skin weren't tricks. They were part of her being—an exceedingly alien being.

"I . . . suppose we should join the others," Anthony said slowly. Yrae's smile broadened, became a conspiratorial grin. Again, she put her arm through his, turning with him toward the house. Her actions seemed thoroughly human—warm, feminine, a bit coy.

His emotions in a spin, Anthony recycled the pressure lock. Halfway up the inner steps from the lower deck, Yrae stopped to look back to the dome. She dawdled, talking about the things she'd seen there, stalling. Anthony grasped her motives; she was punishing Taisso for daring to intrude by sending Majlur to fetch her—another human reaction, getting even, while pretending to do something innocuous. She sensed that he had fathomed her tactics and laughed. Eventually she decided the Committeeman had waited long enough; she continued the rest of the way up to the main room.

When they arrived, the others were on their feet. Taisso, Majlur, and Kyinell were in a huddle, a common reflexive group embrace normal for felinoids—as normal as their polyphasic "catnap" sleeping habits and erratic starve-and-binge eating patterns, according to the edu-vids. Seeing the Whimed trio clasping each other tightly, turning slowly, and uttering muffled noises that almost sounded like animal growls didn't bother Anthony. He'd seen them before, on those tapes he'd produced. Yrae's trance, however, still troubled him. He'd had no prior knowledge of *that*, as he did of huddling.

Yrae didn't join her fellow Whimeds in their snarling knot. That was unusual. The felinoid diplomats serving as advisors on the edu-vids said huddling was instinctive, drawing in any Whimed within reach. In her standoffishness, Yrae Usin Hilandro was as special in that matter as in many others.

Abruptly the huddle broke apart. Taisso, beaming, full of enthusiasm, rushed to shake hands with Jesse. The Committeeman overdid it. Jesse fought to free his fingers without being obvious about it. If the Whimeds were sometimes puzzling to Terrans, a few human customs were still mysteries to the felinoids, despite their extensive advance preparations for the Interspecies Trade Conference. That was one more misunderstanding that would have to be cleared up on Colin's world.

Yrae drew near Taisso and spoke to him in Whimed. Anthony picked up enough words to know she was chastising him for nagging her earlier. He fluttered his hands and replied soothingly, but he didn't grovel, as Majlur had. Status difference? Or the familiarity of long-time acquaintanceship? Taisso *was* Yrae's acting coach, which implied closeness.

Jesse, having escaped from Taisso's grasp, edged toward Anthony and whispered, "Looks real good, kid. Terrific terms. Wanta read 'em?" A ritual query, needing no reply. At this stage of the game, the men trusted each other completely and thought alike. Once Anthony had given his friend the go-ahead by his subtle nod, Jesse would have negotiated the toughest contract possible. More loudly, the associate producer said, "I agreed to take the Committee on a guided tour of the Studio now, give them an idea of the layout, touch bases with the staff, and deliver those super echinoderm hides to Margaret so she can get started making Lavrik's cape. Okay?"

"Sounds fine," Anthony muttered, unable to muster an energetic response. So. They were committed. Or perhaps they *ought* to be committed! Jesse was delighted. For Anthony, that balance between potential and risks was still prominent in this thoughts. But he'd allowed himself to be persuaded. Stupid, maybe. Or brilliant. Time would tell him which.

Pilar was buttering up Governor Yamashita shamelessly, inviting him to join the Studio tour, working hard for the project's benefit and her own. Anthony couldn't fault her on that score. If things went well, this collaborative deal could go a long way toward wiping out the red on Saunder Studio's books. *If*. He tried not to think of failure. He dared not.

Yamashita burbled, "I'll expedite the necessary permits, of course. Glad to be of service. Anything my departments can do to assist, just let us know." Jesse smirked, putting Anthony in mind of a crustacean who'd found a choice morsel hidden behind rotting seaweed.

Expedite, meaning cut red tape—that was essential and long overdue.

"So grateful you could come today, sir," Anthony said, donning his best Mr. Charming suit. So he'd be the businessman, currying favor, stroking egos—just so it paid off in profits!

"Oh, certainly. Wouldn't have missed it." Yamashita strutted while standing still, he was so satisfied with himself. "We had been considering a number of . . . ah . . . interesting proposals from alien merchants. *This* one we hadn't . . . well, it just came out of the blue, so to speak. Remarkable. Don't you think this is a good omen for the success of the ITC, my boy? Ah . . . you won't object if I call on you tomorrow, will you, Anthony? Not interfering with your rehearsals or anything like that, naturally. Shall we say about 2100? All right?"

Behind the Governor's back, Jesse was sending frantic signals. Anthony wasn't sure what his friend and the politician were up to, but he followed Jesse's lead. "2100 will be fine, sir." He waved toward a terminal. "If you wish, you can contact me on the com. That'll save you travel on the canals and spare *your* busy schedule."

"How thoughtful of you. I *do* have a late appointment list tomorrow," Yamashita admitted. "Very good. We'll be in touch." He bowed low and added cryptically, "I look forward to our working together."

Anthony put his mouth on automatic, going through the forms. Conversation buzzed around him. Taisso and the Governor were making plans to pool Procyon Five's official comlink channels with the Whimed Committee's diplomatic contact system. Pilar promised to use her backers' legal resources to hurry along the contract finalizations. Anthony absorbed the chatter without conscious thought, his gaze lingering on Yrae Usin Hilandro. He wanted to prolong the moment—and he wanted to cancel the whole thing out and run back to safe waters, well away from the entrepreneur and this crazy deal she'd lured him into.

As the guests began to file down the outer staircase, Anthony moved to follow them. Jesse caught his arm. "No, you don't. It's homework time. Get busy." He tossed the Dempsey-Janyavee script tape to the younger man. "Lot of planning for you to do, director."

"Slave driver."

Yrae paused on the outer door's threshold and said, "It is an excellent drama."

"See? And I'll bet she's already letter-perfect, and that Lavrik is, too," Jesse said. "So get cracking."

Anthony felt a momentary irritation. Why was Jesse pushing so hard? Still, there *was* a hell of a lot to do in a hurry, and they both knew it. Click-click teamwork. They'd used the method well for years. It was what had brought Saunder Studio as far as it had come. What was different about *this* project?

Yrae stared at him, and again Anthony shivered. *She* was different. Kyinell, Taisso, and Majlur were different. His brief meeting with his collaborators-to-be had given Anthony a glimpse of what he'd be coping with for the next few weeks. He usually relished a directing challenge. But this time he feared he'd bitten off more than he could chew. Possibly more than *any* Terran director could chew.

"Go on down," Jesse told their guests. "I'll be along in a minute." As the others left, he closed the door partway and turned to Anthony, on the defensive.

The younger man hadn't missed the clues. He demanded, "What is Yamashita talking about? Why does he want to call me tomorrow?"

"From the hints he dropped, I think he's going to invite you to join Five's ITC delegation. In fact I think he's going to speedboat you to the head of the line, make you chairman." Anthony was stunned, and Jesse rushed on, saying, "Hey, I know it's an extra load on top of all this stuff. But I'll keep him out of your hair as much as I can."

Anthony finally found his voice. "He's going to appoint *me* head of the delegation? After treating us like non-contribs for so long—"

"Cool off," Jesse said, shaking his friend lightly. "So he's switching currents because of the Whimeds. Who cares? It's our chance to get some prestige for you and the Studio, kid. The settlers will finally see what an asset we are. Our Studio will be right up there alongside Incorporated Seabed Manufacturing and those mucky-mucks from Oceanic Genetic Engineering Exports and Mineral Development Unlimited. Not to mention you'll rub elbows with Yamashita and Commerce Secretary Blumfield . . ." He hesitated, eyeing Anthony anxiously.

The younger man was hunting for the stinger in the honor. "Really? It doesn't take much intelligence to spot the reasons. The Governor wants a famous-name figurehead."

"Figurehead, shmigurehead. Take it. It'll get us a decent business rating—and a long time coming, kid. After this, none of Five's industries will thumb their noses at us," Jesse said with heat. "It'll mean better credit, free advertising—"

"I'll be a puppet," Anthony snapped. "Well, I should have expected it. Yamashita can't be blamed for assuming a clone couldn't be any kind of serious businessman, though I *can* be a pretty face and a useful name."

Jesse shook him again, much harder. "Cut that out, dammit! I won't let you play that stupid game. Sure, he's snubbed the Studio in the past. But it wasn't because you're a clone. It's because we're show biz. To some of those elitists, our industry isn't as solid as skinning and cooking echinoderms or harvesting mineral nodules. You'll show them they misjudged us."

"Correct. I will," Anthony said, startling his friend. "The Governor's going to get a surprise. I'm no puppet. If he wants me as delegation head, he'll find he has one with a mind of his own. Procyon Five's going to get the best damned ITC leadership I can give us. By the time I get through boning up for the Conference, I'll know more about seabed mining and mineral extraction and genetic engineering than those companies' bosses do themselves!"

"Hey, kid, don't overdo it," Jesse begged. "That'd be too much, going along with this Whimed project. Just you concentrate on those rehearsals. Yamashita's not looking for——"

"But he's going to get it. Oh, don't worry, I'll be the soul of finesse. By the time he wakes up and discovers I'm actually doing my job with the delegation, he'll be convinced that's what he planned all along. And the Whimed Committee will get their project delivered on time as well." Anthony studied the older man's worried face. "Don't you think I can handle it?"

"Does it matter what I think? You've decided, haven't you? But hell, I'm thinking what'll it cost you, kid. You'll exhaust yourself."

Anthony seemed to be standing somewhere outside himself, scanning a disembodied person wearing Patrick Saunder's features. "I doubt any damage will be permanent," he said carelessly. "And it's worth it if it makes us solvent. Once we're inside the door the Governor's opening, he won't kick us back out again. And neither will the Whimeds."

"It's just like the time you took on all those productions at once, five years ago, when we were starting the Studio," Jesse wailed. "Damned near killed yourself from overwork."

Anthony was touched by his friend's concern. "It paid off. Gave us the stake to keep going. Speaking of money, is the Governor planning to pay our bills for attending the Conference in exchange for my playing figurehead chairman?"

"Hah! He's not *that* grateful to get you as a front man. From his standpoint, we ought to pay him for the privilege. Don't worry. I'll finagle some of the expenses out of overhead from the Whimed project. Perfectly legal. Incidentals and so on," Jesse said, seeing the alarm in Anthony's expression. "None of that

Tracy Rutledge nonsense. Trust me. Listen, it could be worse. Yamashita mentioned that the ITC host has to foot more than a third of the overall cost for the attending delegations. Housing. Supplies. On-site transport. All that stuff."

"Colin's paying a third?"

"Or more. Ironic, huh? Just wait till he finds out he'll be paying part of *your* bill, kid, *and* mine, *and* our Studio crew's, while we're assisting on the Whimeds' presentation. I'd sure like to see Colin's face when he hears you'll not only be there, but heading up a delegation."

"A delegation of trogs," Anthony said. "Not exactly among the top echelon of attendees from his point of view." He envisioned hordes of humans and aliens converging on Colin's world, and the ITC host picking up the tab. The Conference would boost Procyon Four's economy, but not enough to offset such huge expenses. And Colin would have to be spendthrift. He'd stepped on a lot of V.I.P.s' toes to bring home the prize of managing the first Interspecies Trade Conference staged in the Terran sector. Plus he'd be piggybacking Myron Simpkins' campaign for C.S.P. President during the ITC, and that would mean still more expense. Well, Colin had wanted the honor of the thing, and now he had it, with all its stingers attached. As Jesse said, that was ironic.

"You mad?" the associate producer asked timidly.

"No."

"Sure?"

Smiling, Anthony said, "I'm sure. Why should I be mad?"

"Because of this stuff with Yamashita. I didn't know how you'd take it. And, well, you looked kinda shook when you and Her Nibs came up from the dome. I was kinda shook, too, what with all the cat folks' huddling and the wheeling and dealing with them and Pilar."

"I suppose we can't back out of the deal now."

It took a moment for Jesse to realize that he was being teased. He glowered comically and punched Anthony's bicep. "You know damned well it looks unprofessional to pull back when we've gotten to this point in the contract talk, kid. So just stow that. Okay!" Jesse threw back his shoulders and said, "I'll go play tour flunky. And *you* study that script."

"Try not to get caught groping while you're showing Pilar around the Studio," Anthony said slyly. "It looks shabby for my associate producer to do that. Or were you pretending that wasn't what you had in mind? Then quit drooling on her boots; she'll get the wrong idea."

"Smart-ass kid!" Jesse retorted, but the worry line had disappeared from between his shaggy brows. He shook with laughter as he hurried down the steps.

Anthony peered into the dimly lit staircase. Jesse had already reached the bottom and was out of sight; the overhang cut off a view of the dock. Anthony heard Jesse's and other voices, human and alien. Then a boat motor roared to life—big craft. The Governor's? Odors of fuel and canal water tickled Anthony's nose and he heard thumping sounds. The boat was pulling away from the pier, heading downstream toward the Crosstown Canal leading to Saunder Studio. Noises faded. A few other boats went past the channel, and finally there was only the slap-slap of water echoing up through the darkness. Anthony shut the door.

He was alone with his jumbled thoughts. Surprises had come one right after another: the Whimed project; Yrae Usin Hilandro; and his probable appointment as head of Procyon Five's delegation. Potential triumph and potential disaster were seesawing back and forth in those balance scales, chafing his nerves raw.

Shaking his head, Anthony walked to the refreshment island and dropped into a chair. He cued the Dempsey-Janyavee script, watching and listening intently. Ian's voice-overs accompanied visual inserts of model stage settings and sketches of the play's two characters, with details, concepts, and stick-figure diagrams of dance sequences combining Terran and Whimed versions of that art form. At the short drama's climax, the hero delivered an emotional speech recapping his first encounter with an extraterrestrial. The heroine countered with *her* first meeting of a human and an ardent plea for interspecies understanding, weaving an amalgam of prose and music. The effect was eerie and powerful. Dempsey of Terra and Janyavee of the Whimed Federation mingled their genius despite wide separation in civilization, race, time, and space.

A movement at the edge of Anthony's vision made him turn toward the window wall. The bobber and the hunting octopoid were gone, leaving no sign of their struggle. The echinoderm had abandoned its search for food and now rested on the black sand slope. Then a sea monster arose from the depths.

The echinoderm tried to burrow in the sand. Trogs called the approaching species of native squid ocean kings. They were five times larger than the octopoid that had attacked the bobber and were the planet's most intelligent indigenous life form—about as smart as a very stupid Terran dolphin. Settlers treated them with respect; ocean kings could crush a sub or wreck a subsea dome, if aroused. Fortunately, the giants rarely bothered humans or their machines. But now and then a biped blundered into an ocean king's territory and paid the price, though no one blamed the beasts for following instinct.

This particular king swam slowly past the window. Light played over its lumpy hide. A hood studded with spiky projections almost hid the creature's baleful eyes. Anthony stared at the animal. The wall was triple strength; he could confront the squid with impunity, from this side of the barrier.

Cephalopods had dominated these waters for eons, until the Terrans came. Since then, humans had used genetic engineering to exploit numerous branches of the species, breeding the beasts. Humans and semidomesticated octopoids worked together to harvest the sea, to the humans' profit. In return, the animals enjoyed a greatly lengthened life span, improved survival rates for their young, and a reliable food supply. It wasn't a true partnership; the octopoids were slaves, no matter how well they were treated.

Not all cephalopods were tame, however. Terrans who had to venture into the deeps prayed they wouldn't run into an angry ocean king. Sometimes they lost that gamble.

Well, that was the way it was.

Settlers were fatalistic risk takers. They had to be. The immigrants had come out to the stars for a variety of reasons, accepting the dangers. For Anthony, the reason had been escape from two vindictive relatives. He'd won that gamble, but he might have lost. Many pioneers did. They all wagered with their lives, on mankind's frontiers. And if they failed . . . no complaints. They were volunteers. No court exiled Terrans to the stars. Nobody forced them to sign a Charter Company's paper or tag along on the outbound ships to take their chances in the Settlements' labor pools. Every immigrant had plenty of guts, even the noncontrib brawlers and fast dealers on the boomtown worlds. Weaklings and the timorous never left the Mother World; they stayed on Earth and rotted.

Anthony and the ocean king regarded each other—air breather and water breather. Compared to that contrast, Terrans,

91

Vahnajes, and Whimeds were blood brothers. Indeed, all humanoid species had some form of iron-based blood; the creature outside the window would bleed blue if it was wounded.

Taking its time, the king drifted back toward the depths. Anthony admired the beast with an odd sense of ownership. This was his planet, and the kings were a part of it.

That brief sighting brought a cold truth home to him, however. On Earth, the rules were known. On the frontier, humanity had to learn *new* rules, and adapt. The rules of dealing with alien humanoids and strange lower life forms or dealing with hostile environments were different. The old, familiar patterns had to change. It was a simple case of survival.

In Anthony's mind's eye, the images of the ocean king and Yrae Usin Hilandro were superimposed, equally alien, equally unknown. The cephalopod was, in its way, beautiful, and very dangerous. Anthony acknowledged Yrae's beauty. And the danger she and her Committee's project might present? The verdict was still out on *that*.

Danger and beauty mixed. They meant risks and rewards for the successful settlers on Earth's frontier, and possible disaster for the unlucky on these weird and alien shores.

CHAPTER SEVEN

oooooooo

Rehearsal

Anthony sat bolt upright, jarred awake, then groaned. He rubbed his eyes, trying to focus them and his brain, and squinted at the chronometer. Another groan.

He'd been home over ten days now. No need for compensation meds, and they wouldn't solve the problem, anyway. What he required was sleep—or being what he had started life as, five identical individuals. Maybe *then* he could accomplish all he had to do without wearing himself to the bone. Maybe.

His beard stubble, sweat, and rumpled clothes would betray him. He had to clean up. Jesse would be here to pick him up soon, and the associate producer's comments would be acid if his friend looked the way he did right now. Yawning, Anthony stripped, shambled into the soni-scrub, and started trying to put himself in shape. Later, freshened and dressed, he *appeared* more alert, but it was sham, only sham.

Just like his boast that he could handle both the Whimed Committee's project and the chairmanship of the ITC delegation with no trouble. That was a laugh. Big man brag, worthy of Colin and his elegant posturing. Anthony had never felt so tired and pushed to the wall as he had recently.

93

The sleeping alcove's terminal buzzed. Another call! Such calls arrived around the clock, giving him no rest. Well, he'd asked for it. And he'd certainly gotten it! Anthony seated himself before the monitor, deliberately donned a bright expression, and made contact. The face of a businessman on a continent a hemisphere away materialized on the screen. "Glad I caught you, Saunder. Wanted to confirm our updated agenda. Putting it through." The printout mechanism whirred, feeding a copy of the delegate's papers onto Anthony's desk.

He scanned the material quickly, nodding. "Looks fine, Bodua. I agree, we want to be sure to attend ITC sessions on aquatic life form engineering and the food-processing seminars. You did understand why I crossed out the lectures on economic potentials of arid habitats?"

The man on the other end of the line grimaced. "Can't imagine why Helga put that in the package in the first place. I suppose the Governor told her to include everything."

"But we can't possibly sit in on every meeting and lecture at the Conference," Anthony said, forcing a smile. "I've consolidated the original schedule as much as I can, and this is the best I could come up with."

"No objections, Saunder. You've done nicely." The industrialist paused, then said, "I admit I had my doubts when Yamashita appointed you our chairman, a week or so ago. Late in the day and all that. Knew what Yamashita was up to, of course. Prestige of your name, heading our list. Didn't really expect more than that, and *some* of our people were pretty annoyed, let me tell you. *They'd* wanted the slot. You're proving out well, though. *Very* well."

He was astonishing them, in fact. However, Anthony didn't say that. He murmured politely, thanking the delegate for his confidence.

"Tell you a secret. Damned happy you're steering instead of that pompous little politician. At least you don't have any of his axes to grind. We can count on *you* to keep our meetings fair. Bodua out."

Anthony sighed and rubbed his eyes again. There were advantages in conducting hastily arranged delegation affairs by Procyon Five's worldwide com net. It canceled out the inconvenience of members being located on both day and night sides. All of them had businesses to run, and they couldn't drop

94

everything and travel to a central point for update sessions constantly. Agenda and planning discussions could be handled much more efficiently this way. But it meant Anthony might be tapped for a decision *outside* the planned remote meetings at any time.

Bodua's comments accurately reflected the situation. There had indeed been resistance when Governor Yamashita had rammed through Anthony's appointment as a figurehead chairman of the delegation. At first no one had taken him very seriously. He'd soon proved, though, that he, too, was a competent businessman and knew how to deal with the necessary paperwork and the various personalities comprising the group. It was important that they accept him—and put aside their differences. Their Settlement had too many problems to deal with to waste time. They had to find better means of controlling the planetary environment, boosting factory outputs, feeding and housing all their people, and holding their own among the other Settlements, as well as attracting immigrants, attracting investors, and correcting the import-export imbalance. Fixing that *last* was a special problem for the trogs. How could they make headway when a prosperous and booming world like Procyon Four was practically next door and blatantly luring trade, potential citizens, and money from the newer, poorer Settlement? It was a brain and treasure drain, not illegal, but . . . Jesse called it sharp practice, and Colin Saunder's commercial company was one of the worst offenders.

A bigger stew was boiling as well, one involving the needs of the entire C.S.P. and the Solar System: expanding interspecies relations; calls for monetary stabilization and compromises; and a crying need for adjustments in calendar misalignments, cross-cultural laws, and tax equity. The growing breakaway movements on the frontier faced the Earth-based Charter sponsors' toughening stance on that topic. Last but not least was the Lannons' threat to boycott the Interspecies Trade Conference. Anthony had searched the recent newscasts, hoping to read that Captain Saunder and her allies had combed down the Lannons' fur and coaxed them back into the fold. But . . . nothing. Not a word.

Other nagging worries involved those troublemakers Ambassador Quol-Bez had mentioned—the Biyelin Vahnajes and the Whimeds' Outer Satellite Faction. Were there other spoilers from other sectors as well, waiting to move in if the ITC should dissolve in chaos?

Anthony yawned again, filed delegation business, and got out his Studio "homework," feeding the vid chips into the playback. He sprawled in his chair, studying the earlier run-throughs critically. The recordings were rough cuts, abrupt, typical of these preliminary directing efforts. That didn't bother him. David Lavrik did. A week's worth of intense rehearsals were behind them, and yet the thing wasn't pulling together—largely because of the Whimeds' handpicked Terran star. Yrae Usin Hilandro was doing magnificently, easing the kinks out and getting on top of all the non-Whimed portions of the drama, polishing it to perfection.

Lavrik, however . . .

What was wrong with him? The actor had showed up right on time, friendly, letter-sharp on the script, and willing to be available for fittings after hours with Margaret, in order to complete the costly echinoderm skin cloak the Whimeds demanded for the presentation ceremonies. He showed no temperament, no ego . . .

And no spark.

Yrae's co-star baffled Anthony and frustrated all his skills as a director-producer. He'd tried alternating gentle, avuncular chats with stern challenges to Lavrik's pride. Nothing worked, no matter what he did to discover what the snag was. They were getting nowhere.

Meanwhile, time was ticking away. The deadline for departure was drawing ever nearer.

Anthony fed the original résumé tape of Lavrik's past career into the player, running it alongside the rehearsal roughs. He saw the same man, the same well-honed dancing and dramatic talent, but with all the emotional spark of a rock. Anthony's best efforts on the emota-sensor equipment hadn't helped. Yrae was putting out tidal waves of powerful signals, even during these practice sessions. David Lavrik's projection was distorted, muffled. It would never convince the most receptive audience, let alone the tough sell of the Interspecies Trade Conference delegates.

Yrae danced, spoke Ian Dempsey's lines, and gave the rehearsals her finest. Anthony should have been solving the puzzle of David Lavrik, but his attention was pulled inevitably toward the smaller, feminine form in those crude images. She *was* a cultural treasure, exquisite, alien, and enchanting. Directing her was exciting, an adrenaline high that counteracted his fatigue and momentarily buried his other concerns. He shouldn't let himself get so wrapped up in the project's leading lady. He should be concentrating, strictly professional. And yet . . .

Irritably Anthony shut off the player and yawned once more. Where was Jesse? He ought to be here by now, and they ought to be leaving for the Studio, or they'd be late.

A light flashed on the monitor, announcing an incoming call. He cued the accept circuit and drummed his fingers impatiently. Who was this? Another delegate needing his or her hand held? That paging light meant the party on the far end had placed the call but was probably elsewhere at the moment, getting other work done. Some people who used the opportunity channel were lazy about coming back to their own screens when their party finally answered. Anthony gave the unknown signaler five minutes; then he'd break the link.

Colin's picture appeared. Tiny numbers in the frame's corner showed that this was an instantaneous transmission. Subspace, for a mere one-third A.U. interplanetary message? What was so important that Colin wasn't using real time?

"Hello! You're difficult to get hold of."

"Good to see you," Anthony lied.

His kinsman's image was very sharp, further proof of expensive priority circuits. Artificial lighting in the broadcast area made Colin's blond hair glow. Jungle foliage swayed against the window behind his head. That backdrop pinpointed his location —his estate near Procyon Four's capital, rather than his secondary HQ in that planet's southern deserts. "I just got the update rosters on the attending delegations. I see you're chairing Five's reps," Colin said. "Congratulations. I guess that means we'll be seeing each other often during the Conference."

"It would seem so."

"Oh, and you're producing and directing the Whimeds' opening presentation, too. What a coup! A bit of a surprise, though, isn't it, considering those—what were they called?—erotic dramas you became famous for?" the blond noted, smirking. "Actually, I would have thought if you worked for any aliens, it would have been the Vahnajes, given your lifelong friendship with Quol-Bez, and all."

Anthony didn't let his annoyance show. "I'm merely acquainted with Quol-Bez. You have the advantage, when it comes to close contact with Vahnajes. Aren't your trading partners from their Alliance? Besides, it was a Whimed Committee that made me the offer. My porn vids didn't affect their opinion. Speaking of opening ceremonies, I understand you selected Veda Ingersoll to—"

"Yes, yes." Colin's smile was weak. "I expect her to liven things up. C.S.P.'s beloved ex-President is a fine fellow, but Pacholski *can* be dull. Veda will lend color to the proceedings."

"She's colorful, no argument," Anthony said tonelessly.

His kinsman leaned forward and spoke in a confidential manner, as if he and Anthony were face-to-face, not on separate planets. "Actually, that wasn't what I called about. I hear that you met Cousin Brenna recently."

Now how had Colin learned that? Suddenly another question —and a possible hopeful answer—struck Anthony. "Has Brenna convinced the Lannon to attend the ITC?" he asked eagerly.

There was a pained silence. Then Colin said, "Oh, that. No, not yet. Not important. The Lannon just want to huff and puff a bit. They'll come around."

His offhanded attitude was disturbing. The ITC host should know how serious the Lannons' threatened boycott was. Colin was taking the situation awfully lightly, in Anthony's opinion. "Brenna didn't think the Lannon were faking," he muttered.

"She tends to overdramatize. Uh . . . Regan was with her, wasn't she?"

Anthony nodded. "Regan, Ivan, and the Ambassador."

"That explains it. Brenna's gang of yes-people. Regan in particular is a bad influence—a lovely child, but too wrapped up in Ames Griffith's son to see straight." Colin's dark eyes grew cold as he went on, "As for Brenna, money makes her universe go round. She's afraid of losing a few profits because of the Lannons' snit. As if SMEI isn't rich enough already! Take her warnings with a grain of salt. But I forgot; you troglodytes have a lot of that, don't you? All that seawater." Colin hesitated and peeered intently into the lens.

What was he looking for? A reaction to his taunt? Anthony didn't give him that satisfaction. And he didn't bother to correct Colin's mistake; Procyon Five's seas *weren't* especially salty.

"You needn't be apprehensive about the Lannon," Colin said. "They'll show up, I guarantee. You don't have my sources of information," he finished, very smug.

Anthony ignored that jab, too. Sources meant Simpkins, Colin's presidential candidate. But was Simpkins's info correct?

Brenna commanded much more clout than Colin, and she wasn't sanguine about the Lannon affair. If it came to choosing a faction to trust, Anthony preferred Brenna's.

"Just put that out of your mind," Colin said, hurrying on. "What I really want to know is, Did Brenna sound you out on your vote on the Conference's monetary proposals?"

Slowly shaking his head, Anthony bought time while he considered the query. Surely Colin knew that chance meeting with Brenna had occurred before Anthony had been appointed chairman of Five's delegation. Brenna's statements then couldn't qualify as a sounding out, because at the time Anthony had no inkling he'd have a vote to cast at the ITC. Hadn't Colin's sources filled him in on such details? "No, she didn't," Anthony replied, his tone flat.

Colin's mask slipped a trifle. Suspicion chased over his square features. "Odd. I would have thought . . ." He caught himself and plastered on his merchant prince's grin. "Well! What *is* your delegation going to do? Are you voting for or against?"

Every group of representatives planning to attend the ITC had been bombarded by lobbyist literature vids. One of the thorniest topics coming up there was the controversial monetary reform amendments, sponsored by Ames Griffith's Progressive Party. Colin's candidate was firmly against any changes in the C.S.P. status quo. From what Anthony had observed, Brenna's—and Regan's—candidate was gathering strength fast. Colin needed to get busy twisting arms to support his man. Was that what he was up to with this call? Why did he think he'd have any influence over a kinsman who detested him or over a delegation he referred to with open contempt as trogs?

The amendments would probably be a watershed in the Charter Settlement Planets' existence. They would determine the future of millions of pioneers, for good or ill. Worlds like Colin's, prosperous and well established, had strong ties to Earth and the Colonies. Their trade was doing fine. They wanted things to go on exactly as they were—with a few convenient adjustments in *their* direction alone, admitting their favored alien clients into the privileged inner circles, then barring any new entrants. Still-developing Settlements like Procyon Five were eager for *more* contacts, both human and alien, and greatly expanded trade, as well as a loosening of the bonds fettering C.S.P. to Earth. They definitely wanted a modernization of the monetary system currently in use on the frontier. That method was out-dated, popular with only a handful of the strong, standpatter old-line Settlements, led by Colin's Procyon Four.

Each of the Saunder kinsmen had a vested interest in those upcoming votes. The difference was that Colin was wealthy and powerful, and so was his Settlement. Anthony and Procyon Five weren't.

Or at least that was the way Anthony had assumed things stood. Colin's behavior and this unexpected call, though, hinted that matters weren't quite so cut and dried. He sounded as if he were actually courting Procyon Five's support. Could it be that C.S.P.'s kingmaker was worried about his candidate's campaign and the certainty of his faction's success at the ITC?

Anthony toyed with the idea of telling his cousin that, yes, Five's delegation *had* made up its collective mind—to back Ames Griffith and the amendments wholeheartedly. That was true. But it would be stupid to admit it. A moment's triumph wasn't worth damaging Procyon Five's future commercial prospects. Colin Saunder was a dangerous foe and a man who carried a grudge. It was unwise to give him any cause to want revenge on his neighboring world, his kinsman, or Saunder Studio.

"My delegation has decided to listen to the debates at the Conference before we make up our minds," Anthony said. "There are valid arguments on both sides of the issues. Our people want to be fully informed."

"That's—that's sensible. I wish more representatives were as unbiased." Colin cleared his throat several times, then said, "When you arrive here, do permit me to introduce your group to some important officials, Anthony. It could be of tremendous use to your delegation and to you."

"Thank you, that's very kind."

"You *are* going to be able to make the trip here without undue problems, aren't you?" Colin asked mischievously. "Oh, of course you will. You're piggybacking with the Whimed Commit-tee. I forgot. But how about the rest of the delegates? Are their arrangements solid? I understand most of Five's ships are getting pretty creaky." The blond chuckled and added, "We wouldn't want them to get stranded in space halfway to the Conference, would we?"

Was that what he was *hoping* happened?

"They'll be there," Anthony muttered.

100

"Glad to hear it. By the way, I assume the Whimeds are paying you adequately. Eben probably negotiated a decent fee for you. Invaluable employee. You're so fortunate to have him. Oh, and I see an entrepreneur is involved. My sources tell me she's a real accomplisher."

Anthony ignored the crack about Jesse's being a mere "invaluable employee." "Pilar Gutierrez is a gem," he said.

"Does she handle other projects than entertainment matters?" Colin wondered, seemingly sincere. "I'd like to speak to her. Is she traveling here with you? Naturally I don't want to poach while your contract with her is running. But perhaps we can work something out. Whoops! Other calls coming in. I must run."

The image winked out, becoming static and disappearing. Anthony mentally replayed the conversation. In her short, tragic life, Olivia Gage had taught her son the beginnings of social amenities, and Colin had built on that foundation. Now he was operating in lofty leagues and knew exactly how to pretend a sudden press of urgent business to wiggle out of a sticky situation. Anthony didn't fault his kinsman for wearing a façade and being manipulative; he used both tricks himself to make his way in the universe. But Colin was getting careless. That claim of being forced away from this chat by other calls was too thin. Anthony was tempted to reestablish the connection and offer to give the merchant prince lessons in subtlety. No, too expensive, and Colin wouldn't appreciate the joke. Not at all. And Anthony was more and more conscious of the dangers of angering the host of the Interspecies Trade Conference.

Colin's disdain of the threatened Lannon boycott still troubled him. So did his cousin's parting remarks about Pilar Gutierrez. What was Colin planning? To lure Pilar into a lucrative deal with Colin's corporate division? That was a common, profitable, and completely legal arrangement. But it might hurt Jesse, not that Colin would care about that. The merchant prince could express concern and pretend friendship with the best of them, and mean none of it.

He learned it from the absolute mistress of that tactic, Carissa. So did I. Carissa taught us to use people and twist them ruthlessly to achieve our goals, but to hide our motives from them. I still do that. Did when I was acting, do now, playing a role, almost convincing myself my feelings are real when I sham affection for Margaret and Chet and the others at the Studio or for women I bed. There's no sincerity in any of it, except my friendship with Jesse.

His distorted reflection shimmered on the empty terminal screen, showing overlapping mirror images of him, Carl, Eddie, Bart, Drake, and a long-dead hero, Patrick Saunder. Yet all of the faces were Anthony's. Not possible! True, Patrick Saunder had been approximately Anthony's age when he died, nearly seventy years ago. Carl, though, had been a teenager when he'd committed suicide. And the others had been mere toddlers when the shadow figures stole them away; they *couldn't* share Anthony's adult features.

However, they shared DNA. They shared Anthony Saunder's physical traits . . . and his emotional nature? They were a part of him, and as long as he was alive, so were his brothers and Patrick Saunder. The idea was unnerving.

"Kid? You here? Let's go." The familiar voice roused him from his speculations. Anthony went out to the foyer and saw Jesse pulling a heavy jacket from a storage shelf. "Better wear this," the older man advised. "Colder'n hell on the canals this morning." As he helped Anthony into the coat, he asked, "You sleep okay?"

"Fine. You?"

"You don't *look* as if you did," Jesse grumbled, then said, "I thought I heard you talking to someone when I first came in, a bit ago."

"It was Colin." Anthony was mildly surprised that his friend had been eavesdropping. "Oh ho! You thought it was Yrae—that she was here."

"No, I didn't."

"Rotten seaweed! And what if she was? You're not my watchdog." He spoke harshly, fatigue shortening his temper. Anthony immediately regretted his angry tone. Why was he taking things out on Jesse? Besides, there were ample precedents for the associate producer's assumptions; Anthony often had affairs with the women starring in Studio dramas. The star of the ongoing production, however, was a far cry from Anthony's usual bed-bouncing partner. Jesse looked hurt and uncomfortable, and Anthony tried to take the bite out of his earlier words, teasing, "What's the snag? If I was bedding Yrae, it wouldn't ruin your plans, because you're spending your nights at the V.I.P. Hostel

102

with Pilar. Not that I'm objecting. I like to see you old folks having fun."

Brightening, feigning outrage, Jesse threw a mock punch. Anthony dodged and laughed. They wrestled clumsily a moment, shouting obscenities. The impromptu roughhouse ended when Jesse began gasping for breath. The associate producer straightened his clothes and growled, "Damned handsome brute-brained chud! Go take out your juvenile aggressions on the lobsters!"

"You're out of shape," Anthony twitted him. "We'd better rent a fitness cubicle for you. Go a few rounds in there regularly, and I'll have you toned up in no time. After all, you can't expect to bounce the entrepreneur every evening and swim with us young octopoids the next morning unless you—"

"Sink and bury that!" Jesse bellowed. They waltzed the phony argument about until they wore out the joke. Sobering, Jesse wondered aloud, "By the way, why did Colin call you? He going to give us a hard tour when we get there?"

"I don't think so." Anthony described the conversation, omitting Colin's queries regarding Pilar.

Jesse frowned, tugging his lower lip. "Vote counting, huh? A priority call, you say? Where from? That sandblasted fortress in the desert or his jungle castle?"

"From Jangala." Anthony added, "Actually, I believe he is glad I'm chairing Five's delegation. By the time the ITC is in gear, Colin will have persuaded himself that he arranged it and that I owe him a favor because of it. I'm really no more than a minor nuisance to him, anyway."

"Don't fool yourself, kid. He's gritting his teeth so hard he's breaking them, hating you. Hell, enough about him. Come on. We'll be late."

A taxi boat waited at the pier below. As soon as the riders were aboard, the driver throttled up, heading for Saunder Studio. Cold spray flew and clammy tunnel air blasted across the taxi's bow. Anthony was grateful that Jesse had warned him to wear warm clothes. He hung on to a safety bar as the craft slewed around a corner and sped past a row of squatters' caves. A team from Equitoria's Board of Health was moored at the waterline below the homes in the rocks. Sanitation was a big problem here, and the teams checked out the squatters' quarters regularly, making sure they obeyed the laws. Anthony approved. These days he was seeing his planet from the authorities' viewpoint. They had the tough job of making this Settlement work for everyone. There had been times when Anthony had been a squatter himself, not on this world, but on others. He empathized with the bottom level of pioneers. But now he was a struggling businessman, chairing the ITC delegation, becoming part of Procyon Five's establishment and wide responsibilities went with the position—responsibility for his fellow pioneers as well as for himself and his company.

If this Whimed presentation project doesn't come off, I may be bumped back down to squatterhood again . . .

He raised his voice to be heard over the motor's noise. "Did you come up with anything?"

Jesse caught the reference instantly. "About our wonder boy from KAI, who isn't turning out to be so wonderful on the set? Yeah. I've been tryin' to get close to the guy, same as you. Tough nut. He doesn't tell me to scram. He just sort of sags and says nothing matters."

"Certainly the rehearsals don't," Anthony commented. "He has to shape up soon or the whole project's dead in the water. Yrae needs a co-star in her league—and it's rather late to hunt up a substitute."

"Probably couldn't, anyway," Jesse said. "The Whimeds picked him special. I'll tell you something, he's not playing it level with us." Anthony peered intently at his friend, waiting for an elaboration on that cryptic remark. The associate producer nodded sagely. "I've been tailing him. Tryin' not to be too obvious. You know, like that potboiler adventure series we produced last year. What was the title? *Spies of the Spaceways?* I found out our boy isn't just boating back and forth from the Studio to the hostel day by day. He ducks out along the way every so often. So far he's managed to lose me each time. Beats me what he's up to, but I'll find out. Don't worry."

"I hope so," Anthony said, sighing. "And find out what the problem is *fast*, will you? I'm tearing my hair out trying to direct him. It doesn't make any sense. He's not the same man in those segments on his résumé, not the same performer at all—not even close. And I'm running out of time to pull the project together. It's less than a week before we have to take off. If I can't drag anything more out of him by then . . ."

"Leave it to me, kid. Just go on the way you have been and

I'll find out what's buggin' the guy. Trust me. Eben's on the job. And you've got too much else to do."

Anthony shook his head. "This far along in the project, even if you discover what's the matter with him, I'll have to sweat blood to tie up all the loose ends before our deadline."

"We'll make it, kid, we'll make it . . ."

Saunder Studio loomed at a dimly lit canal junction ahead. The taxi coasted into the slip and a Studio guard snubbed the mooring line. Anthony checked the time and swore. Late! He and Jesse hurried through front offices, production labs, and edu-vid recording sections. The regular staffers were busy turning out standard releases of the Studio's bread-and-butter packages. The big, new production, however, was still in the gestation process, on Rehearsal Stage One. That unit was at the company plant's heart, circled by on-the-spot costuming, prop, and other support areas. Anthony was pulling out all the stops to back this project and accelerate operations. Materiel and technical assistance wasn't the stumbling block. *That* met Anthony as soon as he entered the cavernous room.

David Lavrik was early, as usual. And no doubt he was letter-perfect in his lines, as usual. The actor was accommodating and unfailingly cooperative—and about as effective as a piece of flotsam, as far as the emota-sensors and potential audience satisfaction went.

"Good morning, David. How are you?" Anthony inquired politely.

"Fine, sir."

The response was as phony as Anthony's had been to Jesse's earlier query, but it seemed wise to take it at face value and hope for the best. Anthony patted the actor's back encouragingly. "Good! Today's going to be a great run-through, David. I'm sure of it." Lavrik put on a confident smile, seconding that opinion enthusiastically. An outsider might have been fooled. Anthony wasn't. He'd faked the same sort of reaction on demand when he'd been acting and had seen it used countless times during his work as a director. The young man's grin and cocky posture meant nothing. There was still something very wrong, an impediment to Lavrik's putting forth the superlative performance his résumé showed he was capable of.

But Anthony had little time to dig out that impediment now; as director-producer of this project, he had dozens of small, essential tasks to tend to. He repeated his cheery "let's go!" phrases to Lavrik, then went to check on his other responsibilities: special effects equipment—techs fine-tuning their gear; music—Terran and Whimed experts adjusting volume sets and nuance enhancers to optimum; environmental control—balanced to a compromise setting for both races; costuming—in good shape, and Margaret Orr was nearly done with the irreplaceable hand-sewn echino-derm cape. Anthony conferred with subordinates on the script, on recording apparatus, and on the gripes and requests of human and felinoid actors and support staffers. The only thing he didn't need a consultation for was the emota-sensor boards; he handled those himself, trusting no one to channel the performers' outputs as well as he could.

Saunder Studio Rehearsal Stage One was a mix of glaring lights and stark shadows. The central area, where Yrae and David would stand, was ablaze with showcase beams and the realistic holo-mode projections of scenery. Around the perimeter, techs and craftspeople hovered over equipment. Standby gear, not being used in this production, was stored against the walls, where it lurked in semidarkness like an inanimate audience.

At first rehearsals had moved very slowly. The kinks in the script had to be ironed out; two species had to learn to work together and adjust their individual attitudes and customs. That was not simple, even though the Whimeds were indeed doing their damnedest to fit into the Terrans' patterns. The e.t.s tried to suppress many of their habits like huddling and their starve-then-binge eating style. It had soon become obvious that this restraint was affecting their efficiency, and Anthony had called a mini-meeting on the set with his combined staff. He appreciated the Whimeds' plan to play by Terran rules, here in the Terran stellar sector—and at the Terran-hosted Interspecies Trade Conference. But if they couldn't help him pull this production together, their attempts to behave as the Terrans did would be wasted. From that point on, there had been more mutual adjusting—and a mutual crash course in learning to operate alongside beings very different from one's own kind.

This morning the various functionaries of the team assembled gradually, getting ready for a run-through. Yrae was center stage, chatting with her dresser, Kyinell. When Anthony approached, the alien actress excused herself and came toward him, nodding. She looked as if she were about to speak, but at that moment

Taisso charged up and exclaimed, "We begin now? *Aaa!* I have new . . . is called business? . . . in final hymn of Janyavee. Discussed Yrae. Okay. Okay?"

Yrae frowned. So did Anthony, saying, "If you want to take over the directing—"

The chubby acting coach burbled apologies. "Oh, no no no no! Is not that. None directing. Anthony Saunder director. Does most *aytan*! This business interpretation hymn-dance. Okay?"

Anthony glanced at the production's star. Yrae's expression was remote, her emotions locked in tightly. "Dancing isn't my forte," Anthony said, shrugging. "And it's Janyavee's hymn, not Dempsey's words. If you want to make changes, that's your department." Taisso seized the human's hand, wringing it. He jabbered effusive thanks. "All right. Let's get moving. We have a lot to accomplish today." Anthony managed to break away, with difficulty.

Terran and Whimed techs assumed their stations and cued their equipment. Taisso climbed into the tall chair he used to oversee Yrae's performance. The Whimed actress and David Lavrik took their places on stage. Anthony settled behind the emota-sensor boards, front and center—his coordination post as both director and as skilled operator of the crucial sensor gear.

Rehearsals, as usual, proceeded in fits and starts. Sometimes lighting or scenery effects didn't look right and everything had to stop and back up until the glitches were corrected. Sometimes the actors bobbled their lines, though there was less and less of that now, this late in the process. There were occasional breaks so the Terrans could fuel up on caffa and snacks, or when the Whimeds were compelled to huddle; by now the humans knew Yrae Usin Hilandro wouldn't join the other felinoids in the huddle, nor did she mingle with humans during the breaks. For that matter, David Lavrik didn't mingle with other humans much, either. The man wasn't standoffish; he simply radiated a morose loneliness that made few stagehands want to strike up a conversation with him.

Now and then a Whimed dropped out of the rehearsals to catnap. As far as Anthony was able to determine, the aliens had set up a schedule for that. Felinoids, being polyphasic, slept in short stretches, and at no predetermined time. For this situation, the Whimed Committee apparently had decided a precise rotation system would serve the production best. No one was allowed to nap unless he or she wasn't needed on the set in that period.

Again, Yrae Usin Hilandro didn't nap at all that Anthony could see. More than her 'cultural treasure' talents set her apart from her race, it appeared.

Coping with alien patterns and alien language was part of the complex process of directing this co-authored script, as was keeping check on the emota-sensors' readouts while assessing the rehearsal's progress. Anthony managed somehow to keep on top of it all. It wasn't easy. Not even close to easy!

Fortunately, they were limiting run-throughs to the play's climax today. Earlier segments had been practiced this past week, and were probably as well-honed as they were going to be. The big finish, however, still needed plenty of work.

Yrae and David Lavrik tried on the lines and actions for size, exploring each other's characters and motivations. As trained actors, they had learned to anticipate a co-star's style and pacing, but not when that co-star was of a different species. In that regard, this production was a discovery process for everyone, particularly for the man in charge of it all—Anthony. Watching the performers deliver their lines and go through the script, he was struck that Yrae's technique at some points was equal to that of Terra's best actresses. At others, her methods were totally alien.

Action. Stop. Check the review tape for flaws. Check all equipment for glitches. Then repeat and repeat again.

The stars were real troupers, willing to duplicate the same expressions, intonations, body language, and feigned emotions again and again. Yrae's responses fed solidly to the emota-sensor boards, pegging the readouts. Anthony wondered if she shouldn't save some of that intensity for the actual opening ceremonies. He feared she'd exhaust her reserves of pretended feelings here on the rehearsal stage. But the woman refused to hold back.

Was David Lavrik *also* giving it his all here? If so, hopes for success at the Whimeds' big presentation at the ITC looked very grim. Anthony studied the man's readouts with dismay. All were the right signals, but oddly warped and damped, ruined by a persistent heavy undercurrent of . . . what? Those sublevels were a mess, conflicting and defying easy analysis. Depression? Yes, that was there. And perhaps fear. Fear of what? Failure? Lavrik had good reason to fear that, at the rate he was going. Where was the brilliant actor-dancer Yrae had selected especially for this plum role? This was Lavrik's chance of a lifetime, and he was blowing it, blowing it not only for himself, but for Anthony, Jesse, the Whimeds, and Saunder Studio.

Lavrik wasn't the only problem on the set. Taisso was a pesky busybody, everywhere and into everything, constantly asking questions when people had no time to give him an answer. Whenever he was called on his actions, the Committeeman burbled with good-natured apologies. He did not mean to interfere. No! He was merely trying to observe these operations, which intrigued him. The Committee hoped to cooperate on other joint projects in the future, and he needed to know how a Terran vid or live production was put together—the proper procedures, the function of all the auxiliary equipment, and the subtle interpretations of commands exchanged by the director and his staff.

The alien's compliments didn't mollify Anthony or anyone else. Why couldn't Yrae's acting coach see that this was neither the time nor the place to take lessons in such things? They were all under the gun, swimming hard upstream against a deadline. Taisso, as nominal boss of the Whimed Committee's entertainment division, ought to be aware of that.

Another run-through of another segment was followed by another pause for adjustments. Hurry up and wait was a slogan that applied as accurately to show business, Anthony had found long ago, as it did to the military. Practice made it possible for him to maintain the calm, even manner essential to keeping rehearsals going. Yelling or venting his impatience was almost guaranteed to hamper the schedule still further. Chewing out actors who'd already made a mistake was likely to wreck their concentration. And they were making progress, moving forward in the script, a paragraph at a time.

Then . . . a flub.

The performers froze in their places. Yrae shot a surprised stare at her co-star, as if she couldn't believe Lavrik had blown his line. He rarely did. *That* hadn't been the problem. Hesitantly Yrae turned to Anthony, seeking the director's judgment on the mistake.

He told her and Lavrik, "We were going fine to that point." Quietly, smiling, Anthony said, "Could we try it again, please? From Script Mark #135."

"I'm sorry, sir," Lavrik said, hangdog. "I'm really sorry. I won't do it again. I'll get it right the next time."

"Good, good! And can you give me a bit more emotional

output for the sensors on the passage beginning 'I wish the others could make planetfall'?" Anthony peered at the sensor boards, checking the readouts just before the goof. Lavrik's channels were an absolute disaster. Counting ten, Anthony forced himself to sound cheery, pep-talking the actors up to a repeat of the previously rehearsed segment.

Taisso butted in. "We go end? See changes dance now? Huh?"

He wanted to get to the alterations mentioned this morning. Anthony grimaced. One damned thing after another! But the Whimeds were paying for the project. If the star's acting coach wanted to uproot the schedule to throw in an unplanned change in the finale, who was the mere director to object?

"Yrae? How do you feel about that? Do you want to do a run-through of Janyavee's hymn and the accompanying art forms?"

She considered, her manner withdrawn and distant. Then she replied with a curt nod. Taisso flapped his hands excitedly.

A new consultation was called for with the crew, priming them for a different slant on this retake. Music techs had to gear up the needed background score and refresh their memories from the script. Anthony touched a lot of bases. That was his job, assuring, reassuring, warning his people not to bitch too loudly about Taisso's meddling and reminding them that the Committee-man understood Terran English, even if he didn't speak it to perfection.

"May we have it quiet, please?" Jesse bellowed.

Kyinell was giving a final pat to Yrae's hair. The dresser took the bulky wrap Yrae wore when not actually rehearsing and retreated to the sidelines with it. Anthony had offered frequently, throughout these past ten days, to boost the stage's ambient temperature for Yrae's comfort. She had declined the offer every time, knowing that what was comfortable for a Whimed would be a heat bath for her Terran co-star.

"David," Anthony said, "this run-through is primarily Yrae's. Don't concern yourself with output. Concentrate on what she's doing and learn the changes Taisso is adding to the finale. Okay. Let's go."

The performers took their positions. Recorders, scenery projectors, and emota-sensor boards glowed, at the ready. The play's characters began their dialogue. They had battled through harrowing dangers on a hostile world. In order to survive, they had joined forces. Their companions, and members of other races, were orbiting above the planet, awaiting the outcome of this chance encounter between species. In Janyavee's original drama, the protagonists had represented warring factions among the Whimed Federation, a slice of the felinoids' past history. In Dempsey's rewrite, Yrae personified all nonhuman civilizations, as David Lavrik would stand for Terra.

Action and dialogue began. At the edge of the stage, Whimed techs' eyes shimmered eerily, reflecting oil-on-water colors, a reminder that half the personnel on this project were e.t.s. Yrae and Lavrik worked toward the finale. The human's emota-sensors readouts seemed a trifle better than they had been, in Anthony's estimation, but still were far below Yrae's projections. Her co-star pointed at a special effects "horizon." A series of planetary scenes seemed to flow from his tracing finger. The techs made images wink on and off smoothly as the actor recited a catalog of civilized humanoid worlds. Ian Dempsey had enlarged upon Janyavee's more limited list of Whimed Federation planets; now the script included representative Settlements inhabited by every race that would be attending the Interspecies Trade Conference. "We are all children of the stars," David Lavrik intoned. "It does not matter where we were born. On Koormayin, Husri, Hung Jui, Thayal, Procyon Five, Chayn . . ."

He didn't attempt to pronounce the final name on the list, that of an Ulisorian world. A Whimed audio crewman plugged in a computerized approximation of the harsh syllables. She'd do so at the Conference as well, since few non-Ulisorians could manage that race's language.

Throughout the drama, Yrae and Lavrik would incorporate various examples of the six species' art forms. Now, as the last section of dialogue concluded, they reprised those passages. In this segment, Lavrik wasn't required to match Yrae's awesome output on the emota-sensors; it was solely his dancing skills that would be needed. According to Anthony's instructions, the young actor stood aside more often than he partnered Yrae, watching her timing and patterns carefully. Anthony hoped Lavrik was soaking in what he was seeing and could reproduce it later, at the opening ceremonies, and at least *try* to match Yrae's extraordinary abilities.

111

The finale began with a polite nod to Terra—a duet of the Charter Settlement Planets' anthem. Yrae led from that into excerpts of Vahnaj, Lannon and Rigotian equivalents. She made only a stab at what the Ulisorians termed "floating prose," required to accept her limitations with that alien stagecraft. Then she launched into her specialty—Whimed ballet/opera. Lavrik became little more than animated scenery. He went through the paces alongside Yrae, observing, while the felinoids' cultural treasure displayed her skills in both dance and song. Her physiology gave her voice a range, color, and timbre a Terran diva would kill to possess. No *Homo sapiens'* throat could create such incredible trills and flourishes. Occasionally Yrae's notes soared above frequencies human beings could hear, for a disturbing subliminal effect.

Whimed music was dissonant and punctuated by strong, erratic rhythms. Over these past days of rehearsals, the Terran stage crew had gotten used to the stuff, and a number of them claimed to like it. Anthony considered that a tribute to Yrae's talent.

She didn't stint on any of the excerpts, not even the Vahnajes'. In earlier parts of the script, Yrae had pushed herself. Now she went full throttle as she began to perform in her own species' art.

Pirouetting, rainbows spiraling about her. The actress wore miniature color wands on her wrists, generating that stunning burst of special effects. It wasn't merely gadgetry; Yrae supercharged the wands' prismatic fountains with biofeedback, as she fed the emota-sensors.

Spinning, again and again. David Lavrik matched her, at least physically, right on his marks. Dancing was his first discipline, and its techniques were obviously well ingrained; he executed the necessary jumps and turns flawlessly.

If only he could do the same with the *rest* of the play!

Yrae reached for the sky. Helical streamers spewed from the color wands. As she completed her last pirouette, she stopped, facing her co-star. The alien actress continued to hold one arm high while the other reached toward Lavrik. They teased the suspense several long moments before they touched.

It symbolized interspecies amity, Terran meeting non-Terran in friendship, peace, and a promise of greater understanding to come. David Lavrik, human, and Yrae Usin Hilandro, alien, were a living tableau of the theme of the Interspecies Trade Conference.

The stage's horizons seemed to leap to infinity. A microcosm of suns and planets spun from Yrae's wands. Music mounted to a sustained, unbearably sweet note. Rainbows of light swam around the actors. It was a sparkling web of starstuff, framing them in all the colors of the universe.

CHAPTER EIGHT

✪✪✪✪✪✪✪✪

Private Rehearsal

The breathless silence lengthened. Techs should have been dim-
ming the lights and lowering a holo-mode curtain around the
actors at this point. A small part of Anthony's mind wanted to
chew out the forgetful crew members responsible for that lapse.
But a much greater part of his being was caught up in the magic
Yrae had created. A special, enthralling tension flowed from her
color wands, and from her alien eyes.

Then a loud popping sound broke the stillness.

Taisso was clacking his tongue. That was a version of wild
applause, among some Whimed social groups.

Yrae stiffened, jerking her hand away from David Lavrik's.
The spell was broken.

Anthony realized he'd been holding his breath and exhaled.
Taisso's applause triggered general approval from all the felinoids
and human stage crew. And the lights dimmed finally, cutting the
glare. As Anthony's eyes adjusted to normal illumination, he
moved on reflex, putting the sensor boards on standby. When he
looked up, he saw that most of his people and all the Whimeds
were gawking incredulously at Yrae Usin Hilandro.

"Lord God, but that was beautiful," Jesse whispered.

Anthony smiled, shaking off the lingering shock of what he'd just seen, and went forward onto the center stage. "Wonderful," he told the actors. "Reached right down into the soul, as some critics phrase it."

Behind him, Jesse and Pilar were trading comments. "It worked, it actually worked. I didn't have a hint what some of those dances and songs were about, but it all came together at the ending," the associate producer crowed.

Pilar's voice was choked with tears. "Who cares about the earlier parts? Those sections weren't written for Terrans and Whimeds. It was . . . just gorgeous. I'll run out of adjectives on the PR."

Praise rang out from all around the stage. "Never saw anything like that, Hilandro." *"Aytan, aytan!"* "Whoo! Wasn't that terrific?" *"Koas ay . . . aaa!"*

"They're correct," Anthony said. Lavrik's face was a frozen mask, as if he were keenly aware he'd failed—again—to project convincing signals to the emota-sensor collectors. The compliments barely penetrated his shield of nonexpression. Plainly he knew that Yrae deserved this tidal wave of praise and that he didn't. Anthony hesitated, not wanting to dent the young man's ego further by requesting "a bit more emotional response on the next run-through."

But there would have to be other run-throughs until Lavrik got it right—or as close to right as was going to be feasible.

Yrae, too, ignored the applause. Unsmiling, she peered past the ring of well-wishers straight at Taisso. The Committeeman continued to pop his tongue noisily, cheering her.

Without warning, Yrae waded into the crowd, thrusting people out of her path. Majlur and Kyinell closed in on Taisso, grabbing his arms and dragging him backwards bodily. He protested, flailing comically. His subordinates were trying to get him out of harm's way, but hadn't moved in time. Yrae bore down on her acting coach, her fingernails slashing the air centimeters from Taisso's nose. Her crest was an auburn crown. In contrast, Taisso's crest turned into a frizzy hat, revealing his alarm.

"Ji! Zahla onrudrur chlee dran! Ji briala kiu!" Onlookers had braced themselves for hysterical shrieks. Instead, Yrae hurled melodic thunder, a tooth-popping alto roar.

Taisso weaved and dodged, hampered by Kyinell and Majlur, who still clutched his arms. Yrae swung viciously, successive roundhouses always missing Taisso's face by a fraction. The Terrans had seen her dance, knew how strong she was, and figured Taisso for bloody ribbons—*if* Yrae decided to connect.

The Committeeman tried to grovel, whimpering, *"Aytan, Hilandro! Aytan! Koas, Irasten Usin, nulow!"*

"Julow!" Yrae corrected, blasting his ears. Anthony spotted that verbal shift; Taisso had said that everything was perfect, but that he *would* do something; Yrae had countered that he *should* have. Past tense. Whatever had set off her anger was already done, and Taisso had to pay the consequences.

Yrae swung again, making contact, though not drawing blood. The chubby acting coach howled as if he'd been stabbed. His scream startled the actress, aborting her attack. She seemed to waken from a nightmare.

On the defensive, she whirled, and those nearest her quickly backpedaled. Yrae's eyes sought Anthony's, and he was peering into a mirror:

Alone!

No one else in the universe could stand in his boots or Yrae's. No one could really understand.

As abruptly as she'd rushed at Taisso, Yrae now ran offstage toward an unoccupied corner of the set.

Humans murmured curiously. Whimed crew members shuffled and mumbled, embarrassed, and pointedly avoided looking at Taisso. Were they sorry for him or afraid to be seen in his company? Majlur growled in the Committeeman's ear, lecturing. Until this incident, the protocol chief had behaved as if Taisso was the man in charge. Now Anthony had reason to doubt that assumption. There was no question that Majlur was laying down the law to the hapless acting coach.

A bit late!

Kyinell had tried to follow Yrae, but the star ordered her assistant away. On impulse, Anthony took up Kyinell's good samaritan idea. Jesse grabbed at his arm and said, "Better let it be. It's the Whimeds' affair."

Pilar added, "Maybe I can help. Yrae knows me, and—"

"No." Anthony's tone was firm. "Kyinell isn't what she needs, and neither are you, Pilar. Stay here. Jesse, crew on standby until we see what's what." A rising mutter stirred as Anthony headed ino the shadowed areas of the stage. He'd had to hand-hold temperamental performers plenty of times since he'd begun operating Saunder Studio. He didn't know what to expect on this occasion, though, and neither did the Terran stage crew. All of them must be trying to see where he was going and what happened when he got there.

Yrae was pacing back and forth in the semidarkness, wearing a two-meter-long rut in the floor between stacks of equipment crates. Anthony was surprised to see the alien woman was dry-eyed. The edu-vids said Whimed females wept for all the same reasons human females did, including angry outrage. Anthony halted a stride away from her, watching. Yrae's pacing slowed; then she paused, looking sharply at him. In the dim light, her eyes were iridescent stars. After a tense moment, she spoke in Terran: "It . . . he was wrong."

Nodding, Anthony edged forward. He touched the actress's shoulder lightly and felt a knot of muscles beneath her pale skin. Moving tentatively, he slid his hand around to the nape of her neck and began massaging. Yrae resisted his ministrations at first. Whimeds generally didn't enjoy touching or being touched by non-Whimeds. But eventually she relaxed a trifle.

"*Ji*." Anthony repeated the epithet she'd hurled at Taisso. "'Fool.' He didn't understand. He applauded you when he should have been paying closer attention. What did he do wrong, Yrae?"

She didn't reply. Her head lolled, her golden hair brushing against his arm, the delicate, intriguing scent she wore tickling his nose. Anthony steadied her as Yrae trembled violently, shaking with tension. She was paying the price for not holding anything back during rehearsals. Terran actors who did that often burned themselves out. Anthony wondered if he should warn Yrae of that danger. But perhaps it wasn't a danger for a Whimed performer. He was in unknown territory here.

With apparent reluctance, she pulled away from his massaging hand, thanking him shyly.

"What was Taisso's error?" he asked. "Tell me."

"It is not possible. A Terran would not comprehend."

"Try me," he insisted. "I'll listen. I'm very good at that. And I can learn. Haven't I learned your language, your customs, Janyavee's script?"

She considered those arguments, then nodded. Anthony perched on one of the nearby crates while she gestured emphatically, imitating the pirouette in the finale's dance-hymn. "*Redur?* The turn? It is to be pah! pah! pah! pah! eh! uh! di-ya—*pah!*"

117

She hammered out the erratic rhythm, pounding her small fist into her upturned palm. *"Sar! Sarige-aytan!"*

"Ethically unsound? Unsatisfactory? That's what you mean? I gather Taisso's alterations weren't an improvement. They threw you off your pace? But I assure you, they came across splendidly. You saw how my technicians reacted."

Yrae shook her head furiously. She didn't care that others had been impressed with her stunning performance. The Whimeds' cultural treasure had judged herself unfavorably. She felt betrayed by her trusted acting coach; Taisso's new "business," despite his promise that such would be *aytan*, had put matters badly out of kilter.

The actress's hand was poised in midair after that demonstration of the dance's proper rhythm. Anthony reached out, and she allowed him to draw her down beside him. "It looked perfect," he said, "but it wasn't as good as you could have done, was it? And Taisso should have seen the difference."

Yrae spat, *"Durin!* Yes. He should see. Taisso is my *aytanio por* . . . my corrector." Not merely a coach, but a source of constructive criticism. She didn't demand a yes-man; she wanted honest correction of flaws, and the chubby Committeeman had done exactly the opposite.

The situation put Anthony in a peculiar spot. He was relieved to find it wasn't David Lavrik's lackluster rehearsal that had set off Yrae's outburst. But Taisso had tangled them in another net. As long as the alien woman was so overwrought, nothing could be done onstage. She was the star, the basic reason for this entire dramatic project. Soothing her and getting her back on track took top priority for the director-producer.

No wonder Yrae had tried to crosshatch the acting coach's face with her fingernails! She hadn't hurt him, though . . . or had she? Human actions and reactions might not apply. Whimeds were like humans in many ways, and very alien in others. For all Anthony knew, Yrae's roaring attack had damaged Taisso psychologically, or perhaps severely dented his status among his people.

Anthony frowned. He had to stop judging Yrae by *Homo sapiens*'s standards. However, that was an easy pattern to slip into. Here, in these shadows, she might be a human actress wearing extreme makeup and a crested wig, plus peculiar contact lenses.

Testingly he put his arm around her. Yrae placed a hand

against his chest, and for a moment he thought she was fending him off. Then he sensed she was probing for his heartbeat. He took her free hand, circling her wrist below the color-wand device, and pressed the pulse point. Whimeds' cardiovascular systems weren't the same as Terrans'; Yrae's pulse normally would be very faint. Now it was pounding like a shuttle engine on overload from stress, the rehearsal, and the blowup at Taisso. She compared her heart rate to Anthony's and looked puzzled. Was she trying to figure out why he wasn't as upset as she was?

At stage center and its periphery, Pilar, Jesse, David Lavrik, and Terran and Whimed support crews chatted, tended to equipment, and marked time, loyal people, reliable and helpful. Yet they couldn't help Yrae in her personal search for perfection. She was utterly alone in that.

"They can't stand in your boots," Anthony said softly. Yrae repeated the words and he transferred his grip from her wrist to enfold her small hand. "No one can stand in mine, either. We're alike in that."

He wished there were more light in this storage area. Yrae's felinoid vision enabled her to see quite well in shadows, but he was handicapped by Terran rods and cones. Even if he could see her face clearly, would that do him any good? How did he gauge her expression, her feelings? With a Terran actress, Anthony would have been more sure, working from past experience. Gambling that Yrae's responses weren't *that* much different from a Terran performer's, he said, "It's damned hard work, what you do. The others don't know what you go through out there. I can guess, because of the sensors. And I was an actor myself, years ago."

Cheap trick? Not if it gained her confidence.

"*Ehi*," Yrae murmured. "There is a Terran word—soul. This is my art. A sick-happiness. A fear-want." He was taken aback by the evocative descriptions. She'd been soaring to the heights, while her guts were in turmoil from elation and near exhaustion combined.

Her hand crept from his chest to the base of Anthony's throat. Yrae detected the pulse there and said, "Heart. Head. You share." Then, shivering, she added a sudden non sequitur, "I have never performed for aliens."

Or *was* it a non sequitur?

"Never? I assumed . . . Most Terran acting troupes I'm familiar

119

with regularly perform for audiences that include some nonhumans. They come to take it as a matter of course. I'm sure Lavrik's had some background in that area . . ." Anthony broke off, the significance of Yrae's wistful comment sinking in. He went on with annoyance, "Who dreamed up the plan of your co-starring in this play? Some Whimed diplomat?" Yrae looked oddly apprehensive as she nodded. His anger grew. "They forced you to jump into this just so they can pull a triumph at the ITC. But if you haven't had any previous acting experience for alien audiences, they should have given you lots more time to prepare. This is a dirty deal!"

Yrae said slowly, "You are not pleased because my skills are flawed?"

He hastened to reassure her. "Hey, you're magnificent! No flaws at all, except from the viewpoint of a perfectionist like yourself. It's—you should have told me that this was your first time working with Terrans. Maybe I could do more to help you."

"I am Hilandro." Yrae had used that phrase often during these rehearsals. It reminded him of a line from Old Earth melodramas: "The Queen commands!" It certainly had that effect. Yrae's catchphrase was a trigger mechanism for the Whimed Committee and all its support people. When she said that, they cringed or jumped to obey, depending on the circumstances. But now she spoke the words with a tone of resignation, as if summing up a curse she had to bear.

She stared thoughtfully at him, visually probing. Did she resent the fact that he didn't jump and kowtow to her at those magic words? Yrae answered that unspoken question with a smile, saying, "Aaa! You are Terran. You do not know Hilandro."

"I know you, though not as well as I'd like to."

Her fingers explored his throat sensuously. "It is so? You wish to know me in more detail?" That starburst gaze glimmered, examining him as he was examining her, as best he could, given the dim light. Eyes, face, body—not human. She was a woman born on a planet many light-years from Earth and the Settlements. He must seem as alien to her as she to him. He viewed his species through her senses, imagining her contradictory emotions and uncertainty—and fascination. Despite the gulf between them, their species had traveled along many of the same evolutionary paths. And on those paths, both races had developed basic drives, canceling out an assortment of other barriers. Anthony forgot his resolve not to jump to conclusions. He couldn't be that wrong about her caresses, about the look she was giving him.

Some humans claimed they found an exotic thrill in intimacy with Vahnajes, but lutrinoid females were repellent to Anthony. Whimed females were another matter, particularly this Whimed female. She wasn't of his own species, was too short, too hippy, too broad-shouldered, and had weird eyes and a boy's chest— and kilotons of sexual chemistry, which was attracting him strongly despite all the factors against such a thing.

"I . . . I am awkward in your art forms," she said. Startled, he denied that. Yrae brushed aside his compliments, murmuring coyly, "No, no, I am awkward. This is embarrassing. I do not wish to perform badly. Perhaps this is the cause of the difficulty you feel David suffers in these rehearsals—my awkwardness." She glanced pointedly toward the Committee people and Anthony's stage crew, gathered under the lights. "I cannot rehearse correctly here."

Ever since he had debuted with Li Lao Chang's company, Anthony had been an expert in reading body language—certain types especially. Even if a come-on was veiled in euphemisms and romantic terminology, he rarely missed an invitation. Yrae Usin Hilandro was sending him one now, loudly and very clearly.

"Rehearsal." He pretended to mull the problem. "What you need is a private rehearsal, without distractions. Of course it's important that you feel comfortable with our art forms. I'll be glad to instruct you, if you'd like."

She sat up very straight. "Private. Yes. That is the word. This is possible?"

Duty nagged at him. There were business pressures, the delegation, and his problems with David Lavrik and finishing this bi-species project on time. Then Anthony acknowledged that his *main* responsibility was to the star of that project—a project that promised to bring new trade to his world and thus aid his delegation. "It is possible. I will need to make arrangements with Jesse and my other people first."

"You will do so? I must not shame the Federation or insult your race at the Conference. There is much I must correct. You will teach me?" Yrae pleaded. Her sidelong gaze underlined what Anthony had already guessed. Similarities in their evolution, indeed! She hadn't picked up that coy technique performing classic Whimed dramas!

Cold rationality intruded. She was alien, unknown. He was entering a void in pursuit of erotic pleasure. What if the temptation backfired? He was still woefully ignorant about a lot of things concerning Whimeds. This situation was damned tricky.

Temptation—and curiosity—won.

"*Irasten*, I would be delighted to serve as your teacher." The fingernails that had threatened Taisso flicked delicately at Anthony's lips and throat, touching off sensuous shock waves. Yrae didn't have much to learn about human erogenous zones, or else such zones were the same for felinoids. With difficulty, he put his hormones on hold.

The support crews, including Jesse, were only pretending not to notice the mini-conference in the shadows. When Anthony beckoned his friend, Jesse hurried toward him at once. Pilar tagged a few steps behind the associate producer. A knowing grin spread over Jesse's homely mug when he saw the director and his star sitting cozily side by side. "I take it the hurricane's over?"

"Long gone," Anthony assured him. "Listen, can you set up the following cleanup slate?" He spelled out all the necessary details of finishing the day's work. Jesse nodded, frowning, and guilt stabbed the younger man. "Sorry to dump all this on you, but it's quitting time."

"No!" Jesse turned to Pilar in mock amazement. "There! No one will tell me that these kids aren't fast on the uptake." He squinted at Anthony and teased, "You're pretty sharp for a greenie. Yes, indeed, as you have observed, it's quitting time. Lord God! It's like pulling teeth to get a straight answer out of you when you're in one of these moods. What's going on, anyway?"

"We're going to the house for a private rehearsal."

Taken aback, Jesse muttered, "That's time and a half. I don't know if I can corral any techs for—"

"None of the crew. Just us. *Strictly* private."

Pilar leaned toward Jesse and said in a stage whisper, "Are you thinking what I'm thinking?"

"Lady, you couldn't repeat what *I'm* thinking, not in polite society," he replied.

Anthony was on his feet, offering his arm to Yrae. She knew that Terran custom very well by now and fell into step beside him. Pilar darted in front of them, blocking their way. They stared at the entrepreneur in surprise. Pilar stammered, "I—I don't want to play wet blanket, but is—is this according to protocol? Yrae? Shouldn't you... well, check with some of your people before you just... leave?" The alien woman was nonplussed. Obviously she didn't have the slightest idea what Pilar was hinting at.

"Where *is* the Whimed Committee?" Anthony asked.

Pilar sighed. "They commandeered one of your Studio offices for a powwow. I think Taisso's getting a talking-to. Or maybe he's telling the others what tomorrow's schedule will be."

"Majlur talks. Taisso listens," Yrae said scornfully. The instant the words were out of her mouth, she looked alarmed. Several lesser Whimed techs standing nearby nudged one another, as if the Hilandro had inadvertently let a cat out of the bag.

What cat? What bag? That it was Majlur, not busybody Taisso, calling the shots? That wasn't too much of a revelation. In many human corporations, the person talking the loudest and giving the orders wasn't necessarily the one with the final okay or veto. Maybe Majlur was some sort of power behind Taisso's paper title. So what?

Yrae drew herself up stiffly. "I am not required to inform any being concerning my arrival and departure. I am Hilandro." End of discussion.

Except that it *didn't* end it. Pilar refused to give way. "Do you know what you're doing? Are you sure this is what you want?"

Suddenly Anthony grasped what was bothering the Earth woman. She was certainly no prude when it came to sexuality. Alien sexuality or Terran sexuality—but *separately*, not combined. He doubted she would have made such a fuss if Anthony had been walking off arm in arm with a human actress. Earth, however, still harbored pockets of xenophobia and lingering prejudice against cross-species "miscegenation." To Pilar, the implications in this setup must smack of unnaturalness. Occasionally the same biases cropped up here in the Settlements. But generally pioneers were much more casual about interracial sexual experimenting. Pilar Gutierrez was reacting like a citizen of Earth, well-bred, sophisticated, and adaptable, but tied to the Mother world's attitudes, nevertheless.

Yielding to their determined pressure, the entrepreneur abandoned her objections. Her expression, though, was distraught.

"What about rehearsals tomorrow?" Jesse wanted to know.

"We'll be there," Anthony promised. He hesitated, then added, "About what we—"

"I'll take care of it. Trust me."

Jesse avoided glancing toward David Lavrik. Anthony risked doing so. Others on the stage were shamming indifference to the scene on the set's storage area. It was plain, though, that responses ranged from guarded wonder through prurient fascination to outright shock—except for Lavrik. The brilliant young actor-dancer stood alone, oblivious to the whispering and jokes buzzing around him. The performer's features were drawn, almost haggard, and his eyes were tortured. Because of his director's and co-star's disappointment in his work? Because of his own shame at his failure? Lavrik's face suggested a deeper despair—that of a man confronting not merely defeat but utter catastrophe.

The associate producer hadn't missed that fact. Without being too blatant, he threw Anthony a thumbs-up, tacitly vowing to get to the bottom of whatever was troubling the production's male lead.

Knowing that Jesse was on that job eased Anthony's mind and conscience considerably. He waved good night to employees and escorted Yrae out.

They walked past doors lit with RECORDING and DO NOT ENTER signs, and Yrae wondered aloud about Studio operations. She still didn't understand Terran time schedules and had to be told that many Studio divisions worked split shifts, since day and night had little meaning in this subsurface Settlement. The fact seemed to intrigue her. The differences between her own poly-phasic species and *Homo sapiens*'s sleep-and-wake patterns were no longer abstracts, now that she'd spent days working alongside aliens. She was absorbing other details with flattering attention as well, asking Anthony numerous questions, always wanting to know more about him and his kind.

Outside the Studio, Anthony hailed a taxi boat and a company guard steadied the lines as his boss jumped down onto the deck. Yrae teetered uncertainly on the edge of the pier. Balancing expertly, Anthony held up his arms, and she tumbled into them. He caught her without effort, holding her close for a moment. Then they settled into the passenger seats and the driver cleared the lines and sped off.

The actress was rigid. Anthony spoke softly to her, and she

managed a weak smile and a nod. She reminded him of an immigrant arriving in new, unknown territory. No one with any brains rushed into such a situation. But if you lived on the frontier, you didn't run away from challenges, either. Yrae wasn't whimpering in fear, but she was certainly edgy. Anthony remembered her earlier comments about Procyon Five's watery environment: "The oceans of my brithplace world are very different from this one." It was always a wrench to adjust, and Yrae Usin Hilandro was having to cope with a great many things in a big hurry: never having performed for non-Whimeds before; rushing into this production full tilt; and dealing with a strange, alien water world. He didn't blame her for being jumpy during a boat ride. His own personal bugbear was heights; when his work took him to planets with mountainous terrain, that had been rough going. Anthony had adjusted, as Yrae was doing—wary, but game. He instructed the driver to take it slow, and he'd pay for the extra time that took.

A memory filled his thoughts—a guest at Saunderhome driving a speedboat in the lagoon near the island complex. The man had the throttle wide open. His woman passenger was shrieking in terror as the vessel careened wildly. The driver was enjoying her panic, getting a cheap sexual thrill from her fear.

Anthony had never been part of the boat stunter's social circle —had never wanted to be. At a very early age, he'd become disdainful of Earth's idle rich, those people who flocked around Carissa and Stuart Saunder. Because of that, Anthony had bypassed completely the usual adolescent "show off and scare the girls" phase. And when he'd reached Terra's frontier, he'd fitted right into the social patterns there. Women in the Settlements weren't timid. Any man who tried to manipulate *them* was stupid; dangerous tricks were likely to get a boot in the crotch, not a tumble in bed.

Early impressions and painful lessons had molded Anthony into a person tailor-made for Li Lao Chang's quickie vids. Patrick Saunder's clone had no real childhood, and for a while, acting gave him a chance to *be* a child. It had been a temporary niche, and he'd moved on as soon as he could to directing, not acting. Looking back, he didn't regret having skipped pubescent hijinks, if that speedboat stunter had been an example of the breed.

Seeing Yrae's tense, brave posture, Anthony tried to divert her by pointing out landmarks and engineering marvels on their route. Gradually she perked up. Apparently Governor Yamashita hadn't shown her Committee these particular local scenes during their earlier tour.

Once, at a canal junction, the taxi boat passed a water bus carrying several Vahnajes in the opposite direction. Yrae, who had been responding interestedly to Anthony's running descriptions, went rigid again, glaring daggers at the lutrinoids. Her starburst pupils were enormous, her crest prickling. The hostile signs didn't ease until the Vahnajes were out of her sight.

The incident had taken only seconds, but it slammed Anthony into an inescapable truth—alien mercantile rivalries were moving deep into the Charter Settlement Planets, touching even his world. By agreeing to handle the Whimed Committee's dramatic presentation, he'd put himself on the side of the felinoids. Which meant Saunder Studio could probably whistle for any trade opportunities in the Vahnaj Alliance, from now on—not that he was much worried on that score. He hadn't anticipated any such openings.

When they arrived at Anthony's dock, Yrae didn't hesitate as long as she had earlier in allowing him to help her out of the boat. And she saved him puzzling over interspecies etiquette rules by taking the lead up the stairs after he'd opened the door with his palm impression.

In the foyer, he pondered his next move, stowing their wraps while Yrae peered around. Was she comparing the residence to the way it had looked the last time she was here? Anthony became conscious of clutter. He'd been home now long enough to give the place a lived-in feel. Neither he nor Jesse had time to do much, and Jesse, in fact, had rarely been in the dwelling recently. Yrae didn't remark on discarded food trays and scattered clothing, but Anthony made a hasty effort to pick up a bit, just the same. When he finished, Yrae was gazing at the window wall.

Rain beat against the triple pane. That steady drizzle filtered the twilight glow dancing on the waves. "If the view disturbs you, I can shut it out," Anthony offered. "The window is polarized...uh, can be made opaque," he added, thinking that the word *polarized* might not be on a Whimed-Terran Dictionary edu-vid.

Yrae blinked, rousing. Had she been indulging in a felinoid

version of wool-gathering? "No, I wish to see your world as it is. Do you have a copy of the play?"

Had he misjudged her intentions? Mutely he gestured to the refreshment island's monitor. Yrae went there and advanced the script tape forward to its finale. Very intent, she watched the diagramed dance sequence, studying it. As she did, Anthony studied her. Frowns, scowls, and mutterings indicated she was comparing her performance unfavorably with what Janyavee and Dempsey had written.

"*Aaa!*" she cried, pointing, and slowed the vid to a crawl. "Taisso's changes. Incorrect. This is the way the hymn must be danced."

Anthony eyed the screen, nodding. "Mm. Your acting coach wanted to . . . what? Fancy up the segment? A special variation for the Conference presentation? Maybe Taisso was afraid your classic rendition might be too odd for alien tastes. Was he aiming for a . . . a more universal interpretation?"

"Incorrect! It must not be changed!" Yrae beat time while the stick figure on the computerized demo pirouetted. She made minute adjustments in tempo, as she had in the storage area of the rehearsal stage. From Anthony's viewpoint, the alterations Taisso had put in were insignificant. But they mattered tremendously to Yrae, and she wanted the new, unimproved version junked.

Why hadn't she overruled the Committeeman when Taisso had suggested the changes this morning? Her anger with his ham-handed tampering with the Whimed classic had triggered Yrae's emotional explosion, to Taisso's grief. Hadn't the chubby acting coach seen that coming? Maybe not. Anthony knew so little about the nuances of felinoid personalities and habits. Taisso had missed the signals, whatever the reasons. And for whatever other reasons, Yrae had chosen to bottle up her feelings until things reached flash point.

She shook her head, her golden hair tossing from side to side. "Taisso promised would be same. Is not! True form is . . . broken." Yrae threw up her hands, irritated that she couldn't find the precise Terran translation she wanted.

"He threw your timing off," Anthony supplied. "You've always danced that pirouette exactly the same, haven't you? Your Whimed audiences expect it, and so do you."

"It is so! That is why my turns were poor!"

127

"Only in your eyes," he said. "But if *you* think that's spoiling the play, let's put it back the way it's supposed to be."

Resolve radiated from her. "Yes. We will do it correctly." Doubt rippled across Yrae's piquant face. "If—if what was is not destroyed."

Her apprehension seemed genuine. Was she so unsure of herself? That didn't jibe with her talents and top-ranker status. Or it wouldn't if she were a human actress.

"Why don't we run through it, doing it the way you want it done?" Anthony suggested.

Her living-pearl skin glowed with her excitement. "*Aaa!* You do understand." Yrae touched her heart and throat. "You understand here and here. Yes. I must learn if I am able to create the turns properly."

"Of course you can."

She immediately began a series of dancer's warm-up exercises. Amused, Anthony busied himself shifting the room's few pieces of furniture against its walls and setting up the script tape's music. He also checked the house's environmental control station and boosted the temperature setting; Yrae was shivering, despite her vigorous bending and stretching routine. Finally he dimmed the lights.

"We will create Janyavee's hymn," she announced, concluding her exercises. But she didn't signal him to start the tape. Instead, she rummaged in her jeweled purse and took out a garishly decorated cap. Carefully, moving with seeming reverence, Yrae placed the headgear around her crest. The effect was startlingly barbaric.

"What's that?" Anthony asked.

Yrae was reluctant to answer. "It . . . is *oryuz*. To be costume at presentation. Very *koas rige* . . . precious."

"An audience-grabber, like the cape David will wear?"

Brightening, relieved at that explanation, she nodded, then gestured. "Begin music."

The Whimed anthem filled the seaside home. Previously Anthony had staged "private rehearsals" here with some of his Studio's leading ladies, with predictable results. His anticipation tonight, though, was skewed, and not merely because of the alien music. The golden-haired, starry-eyed woman was singing and dancing in a manner no Terran female could imitate. He was strongly drawn to her and yet was instinctively on guard. Hormonal reactions warred with genetic chauvinism. A settlers' "child of the stars" philosophy couldn't fully overcome the huge gap between species so easily.

Had he been contemptuous of Pilar Gutierrez's attitudes on this situation? Remnants of that same bias seemed to lurk within him, as well.

Yrae spun across the floor, her hair floating like a banner. Her androgynous body was a petite balance to her absent co-star's height and muscular frame. She and David Lavrik would be female and male, fair and dark, fragile and robust. Yrae still wore her color wands. As the music entered its climactic phase, she activated them. Rainbows from unseen prisms engulfed her and Anthony. She danced around him, swathing him in colored light.

There was no stage lighting, no special effects—just the two of them and that mesmerizing spiral of colors.

The outside world was retreating. Anthony was being wrapped tighter and tighter in Yrae's spell.

Rhythms quickened, the sound building to a crescendo.

He realized Yrae was correct; Taisso *shouldn't* have tampered with the finale. The original form was noticeably stronger, much more powerful. The changes had been crucially wrong, so subtle most observers would not have been aware of them. But Yrae had, and now she made them apparent to Anthony.

In restoring what had been taken from her, she was regaining something infinitely desirable. Joy suffused her face. Her pleasure was infectious. Anthony was increasingly caught up in the alien composition. After repeated rehearsals, the music was familiar, and he anticipated its shifts and pauses as he would those in a favorite Terran selection.

The hymn reached a primitive section of his brain, stirring him disturbingly. His pulse accelerated with the beat. The sensation was that of being on the edge of vertigo, yet never quite going over that precipice.

Suddenly he had moved into David Lavrik's place, stepping through the finale's last bars with Yrae, partnering her. They embraced briefly again and again in the patterns of the hymn. Every contact erased Anthony's reservations.

Yrae was beginning her pirouette sequence. Anthony hurried toward an invisible intersection mark. He was transformed, no longer a dispassionate observer, the director, sitting on the sidelines. He felt driven. He *must* arrive at the appointed spot precisely at the right moment to meet Yrae.

She was turning, turning, hesitating for a number of irregular counts, then turning, turning, turning again!

Breathing hard, she halted a meter away, facing him. She was a living statue, exquisitely beautiful. One hand was held high, activating the color wands. Streamers poured from the device, cascading over them both—artificial starlight shattering, falling soundlessly while rain lashed the window. The hymn's last sweet note hung sustained, holding them in the moment.

A curtain of prismed colors shone in the depths of Yrae's eyes. Her hand reached out to Anthony. Faithful to the playwrights' directions, she teased the dramatic tension, delaying that ultimate touch as long as the music lasted.

Slowly her expression altered. And the direction the rehearsal had taken altered as well. This time Anthony knew he wasn't mistaken. Yrae's quest for artistic perfection had been met. Now another motive was taking over.

The play's closing handclasp of interspecies friendship and peace became a kiss, then a fierce embrace.

Anthony and Yrae slowly knelt in unison as the tape ended.

He was two persons. One was a cynical, detached onlooker, noting inconsequential details, such as that the black sand carpeting was a great deal more comfortable than the real thing. Unlike sand, a carpeted floor didn't feel gritty under the weight of bodies. And the onlooker persona decided, too, that modern clothes were convenient; they peeled away effortlessly, not impeding physical drives. The rest of his being was absorbed by those drives.

Sexual urgency mingled with childlike curiosity. He and Yrae tantalized themselves, holding back the moment of total intimacy, exploring each other's faces and bodies. Tactile enchantments, delighting.

He was swept along on the hormonal and sensual tsunami. Soft nonhuman hair and velvety, pearlescent skin were beneath his hands. Dim light added to erotic intensity. Shadows concealed Yrae's more unearthly features, turning her into an elfin creature who had escaped from a fantasy into his arms.

What was she seeing and feeling? Her superior night vision and her graceful, examining hand must tell her far more about him than he was learning of her. Did she like what she was discovering? Did her hunger match his?

In those dream dramas he had starred in, the culmination of this scene was a foregone conclusion, the only purpose, in fact, of the vid productions. There were numerous ways to prolong the suspense, and he knew them all. The ending, though, never varied that much. Anthony had participated in the act in front of the lenses—and in private—countless times. Experience had taught him a great deal about women's tastes, and he considered himself an expert in playing upon those preferences.

Human women's preferences, and *human* women's bodies.

Anatomy and evolution did make a difference, an incalculable difference. His expertise was limited to the females of one species. All his porn vid experience, his comparative lack of xeno-phobia, and his study of edu-vids about Whimeds couldn't eliminate the barriers.

He still had a hell of a lot to learn.

And so did Yrae.

Despite the spacer pilots' brags and edu-vids' graphic biology lessons, Terran and Whimed sexual organs weren't designed for simple matchups. Nothing was where either would-be lover expected it to be. Certain touches that should have brought ecstasy were repellent or actually painful.

And the more they struggled to achieve a position both thought they wanted, the worse things got.

Anthony went through a gamut of startled reactions. Stunned surprise: *"I hadn't realized Whimed females' hip joints locked that snugly against their pubic regions!"* Frustration: *"Dammit, it's like trying to penetrate a duralloy needle at an extreme angle!"* Bewildered panic: *"My God, I don't think I can pull this off. What's happening to me?"*

That cool, detached observer within his mind shriveled and vanished, leaving him reeling, trying frantically to figure a way out of this mess. His body's urgings interfered with all his attempts to think logically.

There had been times, though damned few, during his amorous romps, when he'd been derailed by impotence. Anthony was intelligent enough to know such a situation wasn't a disaster. And his partners of the moment had generally been sympathetic. This was a *very* different situation. He'd never run into anything at all like this before.

He and Yrae were alien to each other. How could he have overlooked that basic reality?

But they had so much in common: their profession; their striving for excellence; and their desire.

Why was it all coming apart?

Yrae was equally frustrated. She writhed futilely, trying to make their genitals cooperate. Her violent efforts brought her atop Anthony, and he peered up at her. Yrae's crest was spiky, proclaiming her arousal. That strange cap, the *oryuz*, made her topknot resemble a tiara. Four small nipples on the sides of her chest were erect. Her eyes were oil-on-water pools.

This wasn't the first time Anthony had coupled with a woman wearing such exotic features. He'd acted out this scene in dozens of Li's dream dramas. The women in those vids, however, had been human, transformed by clever makeup tricks. Yrae's alienness owed nothing to makeup or a playwright.

Alien, yet she was what he wanted, and wanted desperately—a beautiful, intriguing fantasy image, materialized into flesh.

His hormones were willing to cross that species barrier. His flesh couldn't, not without a lot of experimentation and practice.

Suddenly Yrae froze. There had been no orgasmic release for her; she had simply given up a hopeless struggle. Her face twisted with astonishment, and she clawed the air, crying, *"Ji, Ji, Iala ur ja-ji!"*

Fool. Stupid. Failure.

Angry resentment made Anthony see red for a split second. He was thrown back to a dark age of human sexuality. And his ego was wrapped up in that sexuality. He was male, and the entire success or failure of coitus rested in his strong body. This female had assaulted his pride, calling him a stupid failure! He'd encountered a few women like that and regarded them with contempt. They and their male counterparts were irrational throwbacks to a sexually bigoted era of the old Earth's history.

Then his fury began to fade as he mentally replayed Yrae's cries, hearing modifiers. She hadn't blamed him. She had called herself a fool, cursing herself for falling into this fiasco.

The actress sucked in her breath. Wary of Yrae's mercurial mood changes, Anthony braced himself. What next? Would she lash out blindly, venting her rage on him? Even if she didn't hold him at fault for her frustration, she might be mad enough to hit anything handy—and he was definitely handy.

He was also mad enough to hit back.

Instead of clawing or slapping, Yrae began to giggle.

Again, for a fraction of a second, he bristled, his ego offended.

And then, once more, he listened. Her giggling, like her cursing, was inwardly directed. Yrae muttered, chewing herself out, her words broken by hiccups of hysterical amusement. The sound was thoroughly alien, but it was also an invitation to join her reaction to this sexual impasse.

Hesitantly at first, then more and more freely, Anthony chuckled.

It was all so absurd!

They had been swept away by passion, forgetting the obvious. Only among their own kind were they sexually experienced adults. When they stepped across the species barrier, everything had changed. They'd become rank amateurs. Of *course* they couldn't get anywhere! Not on a first attempt. They'd been as clumsy as the adolescents of any humanoid species groping through an initial exploration of the opposite sex. And like so many adolescents, they'd found that the operation wasn't nearly as easy and painless as others had told them it was.

So much for the spacer pilots' brags about interspecies sex!

The awful tension unwound. Yrae's crest softened. She drew off the garish cap and tossed it aside. They were both growing limp, in more ways than one. The actress sank into Anthony's arms and slid off his chest, curling up at his side. Nature had played a ribald trick on them. There was nothing they could do but laugh at their own folly and accept it for the dirty joke it was. Male and female, human and felinoid, they embraced, letting amusement wipe away chagrin and disappointment.

CHAPTER NINE

✪✪✪✪✪✪✪✪

Questions...and Answers?

They snuggled on the black-sand carpet, recovering their energies. Anthony stared up at the darkened ceiling and saw a lace-
work of stars strewn across its surface. His chuckles made Yrae's
hand, resting on his bare rib cage, move up and down with his
intakes of breath. She mumbled a question and he replied,
"Those color wands you're wearing—they're still working.
You're throwing an entire universe up there above us. I almost
forgot where we were. It seemed as if we were on another planet,
looking at an open sky."

Saunderhome.

He sobered, growing silent. Anthony was light-years away
and decades in the past on Earth, late evening of a soft, Caribbean night. He and a servant's boy-crazy daughter had sneaked to
a secluded garden on the island estate. Thousands of stars had
studded the heavens above their trysting place. For a while he
had forgotten he was a clone, a nothing, an unwanted object
trapped in paradise. And then he found out that the girl was
motivated primarily by prurient curiosity; she had wanted to see
if clones were made the same as "real" boys. They had parted
with mutual loathing for each other.

134

At least this far less successful romp had ended much more pleasantly than that.

A faint noise scattered his gloomy memories. Yrae was singing softly in a Whimed dialect Anthony couldn't translate. Her eyes were partly opened, unfocused. He watched her thoughtfully. Was this another form of trance?

She sat up, moving with lithe grace. Yrae tilted her head far back and held her arms over her head, tracing intricate patterns on the ceiling with her color wands. The muted singsong was an ominous whispering. She poured all of her concentration into the eerie chant. Anthony shuddered involuntarily.

With a sigh, Yrae ceased singing, though her lips continued to mouth a repetition of the alien words. She stared raptly at the weaving light patterns. Finally she closed her hands into fists, shutting off the color devices. Nodding, she laid down again beside Anthony and smiled.

He pillowed his head on one arm, saying, "If you don't mind my asking, what was that all about?"

"It is not permitted. I may not explain. It is the—the returning. A nonfruitfulness. It is Whimed."

She was right. She had *not* explained.

"You are sad?" Yrae demanded. Seeing his puzzlement, she went on, "We were . . . precipitate. If you wish, we will examine other methods. There will be contentment."

He coughed nervously, his ego shaken again. Was she hinting that she wanted another go-around right now? Edu-vids didn't mention that Whimed males were such sexual athletes. He tried to read her shadowed face and the tone of her voice. "Perhaps. I—I don't think we should rush into things the *next* time," he murmured.

"No. We require . . . more analysis? Is that the word?" Yrae was amused by her choice of terms. Her peculiar, nonhuman laughter bubbled, raising hair on Anthony's nape. He had an atavistic glimpse into humanity's past, imagining himself in thick undergrowth hunting, or *being* hunted. And somewhere nearby —too near!—an unseen predator lurked, chuckling. But the predator wasn't chuckling at him, rather at the irony of fate.

"Analysis is called for, definitely," Anthony said, increasingly off balance.

He became aware of an odd vibration. A tremor pulsed along his arm where his hand touched Yrae. Another item from the

135

meet-your-alien vids popped into his mind: Under certain conditions, felinoids produced a muffled vibration to signify pleasure. A kind of purring. Could a trait so far down a species' family tree be retained to humanoid levels? Why not? Scratch *Homo sapiens* and find a primate, or even a primitive insectivore. A human being enjoying a gourmet meal and smacking his lips probably didn't look much different—to nonhuman eyes—from a tree shrew devouring a bug. For Whimeds, one such evolutionary holdover was this purring.

If Yrae was this happy after a failed romp, how loud would she purr if they reached orgasm? Anthony wanted to find out. He *did* have his pride. He wasn't going to let a problem like anatomy throw him off stride. Analysis. Yes! And a rematch!

If possible, between human and alien.

Yrae's purring underlined the difference, as did her eyes, her strange skin color, her crest, her multiple tiny breasts, and her voice.

Yrae Usin Hilandro wasn't constructed like a human woman in even the most basic areas.

And yet . . .

She examined his chest hair, innocently fascinated. Her wonderment was light-years—literally and figuratively—from that long-ago servant girl's cruelty. Yrae's interest was similar to that of Anthony's Oriental bed partners, who also had been fascinated by a Caucasian male's hairiness. Differences didn't necessarily mean a turnoff. He indulged his own curiosity, stroking Yrae's exquisitely soft hair and skin. Neither felt at all human. Were those barriers, after all, too great for them to overcome?

Yrae leaned back, peering at him. He reminded himself again that a felinoid could see perfectly well in dim light. What did she see, and what did she think of it?

"You are not angry?"

Anthony raised an eyebrow. "No. Why should I be?"

She gestured toward their genitals. "Our lack of achievement. Some of my *muruen-che* would be most displeased in this situation. Of course, more mature . . . is that the word? . . . *muruen-che* are not easily discouraged. I did not know how a human would behave."

Her earlier laughter seemed to ring in his head. Maybe his few seconds of outraged dignity hadn't been so unusual for an *immature* Whimed male. Grinning, he said, "I admit some Terran men

136

would be furious. As for me, well, I was upset for a while. But I figured out the same thing you did—that we got in too big a hurry." He paused, then went on, "What was that word you used? *Mur*—"

"*Muruen-che*. It is a chosen releaser of tension. I suppose it is not a common phrase in the translations. Our linguists do not believe there is an equivalent in Terran English. A *muruen-che* is a privilege of Hilandro."

Anthony frowned. "A *muruen-che* is a paid sexual playmate?"

He could almost hear wheels turning in her brain as she sorted out his question. Her slim body stiffened and she said waspishly, "There is no payment. A *muruen-che* is a chosen one." With hauteur, she added, "There are many . . . candidates. Those most eager to become my companion. Taisso does not permit the . . . frivolous self-seeking."

"Mm. I get the picture, I think. I've never lacked releasers of tension myself, but I usually do my own screening. So. Taisso's in charge of weeding out the second-raters, huh? Efficient." Anthony didn't comment that in some human cultures Taisso would be an object of scorn because of that function, as would anyone serving the same function for Anthony Saunder. Perhaps the Whimeds didn't see the job in the same light Terrans did—not when applied to a Hilandro. It sounded like a status thing, an expected perk for people of Yrae's rank. He envisioned a parade of handsome, muscular, and very willing Whimed males standing inspection, each hoping he'd be selected as the legendary Yrae Usin Hilandro's current *muruen-che*. Apparently the position was only temporary, though much sought after. Anthony considered his own life-style; many of his affairs were spin-offs from business relationships. None lasted long, by mutual agreement, with no hard feelings afterward. Perhaps the Whimeds were a trifle more formal in arranging for their cultural treasure's romps. So what?

"Why didn't Taisso select a *muruen-che* to accompany you into the Terran sector?" Anthony wanted to know. The question made Yrae squirm. Had he touched on another of the Committeeman's lapses? Taisso must have really goofed. Lucky for him Yrae had merely threatened him when her temper snapped on-stage, earlier. Even the human members of the combined theatrical team had noticed that the Whimed star was a bundle of nerves. Why hadn't her acting coach? Taisso should have seen those signs of stress and taken steps to correct them. Lucky, again, for Taisso that Anthony Saunder was on hand to pick up the pieces and move in as a replacement *muruen-che*.

Or *was* it lucky? Suspicions stirred.

For all of Taisso's faults, was the Committeeman really as dense as he sometimes appeared? *Had* it been luck putting Anthony in the right place at the right time for a sexual adventure? Or had Taisso arranged things that way?

Anthony cursed his own naïveté. What was the matter with him lately? He wasn't usually this lax. Yrae had lulled him, mesmerized him, putting his well-polished cynicism on hold. She'd even made him forget for a while that she was alien. He kept giving her the benefit of the doubt, extending his trust to her entire species. Foolish. He had to be more careful.

They were still sounding each other out, still learning. Aware of that, he asked gingerly, "Will—will you explain a—a type of Whimed behavior? The day we met, when the octopoid and the bobber were fighting near the dome, you went into a trance." Yrae gave no indication that she was listening. Anthony plunged on before he lost his courage. "What were you doing? I've never read about anything like that on the vids. By now Jesse and I are used to a lot of Whimed habits, but—"

"It is called *diya*," Yrae said tonelessly. "It is a special art. Only a Hilandro may learn the skill."

He'd already guessed that "Hilandro" was a title, not merely part of her name. Now he knew more. *A* Hilandro. Implying there were more of them. An elite group? Extraordinary beings. That was another detail not included in those edu-vids C.S.P. had hired him to produce. He was beginning to think the felinoid advisors on that project had left out a lot of such details, possibly because they didn't want non-Whimeds dipping into their private affairs.

Testing deeper waters, Anthony probed, "Exactly what is *diya*?"

Yrae shrugged. "I believe a Terran would call it concentration. I will now see your sea creatures always. Here." She tapped her forehead. "I will be able to re-create all details of the scene for my people in a future drama dance."

He gasped in admiration. Capturing the total essence of a time and place! What a tool for a performer! Anthony had worked with human actors capable of intense concentration. But *diya* was plainly something more. It had turned Yrae into a frightening living statue and altered her skin color, her breathing, and maybe her brain waves.

"I will use my dance and pretense to convey that moment, to convey its essence," she said.

"You're an emota-sensor. You don't need techs or equipment to boost your signals to a Whimed audience, do you? Complete recall and playback. And you can shut it off at will?" Anthony speculated. "As you did when Majlur interrupted you. Is that part of *diya*, too?" Yrae shrugged, noncommittal. He rushed on, determined to know. "What about the way other felinoids obey when you just look at them? Do you radiate a warning to them? Is it a form of ESP?"

That got a reaction, a strong one. Yrae jerked away from him, sitting bolt upright and swiveling to face him. "ESP? This is the silent talking?"

Anthony also sat up, feeling on the defensive. "ESP is a Terran abbreviation for extrasensory perception. It exists, generally at very low levels, among some gifted humans. And there are suggestions your people possess the ability as well. At *high* levels, it would mean the ability to read another person's mind or move objects by mental power alone."

"I do not do this!" the actress exclaimed. "You speak of Biyelin Vahnajes, not of Whimed, and not of Yrae Usin Hilandro. Only Biyelin *ge-aytan sa-chel!*" She reached for the garish silvery headdress she'd tossed aside earlier and held it protectively against her cheek. The object seemed to be a lifeline, and she was clutching it to herself.

Ge-aytan sa-chel. The most unethical being possible. Those words were at the very bottom of the Whimeds' complex code of ethics. Yrae was damning the Biyelin Vahnajes not merely as mercantile rivals of her Federation, but the lowest of the low, ethically beneath contempt.

"There's nothing on the diplomatic edu-vids about Vahnajes being espers," Anthony said.

The figure opposite him was motionless. The room was so quiet he could hear waves lapping against the window despite its thickness. After a long pause, Yrae inhaled deeply. He got the impresson that she had stepped over a threshold. Her anger was under tight control now. She said with icy calm, "The Biyelin

Vahnajes are silent talkers. They possess ESP, as you Terrans call it."

Flat. No softening of the statement. No mealy-mouthing about a scientific hypothesis. She believed this as fact. Lutrinoids were espers.

No. *Biyelin* Vahnajes were espers. A definite distinction.

The ice in Yrae's voice jumped to Anthony's veins, chilling him. He was back on Loezzi Port, in Brenna's suite, hearing Ambassador Quol-Bez saying, "Biyelin Vahnajes are violence-prone." Quol-Bez also identified Anthony's chance acquaintances, ITC Delegate Fal-Am and his party, as Biyelin Vahnajes. At Clay Station, Fal-Am's bunch had been spied on by Whimeds —agents from the felinoids' Outer Satellite Faction, the Ambassador and Brenna insisted. Troublemakers. Long-time enemies. Beyond the authority of their races' central authorities. And both sets of troublemakers were expanding their squabble into the Terran sector to the Interspecies Trade Conference—possibly into other areas, like that shoot-out near Loezzi—sniffing around the fringes and threatening Terra's stability.

A month ago, Anthony would have worried about these accusations; but as an ordinary citizen, he wouldn't have been in a position to affect the matter. Now, as chairman of Procyon Five's delegation, he felt a great deal more responsibility. Clashes among troublemaking e.t.s. might interfere with Five's hopes of clinching further trade deals at the upcoming Conference. Forewarned was forearmed. He was grateful to Yrae for tipping him off. If the Biyelin Vahnajes really could read minds, that could mean big problems.

In retrospect, it struck him that Ambassador Quol-Bez had been abnormally reticent on this subject. Captain Saunder was the aged diplomat's friend, but Quol-Bez *was* a Vahnaj, and he must feel loyalty to his race. Was he hiding the lutrinoids' warts? That would explain why he hadn't mentioned that the Biyelin Vahnajes were espers. If that was a secret, it was a poorly kept one; Yrae knew about it.

"Are the Whimed Outer Satellite Faction espers, too?" Anthony asked.

"No!" Yrae was vehement, her crest bristling. "Whimed is never *ge-aytan*. Only Biyelin!" She showed the righteous indignation of a true believer.

But that didn't make her claims fact. She could be quoting

popular, though false, Whimed folklore. Many Terran cultures had attributed superpowers to their foes—and ESP certainly qualified as a superpower! Those exaggerated folktales made an enemy loom as almost omnipotent. And when the home team's heroes defeated such an enemy, victory was sweeter as a result; they had beaten a genuine menace, not a straw threat.

Was the Whimed Federation acting out that sort of legend-building on a galactic scale? The Vahnajes had been the Whimeds' foes for centuries. At present, the two species weren't at war. However, their rivalry was very much in evidence. Anthony had seen it at work on Clay Station and in Yrae's daggery glare at that boatful of Vahnajes, out on Equitoria's canals. It was cold-war jostling over stellar trade routes and favored status among the Terrans.

Anthony decided to bend the truth in hopes of sifting fact from fiction. "I know Ambassador Quol-Bez well. He's never mentioned that the Biyelin Vahnajes are espers. And I'm sure he would have, if it were true. After all, the Saunders and McKelveys are his friends."

Would Yrae buy his half-lie? Aliens were well aware that the famous Terran family was on chummy terms with Quol-Bez. Anthony was posing as a member of the Saunder-McKelvey inner circle rather than one of its unimportant appendages, feigning a closeness with the Ambassador he couldn't actually lay claim to.

For a while, Yrae said nothing. Then she sighed and conceded, "Ambassador Quol-Bez is much respected by all honorable beings. He is what Vahnaj should be, if Vahnaj were civilized." The courteous remark didn't disguise her continuing tenseness. More and more Anthony was convinced that she, like the Ambassador, wasn't telling all that she knew. She'd blurted those accusations about the Biyelins. A slip. Once that slip was made, she'd yielded ground, parceling out further tidbits of information—or folklore. It was obvious that she wanted to shut off this line of questioning, but couldn't. "Ambassador Quol-Bez is not a *Biyelin* Vahnaj."

Case closed. The lutrinoid diplomat was an *honorable* foe—not at all in the same loathsome category with the Biyelin espers.

Anthony felt as if he were wading in quicksand. "That goes against everything I know and what I know about Quol-Bez. If what you say is true, the Biyelins are a terrible danger to all of the sectors and to Ambassador Quol-Bez's human friends. Why hasn't he told us about that?"

The actress shook her head pityingly. "Vahnajes do not obey your laws." She spelled out the obvious, saying, "Vahnaj choose to keep Biyelin secret talking unknown. Their concern. Their law."

"Just like the Whimed Federation chooses not to advertise that their Outer Satellite Faction is meddling with commerce in the Terran sector?" Had his needle hit its mark? Yrae's crest was still stiff, but she didn't flare at him.

"No Whimed possesses silent talking." Yrae added disdainfully, "All intelligent species possess some of mind-giving, naturally. This is not true silent talking."

"Mind-giving?"

She resorted to hand motions, tracing undulating patterns in the air. "This is the mind-giving. It is soft. It is not often felt by others. It does not move objects, as you have told. Only with instruments is it detected."

He struggled over her descriptions. "Subliminal telepathy? Very low level ESP?"

"It is not silent talking," she repeated. "That . . . injures."

Anthony scowled. This wasn't making sense. Ambassador Quol-Bez was honorable, but he hadn't revealed that a branch of his species, the Biyelins, were esper devils incarnate. And yet *all* species had some degree of ESP. Then why . . .

Yrae's hand motions changed. She sketched jagged lines in the air rapidly. "This is Biyelin silent talking. They control the mind-giving, prevent if they choose. And if they choose, they may take from others." She hesitated, touching her gaudy headdress. "This . . . *oryuz* . . . defends. It does not permit the Biyelin mind-taking. Their taking causes pain in those they attack. And Biyelins do not share their taking."

He had been following her, up to that last statement. Yrae intended to wear the *oryuz* at the Whimed Federation's opening ceremonies at the ITC. A kind of defiant gesture, telling the Biyelin delegates, "We're on to you, and our Hilandro is protecting herself against your mind-reading tricks." But what in the hell was 'sharing their taking'?

"Are you saying that they won't share their mind-reading skills with other Vahnajes?"

"With any species," Yrae said firmly.

Had he heard her right? She spoke Terran very well, but she *did* have an accent. Perhaps that had distorted her words. "Mind-reading across species lines?" Anthony exclaimed incredulously. "That's impossible. There are too many differences in cell structure and brain organization. Humanoids can't swap tissues or diseases."

That was not strictly true, he admitted to himself, though not aloud. Such instances were so rare, though, that he felt safe in denying her statement.

"And we certainly couldn't read an alien being's thoughts," he went on. "There are too many cultural and language barriers."

Stung, Yrae said with heat, "It is done. Biyelins do so!"

"How?"

"There is . . . a method." Anthony had to lean forward to hear her whisper. "Biyelins could—could share. They will not. We would not allow them to. We would not accept."

He refused to let her off the hook, now that they'd come this far. "*What* method? And if this attack is so painful, all the more reason for the honorable Vahnajes like Quol-Bez to crack down on the Biyelins and remove that method. It's a moral obligation. No, none of this is believable. It goes against all logic."

As if to contradict him, Anthony felt invisible walls going up. Yrae, radiating anger at him without speech. The signal was as tangible as the "do not touch" warning she'd sent that day in the undersea dome. ESP? Either that or an amazing amount of cross-species empathy. And if empathy was possible, why not something more powerful—and dangerous?

"Listen, I—"

"It is true. I discuss no more." She was slamming doors. But dammit, she had started this! "No honorable Vahnaj uses silent talking. No Whimed does so. No being who is *cheleet aytan*."

Whimed ethics, again. *Cheleet aytan*—oath obeyer, one pure of purpose. Top of the scale, as the Biyelins were at the bottom.

Anthony tended to accept at least one of Yrae's claims—very probably the troublemaking Whimed Outer Satellite Faction didn't possess ESP of the Biyelins' caliber. If they did, there would be an interspecies balance of power—stalemate. And in that case, the Whimeds wouldn't feel so threatened by the Biyelins' secret mental weapon and their mysterious method of crossing the barriers and attacking non-Vahnaj minds.

Yrae certainly felt threatened. But was there envy mixed with her fear and revulsion? Was she insisting too much that the Whimeds would refuse to accept the Biyelins' potent ESP method even if it was made available to them? Was that because the potential 'sharers' were the hated Biyelin Vahnajes? Or was it the fear of forbidden fruit?

No golden age for humanoid civilizations, Brenna had said. No matter how noble or altruistic they were or how advanced their cultures, dark elements from their savage pasts haunted them all. There were skeletons in collective closets, throwbacks to more violent eras. Was one of the Whimeds' dark elements a suppressed lust for power over other species' minds?

Yrae was a living emota-sensor, a cultural treasure. How much more honored and beloved might she be if she was a full-fledged esper? Did millions of felinoids nurse that same desire? And were they afraid of it? Their ethical standards were very high. And yet, the temptation! To own such a weapon and keep their ethical pride! Perhaps humanity wasn't the only race with a Faust legend.

She had retreated behind that invisible shield. Anthony doubted she'd reveal any more secrets. He said, "Thanks for telling me this. I may have to deal with Biyelins at the Conference. I'll be sure to keep my people out of their way."

"I have given you information useful to you?" Yrae's crest was softening. She smiled. "Then you tell me things useful to me."

It wasn't a question.

"Sounds fair. What do you want to know?"

"I wish to understand the host of the Interspecies Trade Conference."

Anthony grimaced. "Colin? What about him?"

"Our information concerning your kinsman is incomplete. We must deal with him, as you must deal with Biyelin delegations. We wish, as you say, to stay on our toes. We do not know, for example, why you dislike your kinsman."

Chuckling, Anthony granted that he'd asked for it. Turnabout!

She cocked her head, studying him. "You refuse to reply? I complied with your wish to know."

"Not entirely," he retorted, then shrugged. He'd follow her rules, holding back whatever he wished and clamming up when it suited him. "I do dislike Colin, and he dislikes me. My dislike of him is recent, based on his behavior toward me. He's hated me for years. When we were children, he made some assumptions about me and the life he thought I was leading at his expense. Wrong assumptions. It was a very long time before I realized that he was blaming me, in part, for a number of bad things that had happened to him when he was a boy." Yrae listened attentively as Anthony gave her a bare-bones account of his and Colin's pasts. He completed the terse narration by describing his siblings' deaths. Then his voice trailed off.

"This is very confusing to me," Yrae said, frowning. "These beings who commanded you are also of Saunder. Why then are they so ungenerous to you and Colin Saunder? Why did they not assist you?"

Her childlike question was a knife, digging at Anthony's old wounds. "Because Carissa and Stuart don't give a faint damn about any other Saunder unless that person is useful to them. Colin wasn't. He's lucky Carissa ignored him, once Colin's mother was dead and out of the picture. And by the time I got a chance to escape, Colin had emigrated from Earth, so he wasn't a threat to Carissa anymore. She didn't need me and didn't try to stop me from leaving. And she sure as hell never assisted either of us. Never will," he said, his gut roiling.

Why did he let that bitch and Stuart affect him this much after so long?

Yrae's sympathetic scrutiny added to his self-pity. "What's the matter?" he snapped. "The story doesn't agree with your advance briefings regarding Terrans and the Saunder-McKelveys? What did your experts say? That the high-and-mighty Saunders were Terra's first family? That they all help one another and share the wealth?" He laughed too loudly, bitterness pouring over a burst dam. "Somebody forgot to tell Carissa and Stuart that. If it had been up to either of them to decide, I'd still be back on Earth, rotting in Saunderhome."

Or be food for the fishes, like Carl.

He remembered a time when he and Carl watched Carissa, Empress of Saunderhome, tottering across the palatial estate's terrace, with Stuart following at his mother's heels, like one of Carissa's pet lapdogs, and whining for money. The scene could have been any one of a thousand identical incidents. That particular day, when the surviving clones were in their fifteenth year, something broke inside Carl Saunder. He could no longer bear a seemingly endless, hopeless future in the shadows of Carissa and

Stuart. Carl had escaped into self-destruction. When that had happened, Anthony's own hold on sanity had faltered badly. Without his brother, he was utterly alone, confronting that same awful future that had crushed Carl. He was the only one left to act as a helpless audience for the tyrants of Saunderhome.

Anthony roused from his waking nightmare. Yrae was staring at him with compassion, and he squirmed, embarrassed. Trying to set the record straight, he said, "Some of my kindred have been very kind to me. I owe Brenna—Captain Saunder—more than I can ever repay. I didn't have a credit to my name, but she gave me a free ticket off Earth aboard one of her starships. That was priceless, especially then. Earth was going through a severe economic panic in the late 2080s. Thousands of humans were fighting to get on the Charter Settlement Planets' outbound flights. As tough as things were on the frontier, they were worse on Earth if you weren't rich."

The actress nodded, encouraging him to go on. He avoided her unblinking gaze as he did so. "The Settlements needed skilled workers. Colin had the advantage there; he had a mining tech's regs. Got a contract right away. Me? I was nothing. Carissa hadn't wasted money or effort educating a mere *clone*. I picked up general knowledge from edu-vids, but I had no trade—just my looks and a strong back, and those didn't count. I was lost in the crowd until Brenna gave me a helping hand. She twisted a few arms and got me a berth. I don't know why she bothered to rescue her Aunt Carissa's thrown-out garbage."

Yrae's hands closed around his, communicating, sharing, muting his remembered agony. He shook himself, appalled. What had gotten into him? He hadn't spilled his guts like this for years, not since he'd first begun to trust Jesse. Back then, he'd been wary of the older man for several months before he'd opened up. Anthony had known this alien woman a far shorter time. He couldn't pretend to understand her or call her friend, as he did Jesse.

What had happened to his resolve to be wary and clam up if she dug too deep? The situation almost convinced him she was indeed a spellbinder. There wasn't any other good explanation for the way he'd behaved lately. Yrae had lulled his normal cautionary instincts—again.

"Anyway," he went on lamely, "that's how things went. Colin and I both made it out to the Settlements. And we're both free of

146

Carissa and her son—even if Colin does keep dreaming that he can establish his title as Stuart's kid someday. If the Whimeds want to score points with the ITC's host, find a method of legitimizing Colin."

"Legitimize?"

Anthony told her about the old Earth law. Yrae was flabbergasted. He didn't blame her. Colin's obsession meant as little to a truly civilized alien species as it did to most settlers. "It's nothing but an outdated formality," he said. "A palm print on a document. Something Colin could flaunt as he flaunts his feathered hat. That's another example of his vanity; Procyon Four trades with Vahnajes, and Colin's not as tall as they are, so he makes up the height difference with that." Anthony couldn't resist adding, "Colin's an expert at making people think he's a bigger man than he actually is."

Abruptly, Yrae asked, "What is kingmaker? We were told Colin Saunder is kingmaker. Yet our diplomats assure us Terrans do not maintain monarchies."

Anthony smiled. "Quite true. Kingmaker is a word whose meaning has changed. What it means today is that Colin wants to be the real power behind the next President of the Charter Settlement Plancts' Council. President, not king It will give Colin prestige in his commercial ventures as well as in politics—*if* his candidate wins the election."

Yrae studied him calculatingly. "You do not wish Colin Saunder's candidate to succeed?"

"No, I don't. Myron Simpkins' policies would be a disaster for the Settlements. Colin's man is a dinosaur, in my opinion—not that my opinion counts for much. Unfortunately, he probably already has enough votes to beat Griffith's Progressive Party."

"*Aaa!*" Yrae cried, brightening. What was so thrilling about that snippet of Terran election gossip? Before Anthony could ask, she shifted topics without warning. "Is it painful for you to remember cloning?"

"Being cloned? Or being a clone?" he demanded sarcastically. "No, I don't remember being cloned. Do you remember being born? As for *being* a clone, yes, I find it painful. Very."

"I am sorry. I do not comprehend. All technologically advanced species employ cloning reproduction in certain forms. Why should this cause distress?"

"Because we Terrans may be technologically advanced, but

147

we aren't culturally sophisticated yet," Anthony said testily. "On Earth, our mother world, cloning humans is illegal. Out here in the Settlements, it's a technique for producing livestock and plants. A *human* clone, here, is a bad joke, an unnatural thing. And I'm not too enthusiastic about being a joke."

His illustration seemed to confuse Yrae as much as Colin's bastardy had. She frowned and said, "It is not true. Pilar Gutierrez does not speak of you as joke. She admires you greatly. Jesse Eben does. The governor and other Terran officials and people we have met respect you. No Terran has insulted you in my hearing. I believe you misinterpret. I do not believe you are treated as—as joke."

Touché! Anthony hadn't believed her claims about Biyelin Vahnajes' ESP devices and cross-species ESP. Grinning wryly, he said, "The Governor doesn't exactly *respect* me. He needs me as his delegation's front man. But you're right; he probably doesn't sling insults at me behind my back. And Pilar's an enlightened Earth woman. Jesse? He's my friend. No, I don't worry about them. It's the bigots who give me grief. Obviously you haven't met any of them, but you will if you stay in the Terran sector long enough. No avoiding them."

"You had brothers."

Anthony laboriously shifted mental gears. "Y-yes. Four brothers. Cloned from the same genetic blueprint as I was. I'm the only one who survived."

"You knew them." Yrae's voice ached. "You were born together. You shared. You were kindred." She clasped her arms protectively about herself. "I am separate. Others are two-born and three-born. I am not."

He sorted out the verbal jumble. Two-born and three-born. Twins, the norm, among felinoids. Triplets, less common, but not rare. That was the reason for their females' polymastia. Which didn't explain why Yrae thought her single status was a tragedy. Wasn't she a cultural treasure, adored by all Whimeds? "A lot of humans don't have siblings either," Anthony began.

"I am separate," she repeated morosely. "I am different. I was always different. I will always be different."

An initial impulse was to soothe the alien actress, tell her that things couldn't be all that bad. Then Anthony imagined an only child amid billions—trillions—of felinoid twins and triplets.

And Yrae was set apart in yet another way; she was a Hilandro. Was that cause and effect? Were all Hilandros single-born? It seemed likely. Her extraordinary talents might be connected with her separateness. Had she received the genetic potential of two or more embryos?

The Whimed authorities must have known that she was special at her birth, possibly before. Had they taken her away from her natural parents? Very probably. She couldn't be entrusted to a mere family. She would have become a pampered ward of the state, perhaps growing up in a hothouse atmosphere, tutored and trained for artistic excellence to her present level of perfection.

Yrae seemed to have no friends and apparently no close kin. The Whimed Committee and its staffers were in awe of her and her *diya* powers. Not even Kyinell was emotionally close to the star. Yrae didn't participate in communal huddling. She rarely catnapped in public and didn't binge on food with other felinoids.

Different.

Her people supplied her with *muruen-che*, honored her, granted her exalted status, all but worshiped her—and kept a symbolic distance from their gifted Hilandro.

She was a golden-haired alien girl-child with woebegone starburst eyes. Poor little genius, cursed by specialness.

Alone.

Anthony had been born with nothing but Patrick Saunder's good looks and orator's voice. He'd had to fight his way up and was still fighting. But along the way he'd shared his brothers' affection. And now Jesse filled an enormous niche in his life. Those were compensations for all the lean years, all the hurts. Once he had been part of a five-fold person. But after Carl died, he'd been totally alone for a while. Then, only a year or so later, he'd met Jesse, and the terrible aloneness had eased.

In that interim, though, the emptiness had seemed to stretch on forever, with no prospect of relief.

To have endured such aloneness from infancy, among a species where everyone else had a twin or was part of a threesome, was nightmare!

He was in Yrae's skin, feeling what she felt. Not even an adoring bed partner, a *muruen-che*, could break through such an awful barricade.

"*I am separate.*"

They clasped hands once more, sharing, communicating without words. Yrae's starburst eyes widened as she searched

Anthony's face, probing his soul. He felt a sudden tremendous rapport. Nothing like this had ever happened to him before. Maybe Terrans and Whimeds didn't possess the Biyelin Vahnajes' silent talking, but this was an excellent substitute.

The two had become more than would-be lovers. They had arrived at an exalted, dizzying plane Anthony wanted to cling to as long as possible.

A winking light forced its way into his consciousness. Unwillingly he glanced toward the foyer. An "urgent" signal stuttered on the monitor there. Yrae noticed the light, too, and the rapport collapsed. She drew her hands away from his and said tonelessly, "You are required to respond."

"Damn. It's probably a member of my delegation," Anthony griped and began shrugging into his clothes. He continued grumbling as he got to his feet, trying to deal with the terrible, gaping hole in his being where that rapport had been. "I wonder what whoever it is wants at this time nightside." Yrae remained seated on the floor while he crossed the room and activated the monitor, saying, "Yes? Saunder here. What is it?"

Jesse stared back at him. David Lavrik was beside the associate producer. Lapping water and a glimpse of a boat taxi at the edge of the screen showed that the men were standing on the dock below, using the pager link to the house. "Have to see you, kid," Jesse said, his expression grim. *"Now."*

CHAPTER TEN

❀❀❀❀❀❀❀❀

Revelations

"I—I'm not alone," Anthony protested.

"We know. This concerns the Hilandro and her Committee, too. So she'd better be in on it. Tell her to make herself decent if she wants to, because we're coming on up." Jesse slapped at the palm-print release on the door mechanism, and Anthony hurriedly relayed the older man's words to Yrae. He needn't have bothered; she had heard and was already clothed, waiting, as he was, for the men to reach the top of the stairs.

Jesse barged in breathing fire. Lavrik shambled in his wake. The associate producer headed straight for the refreshment island and hunted through its cabinets. "Where's that bottle of . . . ah! Found it!" He tapped into Anthony's carefully hoarded supply of imported alcohol and thrust a glassful at Lavrik. "Here, drink. Then sit. You've got a lot of talking to do."

Anthony and Yrae watched the scene in bewilderment and, in Anthony's case, consternation. He began, "Jesse, what—"

His friend waved a hand, shushing him. "You'll find out soon enough. I *told* you I'd get to the bottom of what was bugging this guy. Well, I did!" The object of his efforts had gulped some of

151

the liquor and sprawled into a chair. Lavrik blinked woozily, and Jesse demanded, "So? How do you feel?"

"I . . . it doesn't matter. Nothing matters now."

"Quit saying that! It's the same nonsense you spouted at the Studio earlier when I asked you what was wrong. If you'd leveled with us from the first, you wouldn't be in this mess." Jesse shook an admonishing finger at the actor.

Yrae knelt beside the distraught young man. "What troubles you, David? Allow us to aid you."

"He'd damned well *better* allow us," Jesse cut in. He turned to Anthony. "I figured he was going to pull his disappearing stunt again, but *this* time I didn't lose him. Tailed him right to the diplomatic area near the Governor's Canal. Know what? This guy met up there with a whiteface. Got a hand-delivered package from the e.t., in fact."

Lavrik cringed, and Yrae's crest prickled in alarm at this revelation.

"A whiteface?" Anthony said, incredulous. "A Biyelin Vahnaj?"

"You got it, kid. The same aliens Captain Saunder and the Ambassador warned us about. There's some of 'em here on Five, trading, I suppose—a few alien merchants on nearly *every* Settlement. But it didn't seem right our boy Davy would be in a cozy little meeting with one, now did it? When he headed back to the offworlders' hostel, I cornered him. We've put up with enough of his non-contrib behavior at rehearsals. I told him we wanted answers. And he finally came up with some."

Anthony clenched and unclenched his fists, struggling to control his temper. Lavrik's lackluster attitude had jeopardized the entire Terran-Whimed production. The man deserved to have the truth choked out of him. Right now, though, as whipped as the actor looked, such tactics might backfire. Anthony used words rather than physical force. "Let's have it. You owe me, Lavrik, and you owe Yrae. What's this about your meeting with a Biyelin Vahnaj? You're no greenie or Earth tourist. You grew up on a Whimed Protectorate planet. You *know* that the Vahnajes are the felinoids' long-time enemies. What ingratitude! Dealing with a whiteface behind your employers' backs! The Committee is paying you a handsome salary, giving you the break of a lifetime. And this is the way you thank them?"

"Go on," Jesse encouraged the performer. "It gets easier each time you tell it, Davy, believe me."

Lavrik took another long pull on the drink, then set it aside and gripped the chair's arms for support. "I—I was finishing a vid recording series on Settlement Wulf Eight when I got the message about the Committee's project. Y-you're right. This *is* the chance of a lifetime for me. More than I'd ever hoped or prayed for. Everyone working in the series with me wanted my luck to rub off on them. A few days before I was scheduled to make the trip here, they threw a party. A major send-off. Invited half the Settlement, it seemed like. *Wonderful* party!" A bittersweet hint of a smile twitched at his lips. "There—there was this young woman. Norah Kamika. She was . . . was lovely. We clicked, right away. And . . . and . . ."

"You decided to have a private party," Anthony said irritably. "Peace and piece. I'm familiar with the pattern. Get on with it."

Lavrik helped himself to another drink. "Yes, that's exactly the way it went. Things were getting too crowded at the main romp, so we headed off together to Norah's sleep unit. It was . . ." The actor shook off the temptation to reminisce and plunged ahead. "I guess the party turned really wild after we left. I mean, the authorities had to break it up. Messy. Some people assaulting Wulf's police, the whole thing. A lot of arrests. The story even got into the local vidcasts. Norah and I were included in the coverage, despite the fact that we weren't there when things got so far out of hand," he said aggrievedly. "The police didn't file any charge against us, of course. Couldn't. But it was . . . embarrassing, having my name and picture splattered all over the place like that. The only media contact I've had previously has been reviews for my work."

"So far," Anthony muttered, "this sounds like a sloppily plotted cheap erotic vid."

Reddening, Lavrik said, "It—it wasn't like that. Not at all!" Another pause for a sip of his drink and a deep breath. "Uh . . . well, I made my shuttle launch okay a couple days later. It was when I was starhopping to my next transfer station that I met Renzi."

"Who?"

"Uh . . . Dino Renzi. He's a merchant. Nice guy. Has a trade route along the rim worlds. He'd booked the flight couch next to mine, and . . . you know how it is. We got to talking."

Anthony reached menacingly for the young man's collar, then restrained the impulse. "Just the gist of your conversation. Don't give us every extraneous detail!"

"He—Renzi—had seen my vids, and my ballet work when I was touring with the KA Institute. He rally raved about them. We . . . well, with everything else we discussed, he happened to mention a recent outbreak of VN/HS-3 on Wulf Eight. Must have started the day I left. I hadn't heard about it, so Renzi showed me a vidcast replay he had . . . and . . . and . . ." Lavrik buried his face in his hands and gasped, "I don't want to die! My career's just started!"

Cold sweat trickled down Anthony's spine. It didn't take much intelligence to extrapolate from the actor's disjointed account and see where it would wind up. VN/HS-3. The biological exception that proved the rule—interspecies barriers *weren't* absolute. The venereal virus was a mild nuisance among lutrinoids; but transmitted to humans, it was quickly and horribly deadly. The disease had been featured on the news often of late, with discouraging updates. The uniqueness of VN/HS-3 offered a poor prognosis for any solution soon. No one had believed cross-species infection of that type was possible—until the first humans died in writhing agony. Now that the virus had been pinpointed, researchers were coming up blank on any possibility of a cure.

For Anthony, the idea of intercourse with a Vahnaj was a turnoff. Other humans felt differently, and some paid the supreme price for their experimentations. But Anthony had experimented sexually with an alien an hour or so ago. Sex with a Whimed, though, not a Vahnaj. There were no cases of cross-species infection between humans and felinoids.

So far as anyone knew.

He exchanged a searching look with Yrae. Was she feeling the same anxiety he was? If so, it didn't show on her attractive features. And after consideration, he also dismissed his concern. Any chances of a Terran-Whimed version of VN/HS-3 seemed very, very remote; it was virtually impossible for biological lightning to strike twice.

The Terran-Vahnaj virus, though, was quite real—and invariably fatal.

"Let me guess," Anthony said. "One of the victims listed in Renzi's replay vidcast was your friend Norah."

Lavrik raised his head, gawking. "Th-that's right. Oh, God!

154

Norah! They had footage. Parameds carrying her out of her unit and hurrying her to the hospital. A—a deathbed interview. Her trying to talk coherently. She . . . she'd had this affair with a—a Vahnaj trader. Just to see what—what it was like. And the hideous lesions! She was covered with them! And seizures. It was awful! And—and they had her obit. Oh, Spirit of Humanity!"

The actor's complexion had gone ashy white. He gulped more liquor, mustering his courage. "Renzi was sympathetic when he learned that I . . . that Norah and I . . . You see, Dino deals in pharmaceuticals. He had some inside connections. Told me the disease doesn't have to be fatal, that the Vahnajes had developed some brand-new drug to put the symptoms in remission. And that I could go to one of their own planets and take the permanent cure there."

"Cure?" Anthony snapped. "There *is* no cure."

"They have one! They showed me!" Lavrik's voice cracked. "At—at the transfer station. Renzi introduced me to this Vahnaj doctor—"

"A Biyelin Vahnaj?" Yrae interrupted, aghast.

"Uh . . . yes. He—he ran tests, and confirmed I was—I was positive for the virus. He—he didn't want to give me the drug. Said it was only for the Vahnajes' proven human friends, and he'd heard I was working with Whimeds."

"How did he hear that?" Jesse broke in. The associate producer shook his head, amazed at the actor's gullibility. Lavrik had been frantic at the time he described, admittedly. But was that sufficient excuse? "Musta been another spy network finding. Because the Committee's kept a real tight lid on PR till just this last week. Pilar showed me the releases herself."

"Go on," Anthony said impatiently, gesturing to Lavrik.

"The—the Biyelin Vahnaj doctor gave me an injection, after Renzi put in a word on my behalf. Made arrangements for me to have enough of the remission-triggering serum to tide me over as far as Procyon Five. The doctor had a colleague here, and gave me his name."

"The Vahnaj Jesse saw you meet?" Once more Anthony had to fight hard against the urge to shake the performer until Lavrik's teeth rattled.

The man was young, he reminded himself. Young in more ways than one. He was no greenie, but a hydroponic forced growth, put into arts training schools at an early age, nurtured for

155

his exceptional talents, not his knowledge of the sectors' under-bellies, and honed and polished to interpret the work of ballet masters and playwrights. In too many regards, David Lavrik was similar to hundreds of other performers Anthony had dealt with, gifted but very shallow. They were so wrapped up in their craft they tended to live on a plane somewhat apart from the real, rough, and cynical universe.

Even so, Anthony detected a doubting glimmer in Lavrik's frightened expression. Naïve or not, the young man must have begun to have some serious questions. And Jesse had managed to corner him when those doubts were at their worst and Lavrik at his most vulnerable.

"This so-called medical colleague you were to meet on Five was *also* a Biyelin Vahnaj, correct?"

"Y-yes. I meet her every day, and she gives me a refill of the auto-inject serum package. B-but . . ." Lavrik sagged, the picture of despair. "I don't know what to do. A friend of mine died of VN/HS-3 a couple of years ago. I was with him, and . . ." The actor closed his eyes, wincing in horror. "Then—then Norah. I—I just can't think straight. Can't concentrate on anything. The medicine *does* help, or I couldn't go through rehearsals at all. And the special injections the doctor gives me really boost the remission."

"It's the old Doctor Feelgood tactic," Jesse said. "Been around for a long time, Davy, and you aren't the first human actor to believe in it."

"I know that." Anger flared in Lavrik's eyes. "And—and I'm starting to realize that they're using me."

Anthony raised an eyebrow. It had certainly taken long enough to nurse the panicky young man to this point. *Now* they'd heard the root of the scheme. "They want something from you. What?"

"The medic keeps repeating that the only way I'll live is to take the permanent cure on her planet." Lavrik steeled himself, meeting Yrae's unnerving stare. "The Biyelin says she'll do that after the failure of the Whimeds' opening ceremony presentation."

His listeners were silent for a moment, absorbing the implications of his statement.

Then Anthony spun on his heel, bringing his clenched fists down full force on the refreshment island's storage cabinet. The furniture rocked on its base as he thundered, "Damn them, damn

156

them!" Spouting curses, he kicked at a chair, sending it flying nearly to the window wall. He seized another, lifting it over his head, preparing to smash it.

"Stop it, kid! Cool off!"

Jesse gripping his arms, wrestling with him, trying to pull the chair out of Anthony's grasp.

David Lavrik was on his feet, retreating as fast as his liquored-up condition permitted—a sensible move when confronted with a madman.

Why hadn't Yrae retreated as well? She, like Jesse, stood her ground, braced for defense, her crest erect, her alien eyes enormous. She was a humanoid hunter, waiting until another hunter boiled away his fury.

"Damn them!" Anthony repeated. He was rigid with tension.

"Yeah, damn them. But *you* simmer!" Jesse ordered. He said earnestly, "God knows I've nagged you for years to break down and confess you're human, a real man. But right now you're acting *too* damned human, kid. Get ahold of yourself! Or do I have to conk you with this chair and let you sleep it off?"

His words were weapons, lancing Anthony's rage, draining the unfocused, useless motion.

Emotion! Genuine emotion, unshammed and undeniable!

It was human emotion, as *he* was human. He could no longer deny that, either.

The outburst wasn't feigned. It served no manipulative purpose. He'd felt the anger down to the very core of his being.

Sucking in air, Anthony called on biofeedback techniques, trying to calm himself. With conscious effort, he reined in his emotions, channeling them. Slowly he lowered the chair he and Jesse were arguing over and set it back in place with precise, measured care.

Reassured, Lavrik groped his way back to the island. He was badly shaken—from his fears and from the alcohol.

Anthony was in full control now. He glared at Lavrik. Jesse and Yrae flanked him, also studying the hapless young man. "I—I've been their puppet," the actor said. Resentment warred with his terror. "They've—"

"Manipulated you," Anthony supplied. "I know the feeling very well. They're saying they'll cure you *only* if you cause the Terran-Whimed dramatic project to fail. Well, you've certainly done your damnedest to accomplish that."

A spark—the spark that had been missing in David Lavrik ever since he had arrived on Procyon Five—flared. "I was under pressure. A tremendous amount of pressure. Can't you see that? I think I had good cause to be unable to—to concentrate." He gulped audibly. "I'm going to die. I accept that now. One way or another, I'm dead. If I don't cooperate, they withdraw treatment. I'll die just like my friend and Norah. But they can't let me live, can they? Even if I assist them in making the project fail, they—they'll have to kill me. I know too much, could accuse them of blackmail." Lavrik met the others' stares defiantly. "Not that I'm *trying* to make the project fail. I'd never do that!"

"Not deliberately, Davy." Jesse nodded. "We know that, son. As Anthony says, they've been manipulating you."

"And you're not going to die," Saunder Studio's boss finished.

Lavrik scowled tragically. "Don't try to soften it. I told you, I've accepted reality. I'm just sorry it took me so long to realize what was coming, that I've given you all so much grief."

Jesse did what Anthony had longed to—shook the actor out of his morbid resignation. "Dammit, wake up! You swallowed their story hook, line, and sinker! How do you know Norah's dead? How do you know she ever had anything to do sexually with a Vahnaj? Are you sure she even got infected?"

"The vidcast . . ."

"Convenient, wasn't it?" Anthony said acidly. "This merchant, Renzi, just happened to be your seatmate on that starhopper. And he just happened to have that copy of a late-late vidcast of Norah's horrible demise. He knocked you totally off vector, exactly as he and his Biyelin Vahnaj conspirators intended to do. You've been so frantic about the virus you *think* you have, you haven't bothered to use your brain."

"But I feel *terrible*. I can feel the virus eating at me, destroying me."

Yrae spoke up suddenly. "This is not the way of it. Our physicians have examined the disease." Anthony eyed her sidelong. The phrase "Know thy enemy" buzzed in the back of his mind. Was that why the Whimeds had made a particular effort in such an obscure branch of medicine? Their research would come in handy now, no matter its motives, if it could shatter Lavrik's stubborn convictions. Yrae went on, "As we understand, the attack of VN/HS-3 is violent. Abrupt. Is that the word? Victims do not interview with media while they die."

"Th-that's true," Lavrik conceded, startled. "Sam . . . when he was dying, he couldn't talk at all. Just ripped him apart, right from the beginning."

"You are improved by drugs the Biyelins give you," Yrae said persuasively. "Is it not that the Biyelin who tested you at the transfer station created your feeling of sickness?"

The actor blinked rapidly, thunderstruck. "You—you mean they gave me something to make me believe I was catching the virus? Why, they—"

"That's the other side of the Doctor Feelgood pattern, Davy," Jesse said, stressing Yrae's point. "Tricksy. Nasty, too. But very effective—if the con gang has a gullible patsy."

Lavrik reddened, from anger this time, not chagrin. "Used me! Made me think . . . If—if that's true, then maybe . . . ."

"Let's find out." Anthony went to the island's terminal and established a link with the Governor's quarters. The conversation was terse and largely one-sided as he forced his way past the sleepy objections of a night-duty staffer. "I'm aware of the time. This is very important. I insist you wake the Governor now. Tell him Chairman Saunder has discovered something that affects our ITC Delegation."

As the staffer stumbled to obey, Anthony reflected that he hadn't actually lied. If the Whimeds' dramatic project failed, their prestige at the Interspecies Trade Conference would nosedive. And the Vahnajes—particularly the Biyelin Vahnajes—were likely to benefit. Procyon Five's potential trade agreements with alien markets were on the Whimed front, not with Vahnajes. The Settlement's hopes of improving their export and commerce picture would go glimmering along with the collapse of Anthony's production.

Yrae had hurried to the room's other terminal, in the foyer, and was putting through a call on a separate circuit. Anthony strained to hear what she was saying, guessing what she had in mind. But at that moment Governor Yamashita lurched into view on the island's screen. "Wha' is it, Saunder? Sounded like some sort of emergency."

"In a very real sense, it is, sir."

Briefly, wasting little breath on personal opinions, Anthony spelled out the facts Jesse had dredged up. Yamashita's manner shifted from annoyed drowsiness to wide-awake offended dignity. "That—that's an insult to the integrity of Procyon Five! How dare they? Where is this alleged Vahnaj physician? The diplomats' quarter, you say. I'll send my guards to detain her immediately! And what should we do about the rest of this situation?"

Yrae had returned from the second monitor. She stood beside Anthony and said, "We request you do nothing, Esteemed Governor. Our Committee wishes to attend to this matter. Permit us."

"Of course, of course. Are you claiming diplomatic privilege?"

"Perhaps it's better if we let the aliens take care of their own, don't you think, sir?" Anthony suggested. "We wouldn't want to become *too* involved in a non-Terran disagreement. The chance of unpleasant repercussions affecting the Settlement, backlash from C.S.P. Council . . . *that* sort of red tape."

The politician's manner altered. "Yes, yes, quite right, Saunder. I see your point. Very astute. We *should* let them handle it. But how is it to be done?"

"I'm not sure myself, sir. I'll let you know if I learn anything," Anthony said, resolving in advance to limit his report severely. The Governor was a notorious blabbermouth. For the sake of Saunder Studio, the project, and whatever future career David Lavrik might have, it was best that the little official possess no more gossip than absolutely necessary. "I'll get back to you, Governor."

One connection ended. Another, prearranged by Yrae, snapped into focus to replace it. Taisso and Majlur were both very solemn.

"It is function, Hilandro," Majlur announced.

"We establish link you ask," Taisso added. "Inform you when complete."

"Do so," she replied imperiously. "Contact me here at Saunder dwelling. *Nalow tialell xiun. Kwilya!*"

As the screen went dark, the men glanced at the Whimed woman wonderingly. "Subspace?" Anthony guessed. "With diplomatic clout to expedite the procedure. I take it your people are contacting Settlement Wulf Eight?" Yrae nodded, startled. "That's a long starhop—or a subspace connection, even for superfast Whimed Federation privileged communications. How long before Taisso and Majlur have anything to give back to you?"

"Uncertain. It will depend upon what is discovered."

Anthony grunted. "Just in case, let's assume several hours, at the least. Jesse, you'd better call the night desk at the Studio and notify them to put the rehearsal crew on standby until they hear differently." As the associate producer went to tend to that chore, Anthony stabbed a finger at David Lavrik. "And you—you look dead in the water." The actor flinched at the word *dead*, and Anthony added, "Metaphorically speaking, that is. There are beds in the next room. Take your pick. Sack out now. We'll wake you when we have anything."

"I should take the medication."

"No! No more medication. Haven't you got that through your skull yet? You yourself acknowledged the Biyelin Vahnajes and that merchant Renzi used you. Chances are that medication is nothing more than vitamins and stims. You'll get as much good out of that rye Jesse insisted you chugalug. Hope you appreciated it. It cost me plenty. And in your condition, it ought to make an excellent sleeping potion."

"I—I guess you're right." Lavrik lurched to his feet. For the first time since he'd arrived in the seaside residence, he looked like a full-fledged settler. Still scared, but ready to fight his way through whatever dangers he had to in order to survive, or go down bravely. "They aren't going to blackmail me any more," the actor said, his jaw set. "No matter what the Hilandro's agents find out. My—my final performance isn't going to be a failure. I promise you that. I'll give you everything I've got."

Anthony chuckled and slapped the boy's bicep reassuringly. "Cheer up! It won't be your final performance. With luck, it'll be the first total smash of your long and glorious career."

"Are—are you sure?"

"As Jesse would say, trust me. In fact, I'll bet my Studio on it. Now go get some sleep."

Shrugging, the actor weaved his way into the adjacent alcove. Jesse met Lavrik halfway between the refreshment island and the smaller room's door and guided the tipsy "virus victim" the last few steps. Then Jesse rejoined Anthony and Yrae. "Nice job, kid. Couldn't have done a better Dutch uncle routine myself."

"I wasn't speaking solely for his benefit. I *am* betting the Studio. And Yrae's betting the Whimed Federation's opening ceremony at the ITC that David's Biyelin 'doctors' are phony, and this whole thing's an elaborate con game. If we're wrong..."

161

Anthony rubbed his forehead tiredly. "If David's romping companion really *is* dead from VN/HS-3, then we're all finished. The project dies before it's born. David will just die a lot more painfully, and literally, than the rest of us." He hesitated, appalled by his own callous remark, softening it with, "Not that I think for a moment the Biyelins were telling him the truth. Not a chance in hell!"

They waited. Conversation was wooden. No one was inclined to snack or drink, even though Yrae had brought along small food items and a tube of one of her species' potables. She preferred to prowl the room restlessly, stopping often by the window wall and staring out at the rain-lashed waves. Jesse, feeling the aftereffects of his amateur spy activities, curled up in a chair and dozed off. Anthony, after making numerous unsuccessful attempts to check rehearsal tapes or review his delegation's business files, was tempted to do the same. For a while, he was diverted by a call from one of Equitoria's businesswomen—an insomniac and a fellow delegate. She was fretting over an ITC issue of crucial importance to her company, and it took Anthony some time to quiet her apprehensions. When the terminal was clear at last, he yawned widely, feeling drained. Yrae seemed frozen in place, still staring at the sea. So he imitated Jesse, resting his head on his crossed arms and propping himself on the table.

Only for a moment, he told himself.

Someone was talking. Yrae. Speaking Whimed. Other voices, also Whimed, answered her.

How long had he been drifting? Anthony's mouth was crammed with cotton. He pushed himself upright, trying to make brain and vision work in unison. It was not easy. Yrae was intent on the refreshment island's monitor, chattering softly to those at the other end of the circuit—Taisso and Majlur.

The report, apparently, was in.

Outside the window, the rain had ended. The sky was bright with morning. Anthony rubbed his eyes with the heels of his palms, striving for alertness.

What a night it had been!

Had it solved anything? For him and Yrae? And especially for David Lavrik and the joint Terran-Whimed dramatic project?

Yrae peered at him. Her expression was veiled, but by now Anthony was starting to read through that felinoid mask. She was

162

as angry as he had been earlier, but concealing it well. "Anthony? You are awake? Bring David. He must witness this."

Jesse was groaning and stretching when Anthony, half leading and half pushing Lavrik, returned from the sleeping alcoves. He steered the actor into a position facing the monitor and shoved Lavrik into a chair. "Think fast," Anthony said, snapping his fingers under the young man's nose. Lavrik started, blinking. "Yrae's people have contacted Settlement Wulf Eight's authorities. I think you'll be interested in seeing the results of their investigation."

All four of them watched intently as the subspace report unfolded. It wasn't in real time, naturally. Taisso and Majlur had condensed and edited the lengthy communication, eliminating the tiresome time gaps between exchanges. Interstellar space was vast. Alien science was very little ahead of Terra's in that area. Every long-range contact across the light-years involved a pattern of talk, then wait for the other end to get the message and send a reply.

There had been additional time delays on the receiving end. But both the Whimed diplomatic attaché posted to Settlement Wulf and Wulf's officials and police had been extremely efficient. They'd unearthed the requested info in a remarkably short time and returned it in flat, cogent form.

Scenes and words flowed with the punch-punch impact of a solid docu-news vid. A Whimed attaché introduced his near counterpart, a highly placed Terran provincial authority, who introduced the chief of the local investigative division, leading directly to a live-on-vid interview with a woman named Norah Kamika. She was very much alive and very much annoyed at being interrupted at work and forced to answer a lot of—to her —stupid questions.

What did they mean, she *had* to cooperate? Interspecies relations? Sex with Vahnajes? Ugh! How dare they imply she had ever done such a thing!

But hadn't she performed in a graphic edu-recording about VN/HS-3, a disease transmitted sexually between Vahnajes and humans?

Well, yes, but that was *business*. An actress worked on a number of scripts that didn't touch her personally. She'd got that particular job the morning before Lavrik had departed, hadn't she? Well, yes. What did that have to do with anything?

Who had hired her?

Anthony leaned forward. He had learned the hard way to distinguish a skilled performance from the real thing. His director's instinct told him Norah Kamika wasn't faking. Her puzzlement was sincere. She honestly didn't understand why the Wulf cops were grilling her.

For his part, David Lavrik was hypnotized, gaping in astonishment at his supposedly dead one-time bed partner. Norah was obviously alive and healthy enough to be sassy.

"It was some guy named Renzi. Said he was a Dr. Renzi. Contacted me right after the party. You heard about the party? Hey! I wasn't mixed up in that vandalism and that cretin who threw himself off the bridge . . . Okay, okay! I'm getting to it. This Dr. Renzi said it was just a one-day public service recording. I had to wear lots of makeup. Looked just ghastly, you know, like I was dying of that filthy disease. Renzi said I'd be doing my bit to help Terrans avoid catching the virus. But he paid good, too. Hey! I don't have to tell you how much! He sure wasn't cheap. I've got no complaints on that score. Say, you're in touch with David? That's great! He's working for these Whimed guys? Tell him I said hi, and to break a leg on that big show he's doing for the Trade Conference."

The remainder was wrap-up of Taisso and Majlur speaking to Yrae, backing the visuals with precise logs of how they'd made contact and the names of Whimed and Terran officials due thanks from the Federation's people in charge of such things, and the Whimed attaché on Wulf relaying his regards to ITC delegates currently on Procyon Five and chattering his compliments to "the Most Honorable Hilandro."

Jesse muted the sound as Lavrik murmured, "She—she was never sick. Never had anything to do with a Vahnaj." The actor held up his hands, flexing his fingers and staring at them. He was a man given an unexpected reprieve from death. "It was all a lie." He leaped to his feet and shouted, "Used me! Convinced me I was . . ." Then doubt chased over Lavrik's regular features. "How—how do I know who's lying? It could be you. That relay from Wulf could be a fake, too."

"Was that your friend Norah?" Anthony challenged. "Or was it someone else? You had occasion to examine her, shall we say, at rather close range. In your judgment, was that Norah or a substitute?"

164

Lavrik's suspicions faltered. "It—it was her. No question. But after what's happened, how can I trust anyone?"

"You'd better trust us, boy," Jesse said, very stern. "You're running out of options."

Yrae gripped the man's hands, forcing him to meet her alien eyes. "You are of ethical family. You know the customs of our species, David. This is not common among Terrans. Humans are new to our concepts of *aytan*. You understand. You have understood since you were a child. I speak to you as Hilandro. I do not lie. This communication was true. We did not know this Norah existed. You told us of her. We searched for her. We have found her. We bring you her own words. Who deceives you? It is not us. It is the Biyelin Vahnaj who are *ja sarige-aytan*. We do not wish your failure."

Her last statement hit him hard. He nodded emphatically. "Hilandro, you are *aytan*. Yes. I know this. You're right. *They* are the ones who want me to fail, who are blackmailing me. When I get my hands on Renzi and those lying Biyelins—"

A buzz on the terminal interrupted his tirade. Anthony elbowed Lavrik aside and cued the screen. Governor Yamashita seemed to burst into the room. "Saunder? My people have been scouring Equitoria all night! And we extended our search to the rest of the planet, too. That mysterious Vahnaj? Claims to be a doctor? She's gone. Caught an outbound flight aboard one of the lutrinoid trader ships late in the evening."

"Last night," Anthony muttered.

"They musta been tailing me, like I was tailin' Davy," Jesse said, unhappy. "That phony doc's probably halfway to the Vahnaj Alliance by now."

"I assume the alien left no evidence behind?" Anthony asked the Governor. "I see. This does put an unfriendly light on our mercantile dealings with her race, does it not? Certainly with the Vahnaj faction known as Biyelins."

"Definitely! I'm alerting my staff. We won't tolerate such meddling in our planetary affairs," Yamashita huffed, righteously indignant. "Glad you tipped us off, Saunder. This business isn't going to affect the dramatic project, is it?"

"I hope not," Anthony said very softly.

Yrae edged in close beside him, peering into the terminal. "No, Esteemed Governor. The friendship of our two species is to continue. I have been discussing this matter with my subordinates. We are concerned that your delegation has difficulties of travel to Procyon Four. Is correct?"

Anthony spared the politician the embarrassment of replying. "It has been a worry, we must admit. What did you have in mind, Hilandro?"

Taisso broke into the com conversation. "Make journey our ship. Provide for you use. Is full big craft. Assure safe and timely arrival all. Mm?" The Committeeman's smile was as unctuous as a Vahnaj merchant's. In the background, Anthony saw Majlur, lurking in the shadows, nodding absently as Taisso made his offer. The protocol chief *always* seemed to be close by in the background. Taisso said, "Is not good two birds, one basket?"

"Sure is," Jesse said. "Just like breaking enough eggs to mop up the spilled milk." Anthony glowered and the associate producer went on, "It would solve one hell of a lot of transportation problems for everybody."

"Indeed!" Governor Yamashita burbled. "Hilandro! Committeeman! How can we thank you? We would be delighted to accept your most kind invitation."

Anthony wondered what the catch was—and the price tag. There was inevitably a price tag, often a steep one.

"We wish promote interspecies friendship," Taisso said. If he'd smiled any wider, his chubby face would have split. "Do not wish recompense. No, no, no. Is gesture of . . . mm . . . amity. Yes! *Aaa!* Is that delegation accepts?"

"I think we can guarantee that, Committeeman," Governor Yamashita assured the alien. Anthony was irked. Who was chairman of the delegation, him or this pompous little windbag?

"Thank you for your most kind offer, *Irast*," Anthony said, nodding to the image on the screen. He turned to the tiny woman at his side and nodded again. "And to you, *Irasten*. I am aware we have you to thank most of all."

"Indeed, indeed!" Yamashita said, beside himself with glee. He and Taisso were two of a kind. "I'll get right to work on the travel documents needed. Saunder, I assume you can notify the other members of the delegation? Oh, and I suppose you still have some stuff to do getting the dramatic thing ready before we depart, don't you?"

"A *few* things," Anthony said stiffly.

"Then we'll sign off and let you get to it, right, *Irast* Taisso?"

"Thank you both for your prompt cooperation on this matter

of the Biyelin Vahnaj," Anthony said, grateful to get rid of the two busybodies. "Saunder out."

He'd put on a salesman's smile while talking to the Whimed and the Governor. But as their images faded, so did Anthony's inane smirk.

The project! There were scant days left to tie up all the loose ends, and a nearly impossible amount of rehearsing to do.

"What about it, David? We'll arrange for a thorough medical screening for you, if you wish. With local, *reliable* medical personnel. We don't want you to have any doubts that you're clear on the VN/HS-3 virus."

"I . . . I'd appreciate that," Lavrik said. "Though it seems the results will be a foregone conclusion."

"Can we say the same about the Dempsey-Janyavee play?"

Yrae, Anthony, and Jesse confronted the actor. Lavrik was shamefaced. "It—it's my fault, the way things have been dragging. But I'm okay now. *Really* okay." Enthusiasm radiated from him. "I can do it, now that I can give it my full concentration without that—that threat hanging over me. I won't disappoint you, Hilandro, or you, sir. Give me a chance. This is my big opportunity. I wanted to live up to the expectations you had of me, but with what Renzi and the Biyelin Vahnajes had me believing, I . . ."

Anthony gripped the young man's shoulders. "Welcome to the project—finally. You haven't quite been with us until now."

"I'm ready to work! Hilandro?" David gestured eagerly to his co-star. Yrae, looking considerably perkier than any of the Terrans, brightened, assenting.

"I'll notify the Studio crew," Jesse said, forcing a weary grin. "We're back in business, kid. I *told* you we could pull off this deal."

"Maybe," Anthony said, not optimistic. Lavrik was a man brought back from the brink and full of fire. He and Yrae were willing to plunge back into rehearsals.

But they were running out of time. Thanks to a bi-species cooperative effort, they'd solved the riddle of what was blocking Lavrik's wholehearted participation in the drama, but late—*very* late—in the game.

Jesse was calling the crew, reporting, "We can do it. Maggie's finished making Davy's cloak, the one out of the silky skins. And Ray is getting the gang together right now. They'll be ready to go in an hour. That gives us just enough time to scrub up and grab a bite."

Deadline markers danced in Anthony's mind. Three days! That was all they had. And during those three days, he'd have to rebuild from scratch a production crucial to the prestige of his world's alien trading partners. Crucial, as well, to the future of Saunder Studio. He also, just as a sidelight, had to carry a full load of delegation Chairmanship duties, with all the extra work *that* entailed.

"Nothing to it," he said. He headed toward the soni-scrub cubicle, wondering if he looked as much like a man whistling his way past his own grave as he suspected he did.

CHAPTER ELEVEN

✪✪✪✪✪✪✪✪

Colin's World

In the days that followed, Anthony pushed his reserves and his Studio's crew's to the limit and beyond. Yrae had insisted that the play's finale be restored to its original form, so everything David Lavrik had learned during that last rehearsal before the big revelation had to be scrapped.

No one could fault the repentant young actor's resolve; he'd accepted a brutal overtime schedule. The night-long counterspy session in Anthony's home had removed all the scales from Lavrik's eyes. He was hell-bent on making up for the trouble he'd caused the project and proving he was worthy of the trust the Whimed Committee had placed in him. In a way, it was Lavrik's form of vengeance against those who had used him so ruthlessly. Anthony, with his own score to settle against the troublemaking Biyelin Vahnajes and their Terran confederate, matched Lavrik and Yrae, effort for effort.

Would it work? The Whimed Committee wanted a miracle delivered and they wanted it delivered tomorrow.

Burdens fell on the shoulders of the project's director-producer. Hours ticked away. The departure date loomed larger and. larger on the Studio's monitors. That deadline was a tangible threat, hounding Anthony.

Then there was the delegation. As chairman, he was on constant call as the various businessmen and officials assembled in Equitoria and rushed through final preparations. There were meetings on the com net, crises as representatives squabbled over minute adjustments in their agenda, and political jockeying by Governor Yamashita and some of his rivals—other delegates who planned to oppose Yamashita in the Settlement's elections two years hence.

Again, the biggest burdens fell on Anthony. He had to be a peacemaker, a coordinator, and somehow make sure his own small company didn't get buried or brushed aside by Procyon Five's bigger, more powerful industries.

He functioned on adrenaline, caffa, and a dangerous amount of stims. Without help, Anthony couldn't have made it. Jesse, of course, was his mainstay, backing him all the way and doing a hundred chores Anthony had no time to take care of. But aid came from other sources as well. Yrae was the ultimate trouper, and far, far more. Since that hectic night of revelations, she had begun to dominate Anthony's waking thoughts. On the Studio stage, in preparations for the launch, she was becoming as indispensable to him as Jesse. Pilar Gutierrez, too, proved that she wasn't merely Jesse's sexual sparring partner or in this project just for the money; the entrepreneur was a hard worker who contributed greatly. So, to Anthony's surprise, did Taisso. The acting coach, shaken by Yrae's artistic rebellion and the foiled Biyelin Vahnaj plot, busted his fat little gut to be helpful. And an even bigger surprise was Majlur. It was apparent that Yrae disliked the protocol expert, but he was invaluable to the Committee. The way he handled a wide variety of jobs on several fronts was impressive. Just the same, whenever Majlur was in the same room, Anthony, like Yrae, seemed compelled to keep an eye on the pasty-faced alien. The man . . . sneaked. That was the only way to describe his manner.

Time ground on.

A thousand tiny, niggling decisions demanded Anthony's attention—plotting sessions with Studio personnel; laying out the firm's schedule and operating plans during his absence, Jesse's, and that of key people who'd be needed to stage the Committee's dramatic presentation; gradually tightening the reins on the delegation; and tactfully persuading clashing egos to cooperate.

And there was polishing, polishing, polishing the drama and helping David Lavrik perfect lines and actions he hadn't given his full focus to earlier, when he'd been under a death sentence.

There was virtually no time for Anthony to be alone—or to have any privacy with Yrae. He and the Whimed actress had managed an hour or two. They'd had no further opportunity to explore sexual alternatives. Conversationally, in those rare quiet moments to themselves, they tiptoed around each other: *"Do Terran dance forms always start on the left foot?" "Don't Whimeds ever eat slowly?" "Are all Terran males so hirsute?" "Can Whimeds erect their crests voluntarily, or is it a reflex?"* So much they wanted to know about each other, with no leisure to pursue their curiosity.

Departure date neared. The scattered strands began coming together.

The Whimed ship was standing by, ready to go. Some of Procyon Five's representatives had dug in their heels when they had first heard of this proposal to combine travel plans; they weren't sure they wanted to be obligated to the felinoids, this early in the trading game. But the advantage of swift, safe transport to the Conference was too tempting for them to refuse in the end. The Governor had tried to grab the credit for the Whimeds' generosity, but few were fooled. They knew that Anthony's connections with Yrae and her Committee's influence had made the difference. Without that, Five's delegation would be limping its way to the neighboring world aboard Five's wheezing fleet of small shuttles.

Time was evaporating, blurring, and sliding down toward the final moment.

And then it *was* the final moment.

There was a gala send-off at Equitoria's Terminal, with full media coverage, arranged by Pilar, Yamashita's officialdom, and the Whimed Federation. The aliens had sent a holo archivist team to record the Hilandro's anticipated triumph at the ITC. And a number of reporters from the Terran networks had come to Procyon Five to join the party and accompany the bi-species journeyers. Several of the media reps had been assigned to that task by Ames Griffith—with considerable additional leverage supplied by Regan Saunder, Anthony guessed. The actors and

171

Whimed Committee posed. The local delegation posed. The cavernous Terminal began to take on a carnival atmosphere. Speeches extolled interspecies friendship. In that, at least, the Governor was shrewd enough to let Anthony take the lead. Patrick Saunder's genes gave him an orator's voice that produced predictable results. He left them cheering and wanting more. The travelers waved goodbye and ascended the wet, slippery ramp to the boarding tunnel.

Anthony stepped inside the Whimed shuttle and paused to catch his breath. He'd been running so fast around the clock for so many days that he had to remind himself that this wasn't merely another rehearsal. The alien crew members he saw weren't holo-mode projections. The ship wasn't a special effects illusion. He really was aboard an alien spacecraft, preparing to lift off.

Liaison guided the Terrans to their seats and gave them a vidscreen tour of the ship. To Anthony, the high tech goodies displayed were simply odd-looking versions of equipment he'd seen on board SMEI vessels. But Five's industrialists involved in heavy manufacturing and some of the government officials reacted greedily. No doubt the Whimeds knew the size of the Settlement's indebtedness. Procyon Five wasn't able to upgrade its fleet at present. The felinoids hinted at an alternative—a mutually profitable arrangement: cheap rental aboard their ships in exchange for an even bigger boost in their most favored trading partner status.

Majlur was unobtrusively seconding the liaison sales pitch. Anthony eyed the man cynically. Was that Majlur's *real* rank among the Whimeds—machinery-oiler and pusher of his Federation's mercantile expansion? It made sense. But it created the impression that the Committee's big dramatic production was yet another fancy façade for their species' actual purpose in attending the ITC. Didn't that demean the Whimed's cultural treasure, Yrae? She didn't seem to think so.

The alien crew pulled out all the stops in demonstrating their ship. Saunder Studio wasn't remotely in the same class with Five's major businesses, but he understood quite well why the delegates listened with such interest. The Studio's last profit readout on emota-sensor vid sales underlined the situation. Shipping problems were pinching his sales badly. How much worse must they pinch Five's big shots—Carmichael, Herbst, and

Omori. The Whimeds were offering to supply reliable outbound transport, with no more ruined schedules because of breakdowns and no more playing ugly sister to Procyon Four's shuttle fleet. The Governor was practically drooling at the prospects. The Whimed liaison officer conducting the vid-screen tour looked smug.

When the show ended, the shuttle was already underway, moving slowly uphill from the Terminal. Semidarkness on the external monitors ended suddenly as the ship emerged from the subsurface levels. The Whimed crew did a quick, thorough, passenger-by-passenger safety check. Then the craft was skimming along the strip, lifting, and arcing steeply upward.

This was power to spare—high tech goodies and then some!

And this was a mere shuttle. Ahead, in orbit, a Whimed starhopper awaited the travelers. There would be no plodding journey to Procyon Four, but transfer to an FTL ship, a jump to an intraorbital point near Colin's world, and a second shuttle standing by to ferry them down. Neat—and *very* expensive.

It took a while to complete the shift. Any rendezvous in space required a lot of delicate maneuvering. The Whimed starhopper filled the shuttle's view screens as the two vessels lined up gingerly. Those screens, Anthony had noticed, were diamond-shaped; and their color-phasing was garish to human eyes. The couches and safety gear, too, were designed for a nonhuman species. No matter. They adapted sufficiently to suit the Terrans.

Most of the Procyon Five delegates had seen Whimed starhoppers previously—at the Terran sector's spaceports. Few of them had paid much attention to the alien craft before this trip, though. Now they were keenly aware of details. The Whimed FTL ship was longer than Saunder-McKelvey Enterprises Interstellar's models. And there was a peculiar bulge around the alien starhopper's main section. The ship was so large Anthony had heard that the Whimeds had hauled disassembled shuttles all the way from their Federation as cargo inside these monsters, and reassembled the smaller craft here in the Terran regions. Once again, that practice implied a lot of credits. Apparently, money was no object to the Whimeds—not if it helped the felinoids successfully overhaul the Vahnaj Alliance's thirty-year-long trading advantage in Terran markets.

Shuttle and starhopper were of Whimed registry. But the invitation issuing from the speakers was in Terran English. A friendly alien voice informed the passengers that linkup was complete. EVA scooter sleds stood by. Crew members would assist guests in crossing to the big ship.

More luxury! The Whimeds had fed every passenger's data into their comps and were providing individually tailored EVA pressure suits for extra safety. Terrans squirmed into their gear and lined up at the air lock to the scooter bay. Sleds relayed luggage and people across the five hundred meters separating the two vessels.

Pilar Gutierrez hung back at the end of the line. Jesse hovered beside her. As Anthony floated toward the pair, he heard Jesse saying, "You'll be over there and buttoned up before you know it."

"I—I just have to get used to this," the entrepreneur stammered. She hadn't yet put on her helmet and looked lost inside the bulky suit. She was stalling, holding off a moment of truth as long as she could. Jesse glanced appealingly at Anthony and the woman blurted, "I . . . I'm ashamed to make such a fuss. I've taken shuttles out to Mars and Kirkwood Station and the Jovian bases lots of times. But *this*! I just can't seem to handle it."

Jesse patted her shoulder carefully, avoiding spin generated by action-reaction. "Sure! This is different from docking at a spaceport and staying snug inside the tunnels during transfer," he agreed. "But listen, doll, these Whimeds know what they're doin'. Things won't be so bad."

At that instant an external monitor showed an EVA sled hurtling out of the bay. Pilar bit her lip. Then she exclaimed, "I *will* be all right. I will!" She loosened her iron grip on the helmet and pulled it over her head. Jesse helped her guide it onto the lock ring, leaving the faceplate open until the woman accepted the hemmed-in feeling. Pilar's gaze shifted wonderingly from Jesse to Anthony. "You've done this before?"

They chuckled. "Hell, no!" Anthony said. "We ordinary settlers can't afford anything like this. Remember, I'm not one of those rich Saunders you see on the news vids."

"Yet," Jesse added loyally.

Pilar shook her head. "But—but if you haven't ridden these sleds before, how can you . . . aren't you . . . aren't you scared?"

"Sure," Jesse said, amending, "some. We'd be fools if we weren't. It's a risk. But emigrating's a risk, doll. Making planetfall's a risk. Out here you have to go ahead and take the jump, or you might as well stay back on Earth. Right?"

She stared at him for a long moment and finally forced a sickly smile. "Right," Pilar whispered. Her face didn't reflect the confidence of the word. The entrepreneur glanced at Anthony. "You—you go ahead. The vid people are in the sled bay. They want holo-modes of the stars and the director while we're getting ready for transfer. Good PR for the project and for your delegation."

Anthony eyed her anxiously. "Will you be okay? If there's anything I can do to help—"

Jesse added his urgings to Pilar's. "Nah! We're fine, kid. Go do your stuff for the reporters." He hugged the woman and teased, "Who knows? You might get to enjoy EVA."

She scowled and retorted, "I'll go, but I won't enjoy it. Ever!"

Chuckling, Anthony went to join Yrae and David Lavrik. They posed for the Whimeds' archivist, the delegation's historian, and several accompanying media types at length. Between shots, Yrae asked, "Is Pilar ill?"

Touched by her concern, Anthony said, "Just nervous. She'll be all right."

"I am certain she will. She is—what is your term?—a trouper?" Lavrik grinned, nodding, backing up Yrae's judgment.

Anthony surveyed the pair. He read the tension under the actors' PR stance. It was a tension he shared. And it wasn't likely to dissipate soon. For the performers, triumph or catastrophe would be decided at the opening ceremonies. For Delegation Chairman Anthony Saunder, that was just the *first* potential crash-and-burn he'd have to face on Procyon Four. Win, lose, or draw with the project, he'd then have to try to pilot his planet's representatives into some profitable deals—while threading through the mine field of C.S.P.'s electioneers.

Though there were a limited number of EVA sleds, the transfer was completed in good time and without incident. Aboard the starhopper, passengers sorted themselves out, finding their assigned couches, fastening their safety gear. Yrae wasn't the only Whimed who had noticed the entrepreneur's uneasiness. Majlur sent a liaison type to offer Pilar a strong chemical soothant. She started to take it, then saw Jesse's disapproval and declined. The Whimed assured her that the happy pill had been cleared by C.S.P. Medical for Terran use. Pilar looked toward her

175

fellow humans and saw no one else was resorting to artificial courage. Her chin went up. "Thank you, but no. I'm geting accustomed to all of this."

Jesse clasped her hand. "Attaway! You're no greenie! Gonna be a seasoned settler like the rest of us, at this rate."

"Don't count on it," she grumbled, though the praise delighted her.

There was another passenger-by-passenger safety check. Then the starhopper eased away from the shuttle and headed for her FTL launch point. When she made the jump to hyperspeeds, Anthony found that the laws of physics applied whether the ship was Terran or alien: he felt that same painless pressure in his skull that he did when he rode SMEI's big ships.

This journey would be a brief one. Months ago, when Procyon Five's planning staff had set up the schedule, they'd allotted ten full travel days. They'd had to program extra time in case of shuttle breakdowns, delays en route, and acclimation after arrival. Anthony's simultaneous acceptance of the delegation chairmanship and the joint Whimed-Terran dramatic project—leading to this offer of transportation—changed everything for the better. The delegates had been able to depart much later than they'd expected. Instead of days aboard their own planet's uncomfortable ships, they were riding in luxury and would cover the necessary distance in scant hours.

And what would they say when the bill came due? Anthony foresaw gripes, or worse. The Whimeds weren't giving them free tickets. They might not collect in up-front credits, but they would undoubtedly collect.

Obligation, owing, being controlled—was it any different, being controlled by Carissa or being subtly indebted to a bunch of pushy felinoid merchants?

Then Anthony saw Yrae smiling at him and forgot his cynical apprehension. Whatever the eventual bill was, he suspected he'd decide it was worth it.

If things didn't go totally to the bad on Colin's world.

Stars on the diamond-shaped view screens dimmed and brightened as the alien ship followed a vector below the plane of the ecliptic. Gradually she began to arc "upward," closing in on her second intraorbital rendezvous point.

Space shrank. Procyon Four grew from an empty, bracketed area on the monitors to a discernible disk, then to a globe marked by landmasses, oceans, and cloud patterns. Whimed scanners pinpointed objects orbiting the planet. Remote relays from Four's sophisticated satellites provided zoom shots of other ships and space junk that the Whimed craft must avoid. One close-up showed a Lannon interstellar vehicle. She was as big as ten Whimed or SMEI FTL ships. The alien was an ominous cylindrical island. Sunlight glittered on her black hull. She was no merchantman. The ship's ident beacons branded her a war craft. And according to C.S.P., Lannon starhoppers carried *plenty* of weapons, even on peaceful missions.

Anthony wasn't sure if he was glad to see the Lannon here or not. The huge ship's presence implied that the procyonids might choose not to boycott the Conference after all. On the other hand, this massive warship, hovering above a Terran Settlement, was a palpable threat. If the Lannon disliked what was happening below, they were in a good position to back up their displeasure with a nasty display of force.

Another flawless intraorbital linkup was followed by another EVA and readjustment to a smaller vessel's environment. Leaving the starhopper in her parking orbit, they began spiraling down toward Procyon Four.

Com chatter increased. Taisso was sending inquiries ahead about the Hilandro's accommodations. Were all arrangements made? Had certain Whimed V.I.P.s made planetfall yet? The names and references meant nothing to Anthony. Besides, he was busy with his delegation's business, going through similar prelanding com calls with Procyon Five's advance team awaiting them at Jangala's shuttleport. On the screens, their neighboring world appeared to grow larger and larger.

"Much land, less water," Yrae murmured.

"Yes, Hilandro," David Lavrik agreed. "I read up on this Settlement before I traveled here. The oceans here don't dominate, as they do on our director's planet. There's a lot of land-based life on Procyon Four as well. An ideal habitat, as I understand."

"Correct," Anthony said, and the actors looked at him thoughtfully. "No terraforming was needed. My cousin walked into a frontier paradise when he won a miner's work contract down there. Twenty years ago, when he landed, the first settlers had just started to hit pay dirt in the southern desert's hills. They desperately needed skilled techs, and my kinsman had the right regs."

177

"It was not simple," Yrae said, speculating on those past events. "A world must be mastered at sacrifice."

"No, it wasn't easy. It never is for us pioneers. But Colin and his fellow settlers had it easier than most of us did. Certainly easier than Five's trogs."

Lavrik commented, "But the ones who opened Procyon Four had to be tough, too, sir. They had to live long enough to enjoy the profits from their mining bonanza."

"No argument, but those who made it rode that strike for all it was worth, and it was worth a great deal. Those precious metals pushed Four from being an ordinary outpost into an exceedingly prosperous community. And local conditions couldn't help but influence their attitudes. Their world is so Earthlike that it puts them in a very special category. They regard themselves more as an offshoot of the Earth than most Settlements do. And they've shown that again and again in their trade treaties and commerce."

The planet's face reflected the progress made in taming this second Earth on the stellar frontier. Her people had made good use of abundant natural resources. Cities and farmlands girdled a subtropical "temperate" zone. Procyon Four's population centers tended to lie in a band between continent-wide forests and mountainous polar areas. The ecology was that of a pregreenhouse world. In another few million years Four might choke on its own by-products, but that wasn't a problem yet.

The terminator fell behind and rushed over the horizon toward the ship again and again as she entered heavier atmosphere. Whimed technology overcame much of the ionization static plaguing older craft—like Procyon Five's shuttle fleet. Approach was nominal.

After another thorough safety check, restraint gear was locked and everything tied down for landing. Ship's screens were scanning, focusing on such key locator points as Metallon City, a hundred kilometers to the right of the glide path. Colin often bragged about his youthful days working in the desert mining camps at Metallon. He was proud of being a self-made man who'd prevailed despite cave-ins, explosions, and poisonous fumes. Certainly he had a right to boast, though his struggles and those of other settlers on Procyon Four—paled in comparison to those of pioneers on neighboring worlds. Four's light Earth-normal gravity, rich atmosphere, and hospitable terrain made her ripe for the taking. Walk right in, mankind!

178

The scanners shifted their gaze toward the planetary capital, Jangala. Anthony had visited the city last year on a marketing survey. He'd formed a firm opinion of Jangala and Colin's world then, and nothing he saw below today changed his mind. This was a soft, seductive planet that would sap a Terran's strength of will, if he or she wasn't careful. Anthony preferred his own Settlement, telling himself that wasn't merely sour grapes. Procyon Five hadn't been friendly to *her* pioneers! But when Five finally reached the debt-free and fully livable stage Procyon Four enjoyed now, the trogs would be able to say they'd done the job themselves, with no assistance from their barren, watery habitat. As far as Anthony was concerned, Colin could keep his tropical, too-lush paradise—all of it, from Jangala to Metallon City and around to the opposite hemisphere.

According to the Conference PR updates, Colin wasn't spending much time at his former HQ in Metallon anymore. He'd transferred the bulk of his mercantile operations to Jangala, confirming Anthony's theory that his kinsman was getting soft.

The easy-living capital lay dead ahead of the ship now, with multi-storeyed buildings and green belts in the city and suburbs. The ITC site occupied rolling meadows west of the metropolis. Anthony viewed the screen with disdain—a nice place to visit, but no world for a *real* settler.

Jangala Terminal's kilometers-long runways stretched toward the shuttle like the fingers of a welcoming hand. Touchdown was imminent.

Suddenly there was a surge of power.

Anthony's viscera twisted. A seat-of-the-pants sensation told him what was happening before the view screen did. The Whimed ship was going into a violent climb-and-bank maneuver.

Any unplanned change of course—especially during planet-fall—could be deadly.

They were flying too damned low!

Was there enough time for the pilot and crew to get the ship squared away before she smacked the runway and cartwheeled?

Anthony felt the shuttle righting herself slowly, agonizingly. The sickening smear on the monitors steadied as the vessel aimed for a runway parallel to the one she had intended to use.

The view screen also showed why the landing had been altered without warning. Smoke and fire boiled from an adjacent runway. Metallic debris was strewn half the length of the tarmac.

Emergency vehicles were rushing toward what was left of a shuttle. The picture was chillingly graphic. Jesse summed it up: "Some poor guys missed their mark and squashed themselves."

Everyone on board was conscious that the wreckage could have been their own craft instead of the other ship. One tiny mistake and . . .

"Look!" A Terran delegate exclaimed. "See the idents on the tail section? She was a Vahnaj shuttle."

Excited jabber in two languages ran through the cabin. Anthony translated bits and pieces of a bloodthirsty conversation between Majlur and a couple of Whimed Committee aides who were sitting close by.

"An incorrect decision . . ."

"The fools were Vahnajes. They were born to be incorrect."

"How pleasing it would be if it was Fal-Am's party."

"Unfortunately no. That contemptible and dishonorable being arrived on this human world some while ago."

"Ah! But how he deserves death."

"Cease!" Yrae shut up the gloating. To Anthony's surprise, Majlur and his cronies quit talking, but they didn't cower beneath Yrae's angry glare. They seemed almost defiant until she flicked a meaningful glance toward the Terran passengers. In the past couple of weeks Anthony had learned to read her expression fairly well. She had mutely warned the protocol expert that aliens could be listening in, and that some were able to understand Whimed. He grimaced, less abashed than irritated. Apparently Majlur was used to voicing his ferocious opinions about Vahnajes without having to worry about non-Whimeds eavesdropping or about squeamish human standards of conduct. Anthony had no love for Fal-Am's Biyelin Vahnajes—not after what some of them had tried to do to the project! But wishing them fried to bloody ribbons in a shuttle crash was far beyond his idea of vengeance.

The Vahnaj pilot had made a mistake. The Whimed pilot didn't. His landing was right out of the text-vids. As the shuttle taxied toward the Terminal, Governor Yamashita sighed, "The Spirit of Humanity be thanked!"

Most of the Terran passengers murmured agreement, even though some individuals didn't happen to be believers in that modern pseudoreligion. In Anthony's opinion, they ought to thank the Whimeds' skills, not any supernatural force. He had

180

quit believing in prayer and deities a long time ago, at Saunder-home.

Relieved to be on solid ground, the travelers boosted their gravity compensation meds. They wouldn't need to resort to those drugs nearly as much as they would if they'd arrived after days of spacing, as they'd originally planned. And this quick trip aboard the Whimed Committee's ships meant a much faster re-adjustment to planetary conditions.

The passengers anticipated a leisurely hour or so. The sched-ule called for them to wait until their advance teams came to the ship to brief them, then escort their people through customs.

Things didn't work out that way. An update came over the com while the shuttle was still rolling. There would be no grace period. Passengers—Terran and Whimed—were to debark im-mediately when they reached the Terminal. They'd meet with their advance teams outside. Procyon Four's authorities were waiving the normal procedure, and incoming ITC delegates should go directly to the V.I.P. ramp, where dignitaries were waiting to greet them.

There was a flurry of protests until the riders grasped the rea-sons behind the sudden change of plans—the wreck. Those dig-nitaries were probably on hand to welcome the travelers aboard that smashed vessel. Now there was scheduling chaos.

Monitors showed crowds hurrying from one area of the Termi-nal's debark section to another. Media followed the herd, record-ing. A few reporters remained on the adjacent runway, collecting gory tri-dis of the Vahnaj shuttle, or what was left of it. However, if that tragedy chewed up too much news space, it was bad pub-licity for the Conference. The regular show must be put back on the road as soon as possible. Yrae Usin Hilandro's entourage and Procyon Five's delegates were being hustled into the breach.

Colin Saunder's distinctive feathered headdress waved above the crowd of welcomers. Anthony toyed briefly with the possibil-ity of stalling the exit from the shuttle and inconveniencing his cousin. Then he thrust the thought aside. Lives had been lost. And important issues were at stake at the ITC. This wasn't the time or place to play stupid games.

The next few minutes were wild. All of those in the shuttle rushed to prepare themselves. The ship's motion made changing into fresh clothes an adventure. Terrans and Whimeds yelled at their subordinates, elbowed one another, and stepped on toes.

The Studio's wardrobe mistress helped David Lavrik into a stylish outfit. Pilar assisted Kyinell in fussing over Yrae's ensemble. Taisso, Governor Yamashita, and others assembled badges of rank and what fancy garments they could find, emerging in some semblance of order.

The shuttle finally stopped. A thump signaled the debark tunnel mating with the ship. The air lock cycled clean, humid air through the compartment. Advance staffers galloped in and hastily rattled off instructions.

". . . and Yrae Usin Hilandro, Lavrik, and Saunder will lead. The Governor and delegates of Procyon Five will follow directly behind . . ."

It could have been a massive protocol headache. But the trog businessmen and the Whimed Committee were so eager to maintain their tentative trade partnership that no one quibbled about precedence.

A harried-looking Whimed crewman posted at the air lock gestured emphatically to Majlur. Majlur whispered to Taisso. Taisso nodded and spoke to Yrae and her co-star. Stage presence and years of training took over. Heads high, the performers started down the connecting tunnel. The Whimeds' archivist and the delegation's historian, their holo-mode lenses busy, stumbled backwards a few meters ahead of the stars, recording. Now and then they yelled at Anthony, wanting the director to walk closer to his actors and make a threesome.

As the new arrivals began to exit from the tunnel, tumultuous cheers greeted them. A small army of media reps surged forward. Honor guards held a mob of spectators at bay. Anthony wondered how many of those onlookers were hired help. A lot of Procyon Four's settlers owed their jobs to Colin Saunder and his company. If the merchant prince wanted a splashy display for Conference delegates and guests, he could buy one. And he was paying plenty, it appeared. Anthony had rarely seen a more enthusiastic crowd. They waved banners and screamed themselves hoarse. More honor guards led the debarking passengers through a bracketing forest of shouting admirers and delivered them to the waiting dignitaries.

Colin raised his voice to be heard above the din. "Yrae Usin Hilandro! What a tremendous thrill this is! We look forward to your dramatic presentation, *Irasten*, and to your participation in the Conference at large. And you are David Lavrik. I have seen your work. Marvelous! Cousin! So good to have you here!" Colin pumped Anthony's hand, playing to the omnipresent media. Knowing the PR value of this encounter for Saunder Studio, Anthony smiled and responded in kind.

As far as the reporters and onlookers were concerned, this could have been a happy family reunion of two Saunders, blond and brunet, merchant prince and businessman—local dignitary and former star of certain vids. They posed while recorders and network relay scanners soaked up the situation.

While the media was getting its fill, Anthony studied his kinsman. Colin's body language was a giveaway of extreme tension. Why? The shuttle wreck and the fouled-up schedule? Or was the tension caused by shamming affection he didn't feel for his visiting cousin?

Yrae also eyed Colin and Anthony. Was she comparing them? Her expression was maddeningly inscrutable.

Other Terrans pushed forward to welcome the newcomers. Colin's pet presidential candidate, Myron Simpkins, oozed phony cordiality and glad-handed freely. Simpkins's political opponent, Griffith, was absent. He'd sent an aide to convey his good wishes. Anthony preferred that to Simpkins's blatant backslapping. Griffith's aide explained that her boss was heavily involved at present in important pre-Conference strategy meetings. It made sense. And if Yrae felt snubbed by Griffith's no-show, it wasn't obvious.

Simpkins postured shamelessly, wanting to be recorded in proximity with every Procyon Five delegate and all the top Whimed Committee people. It was a strong contrast to Griffith's nose-to-the-grindstone absence. Didn't Simpkins have better things to do than trot out to Jangala Terminal merely to say hello to arriving delegates? These public formalities had little to do with the true business of the ITC.

The man was a total publicity hound. Anthony watched Simpkins's performance with disgust. And this lens hog was the candidate Colin wanted as C.S.P. President? Well, he ought to be easy enough to manipulate, once Simpkins was in office; bring in a holo-mode operator, and the politician would grin and nod and do whatever Colin and the rest of the conservative faction wanted him to. The idea of his kinsman controlling this oaf's strings and ruling the entire Terran sector left a bad taste in Anthony's mouth.

He edged along the reception line as a delegation advance staffer paced him, whispering introductions. Anthony already knew many of the names, but was grateful for the prompting. Colin, he noticed, didn't need any such backup. The merchant prince had memorized every guest's ID, and his command of Whimed was excellent. Almost as solid as his command of Vahnaj must be. Would the common knowledge of his commercial links with the lutrinoids affect the Whimeds' reaction to him?

Not on the surface. Yrae was gracious, accepting Colin's plaudits modestly. Onlookers strained their necks to get a good look at her. It was obvious they and the V.I.P.s had come here for a glimpse of the famous cultural treasure, rather than Procyon Five's trogs. Whimed welcomers flapped their hands excitedly and gushed at Yrae, each wanting a tiny moment in the sunlight of her smile. One felinoid-to-felinoid encounter stood apart from the rest. Yrae bristled when she came to a tall, dark Whimed female. Another Hilandro, according to the woman's ID. Ryseen Simra Hilandro. She barely lifted her arms in the Whimeds' courteous greeting gesture. Yrae was equally cool, inclining her head only slightly. As she walked past Ryseen Simra Hilandro, the taller woman peered sharply at Taisso and Majlur, impaling them with her awful Hilandro stare. The two men avoided her gaze, edging past hurriedly.

Most of the Whimeds also took pains to speak to Anthony, looking him over curiously as they did so. He knew that wasn't because he was Yrae Usin Hilandro's director-producer in the opening ceremonies. It certainly wasn't because he was Chairman of Procyon Five's delegation. His famous name was the talisman. Any Saunder or McKelvey was an automatic target for alien interest.

The same applied in the section beyond the Whimed welcoming line. Representatives of the Vahnaj Alliance, carefully separated by several meters from the felinoids, bowed politely to the latest arrivals. Ambassador Quol-Bez led the group. He was one of the few lutrinoids who could honestly and convincingly extend greetings to the Whimed Committee. Yrae's reaction to this being she regarded as an honorable enemy was warmly respectful.

But the temperature dropped to zero Kelvin further along the line. Other Vahnajes nodded to Anthony and his delegates, but pointedly snubbed the felinoids accompanying them—not that the Whimeds cared; they were returning the Vahnajes' animosity mark for mark. The only Vahnaj who persisted in bowing and bobbing to his species' traditional foes was a whiteface—Fal-Am. Anthony returned the formal courtesy with effort. Yrae didn't bother; she breezed on by without a glance in Fal-Am's direction. He seemed amused by that.

"It is a pleasure to see you again, friend Anthony," Quol-Bez said, trying to smooth over the awkward moment.

"As I am pleased to see you, *Mejuo* Ambassador." Anthony offered his sympathy on the shuttle accident. It was obvious the Vahnajes had come to the Terminal expecting to meet the travelers aboard the wrecked vessel—*not* to welcome Whimeds or a comparatively insignificant bunch of Terran ITC delegates. The Ambassador murmured his gratitude for Anthony's concern. Fal-Am glared murderously at the felinoids.

Ryseen Simra Hilandro peered over her shoulder at the Biyelin Vahnaj. Fal-Am spat a few words that made his companions blink in astonishment. Ambassador Quol-Bez whispered urgently to the Biyelin, like an older, wiser head trying to calm down a hotheaded younger colleague. Wary of being caught in the cross fire between Fal-Am and Ryseen, Anthony moved on.

There were token representatives from other races attending the ITC, stationed at the Terminal to welcome their own arriving delegates—and any alien ones, in passing. When the cluster of Lannons grunted hellos to the Terrans and Yrae's people, Anthony wasn't certain whether he was happy to see the procyonids here or not. Brenna obviously had managed to quiet the Lannon Financial Treaties' threat to boycott the Conference, and that was good for the stability of the sectors. But there was that Lannon warship upstairs, orbiting Procyon Four. Anthony comforted himself with the thought that at least the Lannon were in plain sight, not sniffing around outside the ITC and cooking up trouble.

With the Biyelin Vahnajes already on hand, led by Fal-Am, the Conference would have troublemakers enough!

The Lannon, a taller species than the Vahnajes, and considerably heavier, were led by a huge matriarch. Her smaller husbands, a mere 150 kilos or so in weight apiece, accompanied her. Together they made a formidable package. Abundant body hair, scanty clothing, and boisterous social attitudes gave them a savage aspect. "Ho! Not like hot daylights, you Terrans!" the matriarch boomed. "You mus' 'breciate thing we do you and

185

Whimedy, come here meet little beings!" Typical friendly chit-chat for Lannon. They squinted through their smoke-tinted lens implants at the assortment of "little beings." "We look see your 'musements at ceremonies thing. Much promised. You deliveroo! Ho. *Shau!*" The leader's husbands obediently responded with awful cackling bellows, their version of laughter.

Yrae unleashed her alto roar, startling the Lannon as she thanked them for their good wishes. They listened with interest, grinning.

Several blue-skinned Rigotians made a perfunctory stab at welcoming the incoming delegates and the Whimed Committee. No one got too chummy, though. It was a bit of a coup for the ITC to have lured any Rigotians or Ulisorians to this gathering so far from their home territories. Terra's first contact and trade treaties with both species had been made a scant five years ago. Rigotian merchants were just beginning to open a scattering of their markets to interspecies commerce. As yet, they and the Ulisorians were rare sights in the Terran sector. Anthony tried not to stare at them rudely. C.S.P.'s edu-vids were minimally informative about the Rigotians; diplomatic relations were in the initial stages, and apparently Rigotians didn't open up readily to outsiders. The race was tri-sexual. None of their brooders—females—would attend the Conference. Nor was it likely any drones would. The bulk of the Rigotians' government and trade was handled exclusively by the neuters.

The tiny Ulisorian contingent posted at the Terminal was even stranger than the Rigotian welcoming group. The Ulisorians' native environment was such that on a Terran planet or satellite they had to wear pressure suiting and support their bodies with air-driven suspense-platforms. Normal conversation was impossible. Though the Ulisorians resembled humanoid dolphins, their vocal equipment was radically different from that of the other star-roving civilizations. Translation devices converted the aliens' beeps and whistles into something humans and Whimeds could understand. The Ulisorians pumped the natural float bladders embedded in their throats and waved their small extra arms. An uproarious greeting, by *their* standards. Anthony hoped the egg layers knew that the Terrans' and felinoids' smiles were an adequate counterpart.

Colin, who had been jittering with ill-concealed patience during these welcoming rituals, now signaled his aides. They began herding the arriving Committee members and Anthony's delegation toward the Terminal's parking area, bypassing the skimmer station. Spectators scuttled along a nearby fence, continuing to cheer. No one mentioned troglodytes. Today was devoted to truce and goodwill between Anthony's and Colin's planets.

Grandly Colin ushered his guests into three antique buses drawn by cyborg amphibian giants. Anthony had seen these quaint conveyances during his earlier stopover, but he'd never ridden in one. Usually they were reserved for Procyon Four's thriving tourist trade. Visitors from Earth were said to be fascinated by the rigs and their teams. At first glance, the vehicles looked like crude wagons with seats. Closer examination showed that they were handcrafted works of art. The cyborg teams were the products of genetic engineering. In the first years of this Settlement, her scientists had crossbred imported Terran stock with native fauna. Computerized brain implants and metabolic enhancers converted the beasts into tractable living machines. More recent Settlements, including Procyon Five, were applying the same techniques to *their* indigenous lower life forms. By now, of course, Procyon Four had outgrown its need for animal transport. The only ones still in regular use here were the roc fleets; the flying biomechs were as cheap to maintain as skimmers and self-reproducing as well. All other cyborgs had been phased out and replaced with modern systems, except for a small stable of giant amphibians. Colin kept them around as show-off pieces, an expensive affectation, in a sense, like his feathered hats. But they *were* paying for their breeding and upkeep, thanks to increasing numbers of starhopping tourists.

The buses had plush seats, fringed sun canopies, and a full supply of Terran and Whimed refreshments. Colin or his staffers had thought of everything. Flunkies catered to the guests while media skimmers hovered fore and aft of the colorful caravan, taking holo-modes—more PR for Colin's big bash, the Conference. That merchant prince seated himself close to Anthony, Yrae, and David Lavrik, playing genial host. At Colin's order, the old-fashioned carriages began to roll down Jangala's main avenue.

Anthony saw that his kinsman was still radiating a lot of nervous tension. Colin's square face was more haggard than it had been when he'd called Anthony shortly before the Biyelins' VN/HS-3 plot had blown up. Something was wearing hard on

Colin—perhaps a lot of somethings. He'd bitten off a huge chunk for himself in taking on the Interspecies Trade Conference *and* in being Myron Simpkins's kingmaker. There were limits to anyone's strength. Judging by appearances, Colin was nearly past those boundaries.

The antique buses were superbly engineered. Passengers felt as if they were floating. Transport was slow, but the travelers weren't in any hurry. This meandering ride through Jangala gave them a chance to enjoy the sights and adjust to planetary gravity after their journey.

The capital's streets were crowded. Local settlers and visiting offworlders gawked at the caravan. Many of the sightseers were Conference delegates and aides who'd arrived early and were taking a shopping tour of Procyon Four's tourist outlets. Whimed pedestrians recognized Yrae and applauded her with their stammering cry of "*Aaa!*" Some Terrans identified David Lavrik and ran close to the bus to shake the young actor's hand. That was encouraging. He wouldn't be an unknown when he stepped on stage with Yrae.

The teams plodded on. Buses swayed along wide, paved avenues past government and business buildings, neat residential areas, and parks. Plainly the locals had spruced up for the Conference. This sparkling cityscape testified to a lot of work—and money, much of it Colin's. He really *was* pushing things.

One population element normally seen on every Settlement was conspicuously absent in Jangala. There were no squatters, no brawlers, and none of the usual quota of parasites and noncontribs. Anthony suspected the police had cleaned such types out of town for the duration. Were they forced to live in the forest belt's shanty communities or the desert mining camps until the pressure eased? Very probably. It would be nearly impossible to get rid of them on a permanent basis. More powerful worlds than Colin's —including Earth—had tried. Eventually the planet's lower levels would crawl back, seeking soft pickings in the capital.

It wasn't surprising that the authorities had banished that element temporarily as a matter of civic pride. Governor Yamashita hadn't gone out of his way to show the Whimed Committee the squatters' caves of Procyon Five, its backwash sewage dumps, or the abandoned factories. Colin had even more reason for wanting his world and his capital city to look perfect. This wasn't merely his mercantile HQ; it was part of his sales pitch to delegates and potential voters in the upcoming C.S.P. elections. If they liked what they saw, their approval might transfer into support for issues Colin's delegation would present during the ITC—and into a victory for Simpkins.

The host sensed when his guests were getting bored with the slow ride. Again, he signaled the buses' programmers, and the cyborg team picked up speed. Gradually the caravan left the city limits and wound through Jangala's suburbs and outlying agricultural sections. Lush grasslands stretched out to the west. Hectares of Procyon Four's prime planting and grazing areas had been turned over temporarily to the Trade Conference site.

As the vehicles drew nearer to their destination, the complex began to fill the horizon. Architects from six stellar civilizations had combined their talents. Enclave HQs for the individual attending species ringed the cluster of central meeting edifices. Aerial walkways and passages linked separate structures with support units and each other. A skyscraper housed delegates from Earth, the Terran World Colonies—Goddard, Luna, Mars, the Kirkwood and Jovian satellites—and the Chartered Settlement Planets. The Whimed Federation had built a multistoreyed pentagon crowned with bristling spires. The Vahnaj Alliance's HQ was a helix-shaped tower. The Lannon lived in a hundred-meter-tall plasticrete "tree" that sprouted bulbous "nooks"—lofty platforms where their representatives could view the surrounding countryside. The Rigotians' "nest" was a low, sprawling cellular aggregate. The Ulisorians' home away from home was a pressure dome studded with thousands of small polarized view ports. The whole was an aesthetic nightmare. It was unavoidable. The creators had done what they could to bring harmony out of wildly diverse racial and cultural preferences. That was what the Conference itself was all about—finding common ground.

The landscape was exceedingly green, the air humid and oppressive, the temperature uncomfortably warm for humans. Anthony had been gazing at the Conference complex, wondering how the conflicting opinions and goals of the delegates could be hammered into any sort of consensus. Then the ambiance of Colin's world hit him hard. He'd felt it on his previous visit. But the impact was greater now, with Colin sitting just centimeters away from him in this quaint bus. Unwillingly Anthony recalled other lush scenes and their accompanying physical sensations—

subtropical breezes and the light of a star named Sol filtering across a Caribbean island.

He'd run so far, yet here the past still pursued him.

Saunderhome!

Procyon Four was a frontier imitation of that island paradise Colin had seen only once and had coveted ever since. He must have fought tooth and nail to win a contract with Procyon Four's original Charter Company. And he'd used his miner's regs to swing a job that boosted him up the local ladder fast. Now he'd clawed his way to the very top—big man, superachiever. Procyon Four was Colin Saunder's base world, his jumping-off place for expanding his mercantile empire. And all the while, he was doing his damnedest to re-create a lost dream of ruling at Saunderhome. The dream had been transferred to the stars.

The clone and the bastard could never escape. No matter how far they ran, even light-years from Earth.

Despite the heat and the sticky air, Anthony shivered.

CHAPTER TWELVE

✦✦✦✦✦✦✦✦

Shock and Countershock

The cyborg caravan halted beneath the main plaza's parking arcade. Though the Conference wouldn't open officially for several more days, the area bustled with activity. Staffers ran on errands. Security patrols were in evidence. Skimmers and rocs disgorged passengers and took aboard others.

Colin shouted orders. Terran and Whimed advance teams sorted out their respective groups, herding them toward separate walkways. There was only light personal luggage to carry. The heavy stuff would be brought from the shuttleport later.

As the two groups divided, Anthony felt regret. He'd barely had time to speak to Yrae before their guides were steering them in different directions. He was a bit surprised at the intensity of his longing. After all, he would be seeing the actress frequently at dress rehearsals, the opening ceremonies, and the Conference in general. Nevertheless, he'd come to depend on Yrae's being close by.

Jesse and Pilar were talking busily, and Anthony couldn't help overhearing their conversation. "Did you hear what Taisso said?" the entrepreneur asked. "The Studio crew will be housed in the same wing with Procyon Five's delegates. How convenient! Now we won't have to worry about running back and forth and making connections, and Anthony won't get so exhausted."

"The cat folks must want a trade deal with Five even more than I thought," Jesse said. "I'll bet Majlur twisted some arms, got us these handy accommodation setups."

"Shh! You know the Committee doesn't want us to know."

"That pastyface is calling the shots?" Jesse snorted. "Big secret!"

The mention of the Committee's protocol expert drew Anthony's attention back toward the line of Whimeds heading toward a tunnel entrance. Majlur was muttering something to Yrae. She nodded absently, looking elsewhere—at Anthony. Was she feeling the same pain at separation that he was?

Then a staffer approached Majlur, whispering in the shorter man's ear. Majlur grinned vindictively. It was the same expression he'd worn when gloating over the Vahnaj wreck. This time Yrae didn't squash him. She glanced at the staffer and muttered an order that made him bow toadyingly.

As the man straightened, an instant in Anthony's memory locked in place with powerful impact. He'd seen that alien face before—on Settlement Clay, amid a Terran crowd of enthusiastic React Theater fans. The stranger had met Anthony's eyes, burning laser holes in the air between himself and the owner of Saunder Studio.

Now he was here. Light-years away in travel time and status.

Anthony stumbled, caught himself, and kept moving by reflex. He tried to put the pieces of the puzzle together, without success. His thoughts in a jumble, he put one foot in front of another, following Jesse, the Governor, and the rest along the arcade leading to the Terran delegates' enclave. They came out into a glass-walled lobby. It was another of the complex's compromises, an eclectic mix of styles and tastes. Modern art, plasticrete, antique wood, and pseudomoss carpets. Something to please every human delegate, and offend most of them.

A bank of elevators sat opposite the arcade entrance. Jesse waved to an empty car. "Come on, kid. We've got to unpack, and Pilar's got some calls to make. Our cloud chariot awaits."

"Anthony! Anthony Saunder! Just a moment, please!" Colin and a redheaded man hurried into the lobby. Flunkies and SMEI aides trailed them. As he neared Anthony, the redhead thrust out a big hand and exclaimed breathlessly, "Glad I caught up with you! Didn't get clear of a business meeting until just now. Wasn't aware that you'd arrived." Trying to hide his confusion, Anthony took the proffered hand. The stranger laughed. "Oh, sorry! You probably don't remember me. I'm Reid McKelvey. We met years ago at Saunderhome."

"Of course." Anthony compared this bluff, burly man with the chubby little boy in his mind's eye. "Summer of '85, wasn't it? Brenna brought her wards to the island for a visit. I believe Lee and Lara and Zach came with you, correct? I don't know where Dot was that time; probably having her allergies treated. Let me see. *You* four built fancy sand castles," he added with a smile. While Captain Saunder had conferred with her Aunt Carissa on family matters, the wards had enjoyed an afternoon on Saunderhome's beach. Carissa normally didn't approve of the clones associating with their "real" kindred, but on that particular day Anthony and Carl shared several carefree hours with their younger relatives.

Reid McKelvey gasped in admiration. "That's right! The twins and Crazy Zach *were* there. I'd completely forgotten. What a fantastic memory you've got! Hey, this Conference will be a real reunion, won't it? Zach isn't coming, but Lara's here, translating for the C.S.P., and Lee makes planetfall tomorrow. Dorothea's arriving then, too. Brenna's brother and sister are with her, and Ivan's due soon."

Colin cut in irritably, "I don't want to press you, but I do have things to take care of."

"Oh, sure," McKelvey said, belatedly realizing his reminiscences might be painful for a man who had been exiled from Saunderhome.

"I can't imagine what's so crucial that Brenna needs to see us immediately," Colin grumbled. "Won't a call do just as well?"

McKelvey's manner grew guarded. "You'll have to ask her about that. She said it was personal and urgent. Told me to be sure to round you up the minute Anthony arrived. Wants to see both of you together."

Colin was visibly annoyed. He seemed totally in the dark on this situation, which must be an uncommon dilemma for the merchant prince of Procyon Four. Anthony said in a tone of sweet reason, "We had better go up and see what she wants, hadn't we? After all, Brenna wouldn't waste our time if it wasn't important."

McKelvey turned hopefully to the Conference's host. Colin

managed a tight smile. "Indeed. Shall we go? Mustn't keep Captain Saunder waiting."

Jesse, Pilar, and David Lavrik had been listening curiously. Anthony waved them on. "You go ahead. I'll join you when I can."

The associate producer hesitated until Pilar nudged him and the actor and said breezily, "Fine! We'll take care of the unpacking. Don't be long."

Colin had already started toward a reserved V.I.P. elevator, McKelvey at his heels. Anthony took long strides to catch up with them. Aides crowded into the car as well, and the door whispered shut. Procyon Four's four-fifths Earth-normal gravity made for speedy ascents. The car shot skyward, erupting above the Terran enclave's lower floors and scaling the building's outer wall. A widening panorama of the complex spread out beneath the car's glassene floor. Structures seemed to shrink to the size of models. Anthony was grateful he wasn't an acrophobe. He checked the destination readout and asked, "Penthouse?"

"Nothing but the best for our kinswoman," Colin snapped.

Anthony was unable to resist taunting him. "Why not? She helped charter several Settlements and owns part franchises in half a dozen outposts. Surely that entitles her to some perks—and the top floor." His cousin glowered.

At the tube's upper end, the car braked and coasted to a smooth stop. Reid McKelvey led his kinsmen out along a plushly carpeted hall. Part of the penthouse level had been converted to SMEI offices. Staffers occupied all available space, keeping tabs on Brenna's vast interstellar commercial empire. Colin eyed the scene with resentment. Undoubtedly he was weighing his own influence and wealth—and the votes he could muster for his candidate—against his wealthier and considerably more powerful relative. SMEI security guards had established a checkpoint just beyond the offices. They halted Colin's flunkies there, preventing them from accompanying their boss farther. They were very polite about it, but very firm. To help Colin save face, McKelvey's aides stopped at the post, too, chatting with the guards and Colin's people, acting as if this were standard form for everyone entering this floor. Colin knew otherwise. He was having his nose rubbed in Brenna's clout and prestige. Her guards outranked his, even though Procyon Four was Colin's base planet. Subdued, shorn of his comet's tail of toadies, he followed

Anthony and McKelvey to the end of the corridor. The redhead cued an ident plate and admitted them to a private suite. Regan Saunder glanced up from the monitor she was reading and announced loudly, "Mother, Reid's back."

Babyish laughter rang from the next room. Two small children scampered through the connecting doorway. Brenna chased after them, scooping up the smaller child. The older one eluded her, running across the room straight toward the three men. Suddenly the little boy halted and gaped in wide-eyed amazement at Anthony. "Tewwan Scout!" he lisped, pointing. "He's Tewwan Scout!"

Regan left the monitor and knelt beside the child. "Yes, he is. Nathan, this is your kinsman Anthony. He used to be an actor. Do you know what that is?"

The boy glanced at her disdainfully. "Of cou'se I know. Anthony onwy pwetends to be Tewwan Scout."

Anthony was amused by his young relative's precocity. The dozen or so "Terran Scout" adventures were some of the nonporn vids he'd done for Li Lao Chang years ago. Apparently those silly shoot-'em-ups were still in circulation. Even a toddler was familiar with them. Nathan remembered them and had identified Anthony as his hero. Further, the boy knew the tapes were mere "pretend." Not bad for a four-year-old. Nathan had winning ways, reminding Anthony in many respects of himself at the same age.

"Say hello to Anthony and your cousin Colin," Regan prompted.

The boy gravely shook hands, his poise further impressing Anthony. Then the illusion of abnormal maturity vanished. Nathan's mother and the nursemaid came to fetch the children for their naps. The little girl, Tamara, gave no trouble. Nathan put on a dramatic performance, weeping, digging in his heels, clinging stubbornly until his mother promised him a treat if he would behave. Brenna scowled and said, "You and Rolfe are spoiling these kids rotten, Elizabeth. Use some discipline."

"Yeah, break out the whips and laser prods," Regan suggested slyly. "That's how she kept Ivan, Varenka, and me in line—and look how well *we* turned out!" Brenna was not amused.

Anthony sorted out the relationships as the nurse corraled the kids. He'd met Nathan's and Tamara's mother once before, briefly, at an earlier get-together with Brenna's star-jaunting family. Elizabeth Foix Saunder-Chapin and her brother Blake were Brenna's siblings, the children of their parents' golden years. Todd and Dian Saunder had decided to start a late second family, when Brenna was in her late twenties, to "really enjoy our kids, now that we have the wisdom of experience," as they phrased it. Preserved ova and sperm and the ready availability of surrogate mothers made that practice quite feasible for Earth's wealthiest people—and the Saunders and McKelveys qualified. Staggered, overlapping generations had become almost the norm among Terra's elite during the past few decades. Elizabeth and Blake Saunder were contemporaries of Brenna's own kids.

Ordinary settlers turned up their noses at that system, though Anthony had noticed they accepted the tangled chronology of Terra's uncrowned royalty with little fuss. Money made a big difference, and Captain Brenna Saunder's parents had enough of that to do whatever they damned well pleased, including having kids when they were into their seventies.

Nathan, breaking his promise, wriggled out of the nursemaid's clutches and ran to Anthony. "I'm gonna be 'n actor when I grow up," the boy announced. "Will you show me how?"

Chuckling, Anthony ruffled the tot's dark hair—so much like his own, down to the glints of red amid the black curls. "Yes, if you're good. That means obeying your mother and the nurse."

"You 'member me? Won't f'get?"

"No, he won't forget you," Elizabeth told her son. "Scoot!" The boy continued to gawk at the visitor until he was borne around the corner into the next room. Anthony wondered idly where Nathan's father was. Very probably busy with scientific papers in one of the offices down the hall. Rolfe Chapin was Brenna's top R&D man, a key in SMEI's domination of interstellar transport.

The penthouse level was big enough to hold all of Brenna's brood, plus selected friends and dozens of employees. McKelvey had mentioned his fellow wards, who'd be residing here during the Conference. If Anthony had requested it, Captain Saunder would no doubt have made room for him in her sprawling quarters as well.

One of her friends who *wouldn't* be staying here was Ambassador Quol-Bez; he'd be expected to house at the Vahnaj enclave. Brenna accepted that, certainly, with no fuss. For one thing, it meant that she was guaranteed an ally in a high-level position among the lutrinoid delegations.

The Captain and her daughter were arguing about Elizabeth's handling of her kids. Regan said defensively, "You know how family oriented Aunt Liz is, mother. You can't expect her not to bring the children here to be with Rolfe. And he has to attend all of the pre-Conference sessions."

"Liz is an idiot," Brenna growled. "She shouldn't have traveled at all right now, dammit. She's pregnant again, and you know she doesn't have an easy time hatching kids. Ought to stay put on Alpha Cee until this new one's safely out and about. But not her! She has to score points with her natural motherhood nonsense, proving that even a Saunder can reproduce the old-fashioned way. Bah! Who does she think she's fooling? Any woman with sufficient hormones and luck can do that."

"Mother, no female talk. It bores the men. Besides, you're bragging."

The older woman pretended outrage, but Anthony sensed Regan was on target. Regan's had been a natural birth, carried to term by Brenna herself. It was precisely the sort of thing Captain Saunder was deriding in her sister, Elizabeth, as a show-off stunt. Regan's birth had been braggadocio, proclaiming to the entire sector that Captain Saunder could do whatever she put her mind to—pilot a starship, bear a child, or manage a financial conglomerate. Brenna dismissed Regan's accusations with disdain, then went to the connecting door and called, "Blake, would you come in here, please?"

As her brother complied, Reid McKelvey fidgeted. Finally he said, "You don't need me anymore, do you? I should get back to my meeting."

"With Nakamura's Charter reps?" Brenna asked sharply. McKelvey's face darkened. His former guardian warned him, "Take it slow with that bunch of slick operators. Nakamura's group has a bad habit of chartering new planets before all the data are in. Space Fleet has had to bail out his settlers more than once. And his investors tend to lose their skins, as they did on Arden. If you don't want to put your money in SMEI Charters, why not check out one of our reliable competitors, such as Bolotin? Serge drives a hard deal, but he won't cheat you. You'll get a good return on your credits with him."

"Hey! I'm not planning on buying anything," McKelvey protested unconvincingly. He edged toward the suite's outer door. "I'm just listening to their sales pitch. No harm in that, is there?" Before his kinswoman could caution him further, he mumbled a goodbye and hurried out.

Captain Saunder exhaled loudly, then said, "Damn!"

"He's an incurable optimist," Blake Saunder noted. "I'm afraid Reid envisions a profit in every hunk of rock a planet scout finds." He pressed Brenna's shoulder comfortingly. Seeing them side by side, Anthony was struck by how little brother and sister resembled each other. Blake Foix Saunder was tall and dark and handsome. He plainly had a share of his uncle's genes—the same genes that had given Anthony his good looks. But Blake had no interest in the entertainment field, in front of *or* behind the lenses; his forte was business, and he was very good at it, by all reports.

"It's time Reid grew up and developed some common sense," Brenna said. "He's crazier than Zach. At least Zach pays some attention to his financial advisors, and *he's* richer than I am!"

Colin squirmed, seething with impatience, his mood made worse by the fact that Brenna had dragged him up here and had done nothing but fuss over her family since he and Anthony had arrived. Anthony had plenty of responsibilities waiting for him, too. But he deliberately suppressed any hint of annoyance. If Colin twitched, he would be the model of serenity.

"Hardly *that* rich," Regan was saying with a laugh.

"Well, rich enough. No one has to worry about Zach's future. But Reid's? He dives into everything headfirst. I worry about that boy. Well, it's his party," Brenna finished wearily.

Then there was a subtle shift of tone. Brenna gestured to a half-circle of chairs, inviting Colin and Anthony to sit. She remained on her feet. Colin settled himself and said brusquely, "I hope we can tidy this up fast, Cousin Brenna. I have to leave soon. Another delegation is due to make planetfall in about an hour. I must welcome them." He sounded petulant, almost defiant. Anthony raised an eyebrow. What had happened to the merchant prince's elegant pose?

Brenna ignored the blond's rudeness. "This won't take long, but it *is* important. I insist you hear me out."

Colin opened his mouth, thought better of whatever he'd intended to say, and shut up. Anthony donned a mask of polite interest. Inwardly he was apprehensive. He didn't like the wave lengths Brenna was sending.

She jerked a thumb toward her brother and said, "Blake landed this morning, a straight starhop through from Earth. I'd asked him to bring some SMEI operations updates. There was something else in the packet as well, something those damned lock-and-key legal eagles on Earth have been sitting on for months. The idiots! How long did they think they could hush things up? No doubt they'll say they did it for the good of the family. Covering their own asses is what they *really* mean! So damned tangled in obsolete statutes and Earth customs they can't find their heads. If a former employee of the Earth-based Saunder Enterprises hadn't tipped Blake off, we still wouldn't have this info. Sooner or later it's bound to leak, and then there'll be hell to pay. That *could* happen here at the Conference. And if it does, the media are going to be all over you boys. That's why I wanted to tell you in advance so you can prepare yourselves. Personally, if I were you, I'd keep a lid on it. If no one asks, fine. If it breaks, it breaks, and then the snoops will—"

"Mother," Regan chided, "you're stalling."

"Don't nag me, girl!" Brenna ran a hand through her short-cropped hair and said, "But you're right, I am stalling. I hate this kind of job. Always have. I've been on both ends of it, and it stinks either way. Just the same, I wanted you to hear this from kindred, not some damned vulture of a news digger." Blake and Regan watched the older woman sympathetically, but didn't offer to take an onerous chore off her hands. Brenna sighed and announced, "Carissa's dead."

Kilotons of invisible ocean pressed on Anthony's brain and heart, threatening to suffocate him. He had a sudden irrational urge to lash out at someone or something. And he desperately wanted to talk to Jesse or Yrae.

Jesse, naturally. Anthony understood *that* reaction. But Yrae? Why did he want to share this shock with her? How could the alien woman understand his bizarre emotions? He barely knew the actress. A few weeks of rehearsals and that night in his house didn't qualify her as a confidante. She couldn't even comprehend the complex relationships among the Saunder clan.

And yet . . .

He *did* wish Yrae were here with him. Yrae *and* Jesse. People he could turn to who would magically pull him out of these heavy seas swamping him.

Instead, he had to cope alone, with no one but Colin to share this blow. Brenna and her brother and daughter were outsiders—just as the clone and the bastard had always been outsiders to Saunder-McKelvey affairs.

Carissa Duryea Saunder—dead!

The woman who had paid for Anthony's creation, who had hounded Colin's mother into exile and suicide—Carissa, the evil, seemingly indestructible tyrant Empress of Saunderhome was dead!

Impossible!

But it must be true. Captain Saunder's solemn expression confirmed that. Blake Saunder and his niece were ill at ease.

Colin slowly removed his headdress and examined its bright feathers. His dark eyes were glassy.

Anthony's mouth felt desert dry. He licked his lips and said, "How?"

That simple query after the long silence made everyone jump. Brenna blinked and said, "You mean . . . Oh, it wasn't foul play, if that's what you were thinking. Natural causes. Hell, Carissa was over a hundred, after all."

Colin laughed, an awful, tearing sound. With obvious difficulty, he mastered his hysteria. "Forgive me! I shouldn't be disrespectful of the dead." His tone was unsteady, a ghost of his usual urbanity. "This—this is very unexpected. Natural causes, you say? How ironic! We'd assumed that . . ." and he broke off, reddening.

Anthony spoke with clinical detachment, finishing, "We assumed that eventually Stuart would murder her. He threatened to, often enough."

"Stuart doesn't have that much initiative," Blake said coldly. "The last time I saw him, he was a pathetic wreck, almost senile."

"Stuart's always been a wreck," Captain Saunder cut in. "He's been working hard on self-destruction since before any of you were born. He fed his appetite for every illicit thrill he could find, rotted his body, and was finishing off his gray matter fast 'way back in the seventies. Hasn't been a danger to Carissa for years, and they both knew it. She might as well have put a dog collar on him and matched him up with her damned yappy pets. Nothing's changed on that island for a long time, except that Stuart's gotten more decrepit."

"But he outlived Carissa," Anthony murmured. He imagined the decay of Stuart Saunder, a once-handsome face raddled by disease and dissipation. Brenna was probably right; after this much time, there wouldn't be much left of the man who'd made Anthony's younger days hell, except an ugly, wrecked husk.

And Carissa was dead! She'd been far healthier than her degenerate son, yet old age had finally claimed her.

So Stuart had won at last. Now he had it all. Everything he'd lusted for—Saunderhome, the money, the power.

It came decades too late. What fitting justice! Stuart hadn't defeated his mother. Time had, robbing him of his victory and handing it to Stuart when he was long past caring whether he won or lost.

Abruptly Colin stood up. He had recovered his aplomb. Waving a hand negligently, he said, "Well, I suppose it was necessary to keep us informed on the gossip, but I really don't think this news has much relevance for me; I never met Carissa. And she eliminated any nebulous connections I had to her or my father years ago. I'm quite indifferent to how or when she died."

Anthony cocked his head, studying his kinsman. Had Colin repressed the past so thoroughly? Didn't he remember the afternoon Olivia Gage brought her baby son to Saunderhome and was confronted by its matriarch? Colin *had* met Carissa, though apparently the incident was now buried deep in his unconscious mind. His claim of indifference was a flat lie, betrayed by the hatred in his eyes.

"I don't think anyone will shed genuine tears for Carissa," Brenna said. "Not nowadays. However, there *was* a time when humanity was in her debt. My father described it to me. It happened after the Crisis of '41. My uncle Patrick and grandmother Jael were dead, and Earth and the Colonies were right on the edge of civil war. Carissa was one of the people who pulled us back from the brink."

"I see your point." Colin feigned a bored yawn. "But that's ancient history. Carissa certainly hasn't done anything for Terra in recent years. And as for her heir, nobody owes Stuart anything."

"*I* did," Brenna corrected him. Her smile was grim. "I paid

201

him back with interest, and some help from Yuri's good right cross!"

Colin was taken aback. Regan and her uncle Blake looked mildly embarrassed by Captain Saunder's nasty tone. What was Brenna referring to? It was a secret shared only among her immediate family, it seemed. And her expression hinted that she wasn't joking when she said her former husband had canceled that IOU with a fist to Stuart Saunder's jaw. The scenario delighted Anthony. It was probably embellished legend, as most past events were. Nevertheless, if even part of it was true, he longed to shake Yuri Nicholaiev's hand. Anthony himself had never been able to get even with Colin's father. It was comforting to think that Captain Saunder's ex had brought the high-and-mighty Stuart down a peg or several.

"Damn those doctors," Brenna muttered. "How dare they ground Yuri back on Mars! I'd counted on his help at the ITC. We need him here. And he deserves a chance to strut his stuff and rub elbows with C.S.P.'s big shots for old times' sake."

Regan soothed her mother. "The doctors know best. If they say Yuri shouldn't starhop for a while, he'd better stay put. Besides, Varenka's close by, on Earth. She'll keep an eye on him." The young woman lowered her voice and added, "And that'll keep Varenka out of *our* hair."

Blake shot a warning glance at his sister, but Brenna hadn't heard the remark. It was common knowledge that Captain Saunder's daughters weren't on the best of terms. And Brenna didn't like that fact bandied about. Regan's crack was the sort of thing a media gossip hound would pounce on.

Colin's tension was like an aura. He tried to hide his agitation under a veneer of nonchalance. "I will be on my guard around the reporters, thank you, Brenna." The merchant prince donned his fancy hat and moved toward the door. "And now I really must go. I have a thousand things to attend to."

Captain Saunder followed him a few paces. "Listen, Colin, we should get together later. Mutual concerns we ought to discuss."

"Oh, I'm sure we'll bump into each other during the Conference. But I doubt our interests overlap much. I simply don't operate on the same level as SMEI." Before his kinswoman could say anything more, Colin all but bolted from the suite.

Brenna frowned, piqued. She'd gone out of her way to relay

the info about Carissa. And Colin brushed her off! There were polite methods of staging a hasty exit. Colin had used none of them. Anthony supposed his cousin's excuse was that he was badly shaken. He wasn't the only one! But Anthony didn't plan to duplicate Colin's bad manners. There was no percentage in annoying Brenna, not when Procyon Five's delegation might be hurt by the powerful people running ITC. Anthony reined in his impatience, making a leisurely production out of *his* departure. He dallied, chatting.

"I was relieved to see you persuaded the Lannon to attend the Conference after all," he said.

Brenna's smile was weak. "I can't take all the credit. They had their own reasons for changing their minds. And Quol-Bez and some of the Whimed diplomats and nabobs were a big help, too, especially Ryseen Simra Hilandro. She really knew how to get through to the Lannons' stubbornest matriarchs."

"Ryseen?" Anthony remembered the felinoid woman who appeared to antagonize Yrae. "I . . . I've met her. Impressive."

"Impressive and a half," Brenna agreed. "I think her showing up at the peacemaking powwow surprised even her own top cats. Did you know she's a major ranker among the Whimed Outer Satellite Faction?"

Surprise piled upon surprise. "No, I didn't," Anthony admitted. Hair on his nape prickled. He wasn't sure he wanted the Biyelin Vahnajes' troublemaking counterparts involved in this affair. Perhaps Ryseen Simra Hilandro's association with the Outer Satellite Faction was the reason for Yrae's bristling at the other female.

"Intriguing, isn't it?" Regan said, reading Anthony's speculations. "So many differences and points of view between the species and within each species." She went on solemnly, "So much to learn, and we settlers need to learn it fast."

"And how!" Brenna jerked a thumb toward the ceiling. "You saw that Lannon space-going fortress in orbit? What a beauty! But Fleet's chewing its nails because of that metal monster. Funny. The Lannon chief matriarch told me she sent that military craft here as a *compliment* to the ITC. And she's downright scathing about her traders who got themselves mixed up in the Terran smuggling fracas. Know why? The traders weren't armed. In her books, that made them not only stupid but bad-faith bargainers. Crazy people, Lannons."

Anthony boggled. "And if the traders had been armed, and if they'd tangled with Fleet during the smuggler smash?"

"We don't know what would have happened," Regan said. "The Lannons' chief matriarch probably doesn't know either. She might well have considered it a rousing good fight. I've been studying their species for over a year, and I still can't figure step one about most of their motives."

Her mother sighed. "And yet, because Fleet saved those traders' hides, the Lannons felt obliged to lodge a protest and threaten a boycott of the Conference. They don't follow the rules they gave C.S.P. during our treaty negotiations with the procyonid league, five years ago. Those rules were supposed to tell us how the Lannon culture works. Like hell they do! Dammit, we need their trade and their friendship, but they're making that tough. I don't even want to talk about dickering with the Rigotians and Ulisorians. At least when I worked with Quol-Bez, I knew where I stood."

"And the Whimeds?" Anthony asked warily.

"Oh, I know where I stand with *them*," his kinswoman said. "Well upwind, when they're tangling with Vahnajes."

He didn't envy her or the other leaders of Terran society. Squabbles within and without, as Regan put it. Humanity had its own hefty share of internal debates—how to work out trade deals with alien species, for one, and the future direction of the Settlements, as opposed to Earth's preferred direction.

Regan nodded, again reading his thoughts. "I'm glad you're heading the Procyon Five delegation. The reform packages and the credit exchange realignment sessions are going to need support from the outward-looking worlds like yours. I'm afraid Colin and Alpha Cee and the more established Settlements look only one way—backward."

"Too bad you had to ride in here on the Whimeds' coattails, so to speak," Brenna added. "Regan's right. Once you're through nursing the cat folks through their opening ceremonies, we can get down to serious business. I wasn't sure we could rely on Governor Yamashita to keep a level head. You'll do a lot better, steering your reps."

He tried to slough off the compliments, feeling uncomfortable, turning the conversation to general topics. It was not easy. There were eddies and whirlpools stirring the issues facing the Conference—lofty goals, noble sentiments, and heaping measures of self-seeking maneuvering, politicking, and cutthroating. The Terrans would be hotly involved in the election war between Ames Griffith's Expansionist Party and Simpkins's Pan-Terran Consolidationists, Brenna's and Regan's candidate versus the man Colin wanted to place in the C.S.P. presidential chair. The internal debate inevitably would slant opinions on external ones.

Politics explained, too, why Colin, even under ordinary circumstances, wouldn't have been at ease as a guest in this suite; he and Brenna and her brood were antagonists.

Right now Brenna and Regan were wooing another kinsman's vote. Procyon Five was a minor Settlement, but every delegation could be important in the tricky balancing act the Conference would present. Anthony tried to remain noncommittal, and his relatives didn't press him overmuch, to his relief.

As he edged toward the door, a glow from the window silhouetted the Saunders, creating halos. Symbolism? Nimbi for the uncrowned heads of the Terran sector? This was Colin's world, but it was Brenna's branch of the family enjoying a radiant blessing from the Procyon system's primary star. Was that a cosmic prediction on things to come at the Conference and in the Terran elections?

Anthony finally managed to make his goodbyes and slipped out of the suite. He halted in the semidarkness of the corridor, adjusting to the sudden change from bright light to shadow. Ten meters away, the SMEI security checkpoint was a glow of artificial light. Staffers and Colin's flunkies clustered around the desk. Anthony took a step in that direction, then stopped, his heart pounding.

He wasn't alone in this cul-de-sac.

Someone was an arm's length from him. A dark, indistinct shape huddling close to the wall. The figure made sounds—ominous, unintelligible.

Mastering his initial shock, Anthony peered at the mysterious form. It was trembling violently, shaking like a gray-black holomode that refused to click into focus. The animal mutterings began to coalesce into understandable words.

"Bitch! The Spirit of Humanity bury her on a dead star."

Colin!

What was he doing here? Why wasn't he halfway to Jangala Terminal to meet those V.I.P.s who were supposed to land soon? The merchant prince must have halted in this shadowy area when he first emerged from the suite minutes ago. Apparently he'd been lurking here since then, building a storm of hatred to hurricane force. His voice wasn't hysterical. Rather it was disconcertingly quiet and monotonal.

"Bitch. The bitch. Did this deliberately. Knew I couldn't stand any extra distractions now. She planned it this way."

He seemed unaware of Anthony's presence. Not even the blast of sunlight from the opening door had broken this spell. The man had been badly upset by Brenna's announcement of Carissa's death, but no one had anticipated such an extreme reaction as *this*. Was Colin coming to pieces under stress and too many responsibilities all at once?

Anthony had dealt with intensely emotional actors, those whose talents kept them teetering on the precipice of madness. And in his judgment, Colin was in danger of slipping into exactly such a mode. The smart thing to do was get past him without attracting Colin's attention or jolting him too suddenly out of his current mind-set.

Even as Anthony was considering how to accomplish that, Colin's mumbling ceased. So did his shivering. It was very still in the corridor. Colin had returned to the real world. He was staring at his cousin. The laughter of the security staffers sounded very far away.

"So the bitch finally let you go, too, huh? You should have walked out on her, as I did."

Until that instant, Anthony believed that Colin was cursing Carissa's memory. Now he realized the man's anger was aimed at Brenna. "I couldn't leave when I chose, Colin. I don't have your money and status. My delegation's a small one. I have to be polite to more powerful people, including Brenna."

"You mean you have to kiss her foot." That awful tonelessness was gone. There was plenty of inflection in Colin's voice on these words, though he kept his volume low, wary of being overheard. "Damn her. Thinks she owns the universe. And me. Thinks she can put a noose around my neck and walk off with the whole Conference and the election. She *can't*!" The blond's eyes glittered as brightly as a Whimed's, and the feathers in his hat caught reflections from the checkpoint's lights, shimmering iridescently.

Anthony had the odd feeling that he was face-to-face with one of Procyon Four's native jungle beasts. "I—I wouldn't know about that, Colin. I try not to get involved in politics."

"Liar." The other man continued to speak softly, a serpent hissing in the grass. "Tell that to the cretins who buy your Studio's fiction vids, not to me. You fit right into Brenna's idyllic domestic picture. What a farce. Having those brats there. Sending Nathan to fawn on you, the famous Anthony Saunder. How cute! What else should I expect? You're one of Brenna's pets, like Carissa's lap dogs. The Captain keeps tabs on you, takes care of you—"

Anthony attempted to cut off the whispered tirade. "That's not true. Yes, she keeps tabs on me and you and on every cousin three times removed. That's her nature—custodian of the Saunder-McKelvey family tree. It hardly makes me a special pet."

"Doesn't it? I know what you're doing. Brenna's always supported you. Do you deny it? How did you get passage off Earth, back in '88, if she didn't give it to you? Am I supposed to believe a Charter Ship captain gave you a free ride out simply because of kindness?"

Stung, Anthony sidled along the wall, intending to ditch the pointless argument. Colin lashed out, seizing his cousin's tunic. Reflexively Anthony wheeled, his hands balled into fists.

They stood toe to toe in the narrow corridor, frozen in battle-ready stances. The security point's lights cast eerie shadows on their faces. If Anthony were still an actor, he wouldn't need to worry about projecting real feelings to an emota-sensor board. He'd blow out every channel!

After a long moment Colin released him and stepped back. Anthony held his ground, refusing to let things go so easily. "Yes, Brenna gave me a ticket off Earth. And she's loaned me money from time to time. No strings, ever. I'm not her pet and I never will be. Nor does she want me to be. The only reason she pushes those loans on me is from a sense of duty. She wants to make up for what Carissa did. When my last brother committed suicide, Brenna insisted on helping me get away from Saunderhome and Earth. It was her method of evening the score, one Saunder to another. And that's *all*."

Colin winced at the mention of suicide. "Nice story. But I'm not sold. We both know your original ticket outbound was just the first payoff of many."

It was a knife thrust into Anthony's dislike of his indebtedness to Captain Saunder. "Payoff? Call it a bone tossed to an impoverished relation. Sure, I took those bones. I'm not in a position to turn down gifts. I lack the clout and funds to juggle reservations, for example, and steal a kinsman's shuttle flight."

"I never touched your reservations, you damned clone," Colin flared, forgetting to modulate his voice. Heads turned at the security desk. None of the guards made any move to approach the two Saunders, however. Colin drew himself up regally. "I pride myself on my honesty. It's the motto of my mercantile company. I never took a thousandth of a credit from Brenna or any other Saunder. Earned everything I've got with my own sweat. That bitch isn't going to buy me the way she's bought you—the way the Whimeds bought you!"

Anthony studied the blond. Colin's accusations were getting wilder and wilder. He knew there was no bribe involved in Anthony's deal with the Whimed Committee. Why throw that in? Maybe Colin was seeing ulterior motives everywhere. His e.t. clients were Vahnajes. Was he blindly adopting his customers' antagonisms and adding them to his own?

And Colin did owe Brenna. She'd sent him and his uncle money when they were in exile on earth. Had he forgotten that? It was possible. He'd forgotten that he ever met Carissa. The man was developing a conveniently selective memory.

There was no use restating the case. Colin wasn't listening to anything but his own hate.

The merchant prince shook his head and growled, "I don't owe Brenna, but *you* do. I wasn't sure of that until I watched you toadying up to her in there. You're her property. So I'll give you fair warning: Keep yourself and your damned trogs out of my way. This Conference is mine! I won't tolerate interference from Brenna or any of her fawning acolytes. I keep track of my enemies, and from now on, you're one of them. Stand in my path and you'll get hurt!"

With that, he brushed past his kinsman and stalked off down the hall. His aides tripped over themselves trying to fall into step behind him as Colin rushed by the security checkpoint. The SMEI guards snickered at the pompous parade. Colin was too mad to respond. His little group swept into an elevator and dropped out of sight.

Anthony leaned against the wall, breathing hard, composing

208

himself. It was several minutes before he dared follow his cousin's course, and he did so much more slowly. By the time he reached the SMEI station, he wore an air of sophisticated detachment.

"Have a good talk with Captain Saunder, sir?" a guard asked innocently.

"Yes, fine, thank you."

"Is that Whimed opening ceremony going to be any good?" another staffer wondered.

Smiling, Anthony invited, "If you're off duty then, watch it and judge for yourselves. David Lavrik's a star of tomorrow, and Yrae Usin Hilandro is sensational."

"Yeah? Hey, maybe we'll do just that."

Anthony continued moving at a steady, unhurried pace into the elevator car. He threw a salute to the guards and waited calmly for the doors to close.

They did. And he couldn't remember his assigned floor. Jesse had told him, but the number had slipped his mind. No wonder! After the last hour's events, he was lucky if he could remember his name!

It took a frantic mental search to recall what he needed. Anthony punched in a fourth-floor program and the car began to descend, playing out the earlier ride in reverse. Model-sized structures and figures rushed up toward him. He didn't see them. He was elsewhere—in a shadowy hall, facing Colin. The fair-haired, dark-eyed little boy on Saunderhome's terrace was now a powerful and dangerous adult, packing a storehouse of long-nursed grudges and imagined insults. The news of Carissa's death had touched off an explosion in Colin Saunder's psyche.

It wasn't a game anymore. Colin's hatred had come to a boil. He lacked the guts to tell Captain Saunder what he thought of her. Instead, he had hidden in the darkness outside her door and cursed her. It was Anthony's bad luck to blunder into that hiding place.

The clone had drawn the fire the bastard wanted to aim at Brenna.

But a lot of that fire had been meant for him alone. In this instance Colin had hit him with words. Next time?

The elevator stopped. Anthony stood very still, staring at the green world below—Colin's world, a Settlement Colin had chosen because it so closely resembled Saunderhome, Carissa's castle on the Caribbean that Colin Saunder could never own.

Anthony would never own it, either. And despite his cousin's warped view of the universe, Anthony had never enjoyed any of the sixteen years he'd spent trapped on that paradise island. For him, it had been a literal hell on Earth.

Colin was yearning for the unattainable, without hope of revenge on the woman who had driven him into exile and caused his mother's death.

Carissa was my tyrant, too. She created me, produced my pain. And like Colin, I can't get even with her. She's forever out of our reach.

He swung at the elevator's wall. A fragment of sanity stopped Anthony millimeters from disaster. He pulled his punch, his knuckles almost but not quite touching the unyielding metal. Gulping for breath, he forced himself to open his fists, shuddering. How close he'd come to slipping over the edge! Colin had done that—and made a fool of himself in front of those SMEI staffers and his own flunkies. Now Anthony was showing the same juvenile lack of discipline.

I'm sick of swallowing dirty jokes and smiling at my insulters. I'm sick of sly remarks about clones. And I'm sick of Colin—sick of his lies and mealymouthing and accusations and sick of his thinking he's the only Saunder who ever got a dirty deal. I should have gone ahead and hit him. Maybe it would have knocked some sense into him, and it would have made me feel a hell of a lot better!

He's conjuring up phantoms to hate. What does he have to be angry about? He's on top, rich, a kingmaker. And he envies Brenna, wants more, and sees enemies where none exist.

"*Keep yourself and your damned trogs out of my way.*"

Anthony wondered just how he was going to do that. And why should he? All the Settlement delegations had a job to do here. Sooner or later, he was bound to end up on the opposite side of an issue, not only from Colin but from a lot of important people. The Terran worlds had never moved in lockstep. That was why there was a C.S.P. Council, to try to work out a system that accommodated the varied frontier planets. Colin was demanding the same sort of spineless toadying from Anthony that he accused his cousin of giving Captain Saunder.

Anger became stubborn resolve. He was *not* going to be

Colin's puppet. He wouldn't go out of his way to draw his kins-man's wrath, but he wouldn't allow Colin to push around Pro-cyon Five's delegates, either. And if Colin tried to make trouble because of that, Anthony Saunder just might make trouble for Colin. The merchant prince would find there were other ways to control public opinion besides using money. Give Saunder Studio a juicy propaganda script it could run with, and Colin would be sorry he started this. Anthony had survived Carissa's tyranny and Stuart's. He could cope with Carissa's grandson and Stuart's bas-tard!

It'd be a tightrope walk, avoiding that head-on clash. But as Jesse would no doubt say, "What else is new?" It was just one more burden, like chairing the delegation, directing the Whimeds' drama, and avoiding political involvements that didn't benefit his Settlement.

Nothing to it!

Grinning wryly at his self-directed sarcasm, Anthony tripped the elevator's door mechanism and headed for his delegation's rooms. He had no time to waste if he hoped to succeed in this impossible juggling act.

CHAPTER THIRTEEN

✪✪✪✪✪✪✪✪

Encounters

"Yes, I have your memo with me," Anthony said. "I've already added it to our negotiations package. We'll certainly want to bring up those points during the joint sessions with Whimed Colony Chayn and the Aquatic Settlements Consortium."

"All five of us," the woman on half of the monitor's split screen commented sourly. She spoke both to Anthony and the Procyon Five delegate sharing this mini-conference via Enclave com net. "You get so bogged down in details, L.G., you can't see the ocean."

"Better than you, Jade," the brawny industrialist retorted. "All you're interested in is mining. I'm considering our entire world's future trading interests. If you want to limit our work here solely to mineral extraction, you might as well strike an agreement with Colin Saunder. That's *his* main money-maker."

Jade Herbst flared angrily, and Anthony drowned out both delegates. "There's space for our individual concerns on the agenda, I assure you. I suggest—"

"Haven't got time to argue now, Saunder. Getting ready for that zoo the ITC host calls 'an interspecies social acquaintance facilitator,' L. G. Carmichael grumbled. "You'd better get ready, too, Jade. Takes you longer than it does us."

The business moguls continued to wrangle. Anthony sighed, leaning back from the terminal.

"Sir?" David Lavrik stood beside him, striking a dramatic pose. "I think I have that sentence now. Would you correct me if I'm wrong?" The actor peered over Anthony's head at stage scenery that didn't exist in this cramped little room. "'Trust! Without that, we have nothing. Only . . . chaos.'" Lavrik's gaze snapped back into focus, locked on his director. "Is that it?"

"Sounds very good," Anthony said quite sincerely. "Just the right number of beats. Keep it that way. Boost it even more, if you can, during the performance."

Carmichael and Herbst were still snarling at each other from their separate quarters and, whether he wanted to hear their quarrel or not, at Anthony. He switched the private squabble off, leaving the monitor churning out scenes from the Conference Complex network HQ.

The same promo. It ran constantly. Anthony had caught glimpses of the thing throughout the four days he'd been on Procyon Four, at preliminary delegation caucuses, in the main building, helping set up stage arrangements for the Whimed Committee's opening ceremonies, and during yesterday's lengthy dress rehearsals and the press conference that followed. *That* had been an ordeal and a half for the project's stars, director, and crew, answering inane and sometimes hostile questions for several hours, standing still for countless holo-modes, and coping with translation devices and the unfamiliar behaviors of Lannon, Rigotian, and Ulisorian versions of hard-nosed reporters. At every break, every moment of rest, there was inevitably a monitor somewhere within view, churning out what amounted to a shameless puffery for Colin Saunder.

Anthony analyzed the lens work and editing. Slick but uninspired. His Studio could have done a much better job, punched this thing up, and given it some energy.

There were representative travelogues from major planets of the species attending the ITC, introduced by a beaming, posturing Colin, and snippets of amity-extolling speeches by human and alien dignitaries, interspersed with comments from Colin. Anthony could recite the lofty sentiments and Colin's chatter from memory by now.

And then came a sanitized quick-tour of the Conference host's world, showing lush landscapes, thriving industries, exotic habitats, and a treetop landing pad in Jangala, with a roc on a takeoff run and then airborne. Booster implants gave the cyborg climbing speed and power no ordinary animal could command. The roc soared above the continent-wide greenbelt.

Colin's voice-over continued as the travelogue and tour rolled on. Anthony had assessed his cousin's performance professionally, trying to separate personal enmity from judgment. Colin wasn't bad. No David Lavrik, but capable. But it was a good thing he wasn't doing this vid with emota-sensors; Anthony was sure the blond's projections would reveal the phoniness and insincerity behind the grand words.

More shots showed a fruitful agricultural region in Four's southern temperate zone. Now the roc and its taping crew were flying beyond the agri belt and grasslands, out onto the desert. Telltale shifts revealed where the vid had been condensed. In real time, the roc arrived in Metallon City, at the edge of the southern polar mountains, in slightly over an hour. Those booster implants really flew!

There were more visual summaries and laudatory voice-overs, more scenes of contented citizenry and clockwork-smooth commerce, with no flaws anywhere. No squatter camps, no boomtowns, and no ramshackle huts on the fringes of population centers appeared. No rougher elements and no broken-down mines or abandoned factories or plants were shown.

It was boring and unbelievable. Anthony snorted. His cousin was a fool. Who did he think this promo would convince? Any delegate would know that it was too slick. Did Colin think his extraterrestrial guests were so naive?

He should have come to me. Saunder Studio could put together a package that would really sell Procyon Four for him.

In his mind's eye, Anthony saw an ocean king. The cephalopod seemed to symbolize indigenous life-forms and hostile environments. Everywhere that *Homo sapiens* ventured, terrain, atmosphere, or biota reminded mankind that it was not the first species to occupy that niche. Back on Earth, there were still areas and fauna and flora that resisted humanity's encroachments. Adaptation and delicate balance was the rule, always. On Colin's promo vid, untamed creatures peeped from the jungle foliage. And at his estate outside Metallon, sand drifted into the courtyard

214

despite the best efforts of robot and human caretakers. So why did Colin pretend the laws didn't apply to him and his Settlement?

The star-roving species had to accept the strange new planets they had discovered. That was what set them apart from the stay-at-homes on their planets of origin. The risks *there* were small. The risks on the frontier worlds were great, and so were the rewards. Colin had much to be proud of in Procyon Four. Why did he want to turn back the clock and ape Saunderhome? *This* was his place, his future. He was stupid not to see that.

Now he was host of the Interspecies Trade Conference. And his man Simpkins was a strong candidate for the C.S.P. presidency. Yet neither seemed able to see the reality of what must be—cutting the ties to Earth. It had to be done, sooner or later, hopefully not in anger. Colin's cousin Regan understood that completely, and she was only twenty-one; he had sixteen additional years' experience on the young woman, yet in this matter, he behaved as if he were still four, standing on the lawn of Saunderhome, aching for what he could never have.

The small room's outer door slid open. A flood of sound from the hall poured inside. David Lavrik had been rereading Dempsey's script one more time, striving for nuances. He glanced up, and Anthony turned from the monitor, glad for any diversion. Jesse and Margaret Orr squirmed between the closely arranged beds, luggage, and chairs. "Thought we'd never get through that mob out there!" Jesse exclaimed. "Everybody's revving up for the dog-and-pony show."

Anthony said, "Colin calls it an interspecies social acquaintance facilitator."

"Sure he does. Kingmakers always use fancy words. I say it's a chance for the big shots to show off, and the hell with it. Maggie, do your stuff."

Orr carefully unwrapped the package she was carrying and shook out its contents—the priceless echinoderm cape. Anthony inhaled sharply. "You fixed it!"

"Good as new, almost," the Studio's wardrobe mistress said. "Nobody but me could spot the repairs. Here, David, slip it on. Let's see how it looks." The actor obliged, modeling the cloak, turning rapidly, making the material billow. The effect was all the Whimed Committee could hope for.

Anthony planted a juicy kiss on Margaret Orr's brow. "You're a genius. I don't pay you enough. And starting now, you're getting a raise!" He didn't add his pessimistic conditional clause: "*If I don't go bankrupt because of taking on this crazy project in the first place.*"

Lavrik also thanked the hard-working craftswoman at length. As Margaret headed back out into the corridor, Jesse told the actor, "Okay, enough recess. Get back to work on your lines. Dig, dig, dig!" The young man grinned and ducked into the connecting room to fine-tune his role in relative quiet.

"That cape ought to pass inspection," Anthony said. "But I still wonder where it was, for the day and a half the luggage was missing."

"Missing?" Jesse's expression was dark. "Stolen, you mean. Damn Colin, anyway."

"We can't prove it was his fault. Yrae pointed out that if it was Colin's doing, he'd have stolen and vandalized *my* clothes, not David's costume."

"Same difference." The associate producer glowered at the mute monitor scenes of the Conference host's world. The promo ran in an endless loop, inescapable. "He sabotages Davy's costume, he sabotages you and the production you're directing."

Anthony shook his head. "Yrae convinced me that it was the Biyelin Vahnajes. Makes sense, after what they've already done to try to wreck this project." His friend grunted, unpersuaded.

There was no proof either way—just the temporary disappearance of one set of luggage cases between Jangala Terminal and the Conference complex. The entire Terran crew as well as the Whimed Committee had searched frantically for Lavrik's missing cases—and the expensive, hand-sewn cloak one contained, meeting dead end after dead end. Contradicting Jesse's suspicions, Colin's staffers had helped at each stage of the hunt; they were sincerely upset that a guest's property had been stolen.

Majlur had finally found the cases hidden in a little-used storage area. Conference staffers had been appalled when they saw the vandalized cloak and had offered to replace it. But the cape couldn't be replaced at *any* expense, in time for the Whimed Committee's opening ceremonies. Whoever had slashed the delicate, silky pelts must have known that. Without Margaret Orr's superlative skills, the garment would still be in ruins, and an important advertising feature of the Janyavee-Dempsey drama would be lost.

There had been an attempt to make the damage look like an accident. The cases were dented, as if they had fallen from a skimmer's cargo bay and smashed on rocks. But the only thing inside that had suffered was the cape. That, at least, seemed proof of definite tampering.

"Majlur didn't give you a hint on how he located David's luggage?" Anthony asked.

"Nope. But pastyface isn't exactly a chatterbox. We owe him plenty," Jesse said, "though I wish we didn't. He gives me the creeps."

Anthony nodded. "He gives them to Yrae, too."

"Then why doesn't she fire him? She's the muckety-muck."

"I don't know. Whimed politics, maybe." Anthony pinched the bridge of his nose, prodding at an incipient headache. "Maybe he's her distant cousin and she owes him a favor."

But that wasn't possible. *I am separate. Alone.* Yrae Usin Hilandro had no cousins.

"As long as we got the costume back in time, it ain't our problem, kid." Jesse slapped Anthony's shoulder. "Speaking of business, you'd better get moving. The Governor and the other delegates are gathering out there in the elevator lobby. They'll be looking for their chairman."

"A couple of them are going to be late. I dropped out of a marathon argument between Carmichael and Herbst shortly before you and Margaret got here." Anthony set the ubiquitous monitor to blank screen and began putting on his best tunic and slacks. "I'm tired of playing referee to that pair. Are you coming to the—the dog-and-pony show?"

"Pilar and I will be up in the press gallery," Jesse said with a grin, "watching all you V.I.P.s strut your stuff."

"Be sure to plug the drama and the emota-sensor package the Studio will issue after the Conference."

"Hey! You think I'm going to talk to those reporters for my health? Damned right I'll plug it, kid. And you keep busy down on the main floor. Knock 'em dead with your scintillating presence and famous name."

By the time Anthony made his way to the elevators, L.G. Carmichael and Jade Herbst had also arrived. Apparently they had declared a truce in their ongoing debate long enough to attend the general mixer. Down in the Terran enclave's lobby,

217

things were jammed. Delegations rendezvoused, funneling off toward the arcade leading to the main complex buildings.

The plaza was multispecies confusion. Yrae's delegation was waiting for Procyon Five's. It had been agreed in advance that she would split her time this evening between her Federation's various attending groups and Anthony's. That was part of the deal to boost Terran-Whimed trade negotiations and seal the bargain with Yamashita's settlers.

The alien actress greeted each member of Anthony's team by name and title, flattering and impressing them. She shook hands. The Governor preened and said, "I hope you have not waited long on us, *Irasten*."

"Not at all. Pilar Gutierrez has coordinated time . . . is it timetable? . . . expertly. Shall we enter the social facilitator together?"

A few trogs wrinkled their noses at that term. Governor Yamashita ignored his colleagues' sneers. He allowed himself the satisfaction of escorting Yrae through the huge building's exterior gate. Then, as a canny politician, he yielded the actress to Anthony—the delegation's chairman and director of the Whimed Committee's project. That made Anthony a walking advertisement for Procyon Five and the hoped-for trade alliance with felinoid planets. The assembly area between the gate and the main door swarmed with spectators, lesser staff members of various delegations, and media stringers. Interviews were not allowed here, but nothing stopped the onlookers from taking hundreds of tri-di candids. Yrae and Anthony were a magnet for most eyes—she wearing a white-and-gold gown that fit her like a second skin, Anthony looking regal and confident in a severe, dark-blue business suit.

Things were going well, until they were beyond the hall's entrance. A staff guard stopped the procession, pointing to Anthony. "Sorry, sir. Only accredited delegates are permitted on the central level. Secondary tickets must go up to the press and guests' gallery."

Yamashita cried, "What do you mean? Saunder is our chairman!"

"I just do as I'm told, sir."

Anthony concealed his rage behind a mask of bemusement. This had to be another of Colin's backhanded tactics.

Or did it?

Yrae's crest had stiffened. She was staring at a Vahnaj who stood a few meters away from the combined Terran-Whimed delegate group. Anthony followed Yrae's gaze, trying to identify the alien. A whiteface! Biyelin!

Perhaps this red-tape barricade the staffer was throwing in front of Anthony *wasn't* his cousin's fault. But there was a dark alternate possibility: Colin's mercantile allies were Vahnajes, and he made no secret of it. Were any of those Vahnajes Biyelins?

Before the situation could get nasty, a second Terran staffer rushed up and whispered in the ear of the first. There were nervous coughs and apologies. "There—there seems to have been a mistake. Very sorry for the error, Chairman. Please go right in."

The Biyelin Vahnaj, plainly irked, swung away, long robes swirling. Going to report a failure to a superior? And what would be the report? Had the Biyelins meant to inconvenience and embarrass Anthony and the Procyon Five delegation? Or had they intended to strike at the Whimed Committee? They'd already attempted that with their elaborate scheme to destroy David Lavrik's ability to perform in the Committee's opening presentation.

"Well!" Governor Yamashita said. "That was uncalled for! Who do they think they are?"

Yrae trembled with rage. Anthony said softly, "No harm done. He *did* back off. I wonder whom we have to thank for that?"

The actress's eyes were starry pools, her crest softening. For a heartbeat, he felt that special rapport—sharing Yrae's anger on his behalf and her gratitude for his calm assurance.

Anthony felt other emotions as well. A dread of behaving unethically in the presence of witnesses. Doubt. A yearning for...

The sensuality in that last was powerful. He couldn't be wrong about his reading of that wave length.

Then it was gone. So was the rest of it. Yrae was back within herself, her crest completely relaxed, her manner unperturbed. She smiled at the Governor. "Shall we enter the hall?" Slyly Yrae added, "Now that permission is given."

She led the parade. Heads turned. Yrae Usin Hilandro had planned her effect well. Her shimmering costume was designed to please both Terran and felinoid tastes, and to be a spectacular advance advertisement for tomorrow's drama at the opening ceremonies. The snug white fabric subtly outlined her tiny multiple breasts. Gold sleeves and slashed skirt softened the gown's severity. Anthony's experience in front of lenses and behind them told him he made a handsome contrast to her glittering paleness. He played to the watching media and other delegates shamelessly, a thing he hadn't done since he'd worked for Li Lao Chang.

Then he began circulating, usually with Procyon Five's delegates. Now and then they were accompanied by Yrae; her particular group of Whimed delegates made a point of touring the large room in close proximity with their new Terran trading partners. No one could miss the connection, and several reps from other Terran Settlements struck up friendly conversations, obviously hoping there was business enough to spare in the Whimed Federation. Perhaps there'd be a surplus to export to *their* Settlements. And while they were at it, they'd heard the trogs had some interesting products to market.

Much of the evening would be devoted to the Conference big shots, in on-the-spot interviews and being seen and recorded in the company of the Conference host or important politicians or alien authority figures. Yrae was coming in for numerous such calls on her attention.

But in and around the stars, the little guys were starting the real business of the ITC, making acquaintances, learning about their near and far stellar neighbors, and becoming easier with the customs of humans who followed a very different life-style, or with nonhumans and their cultures and languages.

There were translators, living and mechanical. Staffers and aides were everywhere one looked, eager to fetch and carry or provide information. Broad scan and closeup monitors overviewed the entire affair; the screens ringed the hall's perimeter and studded refreshment areas and the Vahnaj "eating privacy cubicles" scattered throughout the room.

"Hall" was a misnomer. This wasn't a single structure but a melding of six separate mini-auditoriums into one. The arrangement would be used during tomorrow's opening ceremonies, too. After that, workers would break up the enormous gathering place into numerous chambers of graduated sizes for caucuses and trade discussions.

Occasionally Anthony glanced up to a mezzanine level—the press and guests' gallery. Once he saw Pilar and Jesse leaning over the railing and waved to them. Then a potential marketer of

Saunder Studio's releases wanted to talk to him and he had to give the woman his full attention.

That was a rare instance. Most of the time Anthony didn't dare devote his whole focus to any one person or stay in any one part of the hall. He was the delegation chairman, often called on to break up an incipient quarrel between a trog businessman and a competitor from a rival Terran world or to grease introductions between mutually interactive industrialists who might be on the verge of setting up an import and export arrangement advantageous to both planets. He was the Whimed Committee's producer-director, chatting with felinoids Taisso or another member of the Committee brought to him; praising the adaptation of the Janyavee classic and pushing hard the bilingual vid packages —emota-sensor enhanced, of course!—which would be sold in the Terran and Whimed sectors later. And he was Anthony Saunder, a minor twig on the Terran dynasty's towering family tree, accosted by reporters and Conference attendees curious to meet any segment of that famous clan.

Amid it all, he needed to keep his eyes and ears open and learn, the better to lead his delegates, the better to avoid problems between species, and the better to survive in the intensifying political duel that was heating up the Terran sphere of influence.

There were rivalries among humans and rivalries among the aliens.

The Whimed-Vahnaj rivalry was the most apparent. Nominally the Interspecies Trade Conference was a neutral zone. Delegates of all races exchanged courtesies when they met. But the felinoids and lutrinoids made no pretense of friendship. Encounters were solely by mischance, it seemed, and the words traded were cold.

Lannon matriarchs and their entourages of husbands, servants, kids, and who-knew-what-else barged in and out of conversations. They were wheeling and dealing on their own basis, keeping the translators and the cultural interpreters very busy, and dickering with would-be clients—while those clients' advisors cautioned going slow and nailing the Lannons down firmly with an enforceable treaty. The procyonids seemed to enjoy starting conversations—or shouting matches—simultaneously with Vahnajes and Whimeds, as if relishing those two species' awkwardness around each other.

Rigotians and Ulisorians were the newest races to begin attending these Conferences. Their representation here was small and quite tentative. The blue-skinned, nest-oriented Rigotians circled the hall in clusters, eyeing other beings warily, only rarely using their trans-devices to approach someone and feel out the possibility of trade agreements. A very few Ulisorian delegates floated slowly about, riding their air-supported platforms, peering interestedly out of their pressure suits' faceplates at the strange humanoids filling the same space with them. Once, Anthony saw an Ulisorian stop at a Vahnaj product display and conduct a labored attempt at speech with the attending lutrinoid merchants. So it appeared even when the racial divisions were severe, cross-species communication—and with luck, trade—*was* possible.

Anthony mingled, shook hands, and smiled and smiled until he thought his face would crack, dodging masses of Whimeds who had suddenly decided to huddle and avoiding looking at Vahnajes emerging from the concealment of their eating cubicles, lest they be offended at a nonlutrinoid observing them doing such a personal thing; Ambassador Quol-Bez was the only Vahnaj Anthony had ever met who didn't care if other beings saw him dining. He walked from one refreshment island to another, meeting people. The islands were mini-enclaves, re-creating the preferred environments of the various delegates. Dimly lit Vahnaj islands were occupied by quiet, slow-speaking lutrinoids. Those dominated by Biyelin Vahnajes, though, tended to be noisier, and the Vahnajes there noticeably argumentative. Brightly lit Whimed islands hummed with activity. Yrae Usin Hilandro was much in demand at these and had to make a stop at each one of them. Lannon islands were crowded with burly females and their smaller males, bustling around realistic campfires beneath an illusionary open sky. Rigotian islands were fenced polygons crammed with odd art objects and clashing music; nest members gathered there, peering silently at one another as if spellbound for minutes on end. The Ulisorians' island was a shrunken copy of their residence enclave—a miniature pressure dome.

Entertainment was provided on many of the islands. There was plenty of food and drink, including intoxicants; and some delegates were wasting no time dipping into those—liquids, fermented roots, and stinking little cakes of . . . stuff. Anthony suspected *that* particular aspect of Colin's catering service might be a handicap to serious, meaningful discussion. Many of the Terrans Anthony met were plainly several sheets to the wind already.

He'd never seen a drunken e.t. until this night. Now he was beginning to see them frequently. When a dignitary became obstreperous or ill, aides did their best to remove the being before an unfortunate incident could occur. Overindulgence didn't affect the species identically, nor each indulger within those species the same. But a drunk was a drunk; none of the races wanted outsiders to witness their V.I.P.s in less than tautly logical modes. And some of the drunks became very unlogical.

Yrae, Anthony noticed, did little more than nibble on the Whimeds' favorite mood alterant, a potent root imported from their Federation especially for the Conference. Ironically, Anthony knew he *could* function quite well with a considerable quantity of alcohol on board. He'd found that out years ago. He'd found out, too, that he paid a high price in nervous tension to control himself while he was drinking. It wasn't worth it, not tonight. He wanted a totally clear head to cope with whatever came at him down the canal.

"Mejuo, thor-i-saduo . . ."

"So happy to meet you, Vice Premier . . ."

"Irast, midow fo grivell . . ."

"Congratulations on your recent appointment, sir . . ."

"Si chi-ill ying durit coya, Lannon NiJoop . . ."

"Thank you, Madam Chairman. I am happy that you enjoy my Studio's presentation of *A Long Way from Earth* . . ."

Anthony chatted with captains of industry, Space Fleet officers, leading settlers and colonists from dozens of worlds. He spoke, too, with ordinary citizens who'd won their delegates' credentials the hard way. He tended to identify with those.

Once or twice he caught someone eyeing him condescendingly, as if to ask, "What's a small-time company owner like *him* doing here?" or "What's a *trog* doing here?" But no one was rude enough to challenge him or any other member of Procyon Five's delegation. Were the veiled sneers aimed in his direction because he was active in the entertainment industry? That was a low-level contributor to Settlement survival, in some industrialists' opinions. Or were those occasional scowls coming his way the result of his uniqueness as a clone? It didn't matter, as long as the scowlers and sneerers didn't call him out publicly. None did. In fact, he was surprised and pleased by the general respect he received. Maybe, just maybe, Jesse was right about certain things.

"Sir . . . *Irasten.*"

Yrae's course through the room had brought her into Anthony's proximity once more. They had been walking side by side for some time, greeting delegates together as top representatives of the Whimed Committee's project. Now a man wearing an SMEI security badge was bowing to them.

"Captain Saunder invites you to join her on her comfort island." Comfort island? That was a quaint term, common in the last century, but now out of fashion. Brenna was dating herself by using the phrase. The guard said, "May I show you the way?"

Yrae turned gleaming eyes up to Anthony. "I would be most honored to meet your kinswoman." Her eagerness wasn't a courteous pose.

Anthony was sourly amused. No doubt Yrae *would* be honored to meet the most illustrious member of the famous Saunder-McKelveys. He waved to the security guard to lead on.

They followed him through the crowds to the area where Captain Saunder was holding court. Hers was the largest island set aside for the use of Terran delegations. There was no throne, and Brenna was standing, but the effect was that of a royal presence chamber. Her siblings, children, wards, their friends, and their spouses were stopping by here to touch base. Those constant comings and goings reinforced the image of a powerful ruling dynasty. Media hawks hovered nearby, recording. No family member attending the ITC was exempt from the obligation to greet the Captain, not even the clone and the bastard.

Colin was just completing his courtesy visit. Saying the proper things, bending gallantly over Brenna's hand. As phony as an air-breathing octopoid, in Anthony's estimation. The merchant prince's smile was plastered firmly in place. It didn't falter even when he stepped off the platform and saw Anthony approaching. "Good evening, cousin. I trust you and the lovely *Irasten* are enjoying yourself? Stay on your toes. The grande dame of SMEI is in top fettle." Colin touched his feathered hat, nodding to Yrae and to the onlooking reporters, and moved on, trailed, as always, by a flock of flunkies.

"He dislikes us intensely," Yrae whispered, as aware as Colin had been of the media eavesdroppers.

"I'm afraid you're suffering guilt by association with me—and he's hated *me* since we were children."

Brenna prowled the refreshment island restlessly. The aging test pilot wasn't a sedentary type, and she would have preferred roaming the hall instead of having people come to her. SMEI policy dictated her behavior, however. It was more sensible for her to stay put, reigning as a mercantile monarch, so that all those who wanted to speak to Captain Saunder would know where to find her. Anthony regarded her with pity; she reminded him of a caged predator.

His kinswoman brightened when she saw him and Yrae. "So you finally made it over to the old lady's bailiwick, eh? About time! Been watching you two on the monitors." Brenna gestured to the ever-present screens. "You're putting on quite a show. *Ir-asten* Yrae Usin Hilandro, I've been waiting to meet you. Looking forward to your performance."

"I bring you warm greetings from the Whimed Federation, Captain. You are well known to us and much admired. I, too, look forward—to many years of friendly association with you and all Terrans."

"You're off to a good start here at the Conference," Brenna acknowledged. "Don't waste any time, any of you." There was a hint of waspishness in the words. Was Brenna still smarting because Whimed techs were helping Serge Bolotin accelerate Hiber-Ship to an early landfall, with Brenna's former lover aboard? If she was, Anthony's kinswoman didn't let that wreck the conversation. "How do you like working with the owner of Saunder Studio?"

The abrupt change of topic didn't bother Yrae a bit. "It is most stimulating. Anthony is an excellent director. He has guided me and my fellow actor, David Lavrik, well. Our Committee is quite satisfied."

"Better be! Anthony's the best there is at what he does." Brenna stepped back a pace, surveying the alien woman's costume. "What a gorgeous outfit!"

Yrae accepted the compliment gracefully and returned, "Your gown is very attractive, too, Captain. Is it not, Anthony?"

"Yes. She looks good in green. The first time I saw her, she was wearing that color." Both women eyed him wonderingly. Anthony went on, "It was at Saunderhome. Years ago. I was very young."

Brenna was astounded. "That was the night Carissa announced Stuart's marriage to Felicity Emigh! My God! I hadn't thought of that in . . . I *did* meet you boys then, didn't I? You and your brothers."

225

"Three of them," he amended tonelessly. "Drake was dead by that time."

There was a hushed pause amid the jabber and clangor of music in the huge room. Brenna murmured, "I'd almost forgotten that green dress and that time period."

"So had I," Anthony confessed. "It was a painful memory for both of us, in many respects. You were sweating out the development of FTL, and your cousin Morgan had been terribly injured."

"Yes, yes." Brenna plainly wanted to sweep the past out of her hearing. She rushed into other matters. "Do you know everybody here? This is Dorothea."

Anthony extended a hand to another of Morgan McKelvey's posthumous heirs, saying, "We've met. Good to see you again, Dot." There were general introductions, with Anthony helping Yrae over the Terran names and relationships. Dorothea Bigelow McKelvey. Lara and Lee McKelvey, twins, two more of Brenna's wards. Reid was elsewhere at that moment, the Captain explained. James O'Brien, Dorothea's husband, was a C.S.P. official, eager to talk politics. So was Lara McKelvey's lover, Jack Frei, Vice-Governor of Settlement Vaughn. Lara and her brother Lee refused to allow the conversation to be dominated by the current campaign, though. That pair were strikingly different from the other wards, with their oriental features. Lee, like O'Brien, tended to stick to a single line of chatter, but his was business, not politics.

"Lee," Captain Saunder growled, "if you want to talk shop, go on over there and cut some deals with Putnam. We need those tie-ins with the new Charter Corporation she and the Muirs are setting up. Get Blake in on the confab. Amber Muir's had hormones for *him* for months. We might as well put Mother Nature to work for us."

He was happy to obey. "Will do, cousin! Rely on it."

As Lee hurried off, Brenna grinned and said, "I sure can! With him and Blake at the controls, old-timers like me and Yuri can sit back and take it easy." Her expression became wistful as she looked at her younger relatives. "Good thing Lee's a work hog. He and Blake will have to take over the main branch of SMEI some day. Ivan's got his own boat to row. And Varenka's so wrapped up lately in that damned Spirit of Humanity rebirth cult back on Earth she's letting some company stuff slide. And God knows what Regan intends to do with her life."

At that moment, a broad-shouldered young man leaped onto the refreshment island and caught Regan Saunder up in a bear hug. Yrae gawked. Anthony explained, recognizing the young man from newscasts. "That's Malcolm Griffith. He and Regan are . . ." Understanding bloomed on Yrae's face. Surprise became tolerant amusement. Was she pegging Griffith as Regan's "*Muruen-che*"?

No. The alien understood far more than Anthony had given her credit for. "*Aaa!* This is the son of the man you wish to lead your Charter Settlement Planets."

He eyed her sidelong. "Correct, although Malcolm's not in politics like his father. He's an executive with a major Terran communications nets."

"Then he is . . . how is it? In position to influence opinions? He will be of assistance in the renegotiation of debts your Settlements must pay to your birth world." Anthony nodded, and Yrae smiled knowingly at the embracing couple.

It was one of those moments when Anthony felt daunted by the Whimeds' cultural treasure. She knew an awfully damned lot about Terran politics, trade, and monetary difficulties—far more than he knew about the felinoids' internal problems. He'd have to work harder, catch up with her, if Procyon Five was going to enter into future commerce exchanges with Yrae's people. Ignorance in such cases was not only embarrassing; it could become very, very expensive.

CHAPTER FOURTEEN

✪✪✪✪✪✪✪✪

Discoveries

They remained on Captain Saunder's island for some time, chatting with the Saunders, the McKelveys, and their friends, being awed as Lara McKelvey, a linguist, switched flawlessly from one Terran and alien tongue to another, and eavesdropping as Lee and Blake engaged in an earnest conversation with a beautiful blond woman, heiress Amber Muir. Regan Saunder sounded out Anthony on possible investments in Procyon Five's products and expressed her wistful interest in Colin's world and its financial potential as well—"except he won't allow me to purchase any shares or have any input." In Anthony's opinion, Colin was a fool for rejecting that offer; Regan was wise beyond her years regarding C.S.P. affairs, and any Settlement that turned down her money was missing a lucrative opportunity.

Despite his unusual origins, Anthony fitted into the family picture smoothly this evening. Yrae eyed him enviously, seeing him belonging to others, as she did not. When Ambassador Quol-Bez arrived at Captain Saunder's island to tender his greetings, Anthony sensed an unexpected enlargement of that intimate rapport he shared with Yrae. Briefly, cross-species empathy included *three* beings.

Yrae? Empathizing with a Vahnaj? No matter that the Ambassador was that rare thing, an honorable lutrinoid in her eyes, he was one of her species' enemies. What could she have in common with the alien diplomat, except . . . Loneliness!

He had been cut off from his people through those sacrificial "excisions" his government had demanded before he undertook his mission to Earth. And Yrae was separate, was always separate, and would always be separate—but not when she touched without touching Anthony Saunder and the elderly statesman of the Vahnaj Alliance. Quol-Bez could never really go home. Anthony had never *had* a real home. And Yrae felt she had never belonged—really—to anyone or anything. They were each, in their own ways, separate.

That tenuous contact strengthened. The Ambassador did not seem aware of its intensification. Anthony did. He sensed a darker element, surging—that dread of failure, again. Failure of ethics, of meeting impossibly high standards of conduct, and hatred for the necessity of . . .

The rapport was gone, like icy water smashing into rocks.

Yrae was wide-eyed, a plea in her starburst pupils. She silently begged Anthony to keep her secrets.

What secrets? He didn't know what he had made contact with. He had swum in murky currents, finding . . . *something*. There was no name for it.

Yrae blinked, and the barrier was solidly in place. She was totally separate once more, breaking all empathic links with him and the Ambassador.

No, the link wasn't quite gone. There was a lifeline drifting through those dark currents. A minute fragment of what they had shared remained.

Anthony put his body and brain on automatic, going through the social motions, thinking hard. When enough time had elapsed that they could leave the island without the risk of seeming too rude, they rejoined the stream of humanoids in the hall, saying nothing to one another. Anthony suspected that Yrae, like himself, was trying to figure out what had just happened to them.

Shortly Yrae was escorted away to meet more Whimed delegates, and Anthony resumed his routine of pressing the flesh and doing his bit as Procyon Five's chairman. Unlike Lara McKelvey, he was no linguist, though his command of Basic Vahnaj and Basic Whimed was fair. He had to resort frequently to translators, either a nearby staffer or one of the interspecies devices many of the other staffers carried for the attendees' convenience. Sometimes it was necessary to ask for a translation when he was speaking to humans, fellow settlers. Slang sprang up so quickly, and accents were becoming ever more distinctive. He recalled mentioning that problem to Brenna, weeks ago—the gap between the Settlements, the Colonies, and Earth. That truth was being brought home hard here at the ITC. Guests from Earth had difficulty following the speech patterns of settlers, and settlers often had difficulty communicating with each other.

The gaps were widening between the worlds of the C.S.P. and between them and Earth. Regan was sure that faster communication was the answer. But that alone wouldn't hold mankind's scattered outposts together. Earth's history was being repeated on its stellar frontiers—the hill people and the valley people. Mountainous planets and watery environments failed to appreciate each other's problems. Prosperous Settlements and struggling ones, at odds, talked at cross purposes. Concern with their individual situations and goals bred chauvinism—and separation.

If the rifts became permanent, rapacious elements would move in, and not solely human rapacious elements. No military conquest need be involved. Aggressive mercantile interests, encroaching steadily, could sap what remained of the isolated Terran worlds' sovereignty. They'd end up as a series of weak independencies, none of them able to survive without domineering assistance from outside. And in the end, they'd lose their identities, to become mere appendages of Earth or alien cultures.

Had the Vahnajes and Whimeds gone through the same trial? They had pushed their squabbling factions out of their mainstream, making them splinters, not the solid bulk comprising their species' galactic expansions. Were humanity's pioneers going to end up like the Biyelins and the Whimeds' Outer Satellites—unimportant offshoots shoved into insignificant niches in their sectors? No! They had to meet the challenge and turn fragmentation into diversity.

Anthony roused from introspection. A Terran delegate had spoken to him and was awaiting an answer. "Sorry, sir. It's noisy . . . I didn't—"

"Noisy? Hardly! I work with propulsion systems. Now *that's* noisy!" The middle-aged blond man's Terran English had an Earth-style inflection. His blue eyes twinkled as he said, "What I asked you was, Did Brenna give you any tips on what she's planning for the Transportation Sessions? I know she's got Rolfe and his R&D boys and girls working night and day on something. Brenna's brother-in-law never bothers with anything less than a major invention. It has to be megaton-significant. What is it?"

Anthony admired the stranger's nerve. The man was one of those uncooperative types who refused to wear an ID. "I don't believe I caught your name, sir."

"I didn't give it. But for the record, it's Bolotin, Serge Bolotin. *Do* you know anything?" Anthony considered what to say. That evidently supplied Bolotin with enough of a clue to content him. He grunted and said, "I didn't think you did. Figured it wouldn't hurt to try, though. Free info pops up in the damnedest places, even from a . . ."

He didn't finish. Anthony met the older man's gaze levelly, daring Bolotin to call him a clone to his face. Bolotin didn't. Yet he didn't seem embarrassed by his rudeness, either. Anthony had heard rumors that the new owner of Bolotin Charter Settlement Corporation was a character. Serge certainly lived up to his reputation, and it wasn't a reputation Anthony cared to know better.

"Got an opinion on whether or not we can get this gaggle marching together?" Bolotin wondered cheerfully, waving at the multiracial crowd.

"It can be done. It won't be easy, but it's possible."

The industrialist studied Anthony with new respect, nodding. "I think so, too. So does Brenna, and old Quol-Bez, and probably Harthul of the Whimed Federation. Do you agree, *Irasten*?"

Yrae's tour of the room had brought her back into Anthony's vicinity. She blinked in astonishment at Bolotin's brash question, and he laughed.

"You must be the pretty little cultural treasure all the felinoids have been chattering about. They're hardly huddling this evening, they're so eager to meet you. You look as if you'll give the opening ceremonies some spice for a change. Sure hope so! The last Interspecies Trade Conference on Vahnaj world Lat-Sha was a big fat bore. Well, I'll leave you to your drooling fans, *Irasten*. Have to do some more info digging. Brenna's keeping a damned tight lid on Chapin's discovery, whatever it is, but she won't beat me. I'll find out what she's up to." With that, Bolotin stalked away.

Yrae stared after him. "Harthul Ivion Hilandro has said that Serge Bolotin is . . . most energetic. I must agree."

"No doubt he fits right into the Whimed style of doing business," Anthony said dryly. "You knew Bolotin had hired Whimed techs to boost the arrival time of his older sleep stasis starship?"

"Yes." Simple and direct. No attempt to change the subject or bat her golden eyelashes and pretend innocence. Yrae added, "We have been told that project angers your kinswoman Brenna. Does it also displease you?"

He chuckled. She could be as blunt as Bolotin—and equally full of surprises. "No, I'm not displeased. The stasis ship is Bolotin's concern, not mine. And Brenna's anger is personal. It has nothing to do with the business angle of the deal or the Whimed Federation's cooperation with Bolotin. Serge's actions just happen to step on Captain Saunder's memories." Yrae was intrigued, but Anthony didn't elaborate.

"Then you do not object if Project Whimed-Bolotin continues?"

"Object? I'm hardly in a position to do so," Anthony said. "You talk as if I'm a power dealer, a Bolotin or a Captain Saunder."

"Could you not be?"

He raised an eyebrow. What a farfetched, unrealistic view of the Terran sector she had! Anthony Saunder, a clone, a producer of quickie how-to vids and action-adventure series—a power dealer? A man whose mere word could cancel contracts, seal interspecies treaties, or win elections? Absurd!

"No," he said, his tone very flat. "But as to your question, I don't object to the Whimed-Bolotin deal. And neither does Brenna, on legal grounds. The Whimed Federation never signed the old Hiber-Ship pact. There's no reason why Bolotin can't hire Whimed techs to work on his ship, though he couldn't legally hire Vahnajes. Why did you want to know? Is it something . . . ge-aytan? Unethical, by your standards?"

Yrae flinched. He had scored an unintentional hit. She laid a small hand on his wrist and whispered, "It is aytan. Right and proper. You know so much of our customs, and yet you do not. You are correct to doubt. You must not—must not accept all Whimeds as aytan."

It had taken great effort for her to spit out that warning. Which

232

Whimeds was she referring to? And why had she pushed herself to caution him against those unknown unethical felinoids?

A gulf lay between them—a gulf two evolutions and two civilizations wide. There was no rapport at the moment, but he felt her worry. A Whimed worrying about an alien and compelled to speak to him as honestly as she dared—Anthony couldn't begin to guess what lay behind that impulse. She was an enigma. Edu-vids and daily contact and even sexual experimentation couldn't overcome millennia of differences so quickly. Nevertheless, there *was* contact, from her side of that gulf, and he would do no less.

His hand closed over hers. "Don't concern yourself. I'm not as gullible as you seem to think. I never trust anyone blindly, not a Whimed *or* a Terran. But shouldn't I trust you?"

Yrae's chin went up proudly. "I will not lie to you. Ever. I am Hilandro."

A qualifier popped into his mind: *Yes, but you often choose not to tell me the whole truth, Yrae Usin Hilandro.*

Despite his reservations about her motives, he was grateful. Yrae might have revealed state secrets or simply pushed the rules by handing him this tip-off, but it plainly had been a major concession for her. She'd tried to warn him without being too specific. It was fruitless to query her further. From her angle, she'd already told him more than she should have.

So he should be wary of certain Whimeds. Which Whimeds? And why?

As if in answer to his speculations, Ryseen Simra Hilandro and an aide walked briskly toward him and Yrae. The aliens halted a few meters away, and Ryseen locked stares with her fellow Hilandro. The air around the two women crackled with animosity. Yrae claimed a Hilandro's *diya* wasn't ESP, but it certainly radiated like it, if what the Whimeds were engaging in was *diya*. The wordless duel ended when Ryseen lowered her gaze. Did that mean Yrae had won? Apparently. Her mood softened immediately. She now appeared relaxed, almost bored with the other woman.

Puzzles and more puzzles, and there would be no end to them likely at a multispecies Conference.

Ryseen motioned to her aide and the man minced forward. Yrae stood her ground, deigning to let him murmur in her ear. Then the aide hastily retreated to safety behind Ryseen.

233

Again Yrae's mood shifted mercurially. She was rigid with consternation. Anthony eyed her anxiously, then glanced at Ryseen and the aide. Why hadn't Ryseen delivered the message herself—Hilandro protocol?

Anthony had seen the aide before—on Clay and greeting the Whimed Committee when they first arrived at the Conference site. Somehow, Anthony wasn't surprised to encounter the man now as Ryseen Simra Hilandro's flunky. He and Majlur were two of a kind—sneaky, unobtrusive, and always popping up where they were least expected.

Yrae wasn't comfortable around Majlur, though she tolerated him and made use of his skills. Was Ryseen doing that with her aide? Did the term unethical Whimeds include Majlur and this man? Anthony knew he'd be wasting his time to ask—and if he did so within Ryseen's hearing, it might cause trouble for Yrae. No, better to keep his mouth shut, listen, and learn.

Abruptly Ryseen turned and disappeared into the crowd. Her aide trailed her like a faithful pet. Yrae sighed and said, "Anthony, I have news you must hear. Jesse has left the press gallery. Ryseen's people report that he was most upset. I think perhaps your friend needs you to speak to him. He has returned to your quarters in the Terran Enclave. You will find him there."

Anthony was shaken. Jesse ducking out of a PR bash early? The associate producer never did that. "Are—are you sure?"

Yrae looked annoyed. "It is so. Do not doubt."

There was no rapport—Nothing but her word to go on and his own intuition. He wished he could read Yrae's face and body language more accurately. Lacking that, he simply had to accept what she told him as fact. "I'll check it out."

"I hope Jesse is well," Yrae said sincerely. "I will explain your absence to Governor Yamashita and the others, should they wish to know where you are." Anthony sensed that meant she would cheerfully lie on his behalf. This was a little secret the two of them shared.

And how many others, besides Ryseen and her aide?

It seemed like a long way out of the hall and the complex's lobby and plaza. Fortunately, by now the Terran enclave was nearly deserted. All the delegates and many of the support staffers were in the main building. Anthony found an empty elevator without any difficulty.

Jesse was in their room, just as Yrae and Ryseen's aide had

said. He was slumped in a pullout chair, peering unseeingly at the monitor. The channel was programmed to an exterior view of Jangala and its nearby forests at night—compensation for the Enclave's lesser status rooms having no windows. The scene was beautiful, but it was hardly the sort of thing Jesse would normally select as entertainment. He was using the monitor as mental white noise; the flow of pictures provided focus for a man trying to forget something.

The connecting door to the next room in Saunder Studio's block of chambers was David Lavrik's. He, too, was watching a screen—reviewing rehearsal vids, doing homework. Anthony couldn't fault the actor for laziness. He'd been nose to the grindstone as much as Anthony himself had been these past days since Lavrik had learned he wasn't under a death sentence. It seemed politic not to disturb him or to have him listening in on a private conversation; Anthony closed the door, then pulled a second chair out of its storage slot and sat down opposite his friend. "Yrae said you'd left the dog-and-pony show," Anthony remarked lightly. "Problems?"

The older man's face was unresponsive. Anthony touched Jesse's shoulder. "Hey! Remember me? The big dumb handsome chud? Come on, what's wrong?"

"I—I'm not certain." Jesse sighed and murmured, "Pilar." A painful pause followed, while Anthony squirmed inwardly. What was going on? Was the entrepreneur ill? She was having a rough time adjusting to some facets of frontier life. Had her gravity compensation meds backfired? Or had she unintentionally offended an alien media person's mores or been manhandled by security? A dozen possibilities danced in Anthony's mind. His concern was compounded by a deeper fear that trouble hitting Pilar Gutierrez would hurt Jesse as well. He tightened his grip on the associate producer's shoulder, conveying his dismay.

Jesse roused, anger in his gray eyes. "She lied to me—to *us*, kid."

Anthony had been braced to hear something very different. "Wh-what are you talking about?"

"I said Pilar lied to us!" Jesse was a pent-up explosion looking for a place to cut loose.

"Wait a minute. Slow down. Take this a script page at a time. Pilar lied? How? About what?"

"About who she is! About her investors! For all I know, she

235

isn't even from Earth!" Anthony considered calling the enclave's kitchens and ordering his friend chemical soothants or alcohol, then dismissed the idea. Jesse didn't need a fuzzy brain on top of everything else. The older man growled, "Zach Newkirk McKelvey signed Pilar's vouchers, all right. Oh, yeah! And he is putting money into this Whimed project. But he never met Pilar. This whole damned deal, from her end of it, anyway, has been maneuvered from some Earth-based dummy corporation. Cover-up after cover-up!"

Anthony took a deep breath. "That's the way they run things back there. Tax shelters and so on."

"There's more," Jesse said grimly. He examined the lint on his tunic, avoiding Anthony's eyes. "The rest of her idents are phony, too. She's never been to most of those Settlements or met those people. And Pilar was talking up a storm in the press gallery with some baldies and Colin, wheeling and dealing . . ." He hesitated, shamefaced at his tone. He hadn't used that spacers' slang word, "baldies," in a teasing way. That alone was proof of how distraught he was.

"Biyelin Vahnajes? She knows their involvement in that nasty trick on David."

"Nah! These were grayfaces, some of Colin's trading partners. Besides, we shouldn't blame them for what a few Vahnaj scum did." Jesse said, sighing again.

"And Colin?"

"Oh, yeah! Fancy Feathers himself. While you and the girl and the delegation were cruising the main floor, Colin kept making visits up to the gallery, pressing the flesh and all—free PR for Myron Simpkins and Colin's commercial empire," Jesse said with bitter scorn. "*And* draggin' Pilar off for a private chat," he finished angrily.

Guilt stabbed at Anthony. He recalled Colin saying, weeks ago, that he might want to employ the entrepreneur, a comment not relayed to Jesse at the time. Now Colin had followed through, and Jesse felt his relationship with Pilar was threatened.

"She's a businesswoman. The Whimed Committee's dramatic project will be wrapped up tomorrow, after the opening ceremonies. Pilar won't have any further heavy contractual obligations to us or the felinoids, beyond marketing the emota-sensor vids. Naturally, she needs to scout around for her next investment," Anthony said, trying to rescue his friend with logic. "She has to make a living, like the rest of us. It's probably all razzle-dazzle, anyway, her talking to Colin and his lutrinoid trading allies."

"Were you listenin' to me?" Jesse demanded. "Making a livin'? As *what*? Who *is* she? I've been rompin' with her, and I can't even guarantee her ident! How can I be sure of anything about her when her regs are nothin' but lies?"

"Easy, easy," Anthony soothed.

There was pain as well as anger in Jesse's expression now. "Forged idents and faked regs, claiming to be what she's not—that's not razzle-dazzle. It's breakin' the law."

"Maybe. I doubt it's even close to it, back where Pilar came from," Anthony reminded the other man. "It's a tax shelter, I tell you."

"*If* she came from Earth," Jesse retorted. He waved his hands helplessly. "Okay, she probably is from Earth. She's got the accent, and things she told me when we were . . . well, I agree that part of her idents is probably true. The next question is, What's she doin' out here, light-years from the good old Earth, operatin' on faked regs?"

Anthony didn't have an answer. He and Jesse stared at one another. In all their years of working together, they hadn't come up against any situation quite like this.

"Dammit to hell," Jesse said, his voice hoarse, "I like her. A lot."

"I know," Anthony said gently. "So do I. So does Yrae."

"She does?"

"Yes. Yrae's the one who told me you'd left the press gallery." Anthony didn't add that he had his own set of questions concerning how Yrae had learned that fact. He gauged his friend's temper and decided Jesse was no longer in danger of losing control. "How did you find out about these forged credentials?"

Jesse leaned on the chair arm, propping his chin on his hand. "I've been circulatin' myself, up on the mezzanine, makin' contacts. We've got to look ahead ourselves, kid, to *our* next deal. And I think I got a line on something . . ." He grimaced and went on, "Well, anyway, I picked up some other stuff while I was at it. These Vahnajes got real friendly with me." Anthony raised an eyebrow and his friend said hastily, "Yeah, yeah, Biyelins. But they insisted they weren't connected with Fal-Am or the bunch that threw Davy a curve. Don't worry! I don't swallow the whole ocean when they offer it to me—like Pilar seemed to be doin'."

"We *all* should stay away from the Biyelins," Anthony warned. "Remember what Quol-Bez and Brenna said."

"Yeah, yeah," Jesse repeated. "I know what the whitefaces are really interested in is sinking the Whimeds, any way they can. But they talked about other stuff to me, too. Thought they were bein' cute, tippytoein' all over the territory, the way Vahnajes do. But I got the point." He looked very pleased with himself. "Splashed hints at me because I've been rompin' with Pilar. I guess Vahnajes believe in pillow talk and figured if they wanted to get at her they should butter me up. Even asked if I'd bring her over to their section of the gallery and make proper introductions . . ."

"Are you going to?"

The older man was startled; then he grasped the implications and smiled. "Hey! Sure! Why not? She's been chattin' mostly with Vahnaj media types. But the guys talkin' to me were pretty damned business oriented. That would be a way to get on the inside, wouldn't it? Maybe find out what's going on with the Biyelins, and what's with Pilar and those damned faked regs."

"It certainly would," Anthony encouraged.

"Okay! You're right, kid. That *is* the way! Why the hell didn't I think of that? Of course, I could ask Pilar straight out why she's cozyin' up to Colin and . . . nah! That's dumb. No finesse. And it might back her into a corner. There's a better technique."

"I can ask around myself," Anthony said. "Mingling with the V.I.P. delegates should give me lots of opportunities."

"No," Jesse said firmly. "Not you. You're too obvious. You'd make a rotten espionage agent, kid."

"I'm crushed."

"Be glad your face *is* well known," the associate producer chided.

"Only because I'm a pretty clone."

"Don't start that again."

Anthony shook his head. "I won't. It's just that . . . Yamashita treats me like a robot. 'Smile and look handsome for this potential customer for Procyon Five's undersea products, Saunder.' "

"Hell, what do you expect? He's a politician. How are the rest of the delegates treating you? I thought so! Like one of them, huh? I've seen it soakin' in on 'em ever since you became chairman. You sell 'em the Studio and our solid rep, kid—and leave the spy stuff to me. Nobody will notice ol' Jesse sneakin' around.

They don't pay any attention to the guy behind Anthony Saunder."

Or to the mysterious aide behind Ryseen Simra Hilandro?

Anthony pushed that worry into a mental pigeonhole and watched his friend. The older man was entering launch mode, enthusiastic and persuading himself that Pilar Gutierrez might have been conned or blackmailed into carrying forged idents, just as David Lavrik had been used by outsiders. Maybe she was a pawn for a heartless corporation based on Earth, and Jesse Eben would save her! There had always been a streak of old-fashioned gallantry in his nature, and the entrepreneur was bringing it out full force.

"Whoa!" Anthony interrupted. "You're talking some awfully tall scheduling there. The opening ceremonies are tommorow. I need you to help with the crew, setting up."

"Nothing to it! I wear more hats than Colin. Leave it to me! Jesse grinned and said, "You concentrate on directin' Yrae and Davy to a smasho success and headin' up our delegation. Yeah! The rest is my ticket. Subtlety. That's the password. The Vahnajes want pillow talk? Fine. I'll play."

"What sacrifices you make for your work."

Jesse got to his feet and switched off the monitor. He shadowboxed restlessly, the fighter, down and drowning, bobbing back to the surface and ready to move in for the kill. "I'm goin' right back down to the press gallery and get busy," he announced.

"Sure? You were pretty low when I got here."

"Not now!" Jesse tapped a harmless punch against Anthony's lean belly. "See that? Sharp as an ocean king's spikes!"

"All right. Then we're back in business."

"Hit 'em from both sides, kid. I'll do the digging, and you pull off the Whimeds' dramatic presentation and steer our business bunch." Jesse rubbed his hands together briskly and took a step toward the hall door. Then he stopped. "Uh . . . let's keep this thing about Pilar's idents just between the two of us, huh? For the time being at least. Nobody else needs to know. Deal?"

Was he worrying that *another* couple's pillow talk might cross species lines? Jesse had never been concerned about Anthony's blabbing to a bed companion until now. But Anthony's romping companion had never been Yrae Usin Hilandro until now. "Deal," he said.

"Okay! Comin' back to the party?"

239

"Later. You go ahead. I'll wait a while, or it might look as if we've been off in a corner hatching plots."

"Yeah! There's a lot of that going on around here." Jesse sobered and added, "If there isn't a plot hatchin', someone thinks one is. You probably haven't heard, kid, but the rumor's all over the press gallery. I'd better warn you. It's likely to show up on the main floor and cause problems. The Vahnajes are blaming the Whimeds for that shuttle crash."

Vivid images came of a flaming wreck, with Majlur and his cronies crowing over the tragedy and Yrae chastising them for revealing such vicious glee where Terrans could observe them.

And there was another image Anthony had witnessed much more recently—Ryseen Simra Hilandro and Fal-Am circling each other warily at the social facilitator in the main hall.

"*Was* it sabotage?" he wondered.

"Space Fleet doesn't think so. I was jawin' with one of their officers, and he said it was definitely an accident. Fleet's stayin' alert, though. They're afraid the Vahnajes will try to even the score."

"With the Whimeds' Outer Satellite Faction," Anthony finished.

"All I know is *we* stay out of it. Watch yourself when those baldies and cat folks mix it up. It's not our business."

Isn't it? Anything that threatens a neighboring sector's stability threatens the stability of the Settlements and, ultimately, Earth and the Colonies.

Jesse cocked an imaginary Space Fleet sidearm. "And now I go play detective. See you. Be charming." The older man winked, then let himself out of the room.

The anger Anthony had managed to conceal while his friend was present erupted. Pilar, lying! Maybe her motives were as honorable as Jesse hoped they were. Maybe not. They'd know more about that once Jesse did some digging. Whatever turned up, though, her lies had hurt the associate producer. Whether that was Pilar's doing or that of unknown beings pulling her strings, Anthony intended to pay back whoever was responsible.

It was all right to play tricksy games if both parties knew the rules. Anthony had swum that course often—smiling insincerity, a brief romance with a client, or pleasant lies for business reasons, with no one getting injured.

But Jesse *had* been injured, so the fun stopped here and now!

240

Anthony had said that Pilar was probably scouting for her next entrepreneurial project. The Whimed Committee's dramatic presentation would reach its culimination at tomorrow's opening ceremonies. Anthony realized with dismay that soon not only Pilar would be moving on, but so would Yrae. They would cross paths for the duration of the Interspecies Trade Conference as their delegations gathered for various sessions. Things wouldn't be the same, however, once the project ended. He hated that realization. The alien actress was getting under his skin, though he'd known all along that the affair couldn't last. He found himself paraphrasing Jesse's words. He liked Yrae. A lot.

Even though David Lavrik had evinced no romantic interest whatsoever in his co-star, Anthony was jealous of the man. Tomorrow Lavrik would be performing with Yrae, dancing with her, breathing life into Janyavee's and Dempsey's lines with her, feeding intense signals to the emota-sensors with her, and making the audience believe that he *did* care deeply for the Whimeds' beautiful living symbol. Meanwhile, that same audience would have no awareness of Anthony Saunder's presence at the below-stage emota-sensor control boards—or of his relationship with Yrae Usin Hilandro. He'd be an unseen figure, working like hell behind the scenes to bring the bi-species production to a successful conclusion.

That was what he ought to be concentrating on right now—that and the problems of his delegation. There were too many big concerns facing them all: that Lannon warship orbiting Procyon Four; Biyelin Vahnajes accusing the Whimed Outer Satellite Faction of sabotage and threatening retaliation; humans and aliens squabbling among themselves; and predators of all species circling the fray, searching for weaknesses they could exploit.

And he was worrying about his own tiny quota of dilemmas? Anthony shook his head and moved toward the door. He had a job to do. And it was past due the time that he returned to duty and got on with that task.

241

CHAPTER FIFTEEN

❁❁❁❁❁❁❁❁

Opening Ceremonies

The presentations hadn't even begun, and the Conference theme of interspecies friendship and understanding was being badly undermined. C.S.P.'s organizational teams and Colin's staffers had been working overtime for months to lay the groundwork. That had involved persuading some of the participating races to join in the programmed opening ceremonies. Such a concept was unfamiliar to several species and cultural groups within others that *did* comprehend what was being planned. The ITC complex's central building had been converted into a carefully arranged amphitheater. The presentation crews had gathered in the below-stage arena. Separate areas had been established for each group, to avoid clashes. It had looked like things finally were rolling smoothly.

Then the chief of the Lannons' Amusements Committee lodged a loud protest. She objected strenuously to the already agreed upon order in which the presenters would appear before the assemblage. *"Hooja!* Lannon lead. Do not follow."

C.S.P. President Emeritus Pacholski tried sweet reason. "Nijoop madam, your representatives have accepted this plan." Pacholski turned to his interpreter. "Does she receive me?"

"No 'cept! Lannon lead. Lannon come stars first!"

The different species' preparation areas were set in wide spokes around the central below-stage arena where the argument was taking place. It was impossible for any of the orators and actors to ignore the uproar. Anthony gritted his teeth. Wonderful! A major brawl on their doorstep, perfectly calculated to destroy his concentration and Yrae's and Lavrik's, just when they most needed to be at their best!

A Vahnaj elder statesman joined Pacholski in trying to get through to the Lannon Committee. He and the procyonid committeewoman were of equal height but as little alike as an effete Earth citizen and an independent planet scout. The Vahnaj was skinny and balding, the Lannon hairy and brawny, towering over her male subordinates. "*Mejuo* Nijoop Tran-non," the lutrinoid began, off on the wrong foot instantly by mispronouncing the other species' name. "It is . . . urr . . . cor-rection. Tran-non had . . . urr . . . not inter-stellar ve-hicles . . . urr . . . two of your . . . urr . . . *fyush* time u-nits a-go. You a-achieve interstellar tra-vel, Tran-non, since . . . urr . . . con-tact . . . urr . . . our ex-plor-er rock-et your Tran-non col-onies."

"You no truth! *Hooja!* Lannon haff past-light ship long long times! Vahnaj no first! You steal! *Hoop!* We steal back! Hah!" The procyonid female flashed a ferocious grin.

Pacholski tried to quiet the two aliens, with little success. Whimeds, including Yrae, watched the fracas with contempt. The Rigotians lurked in their dressing area, peeking out cautiously. The Ulisorians seemed content to remain inside their pressurized chamber and let the others slug it out, if they chose. Yrae muttered, "Lannon always behave so. Their females must establish position. Without this, there is no exchange."

"That's going to make it difficult to negotiate trade pacts with them," Anthony commented, glowering at the squabble.

Yrae shrugged. "They learn. Our merchants allow them to howl and howl with them. Then they cooperate."

"I don't think Pacholski or that Vahnaj diplomat are much for howling."

David Lavrik was oblivious to the entire matter. He was running in place, an athlete, priming himself for his big race. Margaret Orr stood by, waiting patiently, holding the repaired echinoderm skin cloak. Jesse was Anthony's alter ego, hurrying from stage equipment to support crew to the director and back again, helping coordinate. Meanwhile, the ongoing argument dinned at them all.

"It is... urr... in-deed ac-curate Tran-non be... urr... taught." A whiteface Vahnaj butted into the fringes of the Whimed Committee's preparation area. Taisso bristled, barely restraining his outrage. The Biyelin bowed elaborately and addressed Yrae. "Fee-maid... you be-ings... urr... more dangerous. Urr? You are not as Tran-non. Choose car-ry out... urr... threats. Urr?" The lutrinoid bowed very low. "For-give intrusion. Did not mean dis-turb." With that, he backed away, grinning, pointy teeth gleaming in his pale face.

Yrae was a frozen statue. Anthony put an arm about her shoulders and whispered, "Easy. Don't let him distract you. That's what he wants."

She nodded, relaxing slightly. "He implies my Federation destroyed Vahnaj shuttle. He is wrong. It is Biyelins who retaliate with death."

Her words chilled him. Accusations and counteraccusations flew everywhere!

"What's going on? What's the delay?" Colin, with his usual small army of flunkies, waded into the ongoing argument in the center of the lower stage section. Delays in the Conference schedule were costing him money, and plainly he intended to hammer out the snarls fast. His feathered headdress was ruffled and Colin was sweating. He glared up at the Lannon and shouted, "You will have the third position. It is decided. Your fur-kinship elder aunt declared this. It is done."

"Lannon no follow," the furry alien insisted, though not as belligerently as she had previously. "I am Nijoop Inet Dama of Lannon Financial Treaties League. I lead."

"I am Colin Saunder of the Saunder-McKelveys. I command the Conference. You do not lead. You are third. It is decided." Without turning from his adversary, Colin ordered an aide, "Tomo, call Space Fleet. Tell them to bore in on that floating fortress up there in orbit. If the Lannon do not obey the mutually agreed upon rules of the Interspecies Trade Conference, they may depart."

Anthony gave his cousin credit for courage and fast thinking. The Lannon and her mates gnashed their teeth. But Colin didn't back down a centimeter. And the standoff was over as suddenly as it had begun. The Nijoop smirked. Her grin was as unnerving as her glowers. *"Hooja!* You good trader. Good trader like you fur-kinship aunt, she yours, Brenna."

That soured Colin's triumph considerably. "Indeed," he said flatly. "I thank you, Nijoop Dama. My kinswoman would be honored by your praise."

"Good trader Brenna! Tell us come here or lose deal. She good trader like Ryseen."

Vahnajes listening in reacted angrily to that mention of the female from the Whimeds' Outer Satellite Faction. Something here to offend everyone, Anthony reflected. Well, it was poetic justice; the Vahnajes had tried to disconcert Yrae, and now the Lannon had thrown *their* opening ceremonies team into a snit.

"I will rescind my command to the Terran Space Fleet," Colin said, being generous with an authority he had never possessed in the first place. He turned, waving to all the presentation Committees. "I wish you all success. Your audiences await you."

As he started up the ramp to the main level, Veda Ingersoll darted forward, snatching at Colin's sleeve. Anthony was close enough to hear the aging actress plead softly, "Oh, Colin, dear, you really *must* do something to alter the order of presentations. No one cares whether those stupid Lannon go first. But poor President Pacholski has such an unfortunate position. As representative of all the Terran peoples, he should be prominently featured, don't you think? Couldn't you . . ."

It was one of the ham's better performances. Anthony was tempted to applaud.

Colin dashed Veda's hopes. His mask of elegance had vanished. None too gently, he broke Veda's hold on his sleeve, making her wince. "That's impossible. Didn't you hear what I told the Lannon? The order of presentations is set, and that's final."

She babbled tearfully until Anthony, reading his kinsman's face, said, "It's no use, Veda. Give it up." Colin glared daggers at them both as Anthony went on, "You see, cousin, the lady's merely trying to avoid running into an old Terran show biz superstition—being on last is poison."

"The Terran *sector* is hosting this Conference," Colin snapped, *"not* your non-contributory entertainment industry." Yrae was staring at the blond, and her intense Whimed gaze seemed to rattle him, shortening his temper still further. "Pacholski has the honor of winding up the ceremony, and you will do the interpretive readings, as promised, and that's that!"

245

"Too bad, Veda," Anthony commiserated. "That means the Whimeds' presentation will be *next* to last, exactly as scheduled." Veda pouted, knowing her "interpretation" of President Pacholski's speech would be put far in the shade by Yrae Usin Hilandro's performance.

"Y-you go to hell," Veda said, sniffling. She glanced at Colin and muttered, "You too."

"Shut up, you hag! Be grateful you have any part at all in these proceedings." As Colin and his little army hurried on up the ramp, the actress watched helplessly, her lip trembling. Anthony almost felt sorry for her. She'd wormed her way into this position, and had outsmarted herself in attaching her star to Colin Saunder's coattails. But she was a human being, and he needn't have cast her aside quite so cruelly.

In an ironic way, that whole scheme had turned sour. Colin had thought by putting Veda Ingersoll in these ceremonies, he'd be insulting his cousin. But no one had been fooled. Worse, from the gossip Anthony had overheard at last night's mingler, many of the Terran delegates and politicians were snickering at Colin— believing that Veda was the young man's paramour, and that was the only reason she had a place in these prestigious doings.

The aging prima donna struggled to hold on to the rags of her pride. "Forget what he said, Veda," Anthony advised. "Neither of us is a non-contrib. We both do our jobs and damned well. Closing the show won't be as bad a disaster as you fear. You'll see. The old Earth superstitions don't apply out here."

"But there are people from Earth in the audience," Veda wailed. "I was going to impress them."

"You will," Yrae chimed in. Veda gawked as the beautiful alien said, "I have seen the dramatic recordings which you have made for Saunder Studio. Anthony is correct. You have skill. I am certain you will please those in the Hall."

It was a generous attempt to lift the ham's spirit. Veda wasn't having any charity, though. Her chin went up. "Of course I'll please them, you silly girl! I'm a *star*!" She beckoned to her hairdresser and flounced off.

Anthony grinned. "She'll be all right. She's a bitch, but a trouper, a tough settler, under all that posturing."

Yrae was looking at him with a peculiar, soft expression. "You were kind. I did not believe you cared for Ingersoll."

"I don't. Well, not *personally*. I just thought Colin was too rough with her, and . . . well, live and let live."

A cloud came over Yrae's face. "That is wise. I wish it could be so. It . . . is uncivilized to hate. The beings you hate find causes to accuse you of evil and hate you in return. And yet I cannot forgive the Biyelin Vahnajes for what they have done to my people."

He gripped her arms, shaking her. "Hey! I said nothing about hate. Veda's not my enemy."

"Is Colin?"

Anthony had to weigh his answer. "In a sense, I suppose so. But that doesn't seem in the same category as the Whimeds' centuries-long cold war with the Biyelin Vahnajes." He added with a smile, "There's another Terran proverb that might apply to this situation: Let bygones be bygones."

Yrae remained solemn, unresponsive. Anthony wanted to embrace her and thrust away the darkness shadowing her spirit. But the pace was quickening. They had no time for personal concerns. "Come on," he urged. "The ceremonies are about to begin."

Activity picked up in the below-stage preparations areas. Kyinell assisted Yrae into her costume, arranging the Whimed's hair. David Lavrik was getting help from Jesse and some Studio personnel. Anthony tried to be everywhere at once in the crowded space. Final checks were made on special effects, lighting, audio, and, especially, the emota-sensor equipment.

Upstairs, a rotating showcase platform awaited the performers. Stage crews, orators, and actors watched the monitors as the house filled. Last night's refreshment islands had been removed from the hall. Six separate spectator sections replaced them, circling the central platform, with V.I.P. boxes, seating tiers and galleries, a special enclosed and pressurized niche for the few Ulisorian delegates who had journeyed this far into the Terran sphere of influence, nesting boxes for the Rigotians, and enormous cuplike "chairs" for the Lannon. Ample legroom was provided in the Vahnaj sections so that the lutrinoids could stretch out.

Divisions in physical needs, in language, and in relationships had to be accommodated. Vahnajes and Whimeds were widely separated. Ames Griffith's Progressives and delegates supporting his candidacy left plenty of room between themselves and Myron

Simpkins's bloc. Buffer zones lay between each species, but it struck Anthony that Colin should have arranged for numerous buffer zones *within* each species' seating area.

Taisso pointed to a monitor and cried, "Lannon! The roof! Is gone!"

"Stunting," Jesse said. "They said they had to breathe free and demanded Colin's staffers stop cooping them in under a ceiling. I hope it rains and they get their fur sopping wet!"

The Whimed Committeeman whined that the missing roof section would spoil acoustics during Yrae's dramatic presentation. "No, it won't," Anthony assured him. "My people are experienced. We can compensate."

Taisso continued to bemoan the situation until Yrae laughed at him and scratched his head affectionately. "Do not fuss. We will succeed." At that, he subsided. The Terran stage crew exchanged puzzled smiles at the actress correcting her corrector! Whimeds certainly had a backward way of doing things!

Lights were dimmed and brightened according to the requirements of the species using that seating section. Staffers sorted out squabbles over who had the right to sit where. Late arrivals and dignitaries were still drifting into the emormous building.

Below stage, Jesse traded dirty jokes and sparred playfully with David Lavrik, helping the jittery actor-dancer work off a bad case of overprepared nerves. Anthony pep-talked the young man and Yrae, giving them last-moment directorial instructions. Yrae tolerated Kyinell's fluttering attentions, as unheeding as a doll. Was she in *diya*? Her eyes were unfocused and she seemed to be a million light-years away.

Anthony checked the emota-sensor pickups and receptors for the twentieth time. Steady readouts came from all the broadcasters placed around the hall, and the mini-collectors hidden in the stars' costumes were feeding their bio-signals to the boards loud and clear.

Now if David, in particular, could make those signals jump the right way once the performers were onstage . . .

Neutral music came from upstairs. Monitors showed that the hall was jammed. Colin was in the middle of the slowly revolving stage. Former President Pacholski might have the honor of closing these ceremonies, but Colin Saunder was taking the opening spotlights for himself. He spoke briefly and to the point, the gracious host, lavishing thanks and compliments on key persons in the crowd. Anthony had to acknowledge that his cousin had learned timing—or that he'd had a good coach. Colin certainly could afford to hire some of the best tutors in that field.

Of course, if he'd come to Saunder Studio, I could have shown him how to punch up his delivery even more. And with emota-sensors he could really stun this audience.

The Vahnaj Alliance had the first slot of the general presentations. A chorus of lutrinoids gathered around the edge of the stage and, one after another, spoke flowery greetings from their worlds or groups of worlds. Each was a master in a particular alien tongue and culture. One even knew a few words of Ulisorian. When they completed that welcoming segment, they knelt around a Vahnaj poet, regarded as the heart of his people. He recited to and for his Alliance. Vahnaj verse consisted of a series of single words, pronounced sonorously, with pregnant pauses for reflection between each "stanza." The form reminded Anthony of Terran writings involving rigid metric rules and evoking emotions with specific syllables or stresses. He supposed Vahnaj poetry was very satisfying to lutrinoid listeners. To a non-Vahnaj, it was, at best, interesting.

David and Yrae were doing dancer's warm-up exercises, each using different patterns. Anthony, Jesse, Pilar, and the bi-species stage crew stood back, giving the two plenty of room.

Techs were concealing the revolving stage in an opaque holo-mode curtain as the Vahnajes, their presentation finished, rode a hidden elevator down to the preparation area. A lone Ulisorian was riding up on the second elevator. Anthony fine-tuned the monitor in his group's waiting alcove, curious to see what the Ulisorian was going to present. She had trained long and hard for the ITC and functioned well despite the handicap of her pressure suit. Translation devices converted her language's squeaks and whistles into the various tongues of other delegates. There was no formal greeting. C.S.P.'s diplomats said Ulisorians felt that the presence of being in a given place was its own greeting, requiring no further comment. The alien's artistic offering was what her species called narration. The terminology, even in translation, was virtually incomprehensible. Anthony tried to imagine the universe seen through the eyes of an oviparous race from a watery low-gravity world—a race whose young were born in an egg mass, where the survivors were those who had eaten the losers and where learning was absorbed by eating manufactured brain

249

samples of the Ulisorians' dead sages. The suited performer led into a fairly straightforward account of the first of her kind who learned how to remember—a crucial development in Ulisorian civilization. Faces of her peers pressed against their pressurized seating area. They seemed enthralled. And when the speaker mentioned the Ulisorians' keen interest in adding to their stocks of "remember-enhancing" natural drugs, Terran, Whimed, Vahnaj, and Lannon traders sat up and took notice, scenting a possible future market for their wares.

Lannon Nijoop Inet Dama came next. She was a boomer, mistress of a planetwide fur kinship's most popular art form. Her mates, who were also her co-stars, hopped energetically about the stage while the Nijoop chanted loudly about interstellar friendship. The procyonids in the audience roared their approval. Inspired, the Nijoop broke into a singsong yodel. Surprisingly, Anthony found the music catchy. He might have patted his foot, except that his part of the below-stage area was directly beneath the spot where most of the Lannon males were doing their hopping dance. Whimed Committee people and Saunder Studio crew members eyed the ceiling apprehensively and heaved sighs of relief when the Lannons' performance ended. The Nijoop finished by speaking Terran, more or less, and praising the progress of *Homo sapiens* as a star-roving species. They were "almost as brave and adventurous" as the Lannon. High praise indeed, from the Nijoop.

The Rigotian presentation was brief. This staged entertainment was a strange concept to them, and it was obvious that they did not feel comfortable with it. An octet demonstrated a traditional ritual called a nest weaving. To Anthony's eyes, it was a static series of contorted poses, made unattractive by the Rigotians' penchant for making—from a Terran point of view—hideous and grotesque faces. However, he'd spoken briefly to a Rigotian merchant at last night's social facilitator and discovered that species was most interested in emota-sensor technology applied to visual instruction. If the tentative approaches ripened, that could eventually lead to a new market for Saunder Studio, a year or more from now. He couldn't afford to reject the Rigotian's peculiar idea of art out of hand. They might someday be his trading partners.

He was spared the need to pay too much attention to the blue-skinned aliens' weaving, though, because the Whimeds' presentation would be next. The atmosphere in the dimly lit downstairs ready area near the elevators became taut. Techs tuned equipment and made synchronization checks. Pilar and Margaret Orr adjusted the echinoderm skin cloak David Lavrik wore.

"We know it all," Anthony said softly, nodding to the actors. He touched the sensor boards and added, "Give these your best, and we won't have anything to worry about."

Yrae glanced at Kyinell, and the older woman held out Yrae's bejeweled tote, a priestess offering a gift to her goddess. The Whimeds' cultural treasure extracted the garish *oryuz* headgear Anthony had seen that night in his house and carefully placed it over her crest. Kyinell adjusted strands of fluffy gold hair, anchoring the alien tiara in place.

Then the Rigotians were descending from the stage. A stagehand cued Yrae and David Lavrik and they stepped onto the second platform and began to rise. Anthony tilted his head, watching them anxiously. Yrae's manner was remote and concentrated. David Lavrik was visibly tense, breathing hard, his heart pounding, according to the sensors.

Could he pull this performance off? He'd had so damned little time to get his act together after learning that the Biyelin Vahnajes and their Terran confederate Renzi had shamelessly manipulated him.

The Whimeds' entire Conference sales pitch depended on whether Lavrik could live up to his talents. And if he didn't, the Biyelins would have won. Prestige and honor, in the Whimeds' view, would lie in ruins.

And so would the director's reputation. They'd chosen Anthony to shepherd this production, and he'd allowed himself to be tempted, lured by those six big gross Terran-Whimed exchange credit units and by the fascination of Yrae Usin Hilandro.

Now he'd had his last chance to pep talk David Lavrik. If he hadn't gotten the young actor in gear...

Anthony leaned over the sensor board, balancing his attention carefully between the mini-monitor of the onstage action and the readouts. He had never felt so edgy. His Studio crew manned the vid recorders, with full emota-sensor tracking. This would be the merchandising package of the decade, the one that would put Saunder Studio over the top—or bring the Studio and Anthony crashing down in disaster.

The holo-mode curtain was dissolved, revealing the actors in their places, amid realistic scenery.

There was a disturbance in the hall—noise and shouts. It was impossible to start the drama under these conditions. Anthony spoke into the cue mike relays, telling Yrae and David, "Stay where you are. We'll replace the curtain temporarily if we have to." He saw the actors' puzzled expressions and realized the lighting prevented them from seeing what was going on beyond the stage. For a moment he hesitated, not sure telling them was a good idea, then said, "The Biyelin Vahnajes are walking out. Ambassador Quol-Bez and the saner heads are trying to talk sense to them, but Fal-Am's delegation isn't listening."

"Damned whitefaces," Jesse was muttering. "Think they can insult the Whimeds that way. They're making *themselves* look dumb."

"Stay alert," Anthony warned the stars. "It looks like most of them are out of the building by now. We'll be cueing the music in a moment."

Yrae's face was a study in suppressed fury. She wanted revenge for the Biyelin Vahnajes' outrage. David Lavrik, too, was angry. He'd been hurt plenty by the whitefaces. Now this!

"Don't let them get away with it," Anthony said, grabbing his unexpected second chance for a final pep talk before the performance. "This is Janyavee and Dempsey's classic. This is Whimed and Terra united. We are all children of the stars. Remember that. Go!"

The stage turned slowly. Yrae and David had practiced on a similar platform at Saunder Studio and weren't bothered by the motion. Procyon Four's less-than-Earth-normal gravity made things easier. David delivered his character's first lines. Right on the marks. No flubs.

And the emota-sensors! Full! Breathing fire! Anthony had never seen such output!

Yrae's eyes gleamed, oil on water. Her emota-readings matched David's perfectly. Passion was pumping at the audience; and from the monitor scans, it was obvious the dialogue's effects weren't limited to the Terrans. Whimeds and some Vahnajes and Lannons were reacting, being caught up in the drama.

It was possible delegates from Earth might sniff at the plot. They usually did sniff at Ian Dempsey's ongoing love affair with the stellar frontier. Settlers, though, were thoroughly engrossed,

252

gasping, holding their breath, as the play's characters sought to survive under terrible odds.

And there was the unseen cast of characters, supposedly orbiting the castaways' world—an assortment of aliens waiting to see the outcome of this meeting of disparate species.

The Interspecies Trade Conference, in miniature, was onstage.

Yrae was magnificent, leading smoothly into the brief excerpts of non-Whimed species' art forms, blending them into the story convincingly—Vahnaj verse, Ulisorian remembering, and Lannon booming; Yrae's alto pyrotechnics were almost the equal of the Nijoop's, and out in the audience, procyonids howled happily, flattered by that nod to their race. Blue light played over the scene during the Rigotian "weaving" segment; blue was the dominant color in *all* Rigotian visualized material.

In each instance, David Lavrik was the perfect partner, not trying to outdo, but harmonizing, blending his strong baritone with Yrae's voice and, like her, somehow making the inserted segments seem completely natural parts of the larger drama.

Illusion became reality. Two people, Terran and non-Terran, were learning how to be allies and friends!

The performance wasn't flawless, but the bobbles were minuscule. Anthony suspected only he and the actors were aware of them, and they didn't allow the slight imperfections to wreck the rest of the play.

Lavrik's readouts were the best emota-sensor feeds Anthony had ever seen from a male Terran! The man was incredible. This was the superb technician on that résumé vid, the gifted youngster who had won a scholarship to the Kinetic Arts Institute, wowed viewers on his tours, caught the eyes of the Whimed Committee, and made Yrae Usin Hilandro choose him above all other possible human co-stars. She hadn't been wrong.

And Anthony hadn't been wrong in backing this production!

It was *working*, flowing like unimpeded canal water, effortless—on the surface.

A nervous rustling came from the audience, with now and then a tension-strained laugh or groan. The Lannon responded with a surprisingly soft, excited "*Ssusususu*."

The finale was the exquisite, impossible dance. David was more than a moving piece of furniture. Anthony hadn't thought anything could enhance Yrae's endless series of pirouettes and that spinning wave of starstuff from her color wands. But Lavrik did, in the right place at the right time. Masculine and powerfully graceful, he was the ideal counterpart to Yrae's petite intensity.

They were holding that last glorious pose, hands touching, as Yrae's wands poured rainbows over them.

Perfect, perfect, and perfect—for all practical purposes.

Anthony counted, pacing the systems. Should he cut the recording now, save it while the saving was good? No! Let it run. He sensed what was coming, and it would crown the production in a way no PR, no grandiose swell of concluding music could.

That music was rising now, signaling climax's end . . .

And Terrans, Whimeds, and Lannon were on their feet, each applauding in their species' way. Some Vahnajes, Ambassador Quol-Bez leading them, were standing, too, giving polite homage to the triumph of the Whimed's cultural treasure and her co-star.

Anthony was on his feet as well, letting the boards run by themselves. He was cheering himself hoarse, shaking his fists, feeling the victory to his bones, cheering Yrae, for carrying it through despite the Biyelin Vahnajes' calculated disruption and all the other distractions she'd had to bear, and cheering the techs and the Whimeds' specialists, who'd beaten every equipment glitch and made the effects work.

Most of all, he was cheering David Lavrik. Flushed, grinning, the young actor-dancer stood beside Yrae and accepted the crowd's plaudits. Lavrik's expression said it all. He'd gone from an alleged sentence of death to total mastery of his craft in days!

Jesse pounded Anthony on the back. "We did it! Look at 'em!"

The younger man swept his friend into an exuberant bear hug. "We did, didn't we? Hah!" Anthony's throat felt thick, his eyes moist. No denying the emotions—real, intense, the feelings of a full-fledged human being. It was what Jesse had tried to tell him so long—and what he'd refused to accept. Anthony didn't resist his humanness now, reveling in the storm of responses flooding him.

This was not a sham, nor any self-delusion in order to manipulate others. He wasn't manipulating anyone. He was giving Yrae Usin Hilandro and David Lavrik their honest due—and sharing their triumph.

It took a long time for the audience to let the performers go. But at last the holo-mode curtain enfolded the stage. Illusionary scenery blinked out. The actors rode down to the confused, cluttered below-stage area into a scene of celebration. Taisso and Kyinell were engaging in an impromptu little dance, as light-hearted as children. Whimed and Terran techs congratulated the actors warmly. Jesse and Anthony added their praise. "Great . . . beautiful . . . just incredible . . . like clockwork . . . You gave 'em a wowser, just as Pilar says . . . David, you ought to patent the way you handle that cloak . . . Yeah, Omori's company's going to get hundreds of orders for capes like that when this Conference gets rolling."

Pilar, weeping with joy, finally brought some sanity back into the jumble. "We've got to give them a chance to change out of those sweaty costumes, people!" The techs reluctantly resumed work on the tearing-down process while other supportive staff members hustled the tired performers to their portable dressing cubicles. Anthony supervised closing operations, packing equipment, and clearing his team's baggage from the area. As he tended to chores, that feeling of exhilaration continued to sustain him.

He was still in business. And the success of this project should reflect favorably not only on the Whimeds but also on the Whimeds' newest Terran trading partners on Procyon Five. With luck, Saunder Studio might garner orders for emota-sensor vid packages other than the special issue of tonight's drama.

Up top, onstage, C.S.P. President Emeritus Pacholski was plowing through his address, with Veda Ingersoll providing artistic interpretations. Anthony watched them with pity. Veda had been right to protest being assigned the cleanup slot. The crowd was in no mood for an anticlimax. And anything after Yrae's and David Lavrik's performance *was* an anticlimax.

"Congrats are pourin' in on the coms," Jesse reported. "Yrae even got one from Quol-Bez. She called him an honorable person. Davy's gettin' tons of calls, too. And you. Wanta take 'em, or should I keep fielding them to the delegation staff?"

"Fend them off for now," Anthony said absently. He had noted a surreptitious movement in the Vahnaj section of the Hall and pointed it out to Jesse.

"Huh! The Biyelins sneaking back in with their tails between their legs. There's Fal-Am, tryin' to look as if he meant to do things this way all the time. Bet he's madder'n hell. All that work the whitefaces put in, tryin' to ruin Davy's concentration, got 'em nowhere."

255

"Fal-Am would probably insist that *his* particular group of delegates had nothing to do with the Biyelins masterminding that affair," Anthony said.

"Maybe not. But he sure was the ringleader in that noisy Biyelin walkout."

"Doesn't matter. Ambassador Quol-Bez is steering the Vahnajes and *he* sent compliments to our stars," Anthony reminded his friend.

Pacholski droned on, background noise. Anthony studied faces, those on the monitors and those in the below-stage area surrounding him. Jesse snorted with disdain as the former President spoke of universal goodwill. Pilar was looking grave at his mention of Earth's continuing social and economic ills. In a V.I.P. box, Brenna's family sat with Ames Griffith, his son Malcolm, and an assortment of their key backers. Brenna squirmed as if she'd heard the sentiments in Pacholski's speech thousands of times and was bored. Ames Griffith, smiling cynically, was probably analyzing the old politician's delivery and rewriting themes to his own specs. Regan frowned when the orator urged Terrans to hold fast to the Spirit of Humanity faith. Nearby, in another box, Myron Simpkins, Griffith's opponent, was exuding envy of the man on the stage, no doubt picturing himself occupying the statesman's former rank. But when Pacholski headed C.S.P., no one had called him a bought-and-paid-for puppet, as they now did Simpkins. Colin, the puppet master, sat beside his candidate and tried hard to look enthralled and very pleased with the way his Conference was going so far.

Alien faces: Quol-Bez, serene, attentive; Ozro of Lannon; K-U of Rigotian; Yixier of Ulisor, peering from his helmet; and dozens of other nonhumans Anthony had seen last night or during the preceding days leading up to the Conference's opening ceremonies.

Two people in particular caught and held his attention.

Fal-Am, his white face stiff, his black sideburns flat with anger, and his eyes burning with hate, was frustration personified. No wonder! Ambassador Quol-Bez was pointedly snubbing him, and the Biyelin Vahnajes' rude walkout demonstration had flopped miserably. Worse, Yrae Usin Hilandro, the very embodiment of Whimed culture, had been an absolute smash.

The other was Ryseen Simra Hilandro, leader of the Whimed Outer Satellite Faction. She didn't look like a troublemaker today. She was as unruffled as Ambassador Quol-Bez, savoring Yrae's triumph. A fellow Hilandro, the Whimed Federation's cultural treasure, had achieved an ethically perfect presentation for her species.

Ryseen glanced toward the Vahnaj side of the Hall, homing in on Fal-Am. Could the whiteface Biyelin see Ryseen and feel her aloof scorn? Anthony could! The sensation made him shudder. That cold war between the Biyelins and Ryseen's Faction definitely wasn't in a truce stage.

So much for interspecies amity! Ryseen's was the face of a being who had won, and won big. Fal-Am's was that of a being who had lost . . .

This time.

CHAPTER SIXTEEN

❖❖❖❖❖❖❖❖

Delegation Business

It had been a little miracle of organization to get all of the Studio crew and their luggage assembled here in the Terran enclave's lobby simultaneously. Anthony, Jesse, Pilar Gutierrez, and Taisso had labored overtime to set up the schedule to everyone's convenience. Taisso, Anthony kept reminding the Committeeman, needn't have exerted himself and his staffers so much. But the Whimed insisted he wanted to, that it was part of his job, if not specifically spelled out in the project's contract. The Saunder Studio people not connected with actual ITC delegation affairs would be transported to and from Procyon Four via best transportation—which meant Whimed Federation craft. Anthony's crew would be riding back to Five in style.

There were emotional leave-takings. Margaret Orr nagged Anthony and Jesse to take care of themselves. Ray Wu and the rest of the techs promised they'd be right on top of producing the brand-new vid—the Janyavee-Dempsey live performance at ITC.

A special round of lengthy good-byes involved David Lavrik. He was on hand to see the others off, but wouldn't be traveling with them. He'd be heading in another direction, to a new contract and a new and exciting job. "We'll miss you," Margaret said. He hugged her affectionately and turned to shake hands with all of the Saunder Studio crew.

"Don't forget us when you're hobnobbing with all those classic superstars," Jesse teased.

"I won't! Jesse, Anthony, I can't thank you enough! I owe it all to you," the actor exclaimed.

"It's Pilar you should thank especially," Anthony said, nodding to the entrepreneur. She was beaming proudly, very pleased with her successful efforts on behalf of the brilliant young Terran performer.

"I just put Otto Warschau in touch," she said modestly. "It was that opening ceremony that did it, the way you partnered Yrae. He'd heard of you before, but after seeing you in person, Warschau was completely sold."

"I won't be in competition with the Studio," Lavrik reminded them all, very earnest. "I made that clear to Mr. Warschau right up front. But the *lead* in his upcoming live drama series . . . it's what I've dreamed of!"

"You deserve it," Anthony assured him. "Otto's an old friend, and he's never been my competitor. If he ever *does* decide to record any of those classic, one-of-a-kind artistic spectacles of his, my Studio isn't likely to accept the contract. It's great stuff, but a little too rarefied for our regular customers. Come to think of it, the *only* thing of that sort I've ever produced is the job you and Yrae just did here at ITC." Grinning, Anthony went on, "In fact, I really ought to be thanking *you*. That performance of yours made all the difference—and you know it."

"I'd never have made it at all if you and Jesse and Yrae hadn't helped me . . ." Lavrik broke off, gratitude shining in his eyes. He didn't mention aloud their rescuing him from a supposed death sentence of VN/HS-3. That wasn't necessary. And in the end, he'd pulled himself out of that pit of despair with a superlative display of talent and guts. The actor gripped hands, thanking everyone again for helping him get the terrific break.

"So far the Conference has been good to performers," Anthony noted. "Even Veda got a job as a result of the opening ceremonies. Not in the same class as your contract with Warschau, but—"

"Hey!" Jesse said with a laugh. "She's not complaining. I talked to her last night. She's tickled to her blue-dyed roots to get

259

a tour with Francisco's group. It's a hell of a step up for her from Hassan's ragtag collection."

"I hope things go as well for you," Lavrik wished.

Anthony seconded that, and then he was busy carrying extra bags and accompanying his crew out of the Enclave and onto the plaza apron outside. He had little hesitation, now, in bidding Margaret and the rest fond farewells, and *meaning* it. Every day it became easier for him to acknowledge his humanity. Often the feelings were heady. He'd never entirely shake off his insecurity about his origins, about being a clone. But at least he could yield honestly to emotion—and regret that he had lied to himself so long, being cheated of the pleasures of friendships other than Jesse's for years.

There was an unanticipated delay at the skimmer stand. An arm-waving and shouting crowd clustered on the plaza. Most of the people were Whimeds, but they weren't huddling; their agitation arose from another instinct—anger. Anthony's crew drifted close, listening in as the spectators leaned forward, intent on an eyewitness interview in progress. Anthony knew enough of the language to follow the exchange without difficulty.

"I saw it all! I was ten *ujslus* away, no more!"

"You say it was one of the flying cyborgs, the roc creatures the Conference host has provided for amusement of our distinguished ones?"

"It is so." The interviewee was a middle-level delegation aide, and his crest was spiky stiff with alarm. "The flying beast had left the takeoff place and was rising when it fell suddenly. The Hilandro was . . ."

Anthony, too, felt as though he were plummeting. Jesse grabbed his arm, murmuring, "Easy, kid. We don't know it was Yrae."

The staffer imitated the roc's faltering flight. "It came down thus. Was properly programmed, should not have malfunctioned. Fortunately, Ryseen Simra Hilandro was not hurt."

Anthony let his breath out with a *whoosh*! Then implications of the incident struck him. Had this near tragedy been an accident, or sabotage? Whimed onlookers were wondering the same thing. An ugly muttering ran through the crowd: "Biyelin."

The reporter was summarizing for his species' news net, saying Procyon Four's authorities were examining the wrecked cyborg to learn why it had crashed. The Whimed crowd thought it *already* knew.

As the congestion began to ease and Anthony's crew were able to get to the skimmers they had reserved, he noticed some whiteface Vahnajes watching the Whimed media event from a safe distance. Fal-Am was in the center of the bunch of lutrinoids. A companion was whispering to him. The Biyelin leader looked extremely disgruntled—irked because a plot had failed? The whitefaces turned and entered the Conference hall, grumbling to one another. Behind them, hanging well back and trying not to be observed, a felinoid dogged their tracks. It was Ryseen's aide.

"Kid?" Jesse asked. "You okay? You look shaky."

Anthony managed a thin smile. "I'm fine. And I'm also late. The delegation's supposed to meet with our Charter Company's rep today. Are you certain you don't need me at the shuttleport?"

"Nah! Pilar and I will see the gang off. You go on and tend to business. Uh . . ." Jesse lowered his voice, glancing around furtively, afraid of being overheard. "I may be doing some spy stuff. You know. What we talked about. You got your mini-com on?" Anthony tapped the tiny relay and his friend nodded, reassured. "Okay. I won't butt in on you unless I've got something worth telling."

"Keep in touch," the younger man insisted. "And don't ride any cyborgs."

"Hey, it might be fun! Besides, the Biyelins don't want to sabotage us, just Whimeds. Go on! Mind the store."

Anthony did, hurrying on into the Conference hall. Top members of his delegation were gathering in the exhibit lobby. A few looked at him impatiently as he walked quickly toward them. "Sorry. Thought I'd have my people off and on their way to the Terminal by now, but there was a disturbance."

"We saw," L. G. Carmichael said curtly. "Nasty. The Whimeds ought to squash a few of those Vahnajes, teach 'em a lesson."

Omori made a wry face. "Hardly in accord with our purpose in attending this Conference."

"Huh! You trade with anyone. Just because you're getting all sorts of orders for those slimy echinoderm pelts as a result of Saunder's production. You'd think the Vahnajes would have more pride. Buying those things they saw in a Whimed play—"

"Can't we have any discussion without you starting an argument?" Jade Herbst cut in, annoyed.

"Delegates, please, we *do* have a schedule," Anthony said. He tried to herd his people along tactfully. The exhibit lobby wasn't the best place to accomplish that. They stopped frequently, admiring displays of innovative building materials, mineral resource extraction equipment, a new model subsea vehicle that caught Herbst's eye, and numerous other products the business managers and officials from Procyon Five planned to look into or wished they could afford.

Once they got past the bottleneck of the exhibits, there was another gauntlet to run—wending their way through the polyglot mêlée thronging the halls outside the Conference meeting rooms. The huge building had been cleverly subdivided since the opening ceremonies. Caucus chambers, individual delegation meeting areas, and some larger, general-session auditoriums filled the structure. Terrans and aliens were trying to find their assigned places or using the jammed corridors to carry on business transactions or arguments. Getting through the mess provided a crash lesson in how the ITC's purpose of intra- and interracial amity was—or wasn't—working. A delegate from Asita Hosi was talking to others from Loezzi, their separate Terran accents so thick they were having great difficulty in communicating clearly. Vahnajes and Whimeds were making a big production out of snubbing each other. Groups of Lannon were trying to sell some Terrans on the procyonids' "machineroo thing" materials. The Rigotians were barely making contact with "outsiders." An Ulisorian was floating on her platform above the mob, her transdevice repeatedly paging a Terran she hoped to do business with. There was a chatter of com-links and monitors, broadcasting ongoing major sessions and schedule-change announcements.

The quiet of Procyon Five's designated meeting room was a positive relief. Governor Yamashita and his aides and some of the delegates were already seated, sifting through documents. They smiled in a superior fashion at the late arrivals, and Anthony felt forced to apologize again for not being the first on this scene.

Not that it mattered. The appointment with the planet's Charter sponsors, the main thing on the day's agenda, had been pushed back. So Anthony had to preside over a lengthy rehash of the past four days' proceedings for an hour and a half. The trogs really had made some headway, not swimming free, but not being swamped by the bigger and far more prosperous attending delegations, either. All in all, it was not as good as Anthony might have hoped, but it was better than he could have expected. So far there hadn't been an excess of nibbles for Saunder Studio's manufactures. There was some encouraging fallout from his directing credits on the Whimeds' opening ceremonies. He wasn't planning to retire on the profits, not just yet! Perhaps, though, he'd stepped back a bit from the precipice overhanging bankruptcy.

"How long does the delegation want to wait for our sponsors' rep to put in an appearance?" Anthony asked, figuring they'd stalled long enough. He wasn't the only one in the room annoyed by the delay. "I'll entertain a motion to—"

The door opened, and the representative from Procyon Five's Charter Company swept in. He tossed off a very lame and unconvincing apology for his tardiness and took a seat.

Once there, however, he was efficient, briskly inserting vid wafers in the display player and spreading profit-and-loss graphics over the screens in a performance worthy of Saunder Studio's cruder edu-tapes, Anthony decided. The man was laboring to prove that he was an exceedingly overbooked person and barely had time to spare for this insignificant delegation. His bosses, after all, had far more important investments in Settlements that were paying off their debts much faster than Five was.

The rep wore the latest styles from Earth's Martian Colony. Five's delegates, who weren't shabby, were made to feel like raw peasants by comparison. "Hello! Doug Avalos. I think we've all met, at the earlier sessions. Right? Except I don't believe your chairman and I have had the pleasure." Avalos reached across the table, gripping Anthony's hand in an overdone manly gesture. "Like your outfit's tapes. Own a whole library of them."

"Thank you. Glad to hear it. Now, as to this meeting, we assume you received our request, earlier this year, for renegotiation of our contract? We sent specifics on the setback suffered by our major undersea industries." Carmichael, Omori, and Herbst were nodding emphatically.

Governor Yamashita chimed in, "We really can't expect our citizenry to meet the increased tax structure the Companies are demanding. It's difficult to feed our population adequately at the moment, let alone burden our people further." Around the table, delegates glanced approvingly at the little politician. He'd been showing remarkable sense of late, steadily gaining points with his fellow settlers.

"Yes, yes, we got your communiqué," Avalos said. "The Directors have been considering your proposals for negotiation."

Anthony leaned back, torn between rage and depression. This was his first time on the actual scene of such a meeting, but he was well aware of certain telltale body language. Avalos was simply laying the groundwork for delivering bad news, making sure his unhappy victims knew he was only a messenger, not one of the Charter Company's heartless board of directors.

The board of directors had been appointed by the late Carissa Saunder, and her heavy hand still lay on the profit-loss statements. Or was it Stuart Saunder's hand? He'd be no more concerned with the problems of a struggling frontier planet than his ruthless mother had been. The figures on the monitors told the story in plain black and red. Such grim readouts were the sort of thing that would make an unforgiving investor like Carissa or Stuart lean even harder on the settlers. There would be no renegotiation for a world that wasn't paying off. Procyon Five's taxes *were* helping reduce her enormous debt, but far too slowly.

"This audit was completed just before I left Earth to come here," Avalos explained. "C.S.P. confirms our findings. Now here, where Oceanic Genetic Engineering had a big drop—"

Sakae Omori defended his industry hotly. "There was a series of undersea eruptions! Destroyed half our cephalopod breeding stock and wiped out months of cultivated gem harvests."

Avalos spread his hands, commiserating. "Yes, but the fact remains, your loss seriously affects the Company's anticipated annual dividends."

Delegates frowned, struggling with the rep's heavy accent. They had to translate his words into Procyon Five's version of Terran English before they could begin to reply.

Separations! Fat-cat Earth-based investors, led by Stuart, and their reps had different speech patterns and very different attitudes. They didn't know, or seem to care, what went on in the Settlements.

Anthony's group spoke all at once, arguing, protesting. Avalos was unmoved. At a break in the uproar, Anthony used the orator's voice he'd inherited with Patrick Saunder's genes, saying, "Conditions on the frontier are unpredictable, sir. The same applied when Mars, Luna, and Goddard Station were first being established. Does the Company make no allowances for..." He hesitated, considering what phrase would have the most impact on this man from Back There. "... for The Spirit of Humanity? That Spirit accepts the vagaries of new environments. Terrans must be aided while they carry through that Spirit, or they can't succeed. Surely an extension of the investors' rate-of-payment schedule falls within that category." He dipped into his self-taught education from the history vids and added, "When the New Madrid earthquake of 2027 altered the old North American Union beyond recognition, and when the Long Storms hit Mars in 2090, allowances were made. People *had* to be given time to get on their feet."

Avalos smiled. It was what he did best. "Oh, I agree. A natural catastrophe can be a problem."

A problem? The man was a perfect mouthpiece for Stuart Saunder. He had no genuine concern for anyone or anything but lining his own and his bosses' pockets. He had the nerve to dismiss the pioneers' life-and-death crises as mere problems!

"The Charter Board feels your contract is a fair one. They intend to abide by the clauses faithfully and they expect the same from you. Your Settlement's founders *did* sign the documents. I can show you the signatures. Some of you were among the first landing parties, weren't you? Carmichael? Herbst?"

Yamashita spluttered helplessly. Anthony thrust a few more appeals at the rep without any serious hope of getting through to the man. Jade Herbst switched tactics. "A Settlement can be pushed too far into debt. Do the investors want to risk losing *all* their income?"

There was a startled silence. Avalos's smile weakened momentarily, then returned. "If you're referring to the ill-advised tax-withholding campaigns on other planets, those are being dealt with." He gathered his vid chips and got to his feet. "I wouldn't pin my plans on those futile rebellions, if I were you. The Fleet and the law will back us up. And I've studied your environmental stats; it wouldn't be easy for Five to get by for long without heavy imports of foodstuffs and certain essential materials. Oh, I understand you may be self-sufficient in fifty years or so, but—"

"Are we to assume the Charter Company intends to embargo our trade if we don't meet your unreasonable demands?" Anthony asked. He matched Avalos's smile, but underlined it with a threatened retaliation. "Then you won't mind having another Arden Settlement on your hands, I take it."

"I—I seriously doubt you'd opt for that course," the rep retorted, blustering. "I suggest you weigh the facts before taking any hasty action. I know it becomes difficult for you to see the whole picture out here."

Out here was in the boondocks, from the point of view of a Charter Company rep based on Earth. What did *he* know about the whole picture? It took settlers, people on the frontier's cutting edge, to do that.

Avalos edged toward the door. He smiled. "I really would advise you to increase your exports. That's the way to meet your assessment. Forget this nonsense about withholding taxes or secession. It can't work." Yamashita was gawking at the man in disbelief. So were the industrialists, minor business people, and their staffers. Hadn't the man heard anything that had been said in this room? Apparently not. He'd arrived with his mind made up. "Sorry to be so abrupt. But I have many other meetings to attend. My Company is one of the bigger investment groups, you know—another fact that you might keep in mind. A pleasure seeing you all. I look forward to our next get-together."

And with that, he exited.

Carmichael slammed his big hands down on the table. Jade Herbst winced at the sound, but her expression showed she was as angry as he. Yamashita and Omori were exchanging pithy opinions of Avalos. Anthony sighed and said, "This wasn't a surprise. I know this is my first chairmanship of your group, but your past records indicate this is the reps' usual pattern."

"Every damned time," Carmichael confirmed. "We just go around and around."

"You almost had him," Omori said. "I didn't know that, Saunder, about Earth's big earthquake and the storms on Mars. For a second or two, I thought we might actually get through to him. That's the closest anyone's ever come with one of these know-it-alls from Earth."

Anthony shook his head. "A slight dent in his armor, but no real result. It's the same thing most of the Settlements are running into when they try to talk reason to Earth."

"'Increase production,' he says," Herbst exclaimed, mimicking the rep. "Even if we could do that, export costs will gobble up every credit we gain."

A beep on the door interrupted her. "Who's that?" Yamashita grumbled. "Avalos back with more bad news?"

"Maybe he came to apologize and tell us he finally sees the light," Carmichael suggested sarcastically. "Don't be a chud, Hediki."

Anthony hastily cued the door monitor before the Governor and the irascible businessman could warm to their argument. The screen showed a group of Whimeds waiting impatiently outside the room—Ryseen, Yrae, and several other felinoids Anthony didn't recognize. Yrae said, "We wish to discuss matters of business with your delegation. May we enter?"

Even those who had some reservations about the Governor's plans for trade deals with the aliens were suddenly in the mood to listen to any proposal. Anthony took a quick opinion poll and relayed the delegates' assent to Yrae. The Whimeds filed in and the delegation's staffers scurried about, finding chairs for the visitors. An already crowded small room seemed filled to bursting. Yrae made introductions. The two Whimed males accompanying the Hilandros were Merux and Erith, businessmen.

While the amenities were going on, Anthony looked over Ryseen. She didn't seem injured or nervous. For a being who'd lived through a near-fatal cyborg crash landing, the Hilandro appeared remarkably fit. Ryseen Simra Hilandro was in fine fettle and on the move, proving to the Biyelin saboteurs that they hadn't ruffled her style in the slightest.

Anthony shifted his attention back to Yrae and was shaken by a powerful wave of emotion. Her eyes told him she shared his loneliness. If only they could be with each other. To talk. To . . . Aboard the shuttle, traveling between the worlds, during the rehearsals, the opening ceremonies, and these past four busy days of Conference business, she was always with other Whimeds and he was always involved in delegation matters, with no time to themselves.

Ryseen gestured to Merux, and he led off, speaking excellent Terran English—better, Anthony decided, than Avalos did, for the settlers' purposes. "I am authorized to arrange for cargo space on five of my Cooperative's transports. Terms of payment are to be one-eighth percentage yearly profit. If this is not agreeable, Cooperative is willing to discuss. In exchange, my Cooperative wishes to purchase cephalopod genetic materials for breeding purposes on three of our worlds. We also wish to purchase five

267

hundred kilotons of your processed *Procyonis mollusca* as pharmaceutical base."

The industrialists goggled in pleased astonishment.

Erith took up the proposals where Merux left off. He—or his employers in the Whimed Federation—wanted to buy minerals, echinoderm "silky" skins, and other deep-sea manufacturing products. And they offered to pay handsomely.

Anthony wondered if the pair actually *were* offering such a great deal in Whimed terms. The monetary systems of the two species were as different as the beings themselves were. As yet, Terrans were just beginning their trade ventures into the felinoids' stellar regions. When they penetrated a bit further, would humans make offers to buy objects common on Whimed worlds but rare in the Terran sector? And would they offer to pay in pebbles, while the Whimeds thought they were being foolishly generous?

Taking his chairmanship duties seriously, Anthony guided the negotiations. Several delegates were ready to snap at the first bait the felinoids dangled. Anthony managed to get them to backpedal and consider details, drawing out the Whimeds, dickering skillfully. His fellow businessmen threw him grateful glances, grasping what he was up to and following his lead.

It was a good deal from Procyon Five's angle. No matter if the Whimeds were getting a bargain. Their exchange credits would translate into good hard Charter Settlement Planets' currency and stave off a while longer the necessity of withholding their taxes and going the rebellion route. Anthony foresaw the dangerous risks in that course, yet knew it had to come, sooner or later, for his world and most of the other Settlements. This mutual arrangement with Yrae's race would make it possible for the trogs to build up reserves, though, enough to tide them through the very rough times that lay five or ten years ahead.

Things moved fast. By now he knew they would. Whimeds rarely mealymouthed, and they didn't drag their feet. The alacrity with which Merux and Erith upped their prices and accepted the trog delegates' demands confirmed Anthony's guess. Both sides were getting a nice profit out of this. So much the better.

As the details were settled, Ryseen said, "There is another member of your delegation we have with business to do." She leaned forward, peering intently at Anthony. "Taisso and Yrae Usin Hilandro tell of . . . is word facilities? . . . of Saunder Studio. We wish to use. I represent group wants friendship and trade to

Terran planets. Our knowledge human customs incomplete. Decide the proper procedure is education using Terran interpretation. You supply this? We will create Whimed forms we hope pleasing to Terrans. Maybe persuade them trade with our Federation. Your Studio experienced this method. You interested?"

She wasn't as perfect in Terran English as Yrae, and her speech was rapid-fire. Anthony was taken aback, thinking hard. He wasn't going to jump right in on this proposal any more than he had let his delegates swallow Merux's and Erith's offers immediately. No doubt the Hilandro wanted something out of this deal. What?

Yet it *was* an enormously tempting chunk of bait. Edu-vids were right up his channel! This was the sort of thing Saunder Studio had been turning out all along. It was what he did best. And he'd found out emota-sensor enhancement worked equally well with Whimeds or Terrans. Was it possible he could start expanding his markets? The top-of-the-line special issue of the Janyavee-Dempsey drama would grab the cultural audience, as well as entertainment-starved ordinary settlers. And a series of shrewdly produced Whimed sales pitches would open Terran outlets to the go-getter felinoids. If he handled this right, Anthony Saunder and his company would be in on the ground floor, piggybacking on any resulting interspecies trade that might result.

But was Ryseen's offer *too* good? What was the catch? There was always a catch.

He listened as she spelled out her ideas, hunting for the hidden snags. Whatever they were, she didn't let them show. The woman knew her stuff. In her own way, she possessed a lot of Yrae's riveting magnetism—the Hilandro touch. The delegates nodded, half sold already, even though it wasn't their companies she was pitching to. They were here to boost Procyon Five commerce in general, and one of their members stood to profit nicely, if Ryseen's proposed combined vid production scheme went forward.

Anthony reminded himself that Ryseen was a leading member of the Whimed Outer Satellite Faction—a troublemaker, counterpart of the Biyelin Vahnajes. Captain Saunder and Ambassador Quol-Bez had warned him about both groups. What would he be letting himself in for if he snapped at Ryseen's particularly juicy bait? Yrae's presence here was reassurance. It seemed a tacit support of the taller woman's statements. Perhaps he ought not to be so wary. It was possible this was the break he and Jesse needed most of all, the one that would guarantee the Studio's solvency.

He searched Yrae's face, seeking clues. She'd said almost nothing since this unplanned mini-conference had begun. Ryseen sensed Anthony's uncertainty and set the hook. "We would wish Yrae Usin Hilandro to perform in first combined creation this series vids. Whimed project opening ceremonies most ethical, most satisfactory. We wish to repeat."

She had read his mind! Was she reading Yrae's as well?

For a split second, Yrae glared murderously at the older woman, shaking Anthony's ideas about what was going on between the two of them. Then the actress's manner softened. She turned to him and he sensed rapport . . . touching . . . wanting . . . and afraid to want . . . alien dread and fear of wrong, of failure.

A Hilandro was the highest of the high among their kind, a cultural treasure with standards of perfection to match her superb talents. The worst failure, for Yrae, was to fall short of those personal goals of *aytan*. Striving to avoid that must be one of the things that made her separate, forever apart.

Ryseen was also a Hilandro. Didn't the same rules apply to her? The dark woman didn't seem troubled about ethics or fear.

Anthony said cautiously, "Thank you. This is a most generous proposal. I will need to discuss it with my partner. We certainly will give it our most serious consideration."

Carmichael exploded, "Consideration? What more do you want, Saunder? They're practically giving you their Federation on a plate!"

Anthony raised an eyebrow in amused scorn. The industrialist was quick to tell others what to do with their companies, but would he be quite so quick to jump in feet first if it was his manufacturing business putting its profits on the line?

"I cannot give you an answer at once, Hilandro," Anthony said, and Carmichael scowled.

"Intelligent," Ryseen agreed. "We wait your reply."

The door monitor beeped again, showing Whimed aides. When Anthony released the closure, they rushed in, babbling apologies for the intrusion. "Hilandros, important happens. Session Transport. Much people come. Captain Saunder. Colin

Saunder. The persons Griffith and Simpkins. Iulhar Dae Hilandro requests you come. Speaks esteemed Terran friends attend also."

The delegates were on their feet, goaded by curiosity. If this was important enough to break into the private meeting the Whimeds' Hilandros had sought, it must be important enough for everyone to pay attention to!

∞∞∞∞∞∞∞

CHAPTER SEVENTEEN

Breakthroughs

Procyon Five's delegation gathered with numerous others in the corridors and lobby areas, watching the ITC network's view screens. In a short time, nearly every monitor had been tuned to the ongoing transportation session in the main auditorium. Anthony found himself standing next to Otto Warschau, the impresario from Beno Settlement who'd offered David Lavrik such a wonderful job. "Any idea what this is all about?" Warschau asked.

"No more than you. It sounded like something we should hear, though, so we suspended our meeting."

"Beno did, too. I wonder . . ."

Everyone was wondering. Seats in important sessions like the current one on transportation developments were hard to come by. Those watching from the lobbies were the little guys; the big guys all seemed to have assembled within. It was a capsule survey of the field's V.I.P.s.—Gokhale. Uberto. Bolotin. Amber Muir of the Interstellar Travel Combine. Beauvois of the Société de la Famille Shipping Corporation. Ustin Sihu of the Whimed Federation's top starlane trade route division. Lannons. Rigotians. Vahnajes. Even an Ulisorian delegate or two. More beings arrived in the auditorium even while the onstage addresses were going on. Captain Saunder stood front and center on the dais. With her were Rolfe Chapin, her engineering genius of a brother-in-law, his assistants, and several Lannon scientists.

Brenna was saying, ". . . hadn't intended to make this particular announcement until next week's meetings. However, circumstances have accelerated our plans." She glowered into the audience at Serge Bolotin. The Charter Company mogul didn't act as if he'd had much luck ferreting out the secrets he claimed Brenna was concealing. He shifted restlessly in his chair, muttering to his aides. Anthony guessed that it was Bolotin's prying, though, that had accelerated his kinswoman's plans and triggered this announcement—whatever that was. The old test pilot was going to choose her own time and place to break her news, not allow any business competitor to leak it prematurely.

Inserts from zoom lenses framed the picture of the dais and showed important late arrivals to the session: Pickard of Terran Worlds Council; a prominent Biyelin Vahnaj delegate; and Colin Saunder with his candidate, Simpkins. It seemed significant that they'd gotten the word late; Ames Griffith was seated front row center, with Rolfe's wife, Elizabeth, Regan, and other members of Brenna's family. Colin and his puppet had to join the standees at the rear of the room. No one was willing to give up a chair, not even to the Conference's host and a potential next president of C.S.P.

". . . not a new situation," Brenna continued. A holo-mode of debit-credit reports and a display of the civilian interstellar vehicles currently in use in the sectors winked into being behind her, illustrating her points. "SMEI has been concerned for some time about the lengthening travel schedules and increasing shipping costs necessitated by our expanding civilizations. The New Discoveries Guild of the Lannon Financial Treaties League suffer a particular hardship, since their planets are strung out so far. We're both aware that the Vahnaj Alliance and the Whimed Federation employ, on a limited basis, short-range single-unit FTL shuttles. However, the Vahnaj-Terra treaty of 2080 and the Whimed-Terra Treaty of 2099 confine those craft to their own stellar regions, for mutually-agreed-upon political reasons."

And economic reasons, as every ITC delegate knew. There was an unhappy stir among the audience. Terran transport giants like Bolotin glared at their Vahnaj and Whimed counterparts, re-

273

senting the aliens' protectionist trade laws. Anthony noticed that Merux and Erith were looking pained. Did they fear Captain Saunder was about to circumvent those treaties and thus cut into the Whimeds' trade monopolies in certain areas? Well, they'd learn that competition was what made the sectors go round and they'd adapt or go under, just as any number of Terran settlers had been forced to.

". . . For the past three years, SMEI's R&D Division has been working closely with our colleagues from the New Discoveries Guild. Our labs arrived at similar theories, and we have joined our efforts," Brenna said. "We both need light, cost-effective intra-sector vehicles. Today I am happy to announce the results of our cooperative research. We will be introducing a new line of single-unit FTL shuttles for sale to any market. We believe this innovative transport system will go far toward relieving limitations in import-export schedules and enable small young Settlements and outposts to maintain regular ties with more centralized worlds in our separate sectors."

The murmuring rose to an excited chatter. Some onlookers were ecstatic, others agitated. Regan and her lover, Malcolm Griffith, were grinning and holding hands, approving wholeheartedly of this breakthrough. Serge Bolotin and Colin were scowling, for very good reasons.

Anthony nodded, commenting to his delegates, "It's going to make an incalculable difference. The less established worlds won't need to depend on renting space on the superhaulers. They'll be able to buy their own independent craft, make regular runs out and back. It'll speed up the communication and trade links."

Yamashita and the others brightened, beginning to grasp the full implications of the situation. Throughout the hall, delegates were talking excitedly, laying plans. But some watched the screens glumly. In every case, those sour about Brenna's announcement were employees or heads of powerful C.S.P. subsidiaries, members of Myron Simpkins's standpatters, whose stock would sink disastrously if those worlds backing Griffith's Progressive platform had the power to go off on their own tangents.

Rolfe Chapin and the scientists were handling the presentation on the dais now, exhibiting prototypes of their new ship, fascinating stuff to the engineers in the crowd, but over the heads of most of the rest. Anthony couldn't follow all of the specs and exploded diagrams, but he saw instantly that it would be only a short time before Brenna would be ready to sell these versatile little craft.

"Whimed has single-unit hyperdrive," Erith complained. "Can land on planet, go to stars. Should have sold to non-Whimeds."

"*Ge-aytan!*" Yrae reproved the businessman. "Captain Saunder has spoken of the treaty. We are bound to obey. If we did not wish it, we should have changed treaty. It is proper that ships to be used in Terran systems be discovery of Terran. Anthony's kinswoman is *aytan*. She abides by treaty."

"Captain Saunder also practical," Ryseen added, smiling unpleasantly. "It is satisfying this accomplished. You not agree, Anthony Saunder?"

He shrugged, afraid of angering Yrae; she had pointedly turned her back on the other Hilandro.

Herbst and Omori were cackling gleefully. Governor Yamashita rubbed his hands, jabbering to his fellow delegate, Procyon Five's Commerce Secretary, Blumfield. Carmichael jabbed an elbow in Merux's ribs and said with false sympathy, "Too bad. I guess we may not want to rent cargo space on your ships after all. We'll be buying some of SMEI's new little shuttle-starhoppers and setting up our own fleet."

Blumfield threw cold water on the gloating. "We don't know how much SMEI will charge for the single-unit craft. Maybe we can't afford them."

Jade Herbst pointed to the screen. "Here come the data." She read the stats out loud, and the rest whistled, awed. "Cargo and/or passenger capacity six thousand metric tons to twenty thousand for their biggest models. Cost: Fifty thousand C.S.P. credits, scaling to two hundred thousand for top of the line."

The Governor's jaw dropped. His aides were crunching numbers on their mini-terminals. Blumfield exclaimed, "We can do it! It'll take an extra usage tax for a few years, but at that rate, we should be able to purchase two at a time . . . or more, if our deal with our Whimed allies goes ahead."

Ryseen Simra Hilandro beamed. "The matter of export is not changed. This is wished. Yes!"

Omori said softly, "And if the new ships can do everything Captain Saunder says . . ."

The auditorium was a dizzying blur of reactions—shock, hope, consternation, and anger. Little wonder! A single-unit FTL shuttle! There had been popular-science vid articles about that

275

concept for years. But then there had also been speculative articles about a matter transmitter, too. Skeptics had dismissed both ideas as utterly ridiculous. Even the Whimed and Vahnaj versions of the single-unit craft were inordinately expensive and used mainly by their military and top authorities, not by ordinary citizens. SMEI's invention, in collaboration with Lannon engineers, promised to bring this impossible transport method down within reach of everyone, and put certain starlane monopolists in a financial pinch.

A ship could launch directly from a Settlement, taking her cargo out to FTL point, where it would convert itself to starhopping, shrinking light-years, making the little guys competitive in the Charter Settlement Planets' enormous sphere of influence. Some of the onlookers were speculating on whether this might tighten the links connecting the frontier with Earth. Anthony suspected the reverse would happen. Stellar distances were so vast, and Earth and its Colonies were, by comparison, a single island. The new ships would mean little to them. Instead, the single-unit craft would help weld together the growing independence movement.

It would take careful guidance to steer a course down a path into a suddenly uncertain future. Life on the frontier was always somewhat uncertain, but Brenna's discovery threw a whole new element into the mix. The next few years were likely to be tumultuous ones for the C.S.P. They'd need strong hands on the controls and cool heads making the decisions about where the Terran sector was going.

The Charter Companies might initially see the new ships as a potential bonus for them. Now the indebted Settlements would be able to pay back their sponsors more quickly . . . or choose to sever the contracts and thumb their noses at the gouging credit suckers who had no understanding of what life on Terra's fringes was really like!

There would be fresh rebellions, strikes for autonomy, and renunciations of any obligation to Earth. Worlds on the brink of bankruptcy would be declaring themselves free and turning their eyes outward toward alien sectors and trading partnerships that owed little to Earth.

Yes, strong hands and cool heads would indeed be needed!

Brenna's announcement solved a riddle for Anthony. He saw why she had been so determined to quash the Lannons' threatened boycott of ITC. Not having SMEI's engineering collaborators in on this gathering would have ruined all her plans. The race that so intrigued Regan was going to be a close ally of her family. Anthony felt sure Regan intended to take a very active role in enlarging that connection. With Ames Griffith heading C.S.P. and his son Malcolm—with *his* sector-wide communications net —on Brenna's and Regan's team, there might be no stopping them.

The Lannon would benefit hugely. A few years' partnership with SMEI, and they'd be a real mercantile menace, crowding the felinoids and lutrinoids and everyone else in the markets.

Where did that leave the Vahnaj Alliance and the Whimed Federation? Actually, in pretty fair shape. They'd scramble to hang on to what they had, maybe make a few much-needed engineering breakthroughs of their own. Prices would alter, no doubt. There would be monetary adjustments. But those were overdue and inevitable, within a sector *or* across species trading routes. The new kids on the block, the Terrans and the Lannon, would make up for lost time in transport technology, matching the older guys. There would be balance of a sorts.

Nearby doors exiting from the auditorium banged open. Colin Saunder, Serge Bolotin, and Pickard of Terran Worlds Council rushed out. Pickard was trying to make his companions see the obvious. "We can't stop it. Calm down. Brenna's always had a knack for this sort of thing. Look what she and her cousin Morgan McKelvey did thirty years ago! Gave us the stars. And that brother-in-law of hers, Chapin, is a modern Edison, a Ward Saunder."

"I don't have to listen to this," Colin snarled. "It's not my problem."

Onlookers eavesdropped shamelessly, fascinated by the big shots' conversation. Pickard said, "We have to work together on this, Colin. Be sensible."

"I am," the blond snapped. "I can see where this is going, and I refuse to be dragged down with you." With that, the Conference host stomped away, toward the building's outer doors, leaving in the middle of this very important gathering he himself had fought to obtain! Anthony watched his cousin's departure, noting that Colin met another disgruntled attendee next to the main exit. Fal-Am bowed to the merchant prince, speaking softly to Colin Saunder, and the two went out the doors together. That sudden

277

linkup seemed ominous to Anthony—ominous for the smooth progress of the ITC.

"If we can reach a mutual modus vivendi," Pickard was pleading with Bolotin, making the best of a deteriorating situation.

"Don't give me any of that sunlight," Bolotin retorted. "I knew this was coming. Those damned independent-minded settlers think this will enable them to cut loose, but once they quit floating, they'll see nothing's that easy. But in the meantime SMEI will kick everyone in the teeth, including me. Brenna and her puppy bitch Regan are diversified enough that they'll come out on top no matter what happens. But me? And Colin? We're right to be scared. And that fool Simpkins ought to be, but he's too cocksure to realize Brenna's chopped off his political head and handed it and his platform to Griffith on a platter. The Progressives will win, hands down. Get out of my way!"

The Hiber-Ship and Charter Company sponsor knocked Pickard aside and rushed toward a caucus room with his supporters. Unlike Colin, Bolotin wasn't abandoning the ITC. Captain Saunder's tough but honest competitor was settling down for a regrouping session. No doubt there would be many similar, hastily arranged plotting meetings this day. Human and alien delegations alike would be thrown into an uproar by Brenna's announcement.

"Do you wish to continue our trade talk, Chairman Saunder?" Ryseen asked slyly. A none-too-subtle hint. But he conceded she was right. After some confusion, he managed to herd the group back to their caucus room, and the trading discussions resumed. It was a process Anthony oversaw, but had minimal active participation in. Procyon Five's big industries were the ones thrashing out credit points and contract clauses with the Whimed businessmen. The chairman's job, in this instance, was to make sure they all stayed on track, which wasn't difficult. The rest of the time he sat by, listening with only a fraction of his mind. Yrae sat silently at Ryseen Simra Hilandro's side. The actress's manner was withdrawn. Someone who didn't know her might have taken her expression for intent interest in the negotiations. Anthony had come to know her and sensed Yrae was aching.

As he was.

What was the matter with him? He should be concentrating on his job, not yearning for intimacy with an alien woman. Lust could be much more easily satisfied, and with his own species, than what was prodding him now.

No, it wasn't lust, any more than his newly acknowledged responses to other emotions were mere self-delusion. What he felt for Yrae was a complicated tangle of sexual desire and tenderness. He wanted to embrace her, soothe away that hurt in her starry eyes.

Other things should be filling his thoughts: Brenna's transportation breakthrough and what it meant for his Settlement and his company; the fact that Simpkins's star was setting and Griffith's rising fast, and what *that* would mean for legislation in C.S.P.'s Council, and future trends on Terra's frontier; less system-shaking matters, like the upcoming days' sessions, and his delegation's attendance schedule; serving their interests, handling his chairmanship duties properly. ...

He'd never be able to, in his present state of mind.

The bargaining with Merux and Erith seemed to take forever. But the afternoon was only half over when they and Procyon Five's major industries had reached a tentative accord and agreed to finalize details during the remainder of the Conference.

It was time for adjournment. The delegates all had things that needed doing, personal meetings they wanted to get to, and correspondence with their companies and departments back home to tidy up. Anthony went through the forms, wrapping the day's business. People began leaving the small room, drifting off to their various appointments or returning to the Terran enclave and their quarters.

Yrae and Ryseen lingered. So did Anthony. Ryseen pretended to be occupied in clearing a porta-terminal she'd brought to the negotiating session. Anthony didn't really care that the alien was plainly hanging around to see what happened between the Whimeds' cultural treasure and the director who had guided Yrae to such a triumph at the opening ceremonies.

What happened was instinctive and unplanned. Yrae peered up at Anthony and groped for his hand, her small fingers curling about his. The touch was fire, threatened to explode the accumulating feelings in his breast. And he knew those feelings were reciprocated, though perhaps not identically. How could they be? this fey, lovely woman facing him wasn't human. But...

"I—I wish to be with you. We—we could speak of the project Ryseen offers."

279

It was that moment in Saunder Studio's rehearsal stage all over again, with shifted nuances. Yrae wasn't being coy this time. She was tacitly pleading with him to help them both escape.

"I think our time is our own for the moment," Anthony murmured. "What did you—"

Ryseen suddenly broke in. "There is arboreal place."

Yrae seized on the suggestion gratefully. Her look for the other Hilandro was the warmest she had ever extended to her counterpart. "Yes. Anthony, it is a—a haven in the forest near the complex. The Conference provides this for visitors."

"I'm familiar with the tree hostel. Colin constructed it as a tourist attraction, though, in the early days of this Settlement, it was a common habitat for the pioneers." Anthony hesitated. "I haven't been to the area, but I understand it's quite attractive."

And it was secluded—a treetop sanctuary.

"I will arrange," Ryseen said, smirking, and to Anthony's surprise, Yrae raised no objections to the other alien's taking over, nor to Ryseen's obviously self-serving motives. What difference did it make that Ryseen Simra Hilandro was in effect throwing the two of them together? It was what they both wanted, wasn't it?

He certainly did. And the nearness of Yrae, her willingness to share totally, swept doubts aside.

The short skimmer ride to the arboreal hostel had a dreamlike quality. Throughout, Anthony had eyes only for Yrae. The skimmer's driver was a discreet Whimed staffer; the man might have been a robot, never glancing at his passengers at all. He brought the craft to a skilled hover at the elevated platform of a reserved suite, waited until Anthony and Yrae had stepped out, then dropped away, down into the green shadows of the enormous forest.

The hostel was at the edge of a continent-wide jungle. In the distance, the Complex was a bright cluster of buildings in the late-afternoon sun. Around Anthony towered trees—a blend of native flora with DNA-engineered imports from Earth—each of which boasted a private hostel room, complete with skimmer landing apron. The Whimed delegations apparently had made frequent use of this adjunct to the ITC Complex. Ryseen, when she was seeing the couple aboard their skimmer, had commented idly that the forest cabins reminded felinoids of their home environment. Anthony absorbed the remark eagerly. He knew so little of Yrae's background. Had she grown up in a place like this, an environment thick with leaves and cool depths?

Inside, he forgot his curiosity concerning her background, immersed in the eyes that were stars, eyes that a man could drown in, never wishing to rise to the surface. "Is this—is this what you wanted?" he asked, reining in hormones and tension.

Yrae nodded, returning his stare, reaching into the core of his being, touching. He felt her hunger. Those tinges of fear were there as well, but desire was overwhelming them.

They had learned that cross-species sex wasn't easy. There were variations on the standard methods, however. Some Anthony had employed in bedding Terran women. Some were new to them both. They were learning, perhaps for the first time, what such a relationship could be between a human man and a felinoid woman.

Terran traditionalists and alien purists might well have disapproved. Anthony didn't care. He had never known such intense joy. There was no preamble. They had both read the signals right, and the barriers didn't exist. They found completeness, not ordinary orgasm or release. This was something far beyond, a blending of minds and total presences—that *ehi*, or soul, that Yrae spoke of.

Had Ryseen known this was how it would go? Yrae insisted that Whimeds weren't true espers, but empathy, an offshoot of *diya*, must be a powerful parallel skill, and Ryseen was a Hilandro. She had to have been aware of Yrae's hunger.

Anthony didn't care if Ryseen had acted to provide her fellow Hilandro with a Terran *muruen-che*. He was too sated, too content. And now he discovered how loudly Yrae could purr when she was sated also. Very loudly! She lay in his arms for a long while before she went through that odd ritual she called the returning, the nonfruitfulness, though no color wands played over the shadowed room's ceiling this time.

It had been an incredible experience. Anthony had lost all track of time. He assumed it must be nearing twilight, from the slant of the sun's rays filtering through the leaves outside the room's window. How long dared they stay here? He had responsibilities waiting for him back at the Conference complex. Yrae must, too. He peered at her, trying to read her expression, and he

281

stroked her velvety skin, sharing her contentment . . . and her fear, that damned lingering sensation of fear.

Didn't it ever leave her? Even in these circumstances? Fear of what? Of *ge-aytan*, unethical failure, a fall from . . . from grace. He wasn't sure where he'd heard that term, wasn't certain what it meant. Was it something the Spirit of Humanity cultists believed in? Purity of thought and purpose? The emotion radiating from Yrae implied that.

She caressed him, sending tremors through his body. If she'd never performed in erotic dramas, she should have. Yet she hardly seemed conscious of the effect her touch had on him.

"To share . . . I did not think . . . it is believed such things cannot be," Yrae whispered.

"What we shared wasn't *aytan*?" he asked carefully.

Her head snapped up. "It . . . a Terran would not understand."

"Wouldn't I? Maybe you underestimate me." He attempted to embrace her anew, but she pulled away, inexplicably irritable. Her resistance collapsed as quickly as it arose, though, and she sighed.

"It is so difficult. I have studied—"

"About Terra and Terrans. And you assumed you knew what we were like, that it was impossible for felinoid and *Homo sapiens* to share. Correct?" Anthony demanded. "You do know a hell of a lot about us. About me, rather. I picked up what I thought I knew about your species from spaceship jockeys' gossip. And a hell of a lot of what they say is sheer fantasy." He kissed her gently and added, "The reality is finer than those bragging fools could ever dream."

Yrae explored his face with her fingertips. "You—you are not *muruen-che*." There was an odd note of anger in her voice. "That is an end to the trembling. No more." She touched the base of his throat and said, "A *muruen-che* would never create the new trembling here. Not sharing. Not *ehi*. This has never been for me."

"Nor for me," he admitted readily.

The realization seemed to frighten Yrae. She had known a lifetime of separateness. There was physical release, but nothing comparable to this total sharing. And now she had it all—with a *Terran*.

Her starburst eyes glittered with tears. Anthony held her close, wanting to say and do the right things to make her happy again.

But what *were* the right things? A casual reference might hurt her. Innocent words might be loaded with menace to a Whimed. So much still lay between them—time and space and evolution. No invention from Brenna's SMEI labs could bridge this gap. Anthony Saunder and Yrae Usin Hilandro had found each other, but could they hang on to what they now had?

There had been no permanence in her affairs with *muruenche*, nor in any of Anthony's previous affairs, either. Even when there could have been, he hadn't allowed himself to love. He'd had to accept himself, first, and learn who and what he was before he could open his being to Yrae.

Suddenly, she sat up, wriggling free of his embrace. "Why does Jesse investigate Pilar?"

"What?"

"Jesse investigates. He investigates your kinsman Colin Saunder. Colin Saunder also investigates Pilar Gutierrez."

Anthony blinked, pushed himself upright, turning to face her squarely. "Jesse . . . learned that Pilar's idents are forged. He thinks she may be an unknowing front for some Terran investors, so he's checking up on it. As for Colin—I don't try to keep track of my cousin. I try to stay out of his way. Colin claims he has possible business ventures Pilar may be interested in."

"Colin Saunder has been speaking to Fal-Am."

With a startled laugh, Anthony said, "Yrae, my kinsman is host of the Conference. He talks to all the delegates, even Biyelins."

"No! Not Conference. Other matter. Pilar speaks to Fal-Am. Dangerous! You must keep her away. Keep Jesse away. You have affection for them. You will be hurt if the Biyelins—" She twisted violently back and forth, alarming him. "Your kinsman . . . he . . . the Biyelins . . . *ge-aytan sa-chel!*"

She was frantic. Trying to spit out warnings, slipping into incoherence, reverting to her own tongue. Intense hatred of the Biyelins crippled her speech.

"And you must not . . . *stransir!* . . . *nulow!* . . . *nulow!* . . . not join work Ryseen!"

"What does that have to do with—"

"Must not! Stop! Too much has been done."

Anthony was bewildered. "I thought you wanted to be with me. If I take Ryseen's new project, we'd be working together again. We could continue sharing."

Yrae was jittering, getting to her feet, beginning to pace. Her behavior was a stark contrast to the languor of minutes earlier. Anthony rose and stepped in front of her, blocking her nervous to-and-fro pattern. "You want to be with me—and you don't. What's going on? Is this some sort of game that got out of hand?" She stared uncomprehendingly and he elaborated, "I mean, I don't think you could make up your mind whether you wanted to be with me or not until Ryseen pushed you into it."

"Ryseen did not!"

"Didn't she? Maybe that's not the term Whimeds use, but it's what *I* call it. Is that Hilandro your boss?" Yrae's sputtering outrage was his reply. Anthony shrugged. "Then if you're in charge, you simply say that any future combined Terran-Whimed productions are out of the question. It wouldn't matter what Ryseen wants."

"Too late," Yrae wailed. "Is done. I should not have agreed! Wrong! Wrong! *Ge-aytan!*" Again she lapsed into her own language, and Anthony caught allusions to a plan or a scheme, a "not truth" and a "circling." None of it made sense. "They did not—did not see this would happen. I want no hurt to *you!*"

There was a buzzing, and Yrae started like a terrified animal. "Easy," Anthony said, pressing her arm. "It's my mini-com. Jesse's trying to get in touch with me." He went to the room's terminal and punched in the code absently, his focus still on Yrae.

The connection was made. Jesse was leaning in tightly to the screen, so closely that Anthony could see nothing to tell him where his friend was calling from. "Glad I got hold of you, kid." The older man's tone was furtive, as if he were afraid he'd be interrupted at any moment. "Remember I said Pilar didn't know what she was getting into? And how! I found out she's hip-deep in Biyelin Vahnajes. And Colin's really monopolizing her. He was out at the shuttleport with us, snooping around. Want to hear something else cute? That fornicating bastard who fed Davy that line that he had the Vahnaj plague? Renzi? Well, he's here on Four. Working for *Colin*. Can you beat that?"

Jesse paused, gulping in a breath. "This whole thing stinks, kid. But I'm breaking through, getting right down to the dirt. Tried to talk Pilar out of having anything to do with Colin, but she's not convinced. She—she knows about Carissa, too, by the way. I guess Colin told her. And I think she's following him right now. He peeled off from the Conference this afternoon, headed for big trouble. I'm going after them and yank Pilar back to shore before she's in over her head. We're leaving the complex."

Yrae thrust Anthony aside and took his place at the terminal. Jesse was taken aback as she exclaimed loudly, "You are correct! Pilar is in danger. *You* are in danger. Please! You and Pilar must return to Terran enclave. Anthony and I will come to you there."

"Nice of you to be so concerned," Jesse snarled. "Did you tell Anthony that it was your Whimed Committee who put Pilar up to using those forged idents?"

"No, you do not understand."

"I understand fakes when I see them. You and your people are too damned tricky for my taste," the associate producer said angrily.

Anthony tried to moderate. "Calm down. We can figure this out—"

"Biyelins Vahnajes are danger, not Whimed!" Yrae shrieked, and both men flinched. As Jesse pulled away from his end of the connection a trifle, Anthony caught a glimpse of a plasticene canopy around his friend. Apparently Jesse was making his call from a skimmer. Indicators on the hostel room's monitor were no help; they simply established that his friend was transmitting from a location well south of Jangala. *Where* to the south? Where was Jesse going?"

To rescue Pilar Gutierrez from unspecified danger.

"Go yell at Taisso," Jesse flung at the actress. "I'm not one of your flunkies. Saying 'Hilandro' won't make me jump, lady." He turned to Anthony and said, "Don't pay any attention to her. Pilar and I will be fine. I'll get back to you. Right now I've got a lot of catching up to do, and then some serious sandblasting."

"You must not, Jesse!" Yrae cried. She hammered frantically on the terminal until the unit creaked protestingly.

The associate producer's image was gone. The screen was blank.

"He broke the link," Anthony said, tense with worry.

CHAPTER EIGHTEEN

⊙⊙⊙⊙⊙⊙⊙⊙⊙

Love and Danger

"Reestablish! Must!"

"We can't," Anthony said. "He was in a vehicle, routing the message through the Jangala or Conference com centers. Once Jesse pulled the plug, there was nothing for our terminal to hang on to. He didn't want to talk to you anymore, and he made sure I couldn't call him back. He wants to call the shots."

Yrae swung wildly, her flailing hands almost striking Anthony. He caught and pinned her, wrestling with a hysterical Whimed. She was hampered by her frenzy, and he was able to match her superior strength. "Dammit, cool off! Tell me what's going on!"

"Not understand . . . would not understand . . ."

Anthony's worry and impatience were lines on a graph, meeting. He shook Yrae. "Don't tell me I can't understand. After what we've shared? I understand a hell of a lot more than you believe. Whimeds don't understand Terrans very well, either. You've never seen me *really* angry—but you will! Now *talk*! Why is Jesse in danger?"

The actress opened and closed her mouth several times, astonished. Panic in her eyes dissolved, replaced by that glint of fear.

"It is . . . *ge-aytan*. The—the—circling. There is no word in your language, only in Whimed . . . and Biyelin Vahnaj. Whimeds did seek out Pilar. This is so. We did not supply incorrect idents. Pilar was described as producer of entertainments. We wished to approach Anthony Saunder. We did not learn of her false papers at once."

"But you did learn of them, and you didn't tell Jesse and me."

Yrae flushed in shame. "It—it was decided not to inform you. And it was decided to continue the—the circling. Pilar's intent was to investigate Anthony Saunder and Colin Saunder. This was useful to our purposes—to support *you*, not Colin Saunder."

Anthony released her, staring. "Why?"

"A—a matter of . . . legalities. Pilar investigates your life. She sees if you have committed breaking of Terran laws or if Colin Saunder has done so."

"Why?" Anthony repeated, much more sharply.

"It is concerned with your kinswoman Carissa Saunder. There is an object referred to as a will."

"Oh, my God. Pilar's accent. She's some kind of Earth-based attorney or legal detective. That has to be it. But if Stuart inherits Carissa's estate, what do Colin and I have to do with this?"

Yrae frowned. "Not certain. It is only that Pilar's actions are pleasing to the circling. We assisted her. Vahnajes did not at first know of her intent. Pilar begins to examine Colin Saunder's record and Biyelins become aware. I—I think the Biyelins have discovered something we do not." She swallowed and continued, "The circling. Biyelins ally with your kinsman Colin Saunder. We ally with you. But now the Biyelins seek Pilar because of this thing of a—a will. Jesse is with her, and I am afraid for them. The—the circling is not being obeyed. It was not to harm you. But Biyelins are not ethical. They will achieve this thing called a will for Colin and the circling is won for them."

A tidal wave of confirmation smashed over Anthony. This was far more than interspecies mercantile rivalry, and a lot deeper ocean than he had imagined.

How deep? It went all the way back to Earth, to Saunder-home, to a dead tyrant Empress named Carissa, and to her will.

Was it possible Carissa had disinherited Stuart before she died? That would make some sense out of this mess. Carissa's fortune was too big to measure easily—an enormous chunk of wealth and power, for whomever it was who won the legal right to it.

Earth, Saunderhome, the sordid history of Carissa and Stuart, Stuart's tragic paramour and their bastard son, and the sad tale of the five little clones Carissa had created to foil Stuart and his bastard's claim to the vast Saunder holdings—all that had followed Anthony and Colin out to the stars.

The door banged back against the wall, sending wood chips flying. Anthony whirled, his fists at the ready, adrenaline pumping.

Majlur stood on the threshold. His crest was a crown of quills. The alien's chest heaved and sweat ran down his pasty face. He was holding a thing Anthony had seen in newscasts of Whimed military operations—a "stinger," a sidearm, a "crowd control rod," as the vids put it diplomatically. This one's snout was bloody. Majlur wasn't aiming the weapon at Anthony or Yrae. The stinger dangled from the protocol expert's limp fingers as he panted, "Fal-Am has escaped our watcher. Not in Conference Complex." He studied Anthony, noting the Terran's raised fists, and smiled evilly. "I am not enemy, Anthony Saunder. Fal-Am is enemy."

"Who allowed this escape?" Yrae demanded.

"Not important, Hilandro. Failure has been punished." Majlur hefted the bloody stinger. Yrae punished those who offended her by roaring at them and hitting them with invisible waves of emotion, unnerving, but bloodless. Anthony doubted the failure Majlur had punished had walked away from the chastising.

That watcher—the aide who had watched Anthony on Clay and reappeared here at the Conference?—had been tailing Fal-Am. Part of the "circling," whatever the hell *that* was; it seemed to be a dangerous alien espionage game, played for keeps.

And now Fal-Am was the hunter, probably closing in on Jesse.

"Where's Colin?" Anthony asked.

Majlur grimaced. "Your kinsman not at complex or Jangala."

"You put a watcher on Fal-Am but not on Fal-Am's new ally, my cousin? Dumb!" Anthony drew back a fist, but withheld the punch, conquering his rage with effort. "You cretinous chud! I don't know what sort of cold war nonsense you and the Biyelins are tangled in, but you knew Colin was involved. And you let both him and Fal-Am get away. Now you don't know where

288

either of them is. You've got the worst case of vapids I've ever seen. I've directed kiddie scripts with smarter characters than you! You felinoids don't understand Terrans at all, do you?"

Yrae was sobbing. "Biyelin," she whimpered. "Fal-Am is . . . and your kinsman has much power."

"And Colin's hoping he'll gain even *more* power if he can snag Carissa's inheritance somehow," Anthony said coldly. "I can make a fair guess how he'll operate. If Jesse's right, and I believe he is, Colin, Fal-Am, and his Biyelin Vahnaj flunkies are trying to worm certain information out of Pilar. They may have panicked when they realized you were closing in on them, with your damned 'circling' game. Okay. Okay! I have a good idea where all of them are, but I need transportation, and I need it fast." Majlur nodded dumbly and Anthony added, "I mean, a form of transportation that hasn't been sabotaged."

The alien's expression tightened, revealing the cruel, capable intelligence officer behind Majlur's fawning facade. Anthony had misjudged the man, just as Terrans, Whimeds, and Vahnajes had been misjudging each other throughout this insane episode. The "protocol expert's" gaze darted toward Yrae and he said, "Ryseen Simra—"

"I am Hilandro." That phrase had never packed such power before.

"It will be done," Majlur said hastily, almost groveling.

Anthony yanked on his clothes, as Yrae was doing. "It needs to be done *now*," he warned.

"*Hilandro . . . stransir fo kwilya Irast Aytan Eelay . . . cheleet . . .*" Majlur got no further. Yrae stared at him. He bolted from the room as if she'd set fire to him.

As Anthony and the actress stepped out of the treetop hostel, they saw the espionage agent standing on the edge of the landing apron, waving furiously. A flight of cyborg rocs approached, weaving precariously through the forest, hissing to a hovering stop beside Majlur. He gestured, urging Anthony and the Hilandro aboard. "Has been . . . assured. Modified. Will take much speed."

Anthony was already in the passenger seat, his arm about Yrae. Majlur crawled in next to the driver. The rocs rose, flying out over the adjacent plain toward the Conference Complex. Twilight shadows were snaking across the open landscape, and rain slanted down through the forest and pattered on enclaves and surrounding plazas. Yrae huddled against Anthony, shivering. He drew her closer, sharing his body heat.

"Hilandro," Majlur said carefully, "you must tell us where go."

Anthony spoke for her. "To Colin Saunder's desert HQ in Procyon Four's southern arctic. Near Metallon City." Yrae eyed him wonderingly and he said, "Jesse dropped me a hint. You might say I read his mind. Biyelins and Whimeds aren't the only beings with some degree of esperism."

For an instant, her lips tightened into a thin, angry line. Then she told Majlur. "We obey Anthony Saunder. Seek out Colin Saunder and Fal-Am. Go to Metallon."

The situation was impossible, something out of one of the many adventure melodramas the Studio had produced. But Anthony needed no emota-sensor feed to stimulate the trip-hammer beat of his heart. The rocs sped through the twilight rain, aiming south. Jangala blurred behind them, a dim horizon of trees and Conference towers. The prairie to either side of the cyborg squadron was a green-beige smear. Modified, indeed! The biomech creatures were bettering the speed of most skimmers.

Years ago, Anthony had discovered that his Studio's fictional vids often had far more emotional impact on many settlers than actual happenings on another planet. Now he was trapped in just such an improbable adventure, except that it was *real*. "What about Four's authorities?" he wondered. "Won't they try to stop us?"

"They will not," Majlur said, with no doubt whatsoever. How could he be so sure? Bribery? Or had the Whimeds used stinger weapons to silence key local Terrans? Anthony preferred the former possibility. At least fewer people would be hurt that way. Majlur was listening to his communicator; he turned and reported, "Colin Saunder was in company of Biyelin Vahnajes when left Jangala."

"Not exactly news," Anthony grumbled. Majlur nodded, the nod of a subordinate to a superior officer. In the Whimed's judgment, Colin Saunder was an enemy. It made no difference that Procyon Four's merchant prince was a member of the highly respected Saunders and McKelveys or that the alien civilizations were currying favor with an important Terran trader. Colin had thrown in his lot with the Biyelin Vahnajes, and the Whimeds had no further trust in him. On the other hand, they seemed to be trusting Anthony Saunder completely. He was the admiral of this fleet of rocs, the cyborg he and Yrae were riding and those following, carrying Majlur's backup team. They were all rushing toward Metallon, merely on his say-so.

And what if he had guessed wrong? Jesse had always called Colin's Metallon HQ a sandblasted fortress—and he'd referred to sandblasting in his last communication. It was a big gamble, but it was the only thing Anthony had to go on.

Maybe . . . maybe it was all a false alarm. Fine! Anthony would rather be proved a fool than have any harm come to his friend.

"What about the security staff at Colin's residence down there?" he asked. "They won't just let us walk in, and they'll be armed."

Majlur was speaking into his communicator again. He muttered, "Have persons there. Will assist."

Spies? Whimed spies posted even at Colin's isolated former operations center? How complicated *was* this Whimed-Vahnaj cold war game, anyway? Procyon Four was a Terran Settlement, and the Whimeds and Vahnajes were offworlders. They had no right to use this world and its people as pawns in their so-called circling. Anthony doubted either group of aliens had sought permission from C.S.P. Council or the ITC Board to engage in their not-so-harmless game on Terran territory. It amounted to a small invasion. Espionage agents fighting each other deep in the human sector, disguising themselves as tourists, tradespeople, actors, committee members . . .

Yrae shivered again, and Anthony's earlier annoyance with her melted. She had given the orders and made the decisions that had gotten this show on the road—hopefully in time to do Jesse and Pilar some good. But he suspected Yrae was as scared and uncertain of the outcome of this business as he was.

Damn Colin! If he hadn't joined forces with the Biyelin Vahnajes, none of this would have happened.

But the merchant prince had learned that there was to be an inheritance—an irresistible lure for the exiled bastard. And simultaneously Colin's kinswoman Brenna had dropped a bombshell, ruining the prospects of Colin's C.S.P. presidential candidate and probably seriously damaging the future top-dog status of Colin's chosen base planet, Procyon Four. There had been too many blows, added to the pressures the Conference host had been bearing and the staggering expenses. All the situation needed was a catalyst.

Why not take the Biyelin Vahnajes' bait and flee back to Saunderhome and the empire Carissa had cheated him out of?

The cyborgs flew beyond the tropical belt's rain and greenery, entering the desert boundary. There were no challenges by Procyon Four's patrols, no stern orders issuing on the com for the fliers to retrace their course to Jangala and submit to arrest. Maybe the authorities were busy with other things—such as figuring out where the Settlement's most important man was. The host of the Interspecies Trade Conference had vanished as if into thin air! Where had he gone?

That was a question Anthony himself wanted answered. "What does *eelay* mean?" he asked suddenly. The roc's driver spat a pithy Whimed oath and Yrae and Majlur gasped.

"It—it is arbitrator," Yrae said. "Only equivalent in Terran English."

"Majlur suggested you ought to notify the honored ethical arbitrators. Would you care to explain?"

Yrae closed her eyes; when she opened them, Anthony sensed her barely suppressed fury. Her crest remained flat. The emotion was confined to her face and the empathic waves he was sensing. She groped for her jeweled purse and drew out a familiar object—the *oryuz* cap. Majlur watched reverently as Yrae placed it on her head. "I must prepare. Biyelin may await us," she said, then turned to Anthony. "Ryseen Simra Hilandro has not confided in the *Irasti* Arbitrators. A mistake. You must ask her why this was not done."

Hilandro scorning Hilandro. Two gifted females—very much at odds. Like so much Yrae had told him, this was another riddle with enormous pieces missing.

But then a Terran wouldn't understand.

And few Whimeds could understand just how sick with worry this particular Terran was at the moment.

A journey, even at dangerous speeds like this, had never seemed so long. A dust storm blew up as the flying caravan neared Metallon. The rocs plowed straight on, programmed protection masking their eyes and nostrils with glassene hoods. Inside the creatures' howdahs, the riders were safe from the sand, but not from their fears.

Anthony hoped the driver/programmers knew what they were

doing. If they collided with other rocs or ran into objects in Metallon, they wouldn't have to worry about Vahnaj and Whimed espionage games; they'd all be dead.

Fortunately, the storm eased as they arrived at the mining community's outskirts. A few groves of carefully irrigated shrubs loomed through the murky veil. Then a larger shape arose. Anthony's roc slowed, its cyborg power cells whining. The biomechs soared into a landing at an isolated mansion. Whimed guards stood by the entrance to the courtyard.

As Anthony leaped out of the howdah, he turned his face to avoid blowing grit. Majlur was yelling at the posted agents. They shook their heads negatively. The intelligence agent shouted, "It is failed! Biyelins gone. Your kinsman and Terran woman with them!"

"Where's Jesse Eben?" Anthony thundered. The Whimeds didn't have an answer. They waved vaguely toward the mansion. Another group of armed guards was inside the courtyard, surrounding several bound Terran prisoners. Some of the humans wore spray bandages or slings. There'd obviously been a fight, but these people were merely roughed up, not bloodied by stingers or worse. All but one of the Terrans wore a uniform, standard security issue. The civilian aroused Anthony's ire and, knowing what he'd find, he pulled the man's head back roughly. "You're Renzi, aren't you?"

"I didn't do anything!" the hapless prisoner whined, then spat out sand. "Yeah, that's me. Renzi. I just did what they told me. That dumb actor swallowed the story whole. It wasn't my fault."

Several of the mansion's staffers stirred restlessly. Majlur's guards cuffed them, tightening the glistening alien bonds restraining arms and ankles. Apparently the Whimeds didn't care how many human laws they trampled in manhandling Terran citizens, with no nod at all to the local police. Just move in and . . .

How much extra time would it have taken to get the cooperation of the police—police who owed most of their livelihood to Colin Saunder? Too long. And time was the one thing in shortest supply.

"Damn those whitefaces and the cat folks, too," Renzi said. "Told me I'd get out clean. That judge was goin' to send me to a penal colony, but they managed to pay him off."

"And you agreed to work with the Biyelins. And now you're working for my kinsman," Anthony snapped.

Something in his face made Renzi scream, "No! No! Honest! It wasn't my idea. Wasn't Saunder's either, before those white-faces were finished. They . . . it looked like they were draggin' him with them when they left."

"*Where's Jesse Eben?*" Anthony repeated, jerking ruthlessly at Renzi's mane, pulling the man halfway to his feet. "Talk, damn you!"

"Dunno! *I don't know!* I had to play along. They had weapons of some kind. Told me to stay here when they took off . . . and then . . . and then I heard a shuttle." Renzi tried to turn his head to indicate an easterly direction. Anthony's grip didn't permit that. The man moaned, begging for release.

"You're not hurt, you rotten lump of shit!" Anthony flung Renzi down to the sand and ran up the walk into the mansion. Yrae was at his heels, with him every step as he searched the sprawling residence. On her command, Majlur's crew ransacked the place.

The merchant prince's desert HQ was huge, but most of it was frills, Anthony found—tiny courtyards, atria cluttered with hot-house plants, and alcoves of gaudy art objects and costly furnishings. The house echoed with his and the Whimeds' footsteps. There were no servants or security staff; *those* were under guard outside.

Hope was waning when Anthony opened a sliding door in the innermost section of the sandblasted fortress. He froze. There was someone inside the dimly lit room. Yrae touched the illumination panel, brightening the scene, and that someone screamed in agony.

"Dim it!" Anthony cried. Yrae had already done so, her expression stricken with guilt. Anthony loped across the large chamber and knelt beside a twisted figure lying on the floor. He was afraid to touch his friend. Jesse was curled into a semifetal position, his arms clasped tightly across his belly and his legs drawn up. The slightest sound and even muted room light seemed to hurt him, making him thrash about.

"Jesse? Jess? It's me."

No response. The associate producer was drowning in pain.

Yrae could see better in the half light than a human could. She bent close to Jesse, examining him without making physical contact. All the while she sang, a gentle, sad little tune. The faint noise penetrated the wall of pain between Jesse Eben and the

294

universe. His posture relaxed a trifle and he gasped, struggling for breath.

"Where's he hurt?" Anthony pleaded. "I can't see any blood or wound. Jesse, can you tell me where you hurt? We want to help."

"Biyelin." Yrae pressed her forehead, holding tightly to the *oryuz* cap as if it were a shield, the only thing saving her from death. Her face contorted with hatred. "Biyelin, they have . . . *ja sarige! Wai!*" Her starburst eyes were eerie gems, gleaming. She traced an unseen line along Jesse's brow and temples, her fingers held millimeters from his flesh, never touching. "It is the Biyelin weapon. Forbidden. Yet they have used it upon a Terran. How could they bear this terrible crime, Anthony?" She was weeping, her tears dropping on Jesse's hair.

Anthony stared at the *oryuz* cap. A protection against the Biyelins' silent talking, she had called it. But Jesse had no such protection when . . .

"We've got to help him!" The injured man writhed, and Anthony lowered his voice to a whisper. "What has Colin done to him? You have to tell me, and don't say a human can't understand. I understand that Jesse's been hurt. And so do you. Help me to help him."

She gazed past Anthony, and he turned and saw Majlur's agents framed in the dimly lit doorway. Yrae hurled a torrent of angry Whimed words at them. Anthony picked out mentions of the honored ethical Arbitrators and other references to an unethical horror. The Hilandro was pulling out all the stops, telling the spies to go against orders and damn the consequences.

Majlur thrust his way past his subordinates, coming further into the room. He peered down at Jesse. The hard-faced intelligence agent looked aghast, aching with pity for the injured human. In fact Majlur looked as if he might be sick. He gulped audibly and said, "*Irast Aytan Eelay lishan. Ma Ryseen Simra Hilandro di Taisso.*"

"Taisso did not want to do this," Yrae said in defense of her busybody acting coach. "He argued that we should not agree to Ryseen's . . . You—you will show the Arbitrators into here when they arrive. They must see what—what the Biyelins have done." She broke off, sobbing helplessly, rocking back and forth in her distress.

Slowly the other Whimeds retreated. Anthony was alone with

his suffering friend and his alien lover. Yrae whispered, "We must not move him."

"Hell, I know that. We've got to get medics. There aren't even any blankets here, nothing to cover him and keep him warm."

"He does not feel cold or heat," Yrae said morosely. She sat on her heels and crooned that strange song again. Jesse quieted, turning his head toward the lulling sound. Now and then Yrae interrupted the crooning, explaining what Anthony had wanted to know but dreaded to hear. "Biyelin, the silent talkers, this is their method to—to amplify the weapon. They are forbidden to use. They do use against their own beings, which says much. *Aaa!* They use against Whimed. Have hurt my people. It was . . . I did not think it could be used against Terrans. *Wai!* How was this done?" she moaned. "They—they . . . When Biyelin attacked our Federation, they used Whimed captives. A—a link. One who must possess same species structure. Same brain structure. They invade through this pattern-being. It is your kinsman. He was their link. Biyelins use Colin to take them into Jesse's mind. Much pain. Much injury. Biyelins always hurt and kill."

Anthony's gut was ice. All those warnings he had assumed were racial prejudice. Yrae hadn't been exaggerating. The Whimeds had damned good reasons for designing something like the garish *oryuz* cap Yrae wore as a shield against a terrible, mind-probing weapon.

The weapon caused agony as well as enabling the user to reach into another being's thoughts. What Biyelins did to their own kind was their own business, if a mercilessly cruel one. But with this device, and a link—a member of an alien species to provide a channel into the alien's brain—they could cross racial barriers to probe a Whimed's thoughts or a Terran's.

Speculative articles claimed that true ESP would be a wonderful gift. It would aid communication between peoples. And if it could eliminate the barriers dividing species, it would foster universal understanding.

How wrong they had been.

Had Colin acted as the Biyelins' esper weapon-link deliberately? The concept was devastating. Anthony had no love for his cousin, but he found it difficult to believe even Colin would stoop so low. Sure, the merchant prince was a slick operator, undercutting financial competitors and finagling a kinsman's shuttle reservations away from him. That was small stuff, compared to this atrocity.

Renzi had said that the Biyelins were dragging Colin with them when they left. That implied that the Conference host hadn't gone willingly into this sadistic esper mind-link.

And yet Colin was no fool. He had to have realized earlier that Fal-Am's group wasn't dabbling in lightweight matters. Colin should have known this affair could turn ugly and gotten out of it.

"Kid?"

The word was so feeble that at first Anthony wasn't sure he'd heard it. Rattling phlegm caught in Jesse's throat as he said weakly, "Lord God, it hurts."

Anthony felt ripped apart. "Help's on the way. Lie still. Everything will be okay." He risked touching the older man's shoulder, wanting to comfort. Jesse hardly reacted.

"Some—some kinda thing the whitefaces had. Don't—don't know what it was. Hooked Colin—Colin and me . . . into it. Oh, God. It just sliced my head right open."

In his imagination, Anthony was wringing Fal-Am's white, wobbly neck. Or was it Colin's neck he was crushing? He wasn't sure. He only knew he wanted to pay *somebody* back.

Jesse was groping dazedly, and Anthony took his friend's hand and held it. There was no response. Jesse's eyes were unfocused. But Yrae's singsong eased that agony in his face. After a while he said, "They—they wouldn't stop." His fingers spasmed against Anthony's. "Diggin' things out—out of my brain. And they wouldn't stop. Made me—made me talk. Too—too damn much. Lord, kid, where's Pilar?" Jesse asked suddenly, fear for the Earth woman overcoming his pain.

"She'll be here in a few minutes," Anthony lied. He *had* to make his friend believe that.

It didn't matter. Jesse had already forgotten the exchange. He was limp, his head lolling on Anthony's arm as he listened to Yrae's song, and perhaps sounds within his head that no one else could hear. "Stuart. That's—that's what it's all about, kid. Stuart's dead. Died . . . a coupla weeks after 'Rissa kicked off. Pilar . . . told me. She—she didn't find it out from Colin. Knew it all along. 'Rissa and Stuart can't—can't hurt you anymore."

Anthony choked on his anguish. Carissa and Stuart *were* still hurting him. They were the cause of what had happened to Jesse —they, the will, Colin's interest in that inheritance, and the

297

Biyelins scenting that hunger. Pilar was somehow involved in the events back on Earth and an island paradise named Saunderhome. "Please don't talk," Anthony begged.

And yet he needed to know. Did Jesse grasp that intuitively, trapped as he was in that black hole of pain? The older man rambled on, "Pilar's . . . on your side, kid. Just the idents are . . . are phony. She was tryin'—tryin' to be impartial. Works for a fi-financial conglom . . ."

"Conglomerate," Anthony supplied. If he couldn't make his friend take it easy, at least he could help him spill what had caused his agony.

"Yeah . . . yeah . . . Pilar . . . assigned to investigate for—for executors Earth's Saunder Enterprises. 'Rissa's will. In-instructions. Stuart . . . didn't leave any will. Best heirs are you 'n' Colin."

Comprehension made Anthony shudder and curse Carissa anew. So Stuart had died intestate, and Colin *would* have a valid claim to that inheritance—if Carissa hadn't somehow managed to cheat her son out of his rights. Both of them were dead. And obviously there was some involved clause in that bitch's last testament. Executors sending Pilar Gutierrez to probe the backgrounds of the likeliest candidates for that dual inheritance suggested the terms of Carissa's will weren't hard and fast, that there was something yet to be decided.

Unless Colin, aided by his Biyelin allies, pulled a fast one before Anthony had ever realized what was going on.

Jesse seemed compelled to talk, to tell what had happened. Anthony, his throat aching, didn't try to stop him. He listened. "Pilar supposed to . . . sniff around. Gonna . . . gonna . . . explain it all to you 'n Colin when she got the stuff together. Those Whimeds . . . contactin' her . . . good cover story . . . so she could check up on you. She shouldn't have agreed with 'em . . . shouldn't have . . ." Jesse sighed and was quiet for so long that Anthony grew afraid for him. Then Yrae's soft song seemed to arouse the injured man. "Colin . . . tol' Pilar he had . . . a deal t'talk with her. Supposed to meet her here. Rotten seaweed. Smelled it right away. Caught up with her . . . out there." Jesse might have thought he had gestured toward the desert north of the mansion. In reality, he'd made no move at all. His wounded mind functioned only in some areas. Lungs filled and emptied and the heart pumped blood. Little else was working properly. He mur-

298

mured, "I—I made Pilar see sense . . . that it was a trap. She's stayin' at one of those minin' camps. I came on out here . . . in th' storm. Was gonna snoop around . . . like that—that vid you directed from Abdul's script . . . can't—can't remember the name . . ."

"*Sands of the Lost Settlement*," Anthony said, caught in a waking nightmare of Jesse, playing the gallant rescuer, overtaking Pilar Gutierrez on her way to a professed business meeting with Colin and persuading her to hide at a camp while he went ahead to scout the territory. In the script Jesse had spoken of, spying on potential enemies had been a snap. The hero had pulled it off easily, thanks to the playwright. In real life, Jesse had been taken prisoner and tortured. Was the same true of Pilar? Was she still at that mining camp? Anthony seriously doubted it. The Biyelin device would have made Jesse tell the aliens everything they wanted to know—including the entrepreneur's location.

What would they do with her? How far would they go beyond sabotage, torture, and kidnapping? Murder? Colin wouldn't want that, even if he was accepting their aid to gain his inheritance; Pilar's death would be difficult to explain. Worse, it might destroy Colin's chances to grab the Saunder wealth.

Did the Biyelins grasp that they'd gotten themselves into a nest of snakes—Terran laws and Terran attitudes. They understood those as little as Anthony understood the strange circling game Whimeds and Biyelin Vahnajes were waging in the middle of Terra's Charter Settlement Planets. With Colin's goals made their own, they would now have to carry their lawbreaking patterns back to Earth, to the birthplace of humanity.

And the Whimeds—what did *they* get out of this?

There were Arbitrators involved. What were they arbitrating?

Terrans had been pawns, manipulated and used, one against the other by the extraterrestrials.

Yrae's song had made Jesse's breathing noticeably more comfortable than it had been. Pain still assaulted him, but he could escape it briefly through her music. The cultural treasure broadcast her sympathy and caring with the same special intensity she applied to her dramatic art.

Whimed and Terran were different species, but a bridge between them appeared through Yrae's sharing, as she had shared so much with Anthony.

Was there any medicine to help Jesse? Or was Yrae's song and gentle pity the only solace? Anthony was torn between grief for his friend and a thirst for revenge. And no ready outlet or cure existed for either emotion. Jesse's injuries might even be beyond Terran medical knowledge. Renzi said Colin and the Biyelins were gone, probably taking Pilar with them as a reluctant guest. By now the fugitives could be at Procyon Four's orbital transfer point or further, well on their way to the Solar System to claim Colin's long-overdue inheritance.

There was a commotion outside. The noise disturbed Jesse. Anthony glared at the door; as if in reaction, voices stilled. Then aliens began to file slowly into the room—Majlur and Taisso, Ryseen, and six other unknown Whimeds and Vahnajes, three males and three females, identically dressed in slashed robes and jumpsuits. They stood apart from the others, outside the usual animosity dividing lutrinoid and felinoid. Arbitrators.

Yrae's healing song faltered. Jesse murmured, wanting her to continue. Anthony tightened his grip on his friend's hand while he watched his lover. Yrae got to her feet slowly and walked straight toward Ryseen. The taller woman's stance was oddly resigned.

To Anthony's surprise, Yrae addressed her counterpart in Terran; then he understood why. This was as much for his benefit as it was for the aliens'. "I was told this venture would be worthy."

"It was *hasju aytan*," Ryseen said, defending herself.

"It was *not* a necessary bending of ethics to noble purpose!" Yrae challenged. "You told me no one would be harmed. Jesse has been harmed. Anthony has been harmed, his *ehi* wounded. It may be that Pilar has been harmed. And *I* have been harmed. You have made me behave most unethically. I was not informed fully of many things." Taisso and Majlur looked very relieved that her anger wasn't directed at them. Without turning from her target, Yrae pointed at her acting coach and said, "Taisso was persuaded by you, Hilandro. You were not ethical. You did not tell us what could be. *I* am Hilandro. You may not do this to me—or to them!"

She struck, her nails raking open Ryseen's cheek. The second bolt was a stinging slap, jolting the darker Hilandro. None of the aliens moved to aid Ryseen, and her starburst eyes glazed. Staggering, she fell, sprawling ungracefully beside the door.

✪✪✪✪✪✪✪✪

CHAPTER NINETEEN

Decision

Anthony was shocked by the outburst of violence, yet envied Yrae; *she* had someone to vent her rage upon.

Majlur and Taisso were frozen, afraid to take sides in this clash of Hilandros. The Arbitrators made no move, either. After a few moments, Ryseen came to, struggling upright, leaning against the door. She mopped at her bleeding scratches and smiled at Yrae, looking oddly pleased, baffling Anthony anew. Aliens! They wouldn't explain their motives, brushed off all Terran attempts to learn about them, and tortured and kidnapped humans who got caught in their nefarious plots. The only one of the e.t.s who had shown any compassion or made any concessions was Yrae.

One of the Vahnaj Arbitrators started toward Anthony and Jesse. Startled, Yrae ran after him, trying to intercept and stop the lutrinoid. He paused, speaking to her in her own language. The actress was visibly taken aback. When the Arbitrator went on, she followed him meekly. Wary, Anthony hovered over Jesse as the grayface folded his long legs and squatted beside the humans. The Vahnaj steepled his long fingers, whispering, a high-pitched, almost inaudible muttering. Like Yrae's song, the sound appeared to alleviate Jesse's pain. Yrae's attention shifted anxiously between the lutrinoid and Jesse, as if she were superintending his healing attempts.

The Arbitrator glanced at the others of his kind and said, "It is . . . urr . . . Biyelin device. Much a-bused. Grave . . . urr . . . offense."

"Ryseen said Terrans would not be harmed," Yrae repeated, aggrieved. She was once more tracing that pattern over Jesse's forehead without making physical contact. Her features were soft and very human. "Ryseen is Hilandro. I had believed this to be honorable. A benefit to Anthony Saunder. To avenge those Whimeds attacked by Biyelins. I was deluded. I beg forgiveness from *Aytan Eelay*. I have not understood. I have failed."

The Vahnaj squatting by Jesse said, "You did not fail . . . urr . . . Yrae Usin Hilandro. Others . . . urr . . . mis-cal-cu-lated." His sideburns were flattened, revealing his distress. "There . . . urr . . . have been terrible crimes. Biyelin have . . . urr . . . ta-ken Terran person pri-son-er. Must not . . . urr . . . be per-mitted . . . urr . . . harm . . ."

Anthony groaned. So Pilar *was* a captive, and in great danger. How could he ever break this news to Jesse?

"Biyelins . . . urr . . . guilt-y . . ."

Damned right they were! Of kidnapping and mental rape, for starters!

Nevertheless, the Vahnaj *was* condemning members of his own race. There was hope that not all aliens were monsters.

A Whimed Arbitrator asked bluntly, "Can you cure the Terran, Tib-The?"

"Is . . . urr . . . un-certain."

"I touch him with *diya*," Yrae said. "His pain is eased when *I* sense he is not in pain." She was envisioning Jesse whole again, emotionally re-creating that moment, using her special talents to help him. It wasn't medicine. Anthony didn't know what to call it, but was grateful it existed. Would Ryseen have used her abilities to help Jesse? That was questionable.

Tib-The explained, "There is . . . urr . . . flaw . . . much sev-er-ing. Ef-fect on Ter-ran of Biyelin device is . . . urr . . . not known."

"You and Yrae Usin Hilandro will try," the Whimed Arbitrator said. He wasn't making a suggestion. None of the mediators wore badges of rank, but that felinoid acted like the one in charge.

Yrae suddenly reached out, caressing Anthony's face, surprising him. "I will stay with Jesse," she assured him. "This Vahnaj has training in the counteraction of the Biyelin device. Together we will help."

"Is that possible?" He'd been afraid to speak those words, afraid to hear the answer. What had that damned alien mind-reading thing done to Jesse's brain? Was he going to keep on hurting like this for the rest of his life?

"Healing is possible," the felinoid Arbitrator replied, then added a precautionary, "It is possible with a Whimed."

"But you don't know if it's possible with a human," Anthony said. "Because this never happened to a human before. You and the Vahnajes have been playing some kind of ugly interspecies spy game, haven't you, using innocent people as your cats' paws?"

Vahnajes churred and Whimeds growled. The felinoid running the show said sharply, "There is no game."

"Then what is it? A war?"

That accusation triggered even stronger denials. A lutrinoid said, "Is not . . . urr . . . Vahnaj Al-liance and . . . urr . . . Fee-maid Feder-a-tion which part-i-ci-pate. Is not . . . urr . . . per-mitted."

"Oh, I see," Anthony retorted. "You let your species' trouble-makers slug it out on your frontiers and extend their brutal little war into neighboring sectors. But *you* keep your hands clean. How tidy! I suppose you think that clears you of all responsibility for the blood and suffering the Biyelins and Outer Satellite Faction have caused."

"Anthony, you do not—" Yrae began.

"Understand?" He impaled her with a look, as she had so often done to him. "Explain it to me, then. Are *you* a member of the Outer Satellite Faction?"

Yrae shook her head violently. "No no no no! My worlds, the Zyo, are of Main Federation. I—I had not dealt previously with Outer Satellites. Ryseen Simra Hilandro came to me. With *diya* she showed me the Biyelin attacks upon her planets. Atrocities! The Biyelin device! I saw and felt . . ." The actress broke off, shivering in horror, reliving that experience in all its grisly details. *Diya* was not solely a gift; it was also a curse. Ryseen's Hilandro abilities had enabled her to bring the troublemakers'

303

war to Yrae with stunning impact, forcing Yrae to share each torture and death.

"Your ethics tell you it's uncivilized to hate," Anthony said gently. "But you couldn't forgive what the Biyelins did to the Whimed Outer Satellite peoples. Ryseen's followers weren't Main Federation felinoids, but they were part of your species, just the same."

She nodded, very woeful, a lonely, isolated cultural treasure, sharing her being with no one, not even a *muruen-che*, until she had met Anthony Saunder. Ryseen, though, had appealed to Yrae's sensitivity and caring, involving her in the sufferings of Outer Satellite victims of this spy game. Vengeance was supposed to be an honorable pursuit, or so Ryseen had told Yrae, making her believe. The actress had come to battle wearing her anti-esper Hilandro armor, the garish *oryuz* tiara still on her crest.

Ryseen's operators had come up with a slick scheme—a way to follow the Biyelin Vahnajes right into the Interspecies Trade Conference and foil the enemies there. The plot was tailor-made for Yrae's talents. A dramatic production! An adaptation of Janyavee's classic was being planned. What better vehicle? The host of the ITC was Colin Saunder, a trading partner of Vahnajes, some of them Biyelins, like that evil Fal-Am. The Whimed Committee assigned to the drama project would hire a Terran intermediary, Pilar, and approach Anthony Saunder, a rival of Colin, the felinoids' pawn to match the lutrinoids' pawn.

None of the aliens had fully grasped *why* the two Saunders were antagonists. It served the purposes of the Biyelins and the Outer Satellite Faction—and that was all they had considered.

"Not a war, huh?" Anthony said with a grunt. "Well, you may have a war on your hands before you're through, *Aytan Eelay*. The opponents you were supposed to be arbitrating have let their brutal little conflict slop over into other species' territories, egging on the Lannons, trying to get them mixed up in a Terran smuggler smash, sabotaging Ryseen's cyborg here at the Conference, using me, using Colin, and using Jesse, Yrae, David Lavrik, and who knows how many other beings. You're abusing interspecies friendship past any acceptable limit. Terrans don't like being pushed around by anyone. Not by Terrans and not by aliens."

Whimed crests bristled. Gray Vahnaj faces paled. The Arbitrator in charge insisted, "There is no war. No game. This event is concluded."

Anthony carefully eased Jesse's head down onto the plushy carpet, then got to his feet. "No, it isn't. It's hardly begun. Unless you plan to kill me and every Terran who knows what's been going on, you can't hide it. This isn't your private show anymore. You dragged others into it, especially Terrans, and we're in your game up to our necks without wanting to be. I, for one, intend to learn the rules and fight back with everything I can."

"Not . . . not permitted," the Arbitrators' spokesman protested, aghast. "Terra must not join. Would be unbalance."

"That's exactly what I'm going to do—unbalance your damned game to hell and gone unless I get full and complete answers, and fast!"

There was a hasty muttered consultation among the *Aytan Eelay.* When the Whimeds and Vahnajes emerged from that, their leader said, "It . . . is to be explained to you, Anthony Saunder. We are the definers of limits. There is no war between our races. There has been no war for very long time. War is unethical. War is destructive." Anthony was appalled by the man's tone of icy detachment. "It was decided, many orbits ago, that such encounters must be restricted for the mutual survival of the Vahnaj Alliance and the Whimed Federation. The elements you may term aggressive are allowed to conduct moderate conflict. It is not allowed further. We limit. We are the deciders of satisfaction."

"Satisfaction?" Anthony said. "Meaning who wins each bloody little joust, huh? What do you do? Encourage your malcontents to emigrate to the Biyelin planets or the Whimed Outer Satellites? Get rid of the restless legions, in effect, by letting them kill each other, just so long as they keep it out of your nice safe civilized central worlds."

Despite his scorn, Anthony was thinking of ancient human tribal practices of sending forth the champions from two warring groups. They fought it out to the death. The result decided which people got to use the grazing lands or the best fishing areas or whatever. And there was peace for a while. One of the champions had to die, but his tribe survived.

Terra, Lannon, and probably the Rigotians as well still had hot spots of violence on birthplace worlds and Settlements. But they tried to pass laws to chop down the worst cases and their author-

305

ities usually sat on the throwbacks, attempting to be civilized in fact as well as name.

Vahnaj was a very ancient culture, Whimed a fast riser. Both had roamed the starlanes longer than relative newcomers like humans and procyonids and Rigotians. But the Vahnaj Alliance's and the Whimed Federation's poses of being more advanced, more sophisticated beings were just that—poses. They were siphoning off the dark drives still lurking in their gene pools, isolating a murderous cancer, setting limits, and establishing rules for their events. The troublemakers were to kill only each other. That left the majority of their populations to progress peacefully, presenting outward images of lofty civilizations, free of their savage pasts.

Presumably, both sides regarded that as an admirable solution. Whimeds and Vahnajes were still killing each other, but on a very tiny scale in the cosmic arena. There was no interstellar war; no high-tech planet-killing weapons wiped out entire colonies and outposts. There were no enslaved Settlements, no genocide—just a few Biyelins and Outer Satellite Factions bashing each other.

Plus an occasional member of the races' mainstreams, and a few unlucky Terrans.

"What about Jesse?" Anthony demanded. "What about all the others who have been hurt by your event? Do you just walk away from the mess your troublemakers have created? Do you kill us to shut us up? What?"

The Arbitrators conferred again. The scene was extraordinary. A hundred kilometers to the north, delegations of felinoids and lutrinoids sat on opposite sides of Conference sessions, radiating hostility toward each other. But this racially mixed group was working together toward common goals. Why couldn't their peoples in general follow the same pattern? And how could the Arbitrators stand by and let segments of their populations kill each other?

"There has been a crime," their spokesman announced. "There will be amends. Yrae Usin Hilandro consents to assist Tib-The in restoring Terran Eben to health." It was legal language, stilted, and not reflective of the kindness in the Arbitrator's starburst eyes. "You and Colin Saunder were involved in this event because of your kinship."

"Kinship, history, and because we're Saunders," Anthony corrected. "Yes, we became involved. I can forgive my part in it,

306

if you help Jesse. But thanks to all your interference, the host of the Interspecies Trade Conference has left this Settlement. Whether he was a willing participant or a kidnapped victim makes no difference. When word spreads of his absence, the Terran delegations will be in an uproar. Inevitably they'll find out what's happened, and they'll want to blame somebody. By allowing the Biyelins and Outer Satellite Faction to conduct their nasty games in Terran territory, you broke our laws. Human delegates will line up with their Vahnaj and Whimed trading partners, everyone will take sides, and the Conference is going to disintegrate."

"No! Not so!" The Arbitrators were genuinely frightened by the prospect. Anthony didn't have to hammer home his point; they saw where matters were headed all too clearly. Colin's disappearance—and with it his overall control and management of Conference functions—could be the first step on a slide to interspecies disaster. The Ulisorians, the only completely unallied race attending the ITC, would probably pull out in a hurry. Vahnajes, Lannons, Rigotians, Terrans, and Whimeds would begin wrangling and accusing. Trade negotiations would grind to a halt. Treaties would be rethought, diplomatic relations severely strained. Transportation would be curtailed—and at precisely the time when SMEI's single-unit FTL shuttles promised to *open* new markets and eliminate some of the barriers. There would be months, perhaps years, of organizational chaos.

"The Conference must continue," the Arbitrators' spokesman said. "Essential. How is this to be done, Anthony Saunder?"

"Why ask me? It's not my job. I'm a small businessman, heading a fairly minor delegation. All I want is to pay back the people who hurt Jesse. You started this, you can catch and clean your own problems."

There were cries of consternation, extreme distress, and even terror. Anthony saw grim possibilities in the Vahnajes' and Whimeds' eyes, and began to reconsider his position.

There were things more important than immediate vengeance for Jesse, Yrae, himself, and all the others the troublemakers had used. The fates of billions of beings hung in the scales. This matter might not stop at mere organizational chaos and a temporary derailment of trade development. Small, limited events had a way of escalating into much larger ones. Politicians and alien authorities, all with their own axes to grind, would seize an opportunity to sink their opponents, and the opponents would fight back. A restricted, vicious little game to bleed off the energies of two species' savage throwbacks could provide a trigger for a far wider conflict. Humanoid history was full of such incidents— and sectors-wide holocausts could result.

Terra's Charter Settlement Planets would be on the front line. Procyon Five, like its struggling neighbors, might never get a chance to purchase those new SMEI FTL shuttles. They'd never reach their potential, never become a prospering planetary community. In any such escalation, it was probable their population would be decimated, or worse, their world laid waste, even its indigenous life destroyed.

It wouldn't take much, in the galactic scheme of things, to shove them *all* over that brink in a galactic catastrophe, rising from an interspecies "misunderstanding."

Two time lines extended ahead of Anthony. On one, the Conference came to pieces, and things went rapidly downhill into very dangerous regions.

On the other...

"We have to do something," he admitted, racking his mind to discover what. The C.S.P. was an infant, a loosely united, often squabbling bunch of frontier societies, trading, growing, expanding, working out the snags, and learning to share space with each other and their alien neighbors. That particular future time line must continue and thrive. There were those linked to Earth who might say, "Who cares what happens out there?" They didn't see that there was no turning the clock back, no retreat to the cocoon, now that mankind was established among the stars. They had to go on, or...

Money! Of course. That was the quick-fix answer, the plug in the dike that could hold back a slide into catastrophe.

"Brenna." The aliens stared hopefully at Anthony. "If she would step in and take over as ITC host, that might do it. Some of her competitors will squawk, but they'll also realize the dangers if she doesn't do the job."

A Whimed Arbitrator protested, "Brenna Saunder is ally of Vahnaj Ambassador Quol-Bez and of Lannon."

Anthony glanced at Yrae, saying, "And I'm an ally of a Whimed cultural treasure. Does that make me an enemy of Tib-The and every other lutrinoid? Colin is a trading partner of Vahnajes, some of them Biyelins. You won't get impartiality, no matter who's running the Conference. This is an interspecies crisis, and you of all beings should see that we have to pull together. And you're going to need money to do it. I suppose, in your profession, that isn't a serious concern. It is when the crisis point is located at a mercantile assembly. I speak as a businessman, with some view of what it'll take to hold the Conference in place. Captain Saunder *has* money. If anyone can get you out of this jam, she can. If not, the entire Terran sector will be breathing down the necks of the Vahnaj Alliance and the Whimed Federation. So . . . decide. And I suggest you do it quickly."

They already had decided. That was obvious from the aliens' faces. Their spokesman asked, "You request this of your kinswoman for us?"

"Why should I? You made the mess. Clean it up."

"You are of her blood. You understand," the spokesman said. "You will make Captain Saunder understand."

He didn't know if he was being honored or used—again. After a long hesitation, Anthony sighed. "I'll try. Where's a com?"

It was a strange procedure. Arbitrators made the connections for him. Anthony suspected the call was routed through a series of Whimed and Vahnaj top-level scramblers and secret channels. But eventually the signal reached Captain Saunder at the center of her SMEI HQ ITC. That was quite a feat in itself, Anthony acknowledged. He felt his way into the conversation carefully, unsure who else might be listening in and not wanting to dump everything in his kinswoman's lap at once.

Brenna looked tired. She'd had a hectic day following her triumph at the Transportation Session, wheeling and dealing with customers for the new shuttles, mollifying her company's rivals, and doing her bit to solidify Ames Griffith's rapidly building political fortunes. The aging test pilot listened stolidly to Anthony's veiled explanation, then said, "You're not at the complex, are you?"

"No, I'm at Colin's estate in Metallon. It's rather complicated. And it's important that I talk to you."

"I'll bet it is." Regan Saunder's muffled voice came from somewhere out of the frame and her mother waved a shushing hand and said irritably, "All right! And *you're* right, girl, for a change." SMEI's owner leaned back and sighed. "I'm no fool, Anthony. Something big is cracking. All these Vahnajes and

Whimeds contacting me. Do you know where Colin is? Tell him to get his tail back here. No, scratch that order. I know you and he can't stand each other . . . and Colin definitely can't stand *me*. Is he still on this planet?"

"I—I think we'd better talk about that face-to-face, not on the com."

Brenna nodded. "Agreed. I hate being in the dark."

"I'll come to your quarters," Anthony volunteered, simultaneously worrying how he'd care for Jesse if he had to go back to the ITC complex right now.

"Stay put," his kinswoman said. "I'd rather you—and those cat folks and grayfaces with you—didn't come traipsing up here now. Touchy situation at the Conference. *Real* touchy. We'd better keep this wrapped until we know what we're doing. What should I bring?"

"Just yourself," Anthony said. *Yourself and your money and enormous influence.* "Thank you."

It wasn't a very long wait. In the interim, Anthony did what he could for Jesse; and, under the Arbitrators' instructions, Vahnaj and Whimed assistants took charge of the prisoners Majlur's agents had captured. That was *another* touchy situation in the making; Terran citizens performing their duties had been roughed up and confined against their wills by aliens operating illegally in Terran territory. It was one more batch of feathers and fur Captain Brenna Saunder would have to smooth down. Ryseen and the other Outer Satellite Faction people disappeared, and Majlur had left earlier. Anthony wondered if the Arbitrators had arrested them, but was too preoccupied to ask. Taisso, eager to cooperate, received certain orders from the stern faced bi-species "deciders of satisfaction" and left the estate, carrying out some unspecified errand. By the time Brenna's skimmer arrived, there was no one in the residence but Anthony, Yrae, Jesse, and the Arbitrators.

A commotion outdoors informed Anthony that his kinswoman had made good time. He caressed Yrae's face, trusting her with Jesse's care, and went to meet the Terran party in the estate's central room.

"Okay. Where's Colin?" Captain Saunder said without any preamble. "I've got *part* of the story—and long overdue." She peered at one of her companions, Ambassador Quol-Bez. He seemed pained by the accusation in her stare. Regan and Brenna's brother Blake were the only other people with her. The Captain had brought no aides, staffers, or security guards, maintaining a low, secretive profile. "You should have told me sooner," she complained to Quol-Bez.

The Ambassador blinked owlishly. "It was not permitted, friend Brenna. I am obligated. It is duty. You comprehend."

"Duty has its interpretations," Anthony said bitterly. "We've found out our alien allies can lie to us and use us just as readily as enemies would."

"Where's Colin?" Brenna repeated, her patience gone.

Anthony described the event, his inadvertent role in the e.t.s' cold war, and Colin's. He'd had time to rehearse and condense the account, and his lust for revenge was losing its punch, turning into a festering ache. He ticked off details methodically: the carefully balanced nongame; the sabotage of Ryseen's cyborg; the tricking of David Lavrik and lying to Yrae; the probability of a sabotaged Whimed shuttle; the torturing of Jesse; and the kidnapping of Pilar, perhaps also the kidnapping of Colin, after using him as a mental link to pry into Jesse's mind. "From the Terran angle," Anthony finished, "Gutierrez was sent to investigate Colin's and my backgrounds, finding out if we've been strictly law-abiding, worthy of inheriting Carissa's fortune, and Stuart's. Oh, yes: *he's* dead, too."

His kindred weren't surprised. Regan nodded. "We heard from Varenka today. She's been appointed an executor, though she didn't know about this advance investigation. That was the idea of some thick-skulled Earth-based SME legal idiots."

"Cretins!" Brenna exclaimed. "Always trying to hush things up, hide facts even from those who need to know. Look where that got us!"

Anthony pointed through the open door to the next room, where Jesse lay, tended by Yrae and the Arbitrator. "I don't care about the estate's lawyers and the legal machinations. That's not what I care about. It's the real issue. Bending laws out of shape."

Brenna stared compassionately at Jesse and murmured, "You're right. Injuring the innocent *is* the issue. But laws get bent all the time."

"No doubt. Do you think that reality will keep the Conference members in line and tending to business?"

Captain Saunder winced. "Not damned likely. What the hell does Colin ... Well, if he was kidnapped, I could see it. But he must have had an inkling he wouldn't be hanging around; he gave

311

one of his top staffers his ITC proxy. Good enough man, but not capable of handling a job that big. I give the arrangement a couple of days at best. The worst of it is, until this happened, Colin was doing a fine job. His experience in handling a mercantile empire really shows. Unfortunately, he insisted on hanging on to the whole show himself. Didn't delegate authority worth a damn. None of his flunkies can see the total picture, and Colin could—even strangling on his spite, which he was when seeing Myron Simpkins's candidacy going down in flames." Brenna ran a hand through her hair in exasperation. "I can't believe he'd consider for an instant walking out on the Conference, after he sweated blood and spent so much to win it."

"Maybe there are bigger prizes to be won," Anthony said, his tone flat. "He's a big man in C.S.P. and the interstellar trade routes. But with Carissa's and Stuart's fortunes in his hands, his power would take a quantum leap. Enough, perhaps, to override the setbacks and regain the election for his puppet—if that's what he wants."

"The inheritance," Brenna muttered. "You think that's what pushed him over the edge?"

"It's consumed him since he was a toddler," Anthony said. "Yes, I'm sure that was the last straw. Everything piled up on him, more than he could cope with; and then the Biyelins found out what Pilar Gutierrez was really out here for and tipped off Colin. The chance of grabbing that birthright he believes Carissa cheated him out of was too great a temptation for him to resist. He may have been used and even kidnapped by the Biyelins for their own purposes. But that probate hearing or whatever it is, back on Earth, must have been an overriding consideration in his mind."

"You have to contest," Regan said suddenly, very firm. Her mother and uncle glanced at her as the young woman went on, "Colin's forfeited his moral right to the inheritance. His assigning that proxy shows that he was contemplating abandonment of the ITC before this happened. He's a settler. He knows the consequences if the conference collapses. How could he do this to us?"

Us, the humans spearheading mankind's expansion into the galaxy.

Anthony looked at Regan admiringly. "I agree. But Colin's addiction to the past and to Earth seems to be in his blood. Let him have the damned inheritance."

312

"He can't!" she cried. "Think what that will mean to the Settlements."

"I'm aware that Carissa and Stuart had large investments in the Charter Companies," Anthony began, frowning.

Brenna cut in, "Large doesn't describe it. Try 'immense.' Try controlling interest in nearly a dozen frontier worlds, including your own Settlement. The records aren't public, but then I have privileged information."

Anthony nodded reluctantly. "And with that sort of power, he can—he can damage even you." Brenna's expression acknowledged the truth of that speculation. "He has reasons, from his point of view, to want to strike out at all of us and at a lot of other people and their Settlements. Now he'll have the chance to pay us all back for real and imagined wrongs. Especially the family. Especially me. He still carries a grudge because you loaned me money to get away from Earth and never gave him a cent."

"What?" Captain Saunder spluttered. "He says *that*? Why, that lying little bastard!"

"He *didn't* get any of the money you sent, sis," Blake said quietly. Brenna choked, gawking incredulously. "I didn't tell you earlier because I was afraid you'd blow up, as you did. Anthony isn't the only one Colin's repeated that accusation to. So I did some checking, last few trips to Earth, just to satisfy my curiosity. Took some deep digging in the SME archives and a chat with some old cronies of Colin's late uncle. That sot drank up every credit. The boy never saw it. He was in rags, half starving, while Olivia Gage's brother pickled his liver. The liar managed to fool the SME staffers delivering your checks—told them he was building a trust fund for Colin."

There was a pained silence. Anthony broke it at last, saying, "Then he does have a valid reason for his hate. I was more privileged than he, though I didn't know it at the time."

"Valid motives or not, we've still got a whopping problem, and Colin's absence is the crux of it," Brenna said.

Her daughter agreed. "You *have* to contest his claim to that inheritance—not just for you—for the Settlements and for all those who will be hurt if Colin gets that kind of wealth and power."

"Hurt or worse," Anthony muttered. "Colin and his puppet candidate Simpkins can't seem to see that this is a decision point. From here on, it won't be just Terra out here. And it may not be

313

just the alien races we already know sharing space with us. There's no way of predicting what the future holds. Encounters with nonhumanoids, with a hostile invader from another quadrant? Anything may happen. It's the worst possible time for him to abandon the Conference and the C.S.P. I refuse to follow his course. I have responsibilities to my delegation, my company, the people who work for me, and to Jesse and Yrae."

"You've said it yourself," Captain Saunder cut in. "Responsibilities aren't limited to the here and now. The fact that you grasp everything so well proves you should contest Colin's claim. You'll be fighting for all of us out here—and for Earth as well, though a lot of that world's citizens can't appreciate that reality. They don't see that Earth's a part of the interstellar community now. You do. And I'm not sure Colin does."

"I can't leave Jesse," Anthony said, shaking his head.

"Eben's a tough settler. From what you've told us, he survived that torture better than most would have. What would he want you to do about the inheritance?"

"He's too hurt. It wouldn't make any sense to him at the moment."

"Wouldn't it?"

Captain Saunder and the Chairman of Procyon Five's delegation locked gazes. Then Anthony accepted the challenge. He went into the next room and knelt beside his friend. Yrae was whispering softly to the injured man, reassuring him. Jesse blinked, focusing with difficulty. "K-kid? You still here? Thought—thought you already went after—after Colin. Go get 'im. 'N' bring Pilar back. Can't leave her in that shack. 'S cold out there. 'N' you gotta straighten out that—that thing about th' will. Don't let Colin have it. Doesn' deserve it."

"If that's what you want," Anthony murmured, deeply moved.

"Yeah—yeah . . . g'wan. Gotta bring her back 'n' even the score with Colin. *Tol'* you I was keepin' score. You'll do it?"

"I promise." Anthony meant that as a loving lie, but once he'd uttered the words, they became an unbreakable oath.

Yrae glanced at him. "I will stay with Jesse." That too was an oath. *Aytan.* Honor. Jesse was part of that remarkable sharing bond between the actress and Anthony. He knew he could trust her implicitly.

"I wanta go home," Jesse whimpered. His childlike plea made a shambles of Anthony's remaining composure.

"To the water?" Yrae guessed. "In the home you and Anthony own on Procyon Five? I will take you there. We will wait there for Pilar. You will rest and watch the green water, and the hurting will go away."

She began to croon her singsong again. Jesse yielded to the alien lullaby. The Vahnaj Arbitrator-healer was chanting. Was that another form of ESP? Perhaps it was a benign version of the paranormal weapon the Biyelins wielded—poetic justice, to heal the damage they had wrought with their wild talent. Jesse sighed and sank into a light sleep.

Anthony touched his friend's shoulder and vowed, "I'll be back—with Pilar." Yrae continued singing and weeping. Slowly, loath to leave them, Anthony returned to the larger room.

Captain Saunder was talking to Ambassador Quol-Bez, chiding her old friend. "You should have told us about the Biyelins and the Outer Satellite Faction sooner. Maybe we could have prevented this. I know, I know. Duty to your species. Nothing changes, does it? Not even after all these years." As Anthony drew near, she glanced at him and added, "He wouldn't tell me how to achieve FTL, years ago. Couldn't. Duty then, too, and . . . my cousin Morgan and some good friends paid heavily. So did Quol-Bez, in grief."

"You're going to Earth?" Regan asked.

"I have to try to rescue Pilar, if nothing else." Anthony heaved a sigh. "It seems futile. The Biyelins' ship must be out of reach. And it'll take weeks to get to the Solar System. Plus, what am I going to do about my delegation? They expect me to lead them. I've been . . . ." He hesitated, struck by a startling idea. "Regan, will you accept my proxy? Governor Yamashita and the others would willingly follow a Saunder of your status, and you've already expressed your interest in my Settlement."

"Me?" The young woman was taken aback, then interested. "I . . . it sounds . . . you mean it?" He smiled, amused by the enthusiasm in her manner, and nodded. "Of course! I'm flattered and honored. I won't let you down. Procyon Five will get the best I can give."

"That's the most I could ask." Anthony sobered, confronting the Arbitrators. "What about the Biyelins? What guarantee can

315

you supply that Pilar Gutierrez hasn't been murdered? And why should they allow me to contest Colin's claim to the inheritance? Even if I had a ship that could overtake them—"

"You will," Captain Saunder cut in. "Quol-Bez tells me the Arbitrators will supply a top-of-the-line vessel, military equivalent. You'll overtake and then be on Earth in a bit over a week, ten Solar days, at the outside."

"What about Pilar? The Biyelins' prisoner?" Anthony demanded, absorbing his kinswoman's words abstractedly.

The mediators' spokesman said, "Biyelins informed event is concluded. Their craft must stop. Wait for definers of limits."

"Just so they don't hurt Pilar. Can you guarantee that?"

Doubt flickered in the aliens' eyes. "It shall be attempted."

"Attempt pretty damned hard," Anthony warned them. "What about the Conference, Brenna? Can you manage it?"

She grimaced. "Tricky. You don't know how much vote-swapping and arm-twisting and lobbying Colin went through to nail this thing in the first place. He had plenty of competition from other Terrans eager to bankrupt themselves."

"Why didn't *you* want it?" he wondered.

Brenna's grin was sly. "It's expensive, as Colin was finding out. Oh, SMEI can afford it, but the truth is, when the heaviest wrangling was going on, I was too busy with other stuff to waste money and energy bidding for the thing."

Other stuff—the SMEI transportation coup. Well, that package was off the boards and into the hands of potential customers now. Captain Saunder had a bit more leisure—enough, perhaps, to enable her to step in and save the Interspecies Trade Conference.

Like her daughter, she was beginning to succumb to enthusiasm. "You know, it *can* be done. Oh, not the obvious way. I won't walk in and demand to take over the show. One has to be subtle. Give Serge and Pickard and the others a few days of stewing and muddling under the management of Colin's substitute." Brenna nodded, visibly making plans. "I'm holding a hell of a lot of loyalties and votes. So I drop some hints. A ground swell starts—a delegation here, a lobbying group there, even a colonial delegation or two, deciding it's too risky to let the whole thing fall to pieces. They'll bitch and whine and debate, and there will be dozens of idiotic suggestions before they buckle under.

Then one of my people will make a motion that it's the job of the Saunders to pick up the reins, since a Saunder was chosen to host the Conference." Her smile widened into a predatory smirk. "I'll complain. Tell 'em I don't want it, can't afford it. Remind them of all that's involved. It is going to cost me an arm and a leg, you know. And don't think anyone else tempted to step in isn't going to remember that, and back off because of it. After a suitable display of modest footdragging, I'll accept the popular will and pick up the tab and the hosting title." Brenna paused and asked, "Well, director, how's the script?"

He was forced to chuckle. "Not bad. And it's generous of you to volunteer for such an onerous chore."

"Volunteer, hell. I'm just a sucker for the spotlight." That was not a joke. Captain Saunder had enjoyed flexing her muscles, throwing that bombshell into the Transportation Session. She was looking forward to an opportunity to do more of the same on a Conference-wide basis.

Blake was talking softly to one of the Arbitrators, and the SMEI exec turned and told Anthony, "Their ship is ready for you."

"I'm going to regret this," Anthony muttered. "I want to bring Pilar back safely and find out whether or not Colin was a willing accomplice of the Biyelins. But the rest? There's no point in my going on to Earth to chase that inheritance. I have no connections there, no legal representation."

"It isn't done that way anymore," Blake said. He looked amused by such a quaint concept. "They'll fill you in on the procedures. I'll call ahead via subspace and let Varenka know you're en route. She can be your native guide when you get there. My niece is pretty good at that. She loves to show off the world to visitors from Out Here. As far as the inheritance probate goes, just show up, answer the court's questions truthfully, and await results." Brenna's brother regarded Anthony a moment and added, "If you wish, I'll accompany you. Moral support and family backup."

"No, thank you," Anthony said with a spark of defiance. "Now that I've agreed to go, it's something I'll handle myself." The statement seemed like a bridge, carrying him out to a place where he stood utterly alone. He'd made his choice. And he did want to make the journey—and the decisions—on his own. No kindred need tag along to babysit. And yet . . .

He'd be alone, without Yrae or Jesse to support him, returning to Earth, his birthplace. The clone was retracing his way to dark and painful memories and to a confrontation with the other young victim of Carissa Duryea Saunder, the exiled bastard, Colin Saunder.

CHAPTER TWENTY

✪✪✪✪✪✪✪✪✪

Return to Earth

Anthony's relatives and the "definers of limits" expedited. Carefully selected diplomats, delegations, and top C.S.P. brass began arriving at Colin's desert estate: Ames Griffith; Harthul of the Whimed Federation; Ambassador Quol-Bez's current protégé among the Vahnajes; the Lannons' chief matriarch; the Rigotians' "Nest Commanders"; and important Ulisorians. Terrans and aliens gathered for a crucial powwow. Brenna was coordinating, pulling it together to keep the Interspecies Trade Conference on an even course.

As the big shots were settling in for their discussion, Anthony handed his proxy to Regan, adding as much personal advice as time allowed. Then he was boarding a skimmer, soaring through Procyon Four's twilit night to Jangala's shuttleport. A sleek non-Terran craft awaited him—not a Vahnaj ship *or* a Whimed one, but a compromise design, as the Arbitrators' purpose was devoted to compromise. A handpicked, mixed, elite crew rushed through prelaunch procedures, and then they were away.

The ship was unique in another regard. She was a shuttle with FTL capabilities, like those Brenna's corporation was introducing, with no need for intraorbital transfers. Procyon Four was dwindling fast on the screens as the vessel spiraled upward and outward.

At hyperdrive zero point, that familiar painless pressure grabbed Anthony's skull. On the cabin's Whimed-style diamond-shaped viewplates, stars dimmed and brightened. FTL was tele-scoping space. They were hurtling out of the Procyon system, leaving Colin's world—and Anthony's—far behind. He thought of Jesse and Yrae as he watched his planet become a tiny disc on the screen, a dot, then vanish altogether. When would he see home again, or the people he loved?

It had been anguish to leave them, even though it was obvious Jesse was in good hands. Yrae and the Arbitrator Tib-The had made arrangements to transport Jesse to Procyon Five. What a sensation that arrival would cause in Equitoria! Trogs were used to alien visitors, but not to a Whimed and Vahnaj team, taking up residence in the home of Saunder Studio's boss. All the commu-nications had been taken care of, so officially there'd be no quib-bling. The gossip, though, ought to be intense. Eons ago, Anthony might have considered the situation tailor-made for free Studio PR. Now he was too bitter to care. Ryseen's new project, the edu-vid series Yrae was supposed to act in for the Studio, even the successful Whimed opening presentation—everything Anthony had spent his talent and effort toward was under a cloud. Would there *be* a Saunder Studio when this was over? Or would Colin have the controlling hand, not only on Carissa's wealth, but on the fates of the Settlements her Charter Companies virtually owned?

Anthony watched the screens and translated the chatter com-ing over the ship's coms, waiting and hoping. Were they overtak-ing the Biyelins? Had the troublemakers obeyed the Arbitrators' orders to halt and do nothing to harm their prisoners? The Biye-lins hadn't obeyed the game rules they were supposedly operating under up till now; why should they obey these latest commands?

The crew treated Anthony as pampered supercargo, but they were maddeningly uninformative. He had to put the pieces together himself, building on bits and snatches of overheard conversation and the data streaming into the monitors. The Arbitrators were very firm; their first mission in this pursuit was to extract Pilar Gutierrez from unfriendly hands. They also intended to extract Colin Saunder from those same hands. By the definers' judgment, both Terrans had been most improperly detained.

Was that really the case for Colin as well as for Pilar? Anthony had no way to tell. Jesse's account had contained huge gaps in information. And Renzi, the Biyelins' hireling, had admitted that it had looked as if Colin were being dragged along by the aliens. Were the Biyelins Colin's conspirators or was he their hapless puppet, as David Lavrik had been?

Alternate versions. Alternate viewpoints. He was trying to see the universe through another person's—and another species'—eyes. Why couldn't the answers be simple? But they never were.

Brenna was right. There was no comparison between a journey aboard an ordinary spacecraft and the Arbitrators' advance-design ship. And yet, the cosmos was vast. It would take time to span the light-years separating the pursuing craft from the Biyelins'—hours during which Anthony could do nothing but feel frustrated. No matter how highly developed the race or how sophisticated its technology, they were all ruled by physics, and FTL vehicles probably never would surpass certain speeds.

He made no prayers to the Spirit of Humanity or any other deity. Carissa had been a noisy proponent of prayers, adapting to whatever religious pattern she thought would impress her guests of the moment. Anthony adamantly refused to copy her style.

Carissa was the cause of everything. Even dead, she had the power to hurt him and those he loved.

Alien talk and replies came in via the com. They were closing on target, dropping to sublight, and maneuvering. Then a hated face formed on the viewplates. Fal-Am was churring and gabbling at the Arbitrators. The alien dialect was one Anthony didn't know and couldn't translate, except for a few random words—"saving people . . . loss . . . honor."

Honor! What did that lying, torturing being know about honor?

The Arbitrators suited up for EVA. They refused to let Anthony accompany them. His shouting and arguments got him nowhere. The aliens apologized. They would take no risks to the life of Saunder. They would go to see if the captives were alive and bring them back.

Daunted and chilled by the reminder of the deadly possibilities, Anthony watched the suited figures riding EVA sleds over to the drifting Biyelin ship.

Were the captives alive? They might not be. Cornered, seeing their plan go down in flames, had the Biyelins cut their losses and dumped the Terran eyewitnesses to their crimes? It was possible, if Biyelins thought like a number of human troublemakers. But did they?

Waiting had never seemed so unendurable. He was staring at the viewplates, willing something—anything—to happen. And then a sled emerged from the Biyelin ship's boarding bay. Two Vahnaj crewmen handling the little transfer vehicle were instantly identifiable by their lanky bodies and slow movements. The other two riding the sled were human.

Anthony gripped the monitor until his knuckles whitened. When he heard the banging of entry locks, he pulled himself along the guide rails, hovering by the door to the cabin. A Whimed standing nearby said, "Violence is not permitted."

Fanning the air to maintain his position, Anthony exclaimed, "What are you talking about? I'm waiting to see the prisoners."

"You have anger toward your kinsman. You must not seek physical vengeance. That would be contrary to Terran law."

"You're being awfully careful of Terran laws *now*," Anthony growled. But the alien's comments had defused any subconscious urge to lunge at Colin the instant the blond came through the entry. It had been hours since Jesse had gasped out his story—time enough to think, to weigh explanations, and to doubt.

Pilar had removed her helmet but was still wearing her EVA suit. She sailed clumsily into the cabin, and Anthony and the crew helped her anchor herself to the guides. The entrepreneur was even paler and shakier than she had been on the trip to Procyon Four. She clutched at Anthony and gulped air, plainly on the verge of bawling.

Colin's arrival was less precipitous, but he looked no less rattled than Pilar did. Both of them were ashy, obviously fighting nausea. That didn't figure. Pilar was a bit of greenie. Colin was a settler and a frequent spacer, to boot. EVA shouldn't upset him this much.

"My God—my God!" the merchant prince stammered. Crewmen were helping him and Pilar out of their suits. The former captives were limp, doing nothing to assist the aliens. Colin's eyes lighted on Anthony and he blurted, "Fal-Am . . . those . . . those Biyelin Vahnajes. They—they killed themselves."

The Arbitrators' spokesman joined the Terrans in the cabin. He nodded when he heard Colin's horrified comment. "It was done. The Biyelins chose to atone. Their crimes will not return upon their home world."

Anthony was appalled and disappointed. There'd be no personal vengeance on the e.t.s who'd torn into Jesse's mind. Suicide was a way out, chosen among the defeated of some human cultures as well as the Biyelins'. So they had atoned in order to ensure that the Arbitrators, and perhaps the Whimed Outer Satellite Faction, took no retribution upon the Biyelins' kin and clan.

Neat. And undoubtedly according to the rules of this bloody game.

"I—I never thought we'd get away from them," Pilar was saying, swallowing her tears. "And then . . . this ship came out of nowhere and the Biyelin Vahnajes just . . ." She peered around, a frown replacing her expression of sickened shock. "Where's Jesse?"

Anthony stared at his cousin. "You didn't tell her?"

Colin hung onto a guide rail so tightly his muscles rebelled, twitching visibly. "I—I didn't have the courage. Oh, God!"

It wasn't the reply Anthony had expected.

"Wh-what's going on?" Pilar demanded. "They kept me and Colin apart most of the time while we were on that ship—until just now, when the Vahnajes brought us up to the main control room and—and killed themselves. Then these aliens insisted we come with them."

"They're Arbitrators," Anthony said curtly. "I'll explain later. But there are some things I need to know first. How and where did they capture you, Pilar?"

"At a mining hut. Jesse told me to hide there. I can't imagine how they found me. But they marched right in and dragged me off to their ship. I—I didn't know what to think."

"Totally unpredictable," Colin blurted. "I thought they were my allies. Then when we arrived at the estate, suddenly I was a kind of . . . tool to them. I swear to you, Anthony, they simply took over."

"Took over you *and* Jesse," Anthony said with significant emphasis.

His kinsman licked his lips, still agitated. "That's exactly what they did. Those Biyelins . . . they have to . . . *had* to have been insane! I know you hate my guts, and you have every right to, but don't you think I'm horrified by what they made me do? I tell you, I had no choice! I'd never have agreed to come to the estate

323

with them, if . . . They said it was a prearranged meeting with Gutierrez, to discuss a trade matter."

"Not the inheritance?"

The merchant prince avoided Anthony's stare. He actually looked ashamed. "Y-yes, that, too. Not the inheritance, not then. But Gutierrez had been snooping, and it was apparent something was up. I didn't realize what until . . ." Colin gritted his teeth a moment, then said defensively, "I'd never have cooperated in the slightest if I'd known what that device did. When the Biyelins showed it to me, they said it was like—like a lie detector. And they made it plain that I had to obey. They needed me for the circling, whatever that is."

"You don't know?" Anthony asked with mingled suspicion and contempt. "You should have found out. They were your allies. The Biyelins and a group called the Whimed Outer Satellite Faction are playing a cold war espionage game—for keeps. You got a sample of their tactics when they fail—Fal-Am's suicide. They're just as ruthless when it comes to the other beings they use."

"I had no choice!" Colin cried, very shrill. "You've just confirmed my fears. And—and—they kept insisting the object was protection for Jesse, some sort of baffling device to prevent cross-species ESP shock. I swear by the Spirit of Humanity I didn't know what it would do, and when I saw, I tried to stop it. But they wouldn't let me! They wouldn't let me!" The blond was sweating profusely, even though the cabin was set at optimal temperature for *Homo sapiens*. "When—when they started questioning him, that thing locked onto *me*, too. It's—it's a trap, on both ends of the system!"

"On your honor as an honest trader?" Anthony remarked tauntingly.

But the doubts were growing. He had no proof. And with Fal-Am dead and the Arbitrators being infuriatingly uncommunicative about the inner workings of the cold war, it was unlikely he ever would have proof, unless he applied the same brutal tactics to Colin that the Biyelins had used on Jesse.

Anthony's conscience shrank in revulsion. That would make him no better than the Biyelins and their counterparts. In fact, it would prove that he was part of the same uncivilized, bloodthirsty throwback element they belonged to.

"I swear," Colin repeated, his eyes moist. "They—they told

me they'd kill me. And then . . . when I found out about the inheritance, it was a way out. They wanted me to win it. Somehow that pleased them."

"Points for their side," Anthony muttered. "They keep score. But the Arbitrators have pulled the plug on this particular game. Both sides lose. And so did Jesse."

"What happened?" Pilar had been growing more and more frantic, trying to break in on the two men. "Where *is* Jesse? What did those aliens . . . What's the device he's talking about?"

"How have you been treated?" Anthony snapped. "Did the Biyelins approach you with a box, a machine of any kind, hooked up to Colin?"

"No! I refused!" Colin said, almost screaming.

Bewildered, Pilar glanced uneasily from one cousin to the other. "They—they did come to me once with a box of some sort. But Colin yelled at them, and they went away again. What was it? What does it do?"

"Tears your brain in ribbons," Anthony said with icy calm. "I suppose he would have added incentive for stopping them from using it on you, even if they'd threatened his life earlier. It wouldn't look good at a probate court if the assigned investigator had been tortured."

Pilar gasped, hands to her mouth. Arbitrators steadied her, keeping her from floating erratically from action-reaction.

Anthony studied his kinsman with growing uncertainty. The Biyelins had used Terrans as pawns, not once but several times. And their comprehension of Terran customs and laws was vague, at best. Colin's motives might have been scrambled, particularly after he'd learned about Stuart's death and the potential dual inheritance. But according to the entrepreneur, he'd exerted himself bravely—as well as in his own self-interest—to defend her from the same ferocity Jesse had suffered at the Biyelins' hands.

The blond seemed to be wrestling with himself inwardly. "If you want to squash me, go ahead. I deserve it."

Again, it was the last thing Anthony had expected the other man to say, and it magnified his confusion. He could no longer get a firm grasp on his anger and aim it. The Biyelins, the undeniable villains in this scheme, were dead. Had Colin been their helpless cats'-paw, as David Lavrik had been, and every other non-Biyelin involved?

325

Victims. Pawns. That's what the bastard and the clone had always been, while others jerked the puppets' strings.

No! I'm not a puppet! I'm a human being. If I hate, if I take revenge, I want proof positive. And I'm not going to get it.

"I don't blame you for doubting me," Colin mumbled, almost inaudible. "Your being on Brenna's side put us at odds. And the news about Carissa . . . I—I made some pretty ugly accusations that afternoon outside her suite. I was in shock." Anthony listened, saying nothing. "Are these . . . Arbitrators or whatever they are going to take us on to Earth? I gather there will be a decision made there, and it's appropriate now that we both attend."

Was he yielding his sole grasp on the birthright? Or did Colin feel, deep down, that the issue wasn't in doubt, that Anthony's also coming to the court wouldn't make any difference in the eventual outcome?

"Let's agree to a truce. This terrible situation is the Biyelins' fault, not ours."

"Will you tell me what happened?" Pilar wailed. "No one tells me anything!"

"Fair enough," Anthony said. "You didn't tell us anything, did you? Not even Jesse. If you'd explained about Stuart's death and Carissa's will from the start, none of this would have—"

"I *couldn't*!" the entrepreneur argued, pleading her case. "I—I couldn't. Orders."

Colin floated close to her and said comfortingly, "Of course. We appreciate a loyal employee, don't we, Anthony? And a remarkably efficient one you are, as well. She even got into the closed archives of my company. I'll bet she's been through all of Saunder Studio's records, too. She's a marvel. I wish she was available to work for me."

"If you win the inheritance, maybe she will be," Anthony said with a sneer. "But what would she work *at*? You've walked out on the ITC and your candidate, kingmaker. Don't you think that's going to put a serious dent in your reputation as a shrewd interstellar trader?"

Colin was disturbed by the reminders but unrepentant. "Let me worry about my mercantile operations. You tend to yours."

"And the Conference?"

"My best aide has my proxy," Colin said with airy confidence. "He'll handle it until this is straightened out."

326

Anthony stared. His cousin wasn't shamming; he really believed what he said. In an odd way, that tended to confirm Colin's version of events. Maybe that two-way esper device had damaged his mind. Colin still had his keen intelligence and know-how, but something was obviously distorting his view of things badly.

Were never-quite-healed scars, more than thirty years old, opening and blocking out everything but the inheritance?

"Tell Pilar about Jesse," Anthony commanded, then amended, "or as much as you can remember."

"I—I will." Colin was hangdog, not looking forward to that task.

Pilar bit her lip, fearful of what she was going to hear. "He . . . Colin defended me from them," she said. "He really did."

"I'll accept that. Thank you, Colin, for Jesse's sake. If any harm had come to Pilar, I wouldn't have bothered to hear you out."

"I didn't know it would turn out this way," the blond repeated. "I . . . can we have that truce? It's a long ride to Earth."

"Tell Pilar. Then I'll decide. Anyway, the Arbitrators aren't going to let me bash your head in. Or you mine. Get used to that restriction. This is their ship, and they're running the show from now on. Let's make the best of it, starting with complete honesty."

Colin told Pilar everything and with extreme kindness, leading up gradually to that terrible confrontation at the Metallon estate. The entrepreneur broke down when she heard the details, sobbing helplessly for a long time. Plainly the feelings between her and Jesse were very strong and went in both directions. Anthony wasn't sure yet how this mess would end up, but he resolved to try to keep his promise to Jesse and persuade the woman to return to the C.S.P. with him, once the probate concluded.

What if she wouldn't agree? She cared for Jesse, no question. However, she was a citizen of Earth, and her assignment on the frontier had been an ordeal for Pilar, as Anthony had witnessed. Despite her love for Jesse, she might opt to remain Earthbound. What then? What would that do to Jesse's chances for recovery?

There was nothing to do but wait and hope. A lot of that had been going on recently!

The Arbitrators' ship was among the fastest in space, but it was still a long journey—long in apparent elapsed time to the passengers and long in tension. The cousins kept their distance from one another, Pilar acting as intermediary when necessary. Several times the Arbitrators contacted their teams in the Procyon system, relaying updates on the Biyelins' suicide and allowing Anthony to talk to Yrae and the Healer-Arbitrator, Tib-The. They reported that Jesse was improving. Pilar and Anthony reveled in that, clinging to one bit of welcome news, amid so much cruelty.

Time and space were shrinking steadily.

The ship was a marvel. It had to be. The Arbitrators were required to patrol both Whimed and Vahnaj sectors and referee the troublemakers' events, keeping tabs on those affairs, but not interfering—not until after innocent people had been hurt.

Days passed.

Sol was beginning to register on the viewplates. The ship was crossing Pluto's orbit, Jupiter's, Kirkwood Gap's, Mars' . . .

Finally they arrived at Goddard. No EVA transfer was necessary there. Pilar contacted her bosses on Earth. The "entrepreneur"—now admitting her disguise—was returning with the two prospective heirs of one of Terra's largest fortunes.

A Terran shuttle bore the travelers "down" from Goddard. The Arbitrators remained on the artificial satellite. They would wait until the purpose of this trip to Earth had been settled one way or another. Their presence there, and that of their super-secret single-stage starhopper meant more bent laws. No permits were issued, nor clearances for passage in the Solar System. They and that odd ship weren't even supposed to be in the Terran sector.

But then, neither was the Biyelin device or the circling game they'd engaged in with Ryseen's Outer Satellite Faction.

Mankind's birthworld loomed on the screens. Anthony absorbed the descent views with morbid fascination. This was the first time he had returned to Earth since he'd made his escape, years ago. He had never felt any nostalgia for the place or longing to see it again, and didn't now. He supposed he might be known here, as an interesting entity—the clone of one of Earth's famous heroes. His contact with the planet, though, had been detached, a name in vidcasts. His only real interest in the world was the fact that most of the Settlements' Charter Companies were based here, and thus Procyon Five's survival—and his, Jesse's, and Saunder Studio's—depended on what those financial giants chose to do. He felt very distant from Earth, his home separated from it by more than light-years.

The night side was aglow with the life signs of thousands of cities. That fact alone set Earth apart from her Colonies and the C.S.P. No other world had developed far enough to become overpopulated, nor was likely to. The lights, the lush agricultural areas revealed when the alien ship sped over the dayside, and the networks of man-made transportation and waterways showed a world alive, no terraforming needed, where mankind had evolved. There had been times in human history when toxic wastes, pollution, and war were greater threats to survival than any natural disaster could have been. But at present, most of those threats were under control. Com chatter mentioned the usual run of palace revolutions, famines, and economic crises, and so on and so on. None of that would disappear in the foreseeable future.

There was no golden age, even among the galaxy's highest civilizations.

Earth's scars were visible now, altered landscapes left by earlier holocausts created in the name of national pride. New deserts had been created by misuse of the environment, and glaciers triggered by the same.

More com chatter came through—of ethnic conflict, oppression, struggles for independence, quarrels between high tech and low tech nations, and unemployment. On top of everything else, there was still religious fanaticism, with bloody clashes between sects, and persecution.

And there were plague outbreaks, leftovers from bacteriological warfare contamination during the early years of the previous century.

The shuttle landed on the west coast of the North American Union. Anthony had often heard Captain Saunder mention the port in this area, but he had never been there. When he lived on Earth, clones hadn't been free to travel where they chose.

"Odd," Colin said, gazing at the Terminal as their shuttle rolled to a stop, "but this is the first time I've traveled back to Earth in over twenty years. Just haven't had the time previously."

Or the courage? Neither did I, Colin.

A group of very important executors, top rankers, were on hand to greet the clone and the bastard. Benjamin Inge of Saunder Enterprises' Caribbean branch. Ogden Muir, investment counselor with connections to Saunder Enterprises, Muir Solar System Development Corporation, and numerous Charter Com-

329

panies. Ellen Lefferts, administrator of several multinational conglomerates and a distant relative of Brenna's ward, Reid McKelvey. Maurice Bigelow of SE Antarctic Industrials, Ltd. And Varenka Saunder, Brenna's older daughter, owner of enormous stock holdings in both her mother's Saunder Enterprises and her aunt's division of the same association.

Anthony felt disoriented. He smiled, shook hands, and memorized names. Colin was doing the same, like Anthony in betraying edginess by an occasional stammer. They were both stiff.

This wasn't the Caribbean island where Anthony had spent sixteen years as a virtual prisoner. Nor was it the hellish Brazilian mines where Colin had fought to survive. But it *was* Earth. Both men had exquisitely painful memories of what they had been when they lived here before, and how Earth's citizens had treated them.

Clone. Bastard. Freak. Outcast.

Anthony braced himself for the sneers and veiled jokes. But there were none. The welcomers chatted amiably with the new arrivals, expressing polite interest in their long journey.

"Blake said you'd be arriving on an alien craft," Varenka commented, wrinkling her nose attractively. "It seems you really should have traveled on a *Terran* craft. However, Blake explained the vehicle was put at your disposal as a favor to the Saunder family. Understandable."

Anthony forbore to reply. So did Colin and Pilar.

An ultra-modern mono train stood by to carry the group up to the Saunder Enterprises' Earth branch's exclusive corporate HQ, located in the nearby mountains. That had been established as the site of the probate as well, because, for some idiosyncratic reason, Carissa had elected to file the document in this particular county among all of her worldwide property holdings.

The train ride had a dreamlike quality for Anthony. So did the guided tour of the sprawling, palatial HQ grounds. "This must be pretty tame to you boys after the exciting lives you lead out in the Settlements, eh?" Muir asked cheerfully. "Oh, we have our own share of excitement. But things don't change that fast. It probably doesn't seem much different than it did when you lived here."

"Ogden, don't babble," Varenka Saunder cut in rudely. "Of course it's different. And they didn't live in anything resembling these conditions. Give them a chance to acclimate and quit bothering them." She glanced at the cousins and added, "Or *do* you need to get acclimated? I know you settlers rely on gravity compensation drugs, like the Colonists and unlike us."

"A bit of rest would be nice," Anthony said.

"Hm. It'll be arranged." Varenka's face was broader than Regan's or her mother's. She reminded Anthony more of her brother Ivan, or pictures he'd seen of her father, Yuri Nicholaiev. But the woman, seven years Regan's senior, had the same intent, sharp nature as all of Captain Saunder's brood. Varenka's bias, though, was definitely not aimed toward the Charter Settlement Planets. Her chauvinism, boosting Earth at every opportunity, was blatant.

"Yes, some rest would be appreciated, before we . . . get down to business," Colin agreed. "It's very courteous of you to show us around. Most interesting."

"Particularly since one of you will probably end up owning all of this," Benjamin Inge noted dryly. There was no malice in his words, merely statement of fact. The remark fell flat. The two potential heirs eyed one another and Pilar held her breath, fearing trouble.

Anthony read his cousin clearly. Avarice. Anticipation. The blond was surveying SE HQ like a child with an endless supply of credits in an amusement gallery.

Don't count your clams before you've shelled them, Colin.

"Blake told me the will would be read by the probate judge." That brought an exchange of nervous stares all around. Anthony raised an eyebrow, curious at the reaction his comment caused.

"Yes, Judge Wilkes," Ellen Lefferts said. "Right now, he's enjoying himself on the recreational grounds at our expense."

There was no need for the kinsmen to confer. Anthony spoke for them both. "If the Judge is here, I think we'd prefer to get on with it as soon as possible. We've waited long enough." He half expected a sneering comeback, something to the effect that the clone was getting too pushy and forgetting his place.

Again, none came—no echo of the way it *had* been for Anthony Saunder on this planet, twenty years ago.

"Fine with us," Muir said. "We've all got other places to be and things to take care of. The sooner we get this wrapped, the better." He motioned to an aide. "Notify the Judge. Arrange the hearing tomorrow. 1200 hours ought to be about right. Okay with you boys? Good! Varenka, why don't you show them to their suites? Gutierrez, come with us. We want to talk to you."

331

As Anthony and Colin followed their stern-faced young kins-woman along landscaped walkways, Colin peered back worriedly over his shoulder at Pilar. Was he afraid of what she'd tell the executors in private session? Why? If he had genuinely been a mere tool of the Biyelins, he need have no concern.

Becoming aware of his cousin's scrutiny, the merchant prince straightened and held his head high, feigning total self-assurance. The bastard refused to show his fears.

Anthony wasn't so sure the clone could conceal *his*.

The will was the thing that had brought him and Colin this great distance to Earth, the trigger that had created such upheaval and pain.

Tomorrow it would be opened . . . and the matter finished.

The long, long nightmare done, for good or ill.

CHAPTER TWENTY-ONE

❀❀❀❀❀❀❀❀

Carissa's Will

"What are you so jumpy about?" Varenka peered at Anthony and complained, "You and Colin are so nervous you make me itch."

They were seated in a luxurious private conference room. The executors, Colin, Pilar, and an assortment of staffers were present. Anthony and Colin sat on opposite sides of a large semi-circular table.

The arena reeked of wealth and power—Carissa's and Stuart's, a fortune that had been accumulating since far back in the Twenty-first Century, from the time of the legendary Death Years. The riches and the influence they wielded were tangible.

"Why are you so jumpy?" Varenka insisted again.

"I suppose Earth gives us bad memories."

"Oh, that," their kinswoman said disdainfully. "You mean the cloning, and Carissa's legal shenanigans in disinheriting Colin. Unimportant. Forgotten years ago."

Anthony had to admit that everyone he'd met had treated him with unfailing respect and courtesy. There'd been no sniggering, no looking down their noses at him or at Colin. Was Varenka right? *Were* the past's secrets truly a matter for shame only to the clone and the bastard? Surely there were people still living on the

Earth who remembered those days—servants who'd worked at Saunderhome twenty years ago, men who'd mined with Colin's uncle, security guards who'd chased Olivia Gage and her baby son off the island, or guards who'd kept constant, unsmiling watch over the little clones, Carissa's insurance to hold Stuart in line.

The past was forgotten, as Varenka put it. The executors had talked with the men from C.S.P. about business, very interested in the complicated conversion of Earth's money into spendable currency out there, in trade with alien races, and in the problems of import and export across such distances. But the fact that Anthony and Colin were clone and bastard seemed to mean little. What *did* matter was that the men were Saunders—and that one of them was likely to end up very, very rich after today's events.

And yet the pain, the insults, and rejections could never be wiped away.

Judge Wilkes entered the room. Anthony had read up on the man last night. He was an eminent jurist—tops. Carissa's executors would insist on nothing less. Wilkes had presided over the divisions and reorganizations of several of Earth's largest fortunes. Now, amid this assembly of the powerful, he'd decide yet another case, perhaps his most newsworthy probate of all.

What am I doing here? I'm out of my element, fighting a lost cause. A sham. I shouldn't be contesting.

Anthony pulled himself together. He *was* here. He'd made his choice, and he'd stick with it.

Blake was right. There was no razzle-dazzle, no duel of lawyers. Things weren't handled that way nowadays, in this situation. Instead, holo-mode records were presented. It was an exhaustive examination of the possible heirs: childhood IDs; blood tests; DNA samplings; birth documents; the employment application of a very young and callow Colin, starting work in Brazil; tri-dis of his miner's certificate and of his ticket out; more employment applications and records from several Settlements, as he worked his way up; and his breakthrough on Procyon Four, building his mercantile empire.

Anthony had no real history before he'd emigrated. There were a few interviews with Saunderhome staffers—standard stuff, bland. The stats of that period reflected the clone's total domination by Carissa. Digging deeper, the records revealed the questionable methods by which Saunderhome's Empress had brought the clones into being. Then there was a teenaged Anthony's job-ticket IDs from half a dozen frontier worlds, as he, like Colin, tried to survive in a challenging environment. Then came excerpts from Li Lao Chang's porn vids, references to his growing expertise in sensitive emota-sensor equipment and the other complex gear of his field, more employment data, and his loan papers and contract for time purchase of the property that was to be Saunder Studio. There was nothing to compare to the numerous property listings on Colin's record.

Cross-examinations were conducted by Judge Wilkes, putting Pilar and her bosses, the executors, through the mill. The potential heirs' finances? Anything shady there? Credit records clean? Had either man been involved in scandal? In bribery? Had they broken *any* laws? Been *accused* of breaking any laws? Been banned from a Settlement?

No, only from Earth.

Pilar had been professional and very thorough. Obviously she hadn't spent *all* of her time romping with Jesse.

Gradually the stories were laid out in full. There was no mention of the incident with the Biyelins. Anthony suspected the political powers-that-be, wary of stepping on the main-line-Vahnajes' toes, had instructed the court to ignore that topic entirely. Interspecies offense must be avoided for the good of everyone—and for the good of whichever candidate would receive the fortune. Judge Wilkes intended to keep the proceedings squeaky clean and uncluttered.

That's the way it's done. That's the way Carissa did it. She had the money and power to buy us clones and crush Stuart's mistress and exile Stuart's bastard, with nothing to clutter up the records unduly then, either. Though it was buried in the files. They dug that up for this hearing, but haven't made much of it so far.

The candidates were questioned next. Did they challenge any of the evidence presented? No, how could they? Their lives had been spread out openly for all to see. And there was nothing there for them to be really ashamed of. No Tracy Rutledge type of scandal.

"Very well," Wilkes said. "The clerk will note that testimony is accepted as offered. Now as to the statutes . . ."

What followed was a lengthy, convoluted lesson on one branch of Earth's current rules regarding jurisprudence. Anthony admired the Judge's ability to trim off the fat and get to the meat. He'd have made a good edu-vid instructor. Wilkes did a remarkable job of explaining the facts. In essence, by agreeing to appear at this hearing, both Anthony and Colin were agreeing to abide by Wilkes' final decision. And his conclusion *would* be final; no appeals were permitted.

"Let's watch the terms." The Judge gestured to his clerk.

Anthony hadn't realized the reading of the will would come in hologramic form.

Carissa Saunder materialized out of nothing. She stood in the arc of the curving table, halfway between Anthony's chair and Colin's. The two witnesses to her will, one of them Varenka, were beside her. *Two* Varenkas appeared in the same room, one very real, staring at her tri-di replica.

The holo-mode was Saunder Enterprises technology at its finest. Carissa seemed to breathe. A painful band tightened around Anthony's temples, squeezing.

The tyrant was two meters away—and forever beyond his reach.

"I, Carissa Duryea Saunder, being of sound mind, do this day..."

Formalities, in that familiar little-girl voice, seemed grotesque. The holo showed Carissa in extreme old age, clinging to the illusion of youth—wig, overdone cosmetics to hide the ravages of time, and a gown woefully out of fashion. No matter. This had been one of Earth's most powerful women. She could wear whatever she damned well wanted to and paint her face up for carnival if she chose.

Carissa could have. She never would again. She was dead, gone. Colin half rose, his expression rigid. The holo was a copy of a woman Colin claimed he'd never met; but the look on his face was one of recognition and hate. He was a small boy again, standing with his mother on Saunderhome's lawn. And Carissa and her guards were coming to evict them.

Anthony clenched and unclenched his fists, and his gorge rose as he fought his emotions with intellect: *She's dead, Dead, DEAD!* Somehow he managed to relax. Varenka was eyeing him with concern. Had he looked as if he were about to go berserk? Very probably!

Carissa began reciting bequests. "...and to my loyal kennelkeeper, John..." The crone's hands trembled. False

336

eye lashes fluttered. She was a physical wreck beneath the simpers, the layered makeup, and the girlish dress. ". . . my maid, Beatrice . . ."

That awful voice ordered Saunderhome's staffers to round up the little clones and put them out of her sight; they were annoying the mistress.

". . . my Chief of Security, who . . ."

Hard-faced private police strong-armed a weeping woman and a blond little boy down to a boat landing, thrusting them into the vehicle none too gently.

"Now to the principal items of my will."

Anthony blinked and sat up very straight. That hated voice was pronouncing his future.

"To my son Stuart I leave eight thousand shares of Amalgamated North American Union stock."

Varenka leaned toward Anthony and whispered, "That's a fair chunk, for most people. A good ten million a year or so." Anthony nodded mutely. So. Stuart hadn't been cut off without a penny; and with Stuart dead, there would be no other logical heir but his natural son.

The holo-mode froze. Judge Wilkes had stopped it. His aides brought forward two additional tri-di documents. Another image formed in the space beside Carissa and her witnesses. A blond woman, beautiful—Olivia Gage. She wasn't crying, as she had been when Anthony had seen her so long ago. Stuart's mistress was stiff-lipped, defending herself and her son. ". . . attest to these matters . . ."

Sexual cohabitation, an antique legal term, had occurred with Stuart Saunder on such and such dates—before Anthony and his brothers had been created. A doctor's image replaced Olivia's, citing his credentials as an expert in paternity determinations. ". . . attest I have examined specimens on public record of Stuart Saunder and the male child, Colin Gage Saunder. Results are positive . . ."

Someone—Pilar?—had dug exceedingly deep. Anthony once assumed that Carissa had destroyed such tests. But perhaps duplicates had been hidden away for safekeeping, and they were surfacing now. The bastard was finally seeing the proof that Carissa had tried to crush. Colin was Stuart's son, irrefutably, scientifically confirmed.

The merchant prince was struggling to conceal his tears. The

337

exile, his nightmare childhood, his purgatory in the South American mines, his mother's suicide . . . none of it needed to be. If only this proof had been admitted to a court of law thirty-seven years ago . . .

Anthony regarded his kinsman with empathy.

I know what you're going through. They stomped both of us and taught us to hate each other as well as them.

The Judge waited until nervous coughing and squirming quieted, then said, "This evidence pertinent to the case was entered in the court's records earlier, upon the event of Stuart Saunder's death. No other claimant has presented evidence of any conflicting relationship. Therefore, the court finds that Colin Gage is the true and natural son of Stuart Saunder and is Stuart Saunder's sole issue. Since Stuart Saunder died intestate, the laws of this jurisdiction decree direct transfer of his property to his heir. Let the record show this is done. The stated bequest of Carissa Duryea Saunder to her sole issue, Stuart Saunder, is to become his heir's . . ."

Colin had been hanging his head. Now he looked up at the Judge in dazed disbelief. The merchant prince had yearned for this so long—to be acknowledged as Stuart's son. Everyone had known the truth, but no one could do anything about it while Carissa and Stuart lived. The tyrants were dead; long live the new heir.

Anthony sighed tiredly. He'd *told* Brenna this journey to Earth was futile. Why had he yielded to her arguments and Regan's to come here? All of this had been a performance. Judge Wilkes and the executors must have made up their minds weeks, perhaps months earlier, perhaps even before Carissa's and Stuart's deaths. No doubt the Judge had been through this procedure many times. The rituals of blood tests and depositions and collected documents were cut and dried.

Why had the executors spent money and wasted time having Pilar pry into Anthony Saunder's affairs as well as Colin's? That had to be part of the performance, too. Legal stage dressing, to make it look right. Otherwise they could have simply used subspace com to notify Colin that everything he'd ever dreamed of was now his for the asking.

And Jesse would never have been hurt. Anthony would never have come to know and love Yrae Usin Hilandro. The Biyelins and the Whimed Outer Satellite Faction would have had no rival

338

Saunder cousins to manipulate for their cold war games. Colin might still be hosting the ITC. He'd have had little reason to chuck a lifetime's work and come flying back to Earth, if he'd known all of this was already his.

Both of them had been used.

The holo-mode of Carissa resumed talking, on Wilkes' command. ". . . remainder of my properties, real and intangible, to be assigned in toto to that person of direct Saunder lineage who shall be deemed by my executors, named in this testament, to be most worthy and most capable of continuing the traditions and success of Saunder Enterprises."

Anthony had been dropped from a great height, striking water with stunning force, and bobbing back to the surface. He felt blinded by a sudden burst of brilliant sunlight.

The *remainder*?

"Wondered when Wilkes was going to get around to the rest of the bequest," Varenka muttered, "now that we've got the minor stuff taken care of." She saw Anthony's astonishment and said as if to a child, "We thought you knew. You were supposed to be briefed this morning. Someone always slips up. Can't get decent staffers, these days."

"But . . . but the ten million a year Colin inherits—"

Brenna's eldest daughter chuckled. "That? Legal footwork. Carissa's lawyers told her to avoid cutting Stuart off without a cent. He might have fought it. So she left him just enough for him to spend his last days in his usual state of total, disgusting dissipation. I guess he died happy."

"I doubt it," Anthony said softly, remembering the loathsome, diseased man who'd haunted him and had made a young clone's life hell for sixteen years.

Shrugging, his kinswoman went on, "But Carissa owned *billions*. Maybe more. It's an incredible fortune, even for a Saunder. And she tied it up in all the proper legal phrases so that someone, but *not* Stuart, would get the whole thing."

The reading of the will was complete. To Anthony's relief, the clerk switched off Carissa's holo-mode. Judge Wilkes peered thoughtfully at the men from Procyon system. Anthony held his breath, feeling queasy with apprehension. "I've been studying this situation carefully ever since Carissa's death," Wilkes said. "It hasn't been an easy decision. My team of experts has researched at great length. We have interviewed hundreds of witnesses and gone over records exhaustively to be absolutely sure of the deceased's intentions."

The Judge shifted in his thronelike chair. Its plasticene covering creaked. To Anthony, the sound was as loud and startling as a window wall splitting to let in the ocean. Wilkes laced his fingers together and stared solemnly into nothing for a moment before he focused on the living objects of the hearing.

"Colin Gage Saunder, you are the natural son and heir of Stuart Saunder. That is not open for debate. However, a question is posed: What, precisely, is your relationship in the direct lineage of the Saunders, as compared to Anthony Saunder?"

Colin's mouth opened. Nothing came out. After tremendous effort, he said hoarsely, "I-I'm Carissa's grandson."

Wilkes' features were unreadable. He pointed at a court clerk. "State the findings." She did. Laboratory records. Cloning procedures. Exact dates and methods. Anthony was chilled to the marrow. His life was spread out on a slide. The executors listened with detachment. There were no whispered, snickering remarks, no knowing smirks aimed in his direction. Jesse had *said* he was oversensitive on the subject, and now the reactions on every side proved it. Earth no longer attached much stigma to his unusual origins. But did it attach *legal* significance to that fact?

The clerk finished. The Judge cleared his throat several times, then said, "Now, for you, Anthony Saunder. There is no legal precedence to cover the existence of clones. Cloning is illegal for human beings, of course. But the crime must be the responsibility of those performing the act, and not visited upon the innocent victim of such cloning. Hence it becomes necessary to examine whether other precedents may apply.

"Now, by fingerprints, retinal patterns, blood tests, and tissue examination, you are identical with the supposedly dead Patrick Saunder, as has been attested and demonstrated here today. Further, while Patrick Saunder was declared dead, there was no absolute proof of that fact; despite his obvious intent and the massive explosion known to have occurred, no witness to his death or recognizable corpse was discovered.

"There *are* precedents for cases where men have seemingly died and been declared dead, but then have appeared eventually to claim their rights and property.

"I must advise you, Anthony Saunder, that you have the legal identity of Patrick Saunder. You could therefore request a court to set aside *your* death. In that case, Carissa would have been acting as your agent during your absence, but would not have the power to leave any part of this estate by deed or bequest to others, since it would automatically revert to you. In my opinion, you would have a good, though not certain, chance of winning such a suit, as the laws now stand."

Anthony had been borne along on the tsunami of the Judge's words, absorbing, thinking fast and frantically. Now, sensing the questioning pause in the man's address, he said quickly, "I won't sue."

"That's probably wise in view of the time such a case might take. Very well then, let us return to the matter at hand. I find that you, Anthony Saunder, as one who has demonstrated your ability and who can trace most direct descent from the lineage of Ward and Jael Saunder, founders of this estate, are the true and proper heir of this bequest. Such is the judgment of this court."

There was a momentary silence. Colin was standing up slowly. His face was alarmingly red. Anthony stood, too, facing his cousin. Varenka and the executor beside Colin, Benjamin Inge, stood as well, keeping worried eyes on the two. Judge Wilkes glowered sternly at all of them.

"I do not expect disturbances in this court," the Judge said flatly. Shock chased the blood from Colin's face. Inge steadied him, encouraging him to sit down. Colin refused, swaying slightly. Pilar bit her lip and lowered her eyes as the Judge said grumpily, "Frankly, this has been one of the most difficult probate decisions I've ever had to settle. This situation has never come up before."

So much for the appearances of this being a normal hearing. The façade of the court was cracking a bit under stress.

Wilkes continued in a lecturing tone, "I intend to make some recommendations to the United Councils of Earth regarding this matter. In the future, if we are to render judgments on bequests involving clones, the legalities must be clarified. For the present, we operate under our existing laws and common sense. These proceedings are adjourned."

CHAPTER TWENTY-TWO

❄❄❄❄❄❄❄❄

Saunderhome

It had been a long hour. Anthony was still in the proceedings room. The entire feeling of the place had changed. He was somewhat numb, gradually accepting a new reality. Staffers scurried to fetch him caffa, food, and a more comfortable chair. Varenka and the other executors clustered around him, showing him mini holo-modes of his properties and ledgers of assets and stock holdings. Billions or more, Varenka had said. Anthony was finding she had understated. The estate was so vast he couldn't take it all in on such short notice. Judge Wilkes had departed, after shaking his and Colin's hands, and since then Anthony had been easing his way into an outrageously unanticipated role—mogul, tycoon, power broker, controller of Charter Companies, and a man who could determine the Settlements' future as well as his own.

He was swimming on top, gaining confidence steadily. For years Anthony had struggled to cope with his Studio's financial problems. And he had managed remarkably well, despite constant adversity, if he did say so himself. Looking back, he acknowledged it was entirely due to his careful stewardship and thrift that his company had made it as far as it had. That self-education now stood him in good stead. He tackled the new figures as he would have an update handed him by the Studio's accountant. They were staggering figures, and all solidly in the black, not marred by large blotches of red, as he was used to. These were straightforward financial records. He was beginning to view things as a matter of degree. He could cope, but not alone.

There'd be kilotons of work for Chet Deverill to take on. The accountant was going to need lots of assistants. So was Anthony. Saunder Studio wasn't going to be a small-time business anymore. Anthony would have to think in terms of delegating authority and finding people he could count on—until Jesse was back on his feet and able to take his rightful place as loyal partner of the frontier's newest multi-billionaire Saunder.

Delegating authority. Brenna said Colin wasn't good at that. He'd relied on toadies too much. Had Pilar Gutierrez picked up on gossip like that when she was researching, out in Procyon's system? She'd never told Anthony *everything* she'd brought back for the executors. She shouldn't; that was confidential. Yet his curiosity was piqued. It struck him that he now possessed the power to force the answers to such questions out into the light if he chose. He had the money and clout to do exactly what Carissa had always done—make or break those weaker than he.

It wasn't his style. It hadn't been, and it wasn't going to be. The lessons of the past were deeply ingrained.

His biggest chore was going to be diversification and reorganization. All of the funds were Earth-based. Charter Company moneys flooding back to Earth and staying here, for the most part. That must change. Anthony was already making plans for funneling big chunks of his newfound wealth elsewhere—or simply holding it out in the Settlements, where it was needed. There was plenty of surplus to keep Carissa's Solar System branches of Saunder Enterprises rolling smoothly. He wouldn't be crippling the company, not at all. He'd be giving Procyon Five and the rest of the frontier a fresh lease on life and prosperity.

There were so many things he wanted to do: invest in Brenna's new FTL shuttles; promote Terran-Whimed understanding; promote understanding among all the races sharing the starlanes and the worlds Out There; encourage medical research into cross-species diseases; and solve persistent hostile environment problems. So many things . . .

And he had the wherewithal to accomplish them!

Pilar kept studying Anthony from the edge of the circle surrounding him. He'd requested that she stay close by to advise him, and she seemed very grateful for that. He hadn't forgotten his promise to Jesse; he just had to figure out how to fulfill it, without resorting to kidnapping.

"Anthony..."

Colin had been on the other side of the large room, discussing the management of his new inheritance with some of the executors. The blond had peeked furtively at Anthony now and then and had finally gathered his courage to approach his cousin. Colin's hand was out, and he was forcing a smile. The merchant prince! That elegant façade was shaky, but still there. "Congratulations. I've been trying to catch you when you weren't so busy."

"Thank you. Congratulations to you, too."

"Yes, thanks." Colin was smiling to keep from crying, bleeding inside. He had won. And he had lost—and lost big. Whatever had actually happened at the desert HQ outside Metallon—whether Colin had been victim or villain—he was paying a heavy price. To the world, he looked the happy inheritor. To Anthony, his kinsman was almost mortally hurt. "So you get Saunderhome," Colin said, the mask slipping. "And I get the door slammed in my face again. I guess I should have expected that."

The comment was revealing. Saunderhome. Not the incalculable investments. Not the power to take control of the Charter Corporation and alter the direction of C.S.P. Saunderhome, the soul of Colin's quest—and the loss he felt more than any other.

"They've been showing me maps," Anthony said, waving at a table spread with holo-mode mini-projectors and terminals. "It's quite an array. I get the impression not even Carissa knew how much she owned. I'm setting up a tour to inspect the holdings. I've never seen most of them, of course. They'll cover much of the same territory your inheritance from Stuart includes. Why don't we make the ride together?" Anthony suggested. The offer was sincere. Despite memories of Jesse writhing on that floor, he acknowledged that it was possible Colin wasn't guilty of much besides flawed judgment and walking into the Biyelins' trap.

"I... I don't think so," the blond said, scowling.

Anthony ticked off the itinerary. "Tahitian estates. Alaskan and Canadian investments. Indian Surface Transport Manufacturing Complex. Mid-Mediterranean holdings. Brazil." Colin winced, and Anthony added, "Saunderhome."

344

A hesitation showed Colin yielding to the obsession. "Saunderhome," he said faintly. "I haven't . . ."

"Neither have I. Not for a long, long time." Anthony waited. This had to be Colin's decision. He refused to manipulate his kinsman any more than he'd already done.

"I think . . . I think I'd like to see it," the blond finally said.

Their shuttle took off very early the next morning. Pilar and Varenka Saunder, several other executors, and a horde of aides accompanied the cousins. Anthony wondered if he was going to travel in this style, elbow to elbow with staffers, from now on. Probably. For a while, anyway, until he sorted things out.

It was a private craft, Anthony's personal property, now, a top-of-the-line suborbital, latest model, right off the assembly lines at one of *his* factories. It made Procyon Five's vehicles look like junk. Anthony and his companions rode in posh comfort.

Colin wasn't talkative. Anthony didn't prod the man. He was feeling increasingly sorry for the blond. Why? Colin was wealthier than he'd ever dreamed of being. He hadn't won the big prize, but he'd gathered in a very substantial one.

As the shuttle began its descent, the sea below reflected Sol's afternoon light, glittering off deep waters—old waters, salty, not home.

Saunder Enterprises' pilots were the cream of the crop. The landing on a man-made strip near the Caribbean island complex was echinoderm silky smooth. Anthony barely felt the touchdown.

He and his entourage explored the outer reefs, the guest cabanas, the dolphin breeding bays and atolls crowded with servants' quarters, then went on up to the main house, built into the island's rock. None of the staff had met Anthony prior to today. No one was left from the time he and his brothers had lived here—when four of his brothers had died here.

He felt alone, separate, and ached with longing for Yrae, the one other person who fully comprehended what it was to be so alone. Someday he might bring her to Earth and show her these things, not out of pride, but so that she could see and apply her *diya* to this place that had meant so much pain for him.

The original Saunderhome had been destroyed in the Crisis of 2041. Patrick Saunder had crashed his shuttle into the island, killing himself and his mother Jael. Now Patrick Saunder's legal

345

reincarnation strolled the grounds of a new Saunderhome, a re-creation Carissa had raised as a memorial to her dead husband. Here she and Stuart had lived in mutual hate while Saunderhome had become a mecca for Earth's politics and business leaders and a pilgrimage point for visiting extraterrestrials. All that was a collection of facts and statistics, ancient history.

There was a more personal history involved here.

Colin, too, was remembering that. He and Anthony stood on the terrace. The blond gazed about, misty-eyed. He had blocked that incident of more than thirty years ago from his thoughts. But something within him recalled it, and the emotions battered him.

Pilar Gutierrez watched him tensely. Anthony nodded, appreciating her tact in maintaining silence. She was good stuff or Jesse wouldn't love her. Together they let Colin think.

Saunderhome's in-residence superintendent bustled around, trying to please the new owner. "Forty-five rooms in the main complex, sir. And . . . well, we've never tallied the servants' housing. There are the support buildings as well, and—"

"Thank you. I know where everything is," Anthony said tonelessly. "Not too much has changed. I used to live here, you know."

"Did you?" The man shrugged, unconcerned. He had no memories of the new owner's background as a clone. He was just doing his job, respectful and polite.

Benjamin Inge walked down from the main house, waving to Anthony. "How do you like it? Everything all right? Anything you particularly want to know or see?"

"There *is* something. Find someone who can tell me what happened to my three retarded brothers. Carl drowned himself, of course, but the little ones disappeared before they were five. Were they murdered?"

Colin gaped in horror. Varenka and Benjamin Inge looked ill-at-ease. The superintendent made himself very busy at a task well away from the conversation, too far away to be tapped for any answers. Inge sighed and said, "I wondered if you might ask about that. We researched the cloning affair quite thoroughly, before the probate hearing. No, your brothers weren't murdered. They were sickly. Carissa finally had them institutionalized. They were on the mainland for a couple of years, then died of natural causes. They had the best care while they were alive, I assure you."

"Thank you for telling me," Anthony said. "I had to know. They were a part of me. It's very difficult to be one person in five bodies and have four of them taken away from you, one by one."

And as he said that, the shadow figures faded out of existence. They were gone, as Carissa and Stuart were gone. None of them would ever haunt him again.

Colin closed his eyes, shaking off his dismay at witnessing Anthony's purging of his past. Then as the blond opened his eyes and peered around, his gaze locked on the enormous main house. Anthony followed his kinsman's stare and said simply, "Do you want it?"

"What?"

"Do you want it?" Anthony repeated. "Do you want Saunderhome?"

The merchant prince stared at paradise. At least *he* saw it as paradise, this beautiful mansion he'd glimpsed once, too briefly, as a toddler. His mother had told him Saunderhome belonged to Colin's father and that someday it would be his. Then the guards had come and thrown them off the island.

"It's not heaven," Anthony warned. "It's just an island, no better than the people living on it."

"It's—it's Saunderhome," Colin said helplessly. "Do you know what it feels like? You couldn't! You were here. You—you say it was a rotten life, and maybe it was, for *you*. But I would have given anything to share it. I never had a chance." He turned slowly and took in the tropical landscape. Hunger exuded from him. Anthony didn't have Yrae's *diya*, but there was no mistaking the terrible longing in Colin's heart.

"It should be yours," Anthony said on impulse. Colin whirled and gaped at him. Pilar's jaw dropped, too, as Anthony said, "I don't plan to live here. I don't plan to live on *Earth*." It was Varenka's turn to be flabbergasted; she mumbled protests to Benjamin Inge, complaining that Anthony had no conception of things. How could he even think of rejecting this world and returning to those "unimportant frontier worlds"? He ignored that distraction, his resolve strengthening. "I have too many obligations to my Settlement and my company, Colin. You might say I've come a long way since I made those porn vids you regard as trash."

The blond reddened, apologizing. The elegant gentleman, remembering his manners, was embarrassed. It was a mask, but

347

one he had worn so long and so well it had become second nature to him. Possibly that pretense of gallantry had saved Pilar from the Biyelins' infernal mind-reading device. Colin hadn't tried to rescue her out of love, as Jesse had. But the merchant prince might have the right instincts, deeply buried; they'd simply never been allowed to flourish.

He stammered, "Wh-what are you proposing?"

"Well, you own a big chunk of Stuart's stock now."

"Throw the bastard a bone," Colin said bitterly.

"It's a damned juicy bone. I propose you put it together with some of the *other* bones. We've had our differences, to put it mildly. But we're both Saunders. Even the law admits that, finally, and the law handed me a trust. It would be foolish not to take care of all fractions of that legacy," Anthony explained. "And yet I can't stay here to watchdog my Earth-based holdings. I'm offering you a stewardship of this particular property." The irony in that struck him hard. Stuart had never been a steward of this estate or any other family possession; Stuart's bastard was bound to do a hell of a lot better job than his father had—if only to prove that his grandmother had been woefully wrong about Colin Saunder's true worth.

"I—I don't know what to say," Colin whispered. It wasn't necessary for him to reply; his answer was in his eyes. He would agree to anything, sign anything, if it brought him Saunderhome.

Anthony asked Pilar, "Can you arrange the legal forms?" She nodded, sharing his unspoken pity of the man who was staring hungrily at the mansion.

"I'll take good care of it," Colin vowed.

"You realize it'll tie you down?" his cousin warned. "That's what *I'm* trying to avoid. What about your business interests on Procyon Four? Managing Saunderhome and that inheritance from Stuart will force you to spend nearly all of your time on Earth."

"Yes, yes, I know that," Colin said impatiently. The world well lost. He was jettisoning all he'd slaved to acquire during his long exile in exchange for his childhood dream. It struck Anthony that his kinsman hadn't worn his familiar feathered headdress since they had arrived on Earth. The lack of that adornment, and Colin's altered attitudes, made him seem years younger, and much more callow. "I could make over supervisory rights to you," the blond said. "You'll be out there, able to decide what's needed."

Anthony shook his head. "No, it's not my field. I'd need too much help, handling your bunch of companies. I suggest you appoint another Saunder as your agent, someone with the connections to keep things going in the right directions. Someone adaptable, energetic. You'd better think about what you want to do concerning your position at the Interspecies Trade Conference, as well." Colin nodded absently, gazing at the mansion with something very akin to love. "At the very least, you should select an agent to act on your behalf. Regan could probably handle both assignments. How about naming her?"

"Regan? Oh, I guess. Will she accept it?"

Colin's nonchalance, his casual abandonment of his mercantile power in the C.S.P. and the management of the Conference amazed Anthony. If their roles had been reversed, he wouldn't have hesitated an instant to reject Saunderhome and an obligation that would fetter him indefinitely to Earth. "Regan will become your agent, I'm sure," he said. "And she'll do a damned good job."

Captain Saunder's bright younger daughter Regan had been outraged by Colin's actions, saying he had forfeited any "moral right" to his inheritance. The court disagreed with her. And now Colin was going to turn over enormous power to Regan, and ultimately, Anthony suspected, to Regan's lover, Malcolm Griffith, and the political movement headed by Malcolm's father, Ames—C.S.P. President, with all that would mean for the outward-facing proponents of the Settlements. The standpatters, the rigid links to Earth would be dissolving as an effective force. Colin didn't care.

Anthony crooked a finger, beckoning to Pilar. They moved out of Colin's hearing and the Earth woman said, "You're really going to do this, aren't you? Jesse *says* you're one in a billion billion."

With a rueful smile, he replied, "Yes, I'm Patrick Saunder, the sole survivor of five little Patrick Saunders." Anthony shook his head, still trying to absorb the reality of all that had happened to him. "I spent thirty-six years learning to be a full-fledged human being. But I refuse to let the court's decision change me into a man I never knew, a man who died long before I was born. I'm Anthony Saunder, and that's that." He sighed and added, "And as soon as possible, Anthony Saunder is going home."

Home to the stars and Procyon Five.

"Jesse," Pilar said softly. "He's—"

"I used my new subspace net to talk to Yrae again last night. She says he's improving all the time."

Pilar slumped in relief and wiped away tears. "I should have been with him, not in that damned mining camp. If I'd gone along to Colin's desert estate, maybe they wouldn't have hurt him."

"Don't live on maybes. I know how persuasive Jesse can be," Anthony said with a fond grin. "Are you coming with me?"

The Earthwoman reacted with surprise, then examined the invitation. "To . . . the Settlements?" She was tempted, and she was afraid. "I don't know if I'm tough enough."

"You are," he assured her. "All of us immigrants were afraid when we first shipped out there. And some of us didn't make it. It's risky, but it's worth it." He waved toward Saunderhome, symbolically including everything it represented—Earth. "This isn't—not to me, and not to Jesse. Is it to you?"

"I'm not sure," Pilar admitted. "I think I'd like to try being a pioneer, now that I've had a taste of what it's like. Do you think I can pass the test?"

"Jesse believes you already have done so, and that's all the okay you need. There will be an extra seat on my outbound flight. I want you to be in it." Anthony glanced toward Varenka Saunder and the other executors standing several meters away, regarding him with surreptitious dismay. "They don't understand. I doubt they ever will. Weeks ago I told Brenna that Terra can't turn back the clock, can't make Earth the center of the universe anymore. We've been children of the stars for thirty years now, ever since Captain Saunder broke the light-year barrier and made it possible for us to reach out into the galaxy. A generation has come to adulthood Out There. For us, humanity has to keep looking still further outward—as well as back to the world of our origin—to find the future. And my future and Jesse's lie in that direction. Join us."

A slow smile spread across Pilar's plain features. This time the sales pitch had been aimed *at* Pilar Gutierrez, and she was "sold." Anthony said, "Good! Let's make arrangements to turn this place—turn the whole damned local management—over to caretakers. Then we can both go home."

CHAPTER TWENTY-THREE

✧✧✧✧✧✧✧✧

Legacy

The news got to Procyon Five long before Anthony did, even though he rode back to the Settlements aboard one of the fastest civilian starhoppers SMEI made. He traveled aboard his own craft. The Arbitrators had left Goddard Station shortly after the inheritance had been decided. The event, in their judgment, was now totally concluded, and humans had no more claim on them. Through the Saunder-McKelvey grapevine—a private network Anthony was able to tap into at will, due to his new status—he learned that Brenna and other V.I.P.s had hushed up the Biyelin-Whimed Outer Satellite business. The troublemakers had been rounded up and shipped home to their own sectors, and presumably would be watched closely to ensure that their vicious games didn't slop over into neighboring stellar regions ever again.

With his new privileges, new experiences, and incredible new powers, Anthony didn't miss the luxury of journeying aboard the aliens' ship; *his* ship wasn't quite as fast, but was far more palatial. The vessel was only one of many. An entire fleet was at his disposal. Carissa and Stuart had owned this civilian armada and never used it. Earthbound, they farmed the ships out to their execs. Anthony foresaw his *own* execs—loyal Saunder Studio employees, promoted to dizzying responsibilities, and new employees like Pilar Gutierrez, loyal, trustworthy people added to his staff—enjoying the same advantage. But he intended to make plenty of use of the starhoppers himself. He'd have to, to keep in touch with all the C.S.P. investments he'd inherited.

Entire Chapter Companies and controlling interests in others spelled clout—the muscle to strike chains from struggling frontier worlds and allow them room to develop.

Anthony looked forward to that. Requests for his guidance were already filtering in. Congratulations came from Ames Griffith, keenly aware of the way the starwind was blowing, spelling out his monetary reform package in detail, and asking for Anthony's input. C.S.P.'s "settler magnate," the newest Saunder top ranker, would have all the say-so he desired in the way the Council framed its upcoming legislation.

The feeling was heady and humbling. Anthony knew he had his work cut out for him, and it wasn't going to be easy. He'd started by setting in motion a shift of assets—negotiables, credit conversions, and the stuff he'd need out here. Many of the tangibles would have to remain on Earth. The FTL ship fleet was one of the few things in Carissa's and Stuart's inventories that worked equally well for a citizen of the Solar System or a C.S.P. settler.

Update reports from the Conference were flooding in. Even in absentia, Anthony Saunder wielded enormous influence there. Regan called him regularly, consulting. In an odd way, he was steering both his delegation *and* Colin's by remote control—and Regan's good offices. Together they helped Captain Saunder make sure the interspecies gathering stayed on course. Colin's abandonment had been a potential catastrophe. But it wasn't going to wreck things. This project, like another Anthony had accepted with equally strong misgivings, was coming to fruition.

Brenna sent an SMEI shuttle up to Procyon's spaceport to meet Anthony's starhopper. He reflected that in less than a year he'd probably be trading in some of his fleet for new single-stage FTL shuttles from his kinswoman's new product lines. There wouldn't be so many transfer points necessary—for him, and for a lot of other settlers. Frontier planets could be anchored, their tendency to drift apart limited. Trade lanes would be opening for new routes and more frequent traffic.

Crowds awaited him at Equitoria's Terminal. Anthony was taken aback by the warmth of his reception. Settlers grabbed at his hands and tried to touch his clothes and yelled approvingly while staffers attempted to hold back the noisy crush.

"Showed those smart-ass Terrans where they can put their loot, didn't you, Saunder! Good for you!"

"Kick 'em in the teeth."

"Yeah! Teach those stay-at-homes that the Charter Company isn't going to make slaves of us anymore!"

"Saw it on the vids! You did great!"

"Welcome home, trog!"

Anthony was amused by the cheers. Trog—one of their own, transformed from a respected small businessman to a local hero. There was nothing to it! Simply inherit a fortune and announce that you intended to begin diverting Charter Company profits— among other vast incomes—out to the Settlements.

Which was where Anthony wanted to be.

"We've reserved a special taxi barge for you," Pilar said. "It's waiting at the Governor's private landing. Yamashita says to take all the time you need, but they'd like to have you over on Four as soon as you can make it. Things *are* still in a bit of a turmoil since Colin dumped the Conference so precipitously."

Colin. The last time Anthony had seen his cousin, the blond was walking briskly across Saunderhome's sprawling lawn. The former merchant prince of Procyon Four was taking command of his new realm. Colin had a settler's energy and ambition, and he was applying it to conquering that Caribbean island that had been out of his grasp for so many years. As a director, Anthony had learned to get inside the skins of a great many vivid characters in hundreds of scripts. But he couldn't get inside Colin's skin, or his mind. The only answer for that was to take it as it was. Anthony Saunder had his legacy, and Colin seemed content with his. So be it.

The driver of the taxi barge was the same middle-aged woman Anthony had met a couple of months ago, shortly after the market tour. She'd received a promotion in the interim and was happy to chat about her good fortune—and Anthony's. He introduced the driver to Pilar, helping the Earth woman fit into the trog environment. In a year or two Pilar Gutierrez might think of this harsh underground habitat as home, too, and be a proud trog herself.

When they reached the seaside residence, Anthony started to run up the steps, then halted, waiting for Pilar. She'd earned the right to accompany him all the way, and they entered the house together.

The place was very quiet. For a moment, Anthony was worried. He didn't hear Yrae's haunting singsong. Where was she? Shouldn't she be helping Jesse with that strange crooning?

Then the Whimed actress appeared, climbing the steps up from the terrace dome. She froze, staring at Anthony and the Earth woman. They had notified her in advance of their approximate arrival time, but it was tough to be precise across millions of miles. Yrae had said she wouldn't meet them at the Terminal; she would stay here with Jesse.

Now she ran forward, her golden hair flying.

Anthony embraced her, feeling the touch of velvety, pearlescent flesh under his fingers, and seeing the glow of starburst eyes. A thrumming purr vibrated against his chest. He held her close, relishing the sensations.

Pilar looked flustered, as if thinking she ought to make herself scarce and give them some privacy.

Privacy became less. The Vahnaj Arbitrator emerged from one of the sleeping alcoves and bowed politely to the recent arrivals. "I give you . . . urr . . . herro."

"Hello, Tib-The." Anthony peered about anxiously, coming up for air from his embrace with Yrae. "Where's Jesse?"

Yrae pointed to the stairs. "The dome. He is there."

"How—"

"Better. It was not known if the healing would apply to a Terran. However, Jesse is—"

"A tough settler," Pilar supplied, impatient. "I want to see him."

"And he wants to see you," Anthony said. "Let's go."

The Vahnaj Arbitrator remained at the head of the stairs while the others went through the air lock and out into the transparent dome. Yrae whispered, "Tib-The is most likable, for a lutrinoid. I could not have helped Jesse sufficiently by myself."

"Maybe there's hope for the Conference and galactic peace yet," Anthony said, his arm snugly around her waist. That had made descending the stairs a trifle difficult, but he persisted, despite the handicap.

But when they entered the bubble, he released Yrae and circled around the cot placed in the center of the terrace, stopping to face his friend. Jesse seemed to be dozing. The agony in his face

354

was almost completely gone. Traces of the pain lingered, but the improvement was indeed remarkable, as Yrae had promised. Anthony spoke the older man's name and Jesse stirred, blinking. "Kid? Is—is that you?" He sat up straight. That took considerable effort. He was shaky, not yet whole. Getting there, though! Jesse reached out, grabbing at Anthony's hand. "Hey! I wanta take a look at the—the tycoon! Yrae told me all about it. We watched the news. 'S terrific! You really did it!" The associate producer managed a crooked grin. "You beat the bastard!"

"I think it was a tie, actually," Anthony said. There would be time enough later to explain the details to Jesse, to make him understand what it had meant to Colin at last to be a *real* Saunder, and what it had felt like to stand in Colin's shoes and know his lifetime of hunger for a lost paradise. And despite that burning hunger, the former merchant prince had protected the woman Jesse loved.

Yes, it had been a tie, that contest for the inheritance. And in the end, vengeance hadn't been exacted, or required.

He'd explain that to Jesse, too. Why duplicate Fal-Am's complex and deadly game of hate? That game had proved nearly fatal for Jesse. And the game—with the clone and the bastard as its pawns—was finished.

"I brought someone with me," Anthony said.

Pilar came around the chair into Jesse's view. His face was sunrise. "Hey! Hey!" he exclaimed softly in delighted shock.

"I want to talk to you, Eben," Pilar said, pretending to scold. "How dare you leave me stranded in that cold, filthy mining shack!"

"Aw, come on. A man's gotta—"

"Don't give me that. You enjoyed playing detective. You like living dangerously. Probably depend on it to keep your brain in gear!"

Anthony grinned and sidled out of the picture. He wasn't needed here at the moment. The Earth woman was the best therapy Jesse could possibly have to help him on the way to full recovery.

Yrae was also remaining discreetly out of the older lovers' view. She peered up at the water covering the dome. The alien actress wasn't apprehensive, as she had been the first time she'd stepped out of the air lock. These past weeks she'd spent a lot of time in this place, and she was adapting, fitting in well.

"I missed you," Anthony said. The words were too plain, lacking the heartfelt emotion he wanted to express.

But it wasn't necessary to put it into frilly phrases.

"It is felt," Yrae replied.

"Hilandro—"

She shook her head, a strange gleam in her starry eyes. "I am Hilandro not Hilandro." Yrae saw Anthony's puzzlement and went on, "I do not choose. I have spoken to my government. I do not serve those who would allow the *ge-aytan* circling to harm not-Whimed."

He struggled to grasp the alien concept. She had renounced her title? She *couldn't* renounce her talents. However, it sounded as if Yrae had decided not to be at the beck and call of beings like Ryseen Simra Hilandro. Never again! She would not readily act out her gifts for the movers and shakers of the Whimed Federation. Yrae apparently felt she had been used by her entire species, not merely by the Whimed Outer Satellite Faction. *Aytan.* Her standards of ethics had not been met. She was withholding her revered skills—punishing those who had used her, until they cleaned up their act.

"I'm not sure I understand," Anthony said, then chuckled.

There was a lot he never would understand. He and Yrae weren't able to erase space, time, and evolution. They were building bridges between the stars, though, a bridge big enough for two beings to share.

"I will explain," Yrae said.

"Maybe we'd better wait until the Interspecies Trade Conference has concluded," he suggested.

"Yes. Correct. Important. Then we discuss the series of educational Terran-Whimed recordings. It will not be the work of Ryseen Simra Hilandro. It will be our work. Together."

He raised an eyebrow, amused. "I'd like that—very much."

"I will not return to Whimed Federation," Yrae went on, surprising him. Then she tempered her decision. "Not at present. I must learn much first." She moved into his arms again, caressing him.

"You're not separate any longer," he said, "and neither am I." Anthony glanced toward Jesse and Pilar and added, "And neither are they."

Yrae's smile was very gentle. "He will improve now without

356

my song. I will return with you to Conference. Pilar is proper medicine. She and Tib-The will complete the correcting."

"So I see." Anthony's friend and the Earth woman were renewing their interrupted voyage of discovery, unabashed by the presence of onlookers. "Pilar's here to stay," Anthony murmured. "She belongs with us." He paused and went on, "We've all got a lot of work to do yet—learning, touching, and trying to understand. Not easy."

"It is never easy," Yrae agreed, eons of Whimed philosophy —and the philosophy of the Saunder-McKelvey family and all Terra as well—in those words.

"We don't *want* it to be easy," he said, very firm. "If we did, we wouldn't be out here, and the Conference wouldn't be taking place."

Yrae snuggled close, turning so that they stood side by side. She and Anthony gazed beyond the dome. Somewhere in that ocean were creatures that had never known Earth. And here at his side was a woman born of nonhuman parents, under a sun the Saunder family's founders had never heard of.

Yet they all belonged, adapting to each other and the universe.

Farther in the distance, above the waterline, filtered through the green brightness, Procyon's primary star was shining. Anthony's sun! Not Sol—Sol had been just the beginning. It wasn't the end, for him or for humanity. Perhaps there would be no end.

There was a hell of a lot of galaxy Out There, places Anthony Saunder hadn't traveled to, humans and aliens he hadn't met, things he had to do, problems he had to solve.

He'd be sharing . . . with Yrae and with Jesse.

He had the time, now, and the means. He—and the Settlements—were on their way.

Anthony Saunder, expatriate of Earth, human being, had finally come home to the stars.

ABOUT THE AUTHOR

Juanita Coulson began writing at age eleven and has been pursuing this career off and on ever since. Her first professional sale, to a science-fiction magazine, came in 1963. Since then she has sold fifteen novels, several short stories, and such odds and ends as an article on "Wonder Woman" and a pamphlet on how to appreciate art.

When she isn't writing, she may be singing and/or composing songs; painting (several of her works have been sold for excessively modest prices); reading biographies or books dealing with abnormal psychology, earthquakes and volcanoes, history, astronomy—or almost anything that has printing on it; gardening in the summer and shivering in the winter.

Juanita is married to Buck Coulson, who is also a writer. She and her husband spend much of their spare time actively participating in science-fiction fandom: attending conventions and publishing their Hugo-winning fanzine, *Yandro*. They live in northeastern Indiana, surrounded by books, magazines, records, typewriters, and other paraphernalia.

JAUNITA COULSON'S CHILDREN OF THE STARS SERIES

A STELLAR-BOUND DYNASTY; UNITED BY BLOOD, DIVIDED BY GREED.